JOE BUFF

"[Buff] delivers fascinating technical detail [and] white-knuckle undersea action."
Patrick Robinson

"The combined effect of unrelenting action, clever plotting and sheer firepower . . . successfully torpedoes any notion that this long-running submarine series has begun to tire . . . Meticulously described battle scenes both on land and at sea."
Publishers Weekly

"Joe Buff takes the reader through a labyrinth of action and high adventure."
Clive Cussler

"Buff makes for sleepless nights. This man knows his stuff."
David E. Meadows, Capt., USN, author of the Joint Task Force and Dark Pacific series

"The author out-Clancys Tom Clancy . . . Buff gives us terrific battle maneuvers . . . Talk about fun."
Kirkus Reviews

"A superb high-water mark in naval fiction."
Michael DiMercurio, author of *Vertical Dive*

Books by Joe Buff

JOE BUFF

SEAS OF CRISIS

HarperTorch
An Imprint of HarperCollinsPublishers

This book is a work of fiction. The characters, incidents, and dialogue are drawn from the author's imagination and are not to be construed as real. Any resemblance to actual events or persons, living or dead, is entirely coincidental.

HARPERTORCH
An Imprint of HarperCollins*Publishers*
10 East 53rd Street
New York, New York 10022-5299

Copyright © 2006 by Joe Buff
ISBN-13: 978-0-06-059471-8
ISBN-10: 0-06-059471-3

First HarperTorch paperback printing: September 2006
First William Morrow hardcover printing: January 2006

HarperCollins®, HarperTorch™, and ❦ ™ are trademarks of HarperCollins Publishers Inc.

Printed in the United States of America

Visit HarperTorch on the World Wide Web at www.harpercollins.com

10 9 8 7 6 5 4 3 2 1

The whole point of the next big surprise attack against America is that it really will come as a total surprise— not just as to where and when, but especially as to who, why, and how.

The boldest measures are the safest.

—Admiral Horatio Nelson,
one of the greatest and most beloved
naval commanders of all time

NOTE FROM THE AUTHOR

Submarines rank among the most sophisticated weapons systems, and among the most impressive benchmarks of technology and engineering, ever achieved by the human race. Stunning feats of courage by their crews, of sacrifice and endurance, loom large on the pages of history. Since the end of the Cold War, a whole new generation of submarine classes, with astonishing sensors, weapons, off-board vehicles, and stealth, has been conceived and is under construction by the United States Navy.

The world's oceans are the world's highways for the transport of goods and the conduct of commerce. Continued mastery of undersea warfare is vital, because whoever controls the ocean's depths controls its surface, and thus protects much of the world. Sea power, strongly employed, is key to upholding peaceful societies everywhere.

But do America and our allies take our free access through international waters too much for granted? Advanced submarine technology is proliferating among countries who haven't always been our friends. Nuclear weapons are also spreading at an alarming pace, with transnational conspiracies, shrewdly hidden for years, only recently being unmasked. What mortal threats to freedom still remain hidden?

The enemy you don't see coming, because of your own blind spots and preconceived notions, is the one who'll get you every time. The 9/11 Commission Report warned us all of "failures of imagination" and "unprepared mind-sets." Beyond the global war on terror, what shape might the twenty-first century's almost inevitable eventual major worldwide armed conflict take? When faced with so many dangerous future unknowns, the Navy wargames what-if scenarios to learn everything it can; "not implausible" worst cases are very educational. As an award-winning military commentator and seasoned risk analyst, my extreme action-adventure novels aim to do the same thing, based on a firm foundation of nonfiction research. Perhaps the only certainty is that heroic submariners and special operations forces will play a key role in deterring that Next Big War, or in winning it.

Joe Buff
July 20, 2005
Dutchess County, New York

SEAS
OF
CRISIS

PROLOGUE

By the middle of 2011, the global war on terror had flared up and died down repeatedly, with serious losses in damage and blood. Personal freedoms in many countries had also been eroded, while international friendships more and more were a thing of the past. All this was the cost, and the legacy, inflicted or triggered by those whose highest goals were senseless destruction and death. Then, just as the worst of terrorism seemed to have been contained, that struggle was eclipsed by a shocking new conflict of much greater magnitude.

In July 2011, Boer-led reactionaries seized control of the government in South Africa, which was in the midst of social chaos, and restored apartheid. In response to a UN trade embargo, the Boer regime began sinking U.S. and British merchant ships. U.S.-led coalition forces mobilized, but Germany and Russia held back. Troops and tanks drained from the rest of Europe and North America, and a joint task force set sail for Africa—into a giant, coordinated trap.

There was another coup, in Berlin. Ultranationalists, exploiting American unpreparedness for such all-out war, would give Germany her "place in the sun" at last. A secret military-industrial conspiracy had planned it all for years, brutal opportunists who hated the cross-border mixing and feuding of the European Union as much as they resented what to them was seen as America's arrogance and bullying. Big off-the-books loans from Swiss and German banks, collateralized by wealth to be plundered from the losers, funded the stealthy buildup in a perverse but effective form of voodoo-economics bootstrapping and accounting fraud. Coercion by the noose won over citizens not swayed by patriotism or the sheer onrush of events.

This Berlin-Boer Axis had covertly built tactical atomic weapons, the great equalizers in what would otherwise have been a most uneven fight—and once again America's intelligence community was clueless. Compact, energy-efficient, very-low-signature dual-laser isotope separation techniques let the conspirators purify uranium into weapons-grade in total privacy.

The new Axis, seeking a global empire all their own, used low-yield A-bombs to ambush the Allied naval task force under way, then destroyed Warsaw and Tripoli. Those decades of Cold War division, by the overbearing superpowers, into East Germany and West Germany—armed camps in a tinderbox face-off pitting brother against brother—in hindsight debunked the postreunification fairy tale of German pacifism. The most warlike nation in modern history was on the warpath again.

France, stunned, followed NATO's recognized nuclear strategy option of preemptive capitulation, surrendering at once. Continental Europe was overrun. Germany won a strong beachhead in North Africa, while the South African army drove hard toward them to link up. The battered Allied task force put ashore near the Congo Basin, in a last-ditch attempt to hold the Germans and well-equipped Boers apart. In both Europe and Africa the fascist conquest trapped countless Allied civilians, who were herded into internment camps next to major Axis bases, factories, and transport nodes, to be held as hostages and human shields.

It was unthinkable for the Allies to retaliate against Axis tactical nuclear weapons, used primarily at sea, by launching ICBMs loaded with hydrogen bombs into the heart of Western Europe, especially when the murderous fallout of H-bombs dropped on land obeyed no nation's overflight restrictions. The Axis shrewdly avoided acquiring hydrogen bombs of their own. The United States and the United Kingdom thus were handcuffed, forced to fight on Axis terms on ground of Axis choosing: the mid-ocean, with A-bomb-tipped cruise missiles and torpedoes. Information-warfare hacking of the Global Positioning System satellites, and ingenious jamming of smart-bomb homing sensors, made Allied precision-guided high-explosive munitions much less precise. Advanced radar methods in the FM radio band—pioneered by Russia—removed the invisibility of America's finest stealth aircraft.

Thoroughly relentless, Germany grabbed nuclear subs from the French, and hypermodern diesel subs that Germany herself had exported to other countries. The Russian Federation, supposedly neutral yet long a believer in the practicality of limited tactical nuclear war, sold weapons, oil, and natural gas to the Axis. Autocratic and ambitious, Russia was more than glad to take on America by proxy once more—this time she'd let the Germans and Boers do her dirty work. Most of the rest of the world, including China, stayed on the sidelines, biding their time out of fear or greed or both.

American convoys to starving Great Britain are being decimated by the modern U-boat threat, in another bloody Battle of the Atlantic. On land, in theaters of combat and intrigue ranging from the South Pacific to South America, to Central Africa and the Middle East, the Axis have waged campaigns of calculated daring and astonishing callousness, based on razor-thin margins between success and atomic holocaust.

In early summer 2012—almost a full year into the fighting—U.S. and other Allied personnel and their equipment are exhausted. Russia helps Germany and South Africa recover and reequip after each battle. Such biased trading by a neutral with only one side in a clash of belligerents is perfectly legal under international law. Repeated American diplomatic efforts to sway the Kremlin have failed completely.

With so many atom bombs set off at sea by both sides, and the oil slicks from many wrecked ships, oceanic environmental damage is rapidly growing severe. The repeated, ever-closer brushes with Armageddon have themselves become an intentional tool in the Axis' war-fighting doctrine, a weapon of psychological terror like none ever seen before.

Then a destabilizing wild card was unmasked by surprise during combat: a whole new class of nuclear subs, with many breakthrough technologies, is being custom-built covertly in Russia exclusively for German use. This latest treacherous move by a coldly manipulative Moscow could tip the balance of power decisively. Allowing it to continue is militarily unacceptable in Washington. Something must be done to force the Russians to back off, and undermine Imperial Germany at her core—before the entire planet goes up in a forest of mushroom clouds and then freezes in a nuclear winter.

In this terrible new world war, with the mid-ocean's surface a killing zone and elite commando teams sometimes more effective than whole armies, America's last, best hope for enduring freedom lies with a special breed of fearless undersea warriors. . . .

CHAPTER 1

Late June 2012

War isn't hell, it's worse than hell, Commander Jeffrey Fuller told himself. He sat alone in his captain's stateroom on USS *Challenger,* whose ceramic composite hull helped her to be America's most capable nuclear-powered fast-attack submarine. Jeffrey's many successes, during tactical atomic combat at sea in a war that the Berlin-Boer Axis had started a year earlier, had made him one of the most highly decorated submariners in U.S. Navy history. But his Medal of Honor, his two Navy Crosses, his Defense Distinguished Service Medal, and his crew's receipt of a Presidential Unit Citation all put together couldn't dispel Jeffrey's present dark mood.

Challenger was five days outbound from Pearl Harbor, deeply submerged and steaming due north, already past the Aleutian Islands chain that stretched between mainland Alaska and Siberia. She was bound for the New London submarine base, on Connecticut's Thames River, having been sent by the shortest possible route: through the narrow Bering Strait choke point looming a few hundred miles ahead, separating the easternmost tip of pseudo-neutral

Russia from Alaska's desolate Cape Prince of Wales. Jeffrey would sail past Alaska and Arctic Canada. Then he'd sneak through the shallow waters between Canada and Greenland, into the Atlantic, to arrive at home port in two weeks for a reception he already dreaded.

There'd been no medals awaiting Jeffrey or his people at Pearl to recognize their newest accomplishments, despite an earlier message implying there would be. No one was allowed to go ashore. *Challenger* had been told to hide underwater, off Honolulu, taking on minimal supplies and spare parts via minisub. No admirals came to shake hands, no squadron commodore gave any pats on the back. And Jeffrey was sure he knew why.

He'd broken too many unwritten rules—too many even for him—on his latest mission spanning half the globe. He'd stepped on too many toes, made too many well-placed political enemies in Washington, while exercising initiative that had seemed to make sense at the time. In something that verged on a shouting match, he'd quashed an onboard CIA expert whose advice he was supposed to respect. On his own accord he'd clandestinely violated a crucial ally's sovereignty, planting seeds for what could still become a disastrous diplomatic incident. Worst, while obeying ironclad orders to preserve his own ship's stealth at all cost, he and everyone else on *Challenger* had had to listen, horrified, doing nothing but flee the fight while dozens of good men—friends and colleagues—died under Axis attack in the Med on another American submarine.

And when *Challenger* had arrived in Australia for crew leave, one of his star performers, Lieutenant Kathy Milgrom of the UK's Royal Navy, who'd served as *Challenger*'s sonar officer on the ship's most vital missions, had been summarily detached. Jumped two ranks to commander, she was now on the Allied naval staff in Sydney. This was terrific for Milgrom, Jeffrey felt delighted for her, but he'd been disturbed that he found out about it only after she got the orders directly and then told him; the way it was handled by the powers-that-be violated correct protocol.

Jeffrey listened to the steady rushing sound that came from the air-circulation vents in the overhead of his stateroom. The air inside the forward parts of *Challenger* was always cool, to keep the electronics from overheating. Jeffrey was used to it, but this evening for some strange reason he felt chilled. He looked up for a moment at the bluish glare of fluorescent fixtures, like plant grow lights to keep submariners healthy when deprived of sun for weeks on end. He glanced at the grayish flameproof linoleum squares that covered his stateroom deck, then gazed around at the fake-wood wainscoting veneer, and bright stainless steel, lining the four bulkheads of his tiny world.

Outside his shut door, in the narrow passageway, he heard crewmen hurrying about, headed to different stations to perform the myriad tasks that helped the ship run smoothly every second of every minute of every single day. There was no margin for error on a nuclear submarine. Jeffrey dearly loved this endless pressure, much as he'd grown accustomed to the constant, potentially killing squeeze of the ocean surrounding *Challenger.*

He sighed. On his last mission, it appeared, he'd gone too far in some ways, and not far enough in others. There'd be whispers in the corridors of the Pentagon that he was an uncontrollable cowboy, a commander who risked others' lives to gain personal glory. Jeffrey knew he'd done the right thing at every stage of that mind-twisting mission, but what he knew inside didn't count. He had to assume that he was bound now for some shore job far from the action. Soon another man would sit at this little fold-down desk, sleep in this austere rack, put up photos of wife and children, assert his own personality and habits onto the crew. *Challenger* would have a different captain, because Jeffrey's run of luck as captain had finally run out.

Someone knocked. "Come in!"

His executive officer entered, Lieutenant Commander Jackson Jefferson Bell. A few inches taller than Jeffrey, but less naturally muscular, Bell was happily married and had a six-month-old son to look forward to seeing again. Cautious in his tactical thinking when Jeffrey was superaggressive, Bell complemented Jeffrey in the control room during combat. Often he'd played devil's advocate in engagements where split seconds mattered, when the waters thundered outside the hull and Challenger shook from stem to stern as if tossed by an angry sea monster—and Jeffrey's crew looked to him to somehow, some way, keep them alive, while an Axis skipper did his damnedest to smash their ship to pieces and slaughter every person aboard. That hair's-breadth survival, so many times, brought Jeffrey and Bell very close.

Jeffrey grimaced to himself. *Soon Bell will have a new boss.*

Bell had arrived to give his regular 2000—8 P.M.—report as XO to his captain. Bell's words about the ship's status held no surprises. He wrapped up crisply and left, pulling the door shut behind him.

Jeffrey picked up his intercom handset for the control room. The messenger of the watch answered, one of the youngest and least experienced crewmen aboard. Jeffrey knew he was working hard to earn his silver dolphins, the coveted badge of a full-fledged enlisted submariner; officers wore gold. Jeffrey wondered if the messenger would survive this horrendous war or not—assuming civilization and humanity survived.

"Give me the Navigator, please." Jeffrey kept his tone as even as he could.

"Wait one, sir," the still-boyish voice of the teenage messenger said.

"Navigator here, Captain," Jeffrey heard in his earpiece. Despite himself, he smiled. Lieutenant Richard Sessions was one of the most unflappable people he'd ever met, inside or outside the military. From a small town in Nebraska,

Sessions was the type of guy whose hair and clothes were always a little sloppy, no matter what he did. But his indispensable work as head of the ship's navigating department was without fail beautifully organized and precise.

"Nav, when do we pass through five-five north, one-seven-five west?" In mid-Bering Sea, on the way up to the strait. It was at that point, and only then, that Jeffrey was to open the sealed orders in his safe, containing the recognition signals and other data he'd need to complete his final trip without becoming a victim of friendly fire.

Sessions had the answer for Jeffrey quickly. "At local time zero-three-twenty tomorrow, sir." The wee hours of the coming morning.

"Okay. Thanks, Nav." Jeffrey hung up.

Aw, what the heck.

As a small act of defiance against those seniors who'd used him, drained him, and cast him aside when the going got too rough, Jeffrey stood and opened his safe.

He withdrew the bulky envelope. It contained an incendiary self-destruct charge, to cremate the classified contents in case of unauthorized tampering. This precaution was normal for submarine captains' order pouches in this war. As Jeffrey knew well, subs could be sunk during battle. And just as the U.S. had done more than once to derelict Soviet submarines, Axis salvage divers or robotic probes could rifle through *Challenger*'s wreckage if something went wrong, compromising priceless secrets.

Jeffrey very carefully entered the combination on the big envelope's keypad, to disarm the self-destruct. The last thing he wanted was to set it off by accident. The envelope opened safely; he emptied it onto his desk. His heart began to pound.

Among the papers and data disks, and another, inner, sealed envelope, were two metal uniform-collar insignia—silver eagles, which meant the rank of Captain, United States Navy, the rank above commander. The actual *rank* of captain, not just the courtesy title that every warship's skipper received. Jeffrey snatched the hard-copy orders and read as fast as he could.

His entire demeanor changed. He realized that his mind had been playing nasty tricks, in the vacuum of feedback from above, running toward doldrums that were probably a symptom of his own lingering reactions to the traumatic events in the Med.

Challenger's trip to the U.S. East Coast was a cover story. Five mysterious passengers, embarked at Pearl, belonged to a Seabee Engineer Reconnaissance Team; SERTs were elite shadow warriors from among the Navy's mobile combat construction battalions. They gathered unusual intel and did mind-boggling tasks at the forward edge of the battle area. *Interesting.*

Jeffrey was hereby promoted to the rank of Navy captain. He was awarded a second Medal of Honor, though this award was classified. There'd be no bright gold star, for the blue ribbon with small white stars already adorning his dressier uniforms, to denote the second Medal. But the selection boards for rear admiral, Jeffrey reminded himself, would certainly know about it when the time came. *Challenger*'s whole crew had been awarded another Presidential Unit Citation, although this was also top secret outside the ship. *Excellent. Morale will skyrocket.*

Once through the Bering Strait, gateway to the Chukchi Sea, he still would turn toward Canada. In the ice-choked, storm-tossed Beaufort Sea, above the Arctic Circle, *Challenger* would rendezvous with USS *Jimmy Carter. Carter* was an ultrafast and deep-diving steel-hulled sub of the *Seawolf* class, uniquely modified with an extra hundred feet of hull length. This gave her room to support large special operations commando raids, plus garage space for oversized weapons and off-board probes.

Bell was being promoted to full commander. He'd take over *Challenger* from Jeffrey, who from now on was commanding officer of an undersea strike group consisting of *Challenger* and *Carter*. Bell and *Carter*'s captain would be his subordinates. To avoid confusion between these different roles and ranks, Jeffrey was granted the courtesy title of commodore.

Jeffrey read further into his orders, more slowly now to absorb every detail. Crucial portions of the mission required that two submarines be involved, but there was much more to it than *Challenger* and *Carter* together having greater firepower while covering each other's backs. This piqued Jeffrey's curiosity; no explanation was given of what it meant. Even more cryptically, Jeffrey was told to brush up on the Russian he'd studied in college, and to practice his poker face. The SERT passengers would help him on both counts, starting right away. His eyebrows rose, involuntarily, as he took this in.

After the rendezvous and a joint briefing to be held aboard *Carter*, he would lead his two-ship strike group westward, into the East Siberian Sea—Russian home waters. His assignment, the orders warned, was to do something draconian, and utterly Machiavellian, that would decisively force Russia to stop supporting the Axis against America while Moscow outwardly kept claiming legal neutrality. Specifics were inside that inner envelope, to be opened only once the rendezvous was made.

This was exactly the sort of high-stakes mission his command personality needed and craved. Revealing the whole plan in stages, for security, was something he'd gotten used to.

Yet one thing puzzled Jeffrey. For this mission, he came under the control of Commander, U.S. Strategic Command, an Air Force four-star general. In the present wartime military organization, that general oversaw the readiness and possible use of America's thermonuclear weapons—hydrogen bombs. *Challenger* carried no H-bombs, and never had. Her nuclear torpedoes bore very low yields, a single kiloton maximum. H-bombs had destructive power a thousand times as large, and their vastly greater radioactive fallout drifted globally.

The Axis, shrewdly, owned no hydrogen bombs and made sure the whole world knew it. This kept America from escalating past tactical atomic fission devices set off only at sea—not that anyone sane in the U.S. would want to further escalate this war.

Jeffrey began to suffer a rising unease. *Why am I suddenly reporting to Commander, U.S. Strategic Command?*

CHAPTER 2

Jeffrey stood to move around and stretch, breathing in and out slowly, to relax. There were important things to discuss. He returned to his desk, shoving everything back into the orders envelope but not resealing it. He grabbed his intercom and dialed the control room. He no longer felt so cold. He felt as if his blood burned and every neuron fiber tingled.

"Messenger of the Watch, sir."

"Get in here, son, soon as you can."

"Right away, Captain." Jeffrey could hear him jump to attention at the steel he'd put in his tone this time.

The messenger arrived in seconds. The captain's stateroom was only a few paces aft of the rear of the control room. Jeffrey told the messenger to come in and shut the door.

"Yes, sir." The kid wore the blue cotton jumpsuit that was universal garb among enlisted submariners on patrol, and was also popular with most officers. He was typical of many in a fast-attack sub's crew: eager and honest and open, a devoted team player, with the bearing of a techie since every job on the ship required strong technical skill. This young man had a large Adam's apple, and wore eye-glasses—as did about a third of Jeffrey's people—adding to the effect of a likable warrior-nerd. He was apprehensive at first, then quickly picked up on the new electricity radiating from his captain.

"Find the XO and tell him I want to see him in ten minutes. Also the Nav." Bell, and Sessions.

"XO and Nav in ten minutes, aye, sir." Messengers were trained to repeat things back, to avoid mistakes.

"Then go find the one of our passengers named . . ." Jeffrey hesitated. He wasn't positive how to pronounce it. The five strangers had come down the airlock ladder, after the minisub from Pearl Harbor docked, wearing enlisted dungarees and work shirts, as if they were pierside hands. There were no markings on their sleeves to show their rates—enlisted rank—or their ratings—enlisted specialty—but up close they were clearly too old and hardened to be raw recruits. They hadn't even brought luggage, except for whatever they fit inside a single canvas tool bag. To the on-watch junior officer of the deck who met them first, they presented orders that listed no names, then gave him the sealed orders pouch for Commander Fuller to put in his safe.

"Dashiyn Nyurba," Jeffrey said, slowly and carefully. "Tell him I opened the outer pouch early, and we're ready to meet."

Jeffrey didn't know which one of the five was this Nyurba. The group had kept very much to themselves. Because enclosed gathering places were in short supply, they held long meetings, barred to outsiders, in a small compartment crammed with ship's computer equipment. They worked out on the ship's exercise gear when the fewest crew members were around—well after midnight. They slept in enlisted racks on a lower deck, they wordlessly wolfed down meals in the enlisted mess in a booth they would commandeer for barely ten minutes without any mingling, and they seemed to avoid Jeffrey altogether. The crew accepted such behavior, being used to CIA agents and other "spooks" who'd act this way for whole deployments.

"Er, could you spell that name please, Captain?"

Jeffrey did. "I want him to join us half an hour after the XO and Nav get here." Dinner had already been served in the wardroom—where Jeffrey and his ten officers ate—and in the enlisted mess—where the ship's fourteen chiefs also ate, by shifts, in a six-man booth unofficially reserved for them. The whole crew numbered one hundred twenty, which created endless overcrowding. Her weapons stocks fully replenished in Australia, sleeping racks were precluded in the huge torpedo room.

Jeffrey stopped. He'd noticed that he was still thinking too much like a submarine captain, and not like an undersea strike group commodore should. The transition would not be smooth sailing for Jeffrey—or for Bell.

He wished to be hospitable to Nyurba, whom he knew now was seniormost among his guests.

"Have the mess management guys provide us with coffee service for four. And some danish, cookies, whatever they got, warmed a bit, preferably. Time it for when Nyurba gets here."

The messenger repeated this, Jeffrey nodded, and he left.

Using his dressing mirror, Jeffrey undid his commander's silver oak leaves from his collar points, replacing them with his new eagles. The sweet irony wasn't lost that he'd vacate this captain's stateroom a lot sooner than he ever expected.

Sessions was first to arrive. His shirt was neatly tucked into his slacks, and his hair was nicely combed, because of the unexplained summons to see his captain. Jeffrey knew this wouldn't last long, Sessions being Sessions.

"Have a seat," Jeffrey told him, deadpan, watching Sessions react with a jolt when he noticed the different collar tabs.

"Are congratulations in order, Captain?"

"Yes indeed, but hold that thought till the XO gets here." Jeffrey was enjoying himself. Celebratory occasions of this magnitude didn't happen often, and he wanted to savor each moment: the one thing more satisfying that being promoted, as a naval officer, was informing one of your people that he or she had received their own well-earned promotion.

Someone knocked. Bell came in, took the empty guest chair, and did a double-take.

Jeffrey stood. "I won't mince words. Lieutenant Commander Bell, by an act of the United States Senate you've been promoted to Commander. And Lieutenant Sessions, you are now Lieutenant Commander Sessions. Put on the appropriate insignia."

Bell, a bit wide-eyed, removed his gold oak leaves and gave them to Sessions, then picked up the silver oak leaves from Jeffrey's desk and put them on.

Sessions, never outwardly competitive or demonstrative in his ambitions, donned the gold oak leaves of a lieutenant commander. He held his two old twin-silver-bar lieutenant collar tabs in his hand and stared at them dumbfoundedly.

Jeffrey couldn't hold it in anymore. He cracked into a big smile. "I want to do the change of command ASAP, then hold an award ceremony in the morning. . . . Make it at zero-six-hundred, right after breakfast. Enough of the crew should be awake and off watch, to participate. The PUC award."

"Sir?" Now it was Bell who sat dumbfounded.

Jeffrey cleared his throat for dramatic effect. "We aren't going home for a while after all. You're taking *Challenger,* permanently, and the Nav here is being made the XO. You'll both be under me as part of a two-ship undersea strike group that shall form up with USS *Jimmy Carter* once we reach the Beaufort Sea. In my role as strike group commander, I'll present the Presidential Unit Citation, with *you* as the recipient unit's, *Challenger*'s, skipper. It's classified, so no gold stars on top of the one we have, but I'd say, coming from our commander in chief, it's the thought that counts."

"Certainly, Captain."

"*Challenger* is to be my strike-group flagship at all times, for reasons my orders say will be obvious later. Commander Bell, since you'll take over this stateroom as skipper, and Lieutenant Commander Sessions will shift from his officers' three-man stateroom to the XO quarters next door, I'll use the VIP rack and make my office in there." It was standard on American subs for the XO stateroom to have a fold-down second rack for VIP passengers. By Navy custom, not even the President of the United States could displace a naval vessel's captain. "Yes, that part's straightforward enough. . . . Concur?"

"Concur," Bell said.

"We already know certain tactical doctrine and acoustic-link signals for working with another American nuclear sub."

Bell and Sessions nodded.

"We've tons to discuss re *Challenger* getting through the Bering Strait unobserved by our Russky friends."

"Sirs?" Sessions asked. "Who's the new Navigator?"

"Promotion to lieutenant came through for Lieutenant Junior Grade Meltzer. You can give him those railroad tracks." Slang for a navy lieutenant's insignia. "My final act as commanding officer of *Challenger* is to decide to make Meltzer the Navigator. My first act as strike group commodore will be to appoint him my part-time executive assistant."

"Aye-aye, sir," Sessions said.

"As XO, your first act can be to tell him."

"Yessir!"

Jeffrey fixed his gaze on Bell, and became more officious. "I want to make the changeover right away. You've completed your daily walkaround of my submarine?"

"Yes, Captain."

"You're satisfied enough with her material condition and crew competence to sign off on that, this minute?"

"Er, of course, sir."

Jeffrey brought up a form on his computer touch screen, then rotated it to face Bell. "There's the stylus. Render your electronic signature in the places indicated, please."

Bell kept scrolling down the screen, signing at each point required until he got to the end. "Sir, I am ready to relieve you as commanding officer of USS *Challenger*."

"Very well. Commander Bell, I am ready to be relieved."

"I relieve you, sir."

"I stand relieved. Congratulations, Captain," Jeffrey said, shaking Bell's hand. "XO, you too." He shook Sessions's hand.

Sessions beamed. "I wish I could tell my folks."

"You will, after we carry out compelling business."

Someone else knocked. "Speaking of which," Jeffrey said half under his breath. "Enter!"

A tall and muscular man in his early thirties came in. His features and complexion were Asian, maybe Mongolian. By the fierceness in his eyes, the tough set of his lips below a jet-black mustache, and the unmistakable coiled strength in his presence as he merely stood there, Jeffrey thought he resembled a latter-day Genghis Khan.

"Commander Nyurba, CEC, I presume?" CEC meant the Navy's Civil Engineer Corps, officers with advanced degrees who could also lead in frontline combat.

"The pleasure, the honor, are mine, Captain Fuller." Nyurba's voice resonated in the small compartment. His accent was totally American, but his speech had that velvet quality that came from central Asian genetics.

Nyurba possessed a very broad chest. His arms and legs were massive, and toned like a bodybuilder's. Jeffrey could tell all this on sight: Nyurba, for the first time while on *Challenger,* wore nothing but swim trunks and a T-shirt adorned with the Seabee logo—an angry bumblebee gripping a machine gun and tools in its six insect arms.

"Sorry to interrupt your exercise."

"Not exercise, Captain. Now you've read your orders, light dress is to get me acclimatized. It's cold where we're going."

Hmm. "That's what we need to start talking about."

Nyurba nodded soberly—too soberly for Jeffrey's comfort. *Commander, Strategic Command,* he reminded himself.

Sessions yielded his chair to Nyurba, and perched against Jeffrey's filing cabinet. With the four of them packed in the stateroom, it was cramped. Jeffrey preferred to think of times like this as cozy.

Another knock at the door. "That ought to be refreshments. . . . Come in!"

A mess management specialist—also highly trained as one of the ship's paramedics—held a heavily laden tray into the compartment, which Sessions, the closest, accepted. The others passed it from hand to hand until it sat on Jeffrey's desk. Mouth-watering aromas filled the stateroom.

"The pastries are optional," Jeffrey said, "but we're definitely going to need the coffee. . . . You do drink coffee, Commander? We can get hot water and a tea bag if you prefer."

"Thank you," Nyurba said, "but Navy coffee is fine by me. The closer to Mongolia you get in Siberia, the more you see coffee, not tea. Tea is a *Russian* thing. I mean ethnic Russian. Seven time zones west of the village where I spent my infancy."

"Ha. Learn something new every day."

Nyurba smiled warmly, his eyes sparkling in a sprightly way; he had a soft side after all. He also had crooked front teeth, a flaw that made him more human, approachable, not vain.

"My parents moved to Umiat after the Berlin Wall came down."

"Umiat?"

"On the Colville River, in north Alaska. They run a mom-and-pop general store."

"The rustic life? Sounds nice. . . . Well, let's dig in." Jeffrey poured coffee for everyone. "Oh, and from now on, you may call me Commodore." He made it sound routine, matter-of-fact, an afterthought tossed in casually.

The others acknowledged. Bell and Sessions shifted their postures, settling in more comfortably, both physically and psychologically. They already looked older, more mature than when the meeting began. They were growing into their new roles quickly, as they knew they needed to, following Jeffrey's example. He sipped his coffee, strong and hot and black.

"Commander Nyurba, how much can you tell us now about what your team is supposed to do?"

———

Dashiyn Nyurba had prepared thoroughly for this initial briefing, and knew he had to proceed with caution. Commodore Fuller was an intelligent man, and fearless, but there were higher considerations that weighed on Nyurba heavily. It was why he'd been given a cyanide capsule to keep nearby at all times.

"It's not my team, Commodore. I'm second in command."

"I thought—"

"Yes, I'm the most senior of the SERT members you have aboard."

"But . . . ?"

"When we rendezvous, I merge with a much larger group."

"How much larger?" Commodore Fuller asked.

"Seventy-five more." Nyurba knew they were hot-racking— sharing bunks—since *Carter* only had space for fifty riders beyond her regular crew. Seventy-five was a mob.

"*Seventy-five* more Seabees together? What are you guys up to? That's like, what, eight full SERT teams on one mission?"

"We're not all Seabees, Commodore. The complement is a joint one. We have people from special ops groups throughout the U.S. armed forces. SEALs, Marine Recon, Army Green Berets and Delta, Air Force Special Operations Squadrons, and some other air force experts. We were chosen because of our individual skills and our physical fitness. But most of all because of our cultural backgrounds and language fluencies."

"Meaning?"

"The majority of us are combat veterans from the Global War on Terror, who because of our birth and upbringing can pass for native-born Russians or Siberians, or Russian Federation nationalities that serve in their army these days. For instance, I speak Russian and a couple of main Siberian languages, which haven't entirely died out in the Old Country. My family's mostly Evenk, intermarried with Yukaghir." Nyurba saw this drew a blank with Jeffrey. "I spent several tours in Iraq, and have two Bronze Stars and a Purple Heart to show for it, doing SERT engineering recon assignments attached to Marine Corps brigades."

"Okay. I'm suitably impressed."

"My entire current unit, the eighty of us, have been training together, as one commando entity, since the Berlin-Boer War started, as a contingency against a potential scenario. The President has decided to put that contingency, that scenario, into action."

"Meaning?"

"I'm not supposed to say yet, sir. We need to get through the Bering Strait, then go to *Carter* by minisub. As you would know better than me, the Bering Strait is not an easy passage. We can't afford any sort of problem, where this ship or her crew might fall into not-so-gentle Russian hands, while the latter pretend to be helping us poor distressed mariners. Everything they'd learn would be fed to the Germans. In this context, that could prove more disastrous than . . ."

Nyurba stopped himself, leaving an awkward silence made worse by the venom he realized had dripped from his last few sentences; his hatred of the Russians and Germans alike was rather personal. It was something he knew could not be fathomed by those whose ancestors hadn't suffered the eastward expansion of Cossack traders and trappers long ago, the oppression under the czars, Stalin's purges and forced migrations—and then the mass shipment westward of Siberian troops to repel the Hitlerite invaders, as cannon fodder marching on Berlin to be mown down in droves, to keep that same Stalin in power. Stalin's successors had been no better, with Moscow despoiling the pristine Siberian environment in the name of industrial progress and Soviet-Russian national defense; the poisoned ecology killed people slowly and painfully. Nyurba knew all about that last part. He was an expert in nuclear decontamination.

—————

Commodore Fuller put an end to the silence. "Last I heard, *Carter* was under repair in New London after heavy damage and casualties from a failed raid against Axis-occupied Norway."

Nyurba's hackles went up again immediately. "That raid did not fail due to even a single mistake made on site. The intelligence that led to the raid, and the operational security required to support it, are what failed." Operational security meant overall secrecy to maintain surprise.

Jeffrey was taken aback at Nyurba's vehemence. Clearly he was someone with a quick temper, someone to not make angry, especially not off duty in a bar.

"Commander Charles Harley remains in command of *Carter*," Nyurba stated, "for everything that that should tell you. He won the Navy Cross for bringing his ship and the surviving SEALs back in one piece!"

Jeffrey felt a pang of grief. He had a strong hunch that two SEALs he'd grown fond of, who'd been with him on earlier raids staged from *Challenger,* had died on *Carter's* mission to Norway. Because compartmentalization was so strict, none of his efforts to discover the fate of those comrades had yielded one clue.

But that was months ago. And from what he did hear through the grapevine, Captain Harley had reason enough for his own bereavement, from the losses he suffered on that mission, ambushed by waiting German forces through no fault of his own. It said something that, even given the shipyard working round the clock with the highest priority, it took many precious months to make *Carter* ready for action again. Harley's Navy Cross was second only to the Medal of Honor as a naval combat decoration.

Jeffrey barely knew Harley, and wondered what leading him into renewed battle might be like. Would he flinch, after the prior setback, as some did? Would Harley overcompensate and become too reckless? Jeffrey caught himself staring into his coffee mug. He took another sip before addressing Nyurba.

"Why aren't you on *Carter* now?"

"My team had to go for extra training stateside. The rest of the squadron was training too, on an island in northern Canada, pretending to be a science research expedition."

"An ice station?"

"Except on land, not a drifting floe. They were brought south, scattered, then made their way to New London in small groups to not draw attention from Axis spies working in the U.S. It was more secure to fly us five in the SERT cadre to Pearl. It also allowed me to meet you sooner, to perform indoctrination."

"Who's in command of your special ops company?" Jeffrey's orders said the commandos reported to him as strike group boss, but further details rested in that still-sealed inner pouch.

"An Air Force lieutenant colonel, Sergey Kurzin. You'll meet him when we rendezvous with *Carter.* And although we're called a special operations *squadron,* we are in fact organized for this mission like an infantry company."

Jeffrey couldn't hide his surprise. "Why Air Force?"

Nyurba frowned. "I probably said too much. . . . But I do need to emphasize something, to you and your key officers, before another hour goes by. You must have this thoroughly clear before we even begin to approach the strait, because it will affect all decisions you make from here on."

Jeffrey wondered how much Nyurba knew and wasn't allowed to let on yet. He was a senior officer, with the same rank that Jeffrey had held until this evening. At Nyurba's level, he could have been leading a conventional Seabee brigade, over two thousand men. Whatever he was really up to had to be extremely unconventional. "Go ahead, Commander."

"For purposes of this mission, for this mission to succeed, it is imperative that *Carter* remain undetected."

Jeffrey tried to not sound condescending. "I admire your loyalty to Captain Harley's crew and Colonel Kurzin's people, but that's true of every submarine on every mission, Commander."

"Commodore, you don't understand. Perhaps the wording in the orders you've read seemed too routine. My own orders are clear cut. I'm to convey to you in no uncertain terms that this is not in the least routine. *Carter*'s invisibility throughout is paramount. Her having ever been where she will be must remain unsuspected from now until after our mission goals are achieved, and for decades beyond. *Decades.* If necessary to preserve *Carter*'s total stealth, should it come to that, *Challenger* and all aboard, from this moment forth, are expendable."

CHAPTER 3

Thirty-six hours later, at 0900 local time, Jeffrey held a planning huddle with Bell, Sessions, and David Meltzer around the digital navigation table toward the rear of *Challenger*'s control room. The Bering Strait choke point was coming up fast, and critical decisions were needed on routing and tactics.

Lieutenant Meltzer, as brand-new ship's navigator and part-time commodore's executive assistant, was handling himself with commendable professionalism. A Naval Academy graduate like Bell, Meltzer spoke with a Bronx accent that got thicker under combat stress. He always walked, in the ship or ashore, with a strut on the cocky side, chest puffed out, as if daring the Navy—or life in general—to keep giving him more difficult things to do. Jeffrey, who'd grown up in St. Louis and done Navy ROTC at Purdue, liked this attitude; Meltzer was popular and admired among the junior officers as well, and respected without reservations by the chiefs and other enlisted people. More visibly ambitious than Sessions, and more socially poised and outgoing, he took being made a department head in stride.

To Jeffrey's practiced eyes, there was no sign of jealousy among the men who'd remain for a while yet as lieutenants, junior grade. If anything, the feeling shipwide was one of a group bond renewed, and strongly validated, by their shared Presidential Unit Citation. Jeffrey could sense this in the busy control room, packed with two dozen people sitting at consoles or standing in the aisles, each doing some specialized task, or helping or teaching or learning.

The tactical plot was updated for the umpteenth time. The surface wind came from the south, at force four—about fifteen knots—strong enough to cause whitecaps. The same wind created enough noise that *Challenger*'s advanced passive sonars could use ambient ocean sounds, instead of telltale active pinging, to detect any silent collision threat—even an errant mine—in time to avoid it, if people stayed on their toes. With prevailing currents coming from southeast, across a fetch of open water whose temperature in early summer was well above freezing, the risk of encountering an iceberg soon was minimal; the Bering Sea only froze during winter. Jeffrey knew this would change, menacingly, once they got above the Arctic Circle—near the summertime reach of the polar ice cap, and closer to massive coastal glaciers from which the biggest icebergs calved.

Jeffrey had an unobstructed line of sight to the big displays on the bulkheads at the front of the control room, because *Challenger* possessed no old-fashioned periscopes. Instead, data from photonics masts, which retracted into the sail—conning tower—when not in use, would electronically feed imagery to full-color, high-definition plasma screens that many crewmen could observe simultaneously.

"The photonics mast control console," Jeffrey said to Bell.

"Commodore?"

"I don't think you'll be needing it anytime soon. I'd like to take it over, while I'm in Control, as a place to sit and command my strike group."

The console was on the aft bulkhead of Control, its screens

dark now, the seat unoccupied. The console was also near the doors to the radio room and the electronic support measures room. The radio room contained the ship's top-secret encryption equipment. The electronic support measures room contained the equally classified signals-intercept eavesdropping gear. Both doors had security warnings posted on the outside, and were protected by combination locks.

Jeffrey pointed toward the doors. "They'll be handy in case I need either one, and I can reconfigure the console to show me the data I'll want, and I'll also be out of your way but still in easy speaking distance."

"Certainly, Commodore."

That console also happened to be the one closest to Jeffrey's stateroom that he shared with Sessions and used as an office. He could move back and forth quickly and unobtrusively. *On a submarine there's no formality like someone shouting* Commodore *in Control* or Captain *off the Bridge or crap like that.*

"New passive sonar contact on the starboard wide-aperture array," the sonar supervisor of the watch, a senior chief, called out. "Bearing zero-six-five, range twenty thousand yards." East-northeast, ten nautical miles. The northern Bering Sea's bottom was shallow and silty. Sound emanations bounced repeatedly between the surface and the sea floor, and signal strength was lost with every bounce, so detection ranges were short. "Surface contact, designate Sierra Eight-Four."

"Contact identification?" the officer of the deck asked.

"Three-bladed shaft, dead-slow blade rate. Auxiliary machinery broadband, with intermittent transients. . . . Assess as American fishing trawler." A factory ship. Salmon, pollack, and herring were plentiful here, unblemished by radioactivity because the war to date had spared the Pacific.

"Very well, Sonar." The OOD for this six-hour watch, a junior officer from Engineering, also had the conn, in charge of the course, speed, and depth of the ship.

"Conn," the leader of the contact tracking party called out, "Sierra Eight-Four appears to be making bare steerageway, conjecture to hold position against the half-knot current. Our projected closest point of approach crosses within five miles of possible deployed trawling net." Too close for comfort.

Bell glanced forward in concern.

New lines and icon symbols appeared on the tactical plot.

"Very well," the officer of the deck responded. "Helm, left five degrees rudder, make your course zero-four-zero."

"Left five degrees rudder, aye," the helmsman acknowledged. "Make my course zero-four-zero, aye." He worked his joystick, then made more reports to the OOD at the conn.

On the tactical plot, *Challenger*'s projected track shifted to the left, further away from the trawler. Bell appeared satisfied.

These interactions had been going on nonstop for hours. Jeffrey leaned his elbows on the edge of the horizontal navigation plotting table, and tried to tune them out. He followed along as Meltzer summarized *Challenger*'s progress since crossing the Aleutian Islands volcanic chain, entering the southern Bering Sea through one of the deep-water inter-island gaps. The ship's previous track was shown on the navigation display. This verbal summary was needed for clarity, to best establish a context for the next decisions they faced. It was a long-standing Silent Service tradition that every briefing was also, in part, an oral exam. Errors could be avoided, weaknesses identified and fixed, and continuing education maximized if seniors tested juniors—and themselves strove, before a keen audience, to meet the highest standards.

Meltzer continued his first major briefing review. "After the change of command, we altered base course to zero-one-zero and came up to five hundred feet as we reached the Siberio-Alaskan rise. That let us avoid St. Matthew Island

and then St. Lawrence Island, U.S.-owned in mid-Bering Sea, and we also bypassed the very shallow water stretching east of them to the Alaska mainland." Meltzer gestured at the chart with his hands. "It did, however, bring us near to the treaty convention line defining American versus Russian waters." That abstract line on nautical charts, during the Cold War, helped prevent U.S. and Soviet warships from coming too close together unintentionally, thus avoiding an accident or misunderstanding that could escalate. "We've gone progressively shallower, and reduced speed, as water depth decreased to its present one-hundred-eighty feet. We altered base course to zero-four-five when we rounded the western tip of St. Lawrence Island." Northeast. "This put us moving parallel to the treaty line, fifteen, that is one-five, nautical miles on the U.S. side. . . . Excuse me, please, sirs."

Meltzer conferred with the Assistant Navigator, a senior chief, and pointed out that their most recent course diversion was slowly bringing them closer to the treaty line. The assistant navigator calculated when, and by how much, to turn back east, safely past Sierra Eight-Four, and before intersecting that line. The senior chief relayed this data to the officer of the deck, who acknowledged.

"Well, then," Meltzer resumed. "Since, as you can see, the treaty line splits the Bering Strait down the middle, the zero-four-five heading also put us on course for the strait. At our present speed of eight knots, and from our present position, *here,* we'll need to commit to one side of the strait or the other within two hours. That's the next major choice. Do we take the channel on the U.S. side of Little Diomede Island, or the other channel on the Russian side of Big Diomede?" The two islands sat right next to each other in the middle of the strait. "If we take as our minimum acceptable water depth one-five-zero feet, for a covert passage at reasonable speed, then the navigable part of either channel is one-five nautical miles wide."

"The American side seems the much safer bet," Bell stated.

"I concur, sir," Sessions said.

"Okay," Jeffrey responded. "It *seems* the safer, so it's what the Russians would expect."

"You mean," Bell asked, "go through on their side because they'll think that channel's more secure? I don't know, Commodore. Is that even allowed by our rules of engagement?"

"My ROEs give me extensive discretion," Jeffrey said. "And the Russians are neutral, supposedly."

"We're not neutral, sir. We're a belligerent. And their neutrality is, as you say, only supposed. Plus, they're totally paranoid. They could easily open fire on an unidentified submerged contact, *us*, without any warning."

Jeffrey gave Bell a wry smile. "I'm paranoid, too. I'm paranoid of *American* traitors and moles. I have good reason to think there's one on the loose in Washington, with high access. If we pass through east of Little Diomede, our own assets might more likely pick us up. We get injected into the U.S. command-and-control net. If that net is compromised, our position and course get reported right to the Axis."

"Like another Walker spy ring or something?" Meltzer asked.

"Exactly. And our detection systems are more advanced than the Russians', so if we get picked up at all it'd more likely happen on the U.S. side."

Bell shook his head. "We don't know what gadgets Russia has that we don't even know about, Commodore. We do know their anti-stealth radar is better than ours. We do know the Germans are giving them various things, fancy things."

"Antisubmarine warfare is about much more than gadgetry, Captain. By 'systems' I include the *people*. It's a team sport, as you're aware, and I believe our side's team does it better."

"Sir, the Bering Strait is one of the most strategic choke points in the world! For all we know the hydrophone listening posts in the Russian channel are manned by Germans!"

"I still think our side's team does it better. We've had years, *decades* more practice than the Germans."

Bell almost sputtered in exasperation. Jeffrey pretended not to notice. "The decision affects my entire strike group. It's not one you on *Challenger* can view in isolation."

"Yes, Commodore. Of course."

"Very well," Jeffrey said. "We have a schedule to keep. We penetrate the strait through the Russian side."

"What about their antisubmarine patrols and bottom sensors?"

"On that I defer to you, Captain. I've told you where we need to go. You tell your crew how to get us there."

CHAPTER 4

Jeffrey took a short nap and a shower and immediately felt refreshed. He grabbed a quick lunch in the wardroom at 1105, joined informally by some of Bell's officers. Among them was Lieutenant Bud Torelli, the weapons officer—Weps for short. Torelli was from Memphis, and his Southern accent showed it. He had a neatly groomed mustache, brown like his curly hair. His build ran to the fleshy side, with some overhang over his belt, but this was true of many submariners and it didn't slow him down any. Torelli finished eating.

"I'm paying a quick visit to the men in the torpedo room." His shoulders set squarely, he left the wardroom to go below. Jeffrey knew that Torelli and his people might soon be frantic with effort to keep themselves and the rest of the crew alive.

They're a hardened, steely-nerved bunch now that they've got their sense of purpose back. Intercepting incoming fire, and putting weapons on target, required exhausting teamwork as intricately choreographed, and as thoroughly rehearsed, as any ballet. Every torpedo or cruise missile weighed thousands of pounds, much of that volatile engine fuels, high explosives—and fissionable cores of uranium or plutonium. Crush injuries and toxic spills were a constant hazard. A fire or explosion could spell disaster. Operating each tube correctly was a tricky task in itself. Bad flooding through one would doom the ship.

Damage control in Torelli's department was taken tremendously seriously. Sessions, as XO, had assigned the Seabee passengers, when at battle stations, to be an extra damage-control party stationed outside the torpedo room; their talents at improvising machinery repairs during combat might give a decisive extra margin for survival if worse came to worst. One of *Challenger*'s chiefs from Engineering was with them as the man in charge, since the Seabees weren't qualified in submarines.

Lieutenant Willey, the engineer, stopped by while Jeffrey finished gulping his coffee. "Greetings, *mein* Commodore."

"Ahoy there, Enj," Jeffrey razzed him back—a ship's engineer often got the nickname Enj. Willey was respectful, but he did have an offbeat, sometimes edgy sense of humor. Tall and lanky, his face always seemed pinched and his posture slightly stooping, as if carrying a heavy load. Right now he had stubbly five-o'clock shadow and extra-bad coffee breath, and looked like he'd been awake for twenty-four hours straight, at least. His eyes were sunken and bloodshot, but sharply focused.

Jeffrey sympathized: he'd been an engineer on his own department head tour. The hours were especially grueling; the responsibilities never let up. Overseeing the safe and reliable running of a sub's nuclear reactor, and all the rest of the propulsion plant and other mechanical systems, took commitment and heart as well as tons of book smarts and common sense.

Willey wolfed down a slice of sausage casserole, and hurried aft. Jeffrey left the wardroom, stepping into the passageway. The enlisted mess, on the opposite side of the galley, was doing brisk business. Captain Bell had passed the word that he'd be going to battle stations soon. This could be the crew's last chance for a hot meal for a while.

The mess management specialists, normally very attentive to their customers and renowned for their cheerful service, seemed unusually eager for everyone to finish eating and leave. They needed to clean up, then specially sanitize these spaces: in emergencies, the ship's wardroom doubled as an operating theater, and the enlisted mess was the triage area.

A corkscrew twisted in Jeffrey's stomach momentarily, and he knew it wasn't the food. He was remembering times on previous missions when there'd been human blood on the floor here in puddles, and bodies or parts of bodies stored in a sealed-off section of the ship's freezer.

Jeffrey walked forward into the control room, pushing these macabre recollections from his mind. He sat and activated his console, arranging windows on the two large screens, one above the other, to show the data he would need: a copy of the navigation plot and the tactical plot. A copy of the ship's gravimeter display, which used sophisticated sensors and computer algorithms to measure the three-dimensional gravity fields around the ship, and from that derive a picture of the local sea floor and coastline topography. The gravimeter was nice because it was passive, not needing to make emissions that could give away *Challenger*'s presence. It could see through solid rock, because gravity reached through solid rock. It also was immune to loud noise, unlike the sonar systems, though the gravimeter couldn't detect moving objects.

Jeffrey next called up a copy of the main sonar waterfall displays. Lighter solid streaks marked man-made contacts; aircraft could be detected if they came close enough, from their engine sounds passing down through the water. Intermittent bright spots, or a series of dots, indicated whale calls: humpbacks and grays were especially common, feeding on the plankton blooms that nourished these waters at this time of year.

Last, he added to his crowded screens the pictures from the ship's hull-mounted photonic sensors, set in passive image-intensification mode. The ocean outside *Challenger* was murky, due to the rich biologics and their organic waste, and because of erosion silt from heavy runoff as snow and ice melted on the watersheds of the continents looming to both sides.

He was satisfied for now. These readouts gave him the best possible overall situational awareness as the ship approached the Russian channel through the Bering Strait.

Bell strode into the control room, nodding to his commodore as he passed. "Officer of the Deck, I have the deck and the conn."

"Captain has the deck and the conn, aye-aye." All the watchstanders acknowledged, too.

"Chief of the Watch," Bell ordered, "on the sound-powered phones, rig for ultraquiet and go to silent battle stations." The shipwide public-address system, the 1MC, was much too noisy.

In moments, people began dashing into Control, relieving those at some positions. The chief of the boat came in, a salty bulldog of a master chief, Latino, from Jersey City, in his early forties the oldest man aboard. Everyone called him "COB"—like the word "cob," not an acronym—as if that was his only name. He took over as battle stations chief of the watch, at the two-man ship control station at the front end of the space. The helmsman on watch next to him didn't move; Lieutenant (j.g.) Radesh Patel, from Engineering, was the newly designated battle stations helmsman. A former Western Conference football linebacker and physics major, even seated he was a head taller than COB. Normally jovial, and a wicked chess player, Patel had gone from damage control assistant to a very different sort of responsibility—one that would be like doing football, chess, and physics all at once.

Bell took the left seat of the two-man desk-high command console at the center of Control. Sessions assumed the right seat. Metallic *snicks* sounded throughout the space, men buckling their seat belts, which reminded Jeffrey to do the same.

He set up one more small window on his lower screen, so he could instant-message with Meltzer through the LAN. This way they could converse, commodore and executive assistant, without distracting Bell and Sessions as they fought the ship.

Lieutenant Torelli hurried in and stood in the aisle overseeing his first team at the four target tracking and weapons consoles that lined Control's starboard bulkhead. A nondescript lieutenant (j.g.), the new sonar officer—Alan Finch, from Peoria, Illinois—stood in the opposite aisle. The forwardmost of his seven consoles, lining the port bulkhead, was taken by the most seasoned sonar supervisor, Senior Chief Brendan O'Hanlon.

Meltzer entered and stood at the navigation plotting table with the assistant navigator and several of their people.

The phone talker, wearing his heavy sound-powered intercom rig, listened on his big headphones. He answered on the bulky mike that made its own electricity from the vibrations as he spoke, then looked up. "Captain, Phone Talker. All compartments report manned and ready."

"Very well, Phone Talker," Bell said. "Chief of the Watch, rig ship for red."

COB acknowledged. The lighting switched from bright white to a subdued ruby glow. It gave the control room an intimate feel, and helped remind people in some other spaces to maintain ultraquiet. Men blinked to help their eyes adjust to the dimness. Several small pocket flashlights were brought out, to frequently check pipes and fittings for flaws that might otherwise go unobserved. All hunched more closely over their consoles. Their voices became more restrained.

"Chief of the Watch, secure ventilation fans."

"Secure ventilation fans, aye." COB worked switches. The air circulation vents ceased their hushing sound; the gentle cool breezes stopped. The change was portentous, eerie. *Challenger,* like a living thing, was hunkering down for maximum stealth.

The control room slowly began to grow stuffy, from the heat and tense breathing of two dozen men and the warmth of electronics—*Challenger*'s acoustic and thermal insulation kept the chill of the water outside well away from her innards. The crew was used to this, but no one liked it. If it went on for too long, personnel performance would be degraded, and eventually some important part of the combat systems might fail. Jeffrey knew that this was just one of many unpleasant trade-offs an SSN's captain faced. Peering forward, he could see people shifting in their seats, flexing their shoulder blades, moving their heads back and forth, to loosen cramping muscles. The excitement of new mission orders had worn off. It wasn't a game anymore.

"Helm," Bell ordered in a low but firm voice, "slow to ahead one third and make turns for five knots."

The helmsman, Patel, acknowledged, then gingerly touched icons on one of his screen menus. His arm movement was jerky, and Jeffrey thought he could see his hand shaking. In a moment, Patel reported in a near-whisper, "Maneuvering answers, ahead one-third, turns for five knots, sir." Jeffrey heard the strain in his voice. Meltzer would have been handling the stress much better, but he'd been promoted to navigator.

"Very well, Helm. Left five degrees rudder, make your course three-four-zero."

Again Patel acknowledged Bell, twisting his joystick.

Feeling strangely detached, almost as if he'd been plunged back in time to the height of the Cold War, Jeffrey saw the own-ship heading's readout on his console change as *Challenger* swung gently left. *Who am I kidding? We're in a second Cold War with Russia right now that could quickly turn hot.*

He envied the men who had assigned stations they could fixate on. With nothing concrete at the moment to keep him preoccupied, he found his mind beginning to dart from one item to the next. His gravimeter display, set in forward-looking mode, showed rugged Little Diomede and Big Diomede Islands a short distance ahead, slowly drifting rightward on the 3-D picture as *Challenger* continued her turn. He could see the ocean floor, the parts of the islands that rose steeply from the bottom, plus a notional transparent plain that marked the ocean's surface, and the terrain of the islands exposed in the air. The sea floor was almost perfectly flat, at a depth of only one-hundred-sixty feet.

On the left edge of the image, a mountainous knob three miles wide rose suddenly from the ocean floor to altitudes of over six thousand feet above sea level: the beginning of mainland Russia. On the right edge, on both the gravimeter and the navigation chart, Cape Prince of Wales and the Prince of Wales Shoal were visible. This jutting part of the Alaskan mainland was tipped by a mountain, too, though only half as tall as the Russian ones.

Jeffrey eyed the tactical plot. All merchant shipping had been left behind, and none was detected in front. Every one of the handful of contacts held on the display, surface or airborne, was denoted by an icon that meant it was military, and Russian. If something submerged was lurking in ambush, a submarine or an unannounced minefield, *Challenger*'s sensors and technicians hadn't spotted it yet. Not that they weren't trying. A few of the sonarmen and fire-control specialists were already wiping sweat off their foreheads.

Rules of engagement for neutrals were words on paper, Jeffrey reminded himself. Russia didn't have a stellar record putting them into practice in the field. In 1983, when local commanders ordered Korean Airlines Flight 007, from JFK to Seoul, be shot down by a fighter—without properly verifying the 747's identity first—the Kremlin was humiliated before an angry world. Hundreds of innocent civilians were killed. The blunder helped bring down the Soviet Union. Though that was almost thirty years ago, the newest Russian Federation regime was autocratic, and talked very

tough about self-defense, with rising investments in hardware to back up the talk. It was unclear if local forces would
open fire on an unidentified undersea contact.

Jeffrey was second-guessing his own decision, too late.
The navigation plot showed *Challenger* miles beyond the
treaty line already.

———

Bell ordered several more course changes to get the ship
into position to transit the Bering Strait. Jeffrey's displays
showed *Challenger* nearing the mouth of the Russian-side
channel. The constricted part, the strait itself, was only
three miles long from start to finish before widening out
again, so depending on Bell's tactics they could be through
it very quickly. He'd chosen to aim for a path about two-
thirds of the way from Big Diomede to the protruding knob
at the tip of Siberia. Closer to the mainland, the water
should be cloudier from soil erosion and thaw runoff. The
Russian side was also more nutrient-rich—more productive
biologically—and phytoplankton could turn the surface
yellow-brown or milky white; even droppings from numerous sea birds helped obscure submerged visibility.

This would make it harder to detect *Challenger* via optical sensors: dipping blue-green lasers called LIDAR, or
airborne cameras linked to supercomputer software—
called LASH—able to notice anomalous color gradations
and shapes deep underwater.

Out of curiosity, and to audit the proper preparedness of
Challenger's brand-new command team, Jeffrey called up
a copy of the main weapons status page. He saw that Bell
had four tubes loaded with high-explosive Mark 48 Improved ADCAP torpedoes, the standard heavyweight fish
of the U.S. submarine fleet. The other four tubes held Mark
II brilliant decoys, which could be programmed to imitate
Challenger, or another sub, by giving off an acoustic signature meant to be noticed by the enemy.

He typed a message to Bell: "Why no off-board probes to scout ahead?" Remote-controlled probes could be deployed through the torpedo tubes, too. Similar in size and shape to an ADCAP, they were fitted with a mix of active and passive sonars, passive photonic imagers, and active laser line-scan cameras.

Bell answered right away, typing, "Path here known clear of shipwrecks." A pause. "You're welcome to stand by my console."

Jeffrey got up and eased forward through the compartment's cramped left aisle. He stopped next to Bell's console, with his back touching the sonar supervisor's chair. Bell turned from his horizontal screens and looked up at Jeffrey. He responded to the query more, his voice lowered to be barely audible. Bell spoke softly mainly to not break his crew's concentration on their console displays, since a threat could appear out of nowhere at any time. But some of it was purely mental: at ultraquiet people walked and talked and even thought on pins and needles.

"Because probes might be detected, Commodore, and Russian subs wouldn't use them in their own safe corridor. It would show right away we're not friendlies. Besides, in these conditions our own probe sensors in passive-only won't give us much we can't get better on *Challenger* herself."

Sessions joined in from the seat next to Bell, his soft features softened further in the dim red lighting. "The Captain and I discussed it, Commodore." While Jeffrey had been in the wardroom, apparently. "Since we can't afford to radiate, we can't use the acoustic link to control any probes. If we use a fiber-optic tether instead, and it breaks, we can't recover the probe and then we've left a clue we were here. . . . Plus, to send a probe on ahead of us slowly and quietly, by far enough to make a difference in tactically useful data, would take too long when we want to minimize our dwell time by the strait."

"What about antisubmarine mines, if this path you

picked isn't in their safe corridor of the day? The whole channel's fifteen miles wide. What if we're too far right or left of where Russian subs know they should go?"

"No notices to mariners, sir," Sessions reminded Jeffrey politely. "No minefield."

The reminder was unnecessary—Jeffrey had been quizzing him. By international law, all naval minefields had to be publicly announced, with all mines moored or otherwise held stationary. Modern mines could be programmed to ignore surface shipping, and to go off only when a submerged submarine went by. They could also be armed and later switched off via remote control, altering safe pathways through a solid field of mines.

Jeffrey nodded sourly. "If there's one good thing we can say about Moscow, they're sticklers for the outward letter of international law. . . . Axis subs using the strait?"

"Intel says our forces have them too well bottled up on the other side of the world, sir."

These were good answers. "Okay." Jeffrey eyed the tactical plot vertical display on the forward bulkhead. Something genuinely puzzled him. "Why do you think the U.S. doesn't have any surface ships or aircraft patrolling the American channel?"

He felt the sonar supervisor sliding sideways in his seat. Jeffrey glanced at O'Hanlon, a self-assured expert who liked to go clean-shaven, and almost bald with a razor cut, accentuating the way his small ears stuck far out from the side of his head. Senior Chief O'Hanlon, in his mid-thirties, was a battle-hardened sailor, and Jeffrey could see the very top of a chest tattoo above the collar of his undershirt, worn beneath his jumpsuit. He had a pair of sonar headphones draped around his neck, so he could don them in a jiffy if he wanted to. A small lip mike was positioned to one side of his very square jaw.

Jeffrey stepped back to not block his view of the captain and XO. "If I may?" O'Hanlon asked. Bell nodded.

"Sir," the chief told Jeffrey, "we conjecture it's to minimize signal-to-noise ratio for U.S. bottom sensors and our own subs sneaking through or doing barrier patrols."

"Makes sense," Jeffrey said. By flying around and charging all over, engine and machinery sounds from aircraft and ships created underwater interference. This would make it harder for bottom hydrophones, or the sonar arrays of a lurking American submarine, to pick out a hostile sub's giveaway broadband and tonals from amid the extra background clutter. *But* . . .

"That would be true for Russian bottom sensors, too."

"Of course, sir," O'Hanlon said.

"Then why are they making things harder for themselves?"

"We conjecture that with the water so shallow, and no pronounced sonar layer, they use a completely different approach from us, relying mainly on surveillance from above instead."

"Which is why you're keeping the ship as deep as you can," Jeffrey stated to Bell, who nodded.

"There's another factor in these waters, Commodore," Sessions murmured. "The entire strait's bottom is just within reach of divers using compressed air rigs. If they work out of a seabed habitat, they can spend long hours inspecting the bottom, day in, day out, and map or even disable a bottom sensor grid."

"You mean, SEALs deploying out of a SeaLab type of contraption, saturation divers, sneaking to the Russky side and jiggering with their security measures?"

"Something like that, sir," Sessions said.

"Suppose so. Then what prevents Russian divers from doing the same thing to us?"

"Presumably the SEALs would be standing guard against that, or they could have sensors specifically meant to watch for human intruders crossing the treaty line."

"So saturation diver SEALs defend our channel's hydrophones, and can sabotage any Russian ones? The Russians don't even try to compete for the low ground, they just use surface and airborne surveillance platforms instead? That didn't even occur to me."

Bell summoned up a different type of display. The spikes and jiggles showed a graph of sound intensity versus frequency, which Bell had set to focus in on the relative bearings near one-eight-zero—rearward. *Challenger* hadn't deployed a towed array, because it could drag or snag on the bottom, creating giveaway noise. He was using the sonar sphere at the bow, with its all-around coverage, to check on his own ship's signature.

Bell turned to Sessions and pointed to spikes on the display. "We need to quell our self-noise more."

"Concur, sir."

"Chief of the Watch," Bell ordered in a stage whisper. "Stop portside auxiliary turbogenerator. On the sound-powered phones, rig ship for reduced electrical."

This would turn off more unnecessary equipment, large and small, making *Challenger* as silent as a church mouse.

Jeffrey shimmied back to his console and sat. He cringed as his backside rubbed against the vinyl, squeaking. His brain told him this couldn't possibly get through *Challenger*'s state-of-the-art quieting technology, to be heard outside the ship. The sudden tightness in his gut showed that the rest of his body didn't believe his brain.

Bell ordered one more course change. Patel acknowledged, and Jeffrey's displays shifted their pictures leftward. The maw of the strait was dead ahead. Bell had Patel reduce speed to three knots, about 3.5 miles per hour—a brisk pace for a person on a sidewalk. The current coming from behind, of about a half-knot, gave them a small extra push with no noise penalty.

"Helm, rig for nap-of-sea-floor cruising mode."

Jeffrey's repeat of the helm displays now showed a different type of information, with steering cues and warnings of gradual dips and rises in the bottom in front of the ship, as revealed by the gravimeter's sharp resolution at very short range.

"Helm, maintain clearance beneath the keel of one-five feet. Engage autopilot but be prepared to override." Jeffrey knew Bell well enough to hear a subtle quiver in his voice; what he'd ordered was no easy task, with a ship as long as a football field including both end zones.

Even with computer assistance from the ship control station's autopilot, depth management by Patel and buoyancy and trim control by COB were critical now. The slightest mistake and the bow or stern would hit the sea floor. But *Challenger* needed every foot of distance from the surface that she could get: LASH worked best at the peak of daylight, and outside the ship it was noon. Every soul aboard was aware, based on horrible experience, of how deadly an antisubmarine weapon LASH was.

Tension in the control room thickened palpably, becoming almost suffocating. Crewmen pulled off sweaters, or unzipped the tops of their jumpsuits. Others rolled up their sleeves, to stay fresh as the air grew increasingly stale. This was only the beginning of the ordeal of making it through the strait.

Jeffrey shuffled his windowed displays, to give more room to the pictures from the hull's photonic sensors. In passive image-intensification mode, he caught glimpses of fish swimming by, and watched the soft, silty bottom receding behind the ship as she moved forward. He saw rocks, transported over the centuries in icebergs calved off glaciers along the coast; as the bergs melted, their burden, released, fell through the sea.

The tactical plot showed two Russian surface ships just past the northern end of the strait. One was a destroyer, of the type NATO gave the code name Udaloy. Though they tended to be plagued by onboard fires, when they worked right they were formidable. The Russians called the Udaloy class a "Large Antisubmarine Ship," and to Jeffrey this said it all. The other was a Grisha-V antisubmarine corvette, much smaller than the Udaloy.

At low altitude, on a racetrack-oval course that ran east-west beyond the strait, the plot also showed sonar holding intermittent contact on an Ilyushin-38 four-engine turbo-prop plane, NATO code name May. The Mays had been modernized since their introduction in 1969. Finally due for retirement just when the war broke out, Russia kept them in service. Each one could carry a dangerous mix of air-dropped torpedoes, sonobuoys, and depth charges. They also bore a magnetic anomaly detector—MAD—on a boom behind their tail, which if properly calibrated could find *Challenger* in water this shallow. Though her hull was made of nonmagnetic ceramic composite, there was enough steel and iron inside to register at short enough range.

Challenger could easily outrun an Udaloy or a Grisha, but not the Udaloy's two antisubmarine helicopters. She might or might not manage to escape their lightweight torpedoes. The May maritime patrol bomber, *Challenger* could never outrun. If that aircraft was carrying APR-2 or APR-3 rocket-propelled torpedoes, and her crew drew a bead and chose to drop the weapons armed, in such confined waters *Challenger* was finished.

CHAPTER 5

J effrey was staring tensely at the pictures from outside.
        "What's that?" COB hissed.
        Through the murky water ahead, Jeffrey saw a long
and thin object projecting high off the bottom.

"Helm left thirty rudder," Bell snapped, the risk of collision too real. "Back one third."

"Aye, sir!" Patel said, his voice cracking, too panicked to
acknowledge properly. The ship swung left. In front of them
were more of these towering objects. *Challenger* had too
much momentum to be able to stop or turn out of their
way.

"Helm maximum rise on autohover!" Bell kept his voice
deep with great effort. The only thing remaining was to try
to go up and over the obstacles.

"Autohover, aye, rise!"

"Chief of the Watch, pump all variable ballast!"

COB acknowledged crisply. His hands worked his console controls and keyboard like a concert organist giving
the performance of his life. Bell was doing everything he
could to get the ship going straight up on an even keel. To

use the bow and stern planes would make her pivot about her center of buoyancy too much, especially with a jittery helmsman, and her rudder and pump-jet propulsor would smash into the bottom's muck and stones. The autopilot computer assists could aid Patel only so far.

Challenger's depth began to decrease. The unexpected spires were still there.

They must be forty or fifty feet high, Jeffrey thought. *What the hell are they? . . . We're going to hit them.*

"Helm back two thirds!" Bell's order came out at a higher pitch this time. "Chief of the Watch, on the sound-powered phones, rig for depth charge." As a modern expression, this meant to prepare for possible shock and damage from enemy weaponry, including not just depth charges but mines, torpedoes, cruise missiles, or bombs. No one knew what might happen next.

"Propulsor is cavitating," O'Hanlon announced, his Boston Irish accent especially thick. The power Bell had demanded, with the comparatively low sea pressure at such mild depth, meant that the pump-jet turbine blades, thrown hard into reverse, began to suck vacuum, fighting *Challenger*'s nine thousand tons of inertia.

"Chief of the Watch, on the sound-powered phones, silent collision alarm."

COB acknowledged. Phone talkers in each compartment, monitoring the circuit, would pass the word to all hands.

The ship's rise began to accelerate, even as her forward speed slowly came off. Everyone braced themselves and watched the photonics imagery, and prayed. A crash would be disastrous for stealth, and could seriously damage the bow dome or bowplanes—or worse.

As the pump-jet propulsor strained, and internal pumps emptied the variable ballast tanks' water into the sea, *Challenger* moved upward past the tips of the spires.

Jeffrey caught glimpses of their profiles: each had a slim, teardrop-shaped cross-section, with the razor-thin edge pointing at him, into the current. They showed no sea-growth fouling. He realized they bore a slippery, echo-suppressing outer sheath.

This configuration would minimize their water drag and flow noise, and make it very hard to get a return with any obstacle-avoidance sonar ping—which Bell dared not use for fear of destroying their stealth. *No wonder we didn't hear them on passive sonar.* Jeffrey's heart was racing, his breathing ragged and short. The spires' tops bore rounded fairings that probably housed hydrophones, or sensors to measure unusual turbulence or vibrations, or all three. He badly wanted to bark out instructions, but this was Bell's battle, not his.

"Sir," Patel called to his captain, "my depth is one hundred feet and decreasing rapidly."

Reported ship's depth always meant at the keel. *Challenger*'s hull was forty feet in diameter, and her sail projected twenty feet higher than that. The top of the sail was barely forty feet under the surface now, less so by the second.

Bell needed to make some very fast decisions.

"Helm, maintain depth one hundred feet on autohover. Chief of the Watch, flood variable ballast to restore neutral buoyancy. Helm, all stop. On auxiliary maneuvering thrusters, rotate our heading to westward, then translate the ship sideways north."

Patel acknowledged, his words slurred. COB leaned over to give him help with one hand while he did things on his own console with the other.

Jeffrey watched his displays. The ship's depth had risen dangerously to eighty-four feet before her upward motion came off. The small thrusters at bow and stern were swinging the ship parallel to the line of spires, and those thrusters and the current were moving *Challenger* over and past the spires.

An antisubmarine booby trap. Simple and fiendishly clever. We barely missed hitting it . . . but these movements, cavitation noise, and mechanical transients can't go unnoticed.

Now Jeffrey understood with horrible clarity how the Russians intended to block their channel to foreign submerged submarines: they *wanted* unfriendly captains to think it was safest to stay deep. Who'd built this peculiar snare of a fence? Jeffrey answered his own question. Russian saturation divers. It had to be recent, since its surfaces were so clean. Why wasn't this in the intel reports he'd been given? He definitely had a need to know. The U.S. must not be aware of it. Construction could have been achieved unobserved, given how short the acoustic detection ranges were locally, especially with Big Diomede totally blocking any hydrophones near Little Diomede.

Challenger was past the fence, slowly moving sideways further north into the strait; Bell was making the most of the current to drift quietly out of the area.

"Aspect change on Masters Nine-Five, Nine-Six, and Nine-Seven," O'Hanlon stated. The Udaloy, the Grisha-V, and the May bomber. "Blade rate increase on Masters Nine-Five and Nine-Six. Bearings to contacts now constant, range decreasing." The destroyer and the corvette were steering toward *Challenger* and speeding up. The bomber was headed their way, too.

"Helm," Bell ordered, "on autohover, make your depth one-five feet from the bottom. On auxiliary thrusters, maintain distance four-zero feet upcurrent from bases of spires."

Patel acknowledged more calmly. The pictures from outside showed no end to the line of spires to east or west. They were spaced evenly, twelve or fifteen feet apart, the gaps too narrow for even a small diesel boat to slip through. *Challenger* began to descend. Soon she hugged the sea floor, and hugged the backs of the spires from inside the strait, as closely as Bell dared.

"Overflight, north to south!" a sonarman shouted.

"Quiet in Control," Bell snapped. People were too agitated.

"Master Nine-Seven passed almost directly overhead,"

the same sonarman stated with a mix of sheepishness and fright.

The whole control room became deathly quiet. If Jeffrey had miscalculated about Russian attitudes, then an air-dropped torpedo—impact with the sea cushioned by a parachute—might have already left the Il-38's bomb bay. An eternity passed, but Sonar announced no noise of a weapon hitting the water.

"Let's hope these spires have some steel in their cores," Jeffrey said. "It might confuse their MAD."

The Grisha-V was charging toward *Challenger* at thirty knots, her top speed. The Udaloy, further off when *Challenger* hit the booby trap, was coming their way just as quickly.

"New passive sonar contacts on the bow sphere," O'Hanlon reported. "Airborne, bearing three-five-five, range is short, closing rapidly. . . . Turbine engines and helicopter rotor noise. Assess as two Helix-As, scrambled from the Udaloy."

"Very well," Bell responded. "Activate sonar speakers." The noise of the helos filled the control room, in surround-sound quadraphonic, giving a three-dimensional sense of the location of the contacts. Engine turbines roared and whined, the helicopters' transmissions screamed, and their twin counterrotating main rotors, mounted one above the other on each aircraft, made steady throbbing, thudding beats. "Stand by to suppress active sonars with out-of-phase return emissions." *Challenger*'s sonar arrays, mounted in different places at her bow and along her sides and on her sail, could actively cancel enemy pinging—if the enemy systems weren't too powerful or too sophisticated.

Jeffrey heard sharp smacking sounds. He almost jumped out of his seat.

"Surface impacts!" O'Hanlon continued his running commentary.

People ducked, as if cowering from a depth charge.

"Assess as sonobuoys!"

The sonobuoys went active, making musical bleeps, taunting, high-pitched, nerve-shattering. They used small hydrophones to pick up echoes, relayed back to the Helix-As by radio. The helicopters in turn might be relaying the data to the Udaloy's computers for thorough analysis. The only good thing Jeffrey could say about them was that because they had to be small and battery-powered, sonobuoys were not the most dangerous threat.

A deeper tone sounded. "Contact on acoustic intercept!" a different sonarman called out. "Grisha-V hull-mounted Bull Horn system." Bull Horn was another NATO code name.

"Helicopters departing," Sessions, as Fire Control Coordinator, said to Bell, sounding hopeful.

"Too easy," Bell retorted.

A new bright line appeared on Jeffrey's waterfall display, streaking across it diagonally like a comet.

"Overflight!" came from O'Hanlon. "South to north!"

This time, on the sonar speakers, the droning rumble and roar of a four-engine turboprop fixed-wing aircraft punished everyone's ears, then receded.

Sonar made formal reports, belaboring the obvious.

"The helos backed off so the May could get a better MAD fix," Bell said. Jeffrey knew he was right.

"Helos returning!" Sessions was too overwrought not to shout.

Turbines, transmissions, and rotor noises increased in intensity, almost drowning out the *plop* and *bleep* as more active sonobuoys fell and switched themselves on.

"They're keeping us pinned until the ships get here." Now Bell was giving his own running commentary. "Sonar, are they getting solid echoes off us?"

"Negative," O'Hanlon said. "Am able to suppress."

So far. The control room had begun to feel roasting hot, like an oven. Sweat dripped from Jeffrey's chin, and his underarms were drenched with it. The atmosphere tasted foul, and smelled rancid—the stench of two dozen men's fear.

Challenger had Polyphem antiaircraft missiles, which could knock down helicopters and maritime patrol planes. They were loaded and fired four at a time through a torpedo tube. Using them now was entirely forbidden by U.S. ROEs—and they'd merely prove *Challenger*'s exact location to the corvette and destroyer getting closer by the minute. Torpedoing those ships was absolutely not an option, and useless besides since the Russians would only send more.

Another deep tone filled the air, followed by a weaker, higher-pitched one.

"Bull Horn from the Grisha-V again. Udaloy has gone active with hull-mounted Horse Jaw." The Udaloy's sonar was more powerful than the Grisha-V's, but the Udaloy was further away.

Jeffrey watched the tactical plot and listened to the sonar speakers. The helicopters began to circle, sometimes coming very close to *Challenger*.

The Grisha-V announced its arrival on scene with a louder blast from its Bull Horn system. The tactical plot showed her slowing, reducing her self-noise to get clearer sonar returns.

"Sit tight, people," Bell said. "We can't sneak further into the strait or they'll track us for sure, by a Doppler shift in whatever fragmented echoes they're hearing. Just sit tight." An object in motion toward or away from an active sonar caused the returning ping to be higher or lower in frequency, enough to register on the active sonar's signal processors—a dead giveaway of a genuine target.

Everyone waited for the Russians to make their next move.

People were jolted by three loud *bangs* in quick succession.

"Signal grenades," Bell said before Sonar could.

Three grenades dropped one after another was the international signal meaning, "Unidentified submarine in my territorial waters, surface and indicate your intentions."

"Sit tight," Bell repeated. Three more grenades went off, much closer. "Commodore, any directives?"

Jeffrey stood and eased gingerly past the sonar officer, Finch, over to Bell. "Whatever we do, don't surface," he whispered. A junior enlisted man let out a yelp as three more grenades went off, closer still. "We don't know for sure that they know that we're here."

"You do like to gamble, Commodore."

"Get inside their minds. They don't have a solid sonar return off our hull, with our out-of-phase suppression. They might think what they're getting are garbled bounces off the backs of the spires. Whatever sensor data zeroed them in on this location could just be dismissed as a false alarm, or a whale."

"Maybe." Bell was starting to sound sarcastic.

Jeffrey brought his face a few inches from Bell's. "They can't be positive of an MAD contact because of these spires."

"Only if they do have steel in them."

"Yes, there is that."

"The bomber might have gotten a lock on us, twice, by LASH."

"I think the water's too opaque."

"And *I* think we should sneak away on auxiliary maneuvering thrusters. The longer we stay here, the better their chance to be certain they have a non-Russian sub in their sights."

"We can't move away from the spires. You said so yourself."

"Not *away*, Commodore. *Along.*"

"You mean follow the fence east or west?"

"Yes."

"No. If we move at all, their readings at this spot on sonar and MAD and even LASH will alter. They'll grow more suspicious, instead of doubting they've got a real contact."

Three more grenades went off: The Udaloy had arrived. In a few seconds, everyone in Control heard three more loud *bangs.*

"Commodore, how long before those become depth charges?"

"I don't think they'd actually depth-charge us or launch a torpedo. They certainly *might,* but I don't think they will."

"Getting inside their heads is a much too iffy thing for me. Commodore, I cannot unduly endanger my ship. The people up there could be tired, or drunk, or just plain trigger-happy. Who knows what foul-ups are possible in Russian command and control?"

"That's what I'm counting on them thinking, too. That a submarine actually here would surface, and blame everything on navigation error, then just sail away. Submerge again once back in U.S. waters. . . . The fact that nothing surfaces helps them convince themselves that nothing's here."

"What if they think we're here, and won't surface because we have a covert mission?"

"There's covert and then there's suicidal, Captain. They won't expect even a ballsy U.S. spy sub skipper, on neutral Russian turf in time of war, to be genuinely suicidal."

"Concur, Commodore, except . . . except I'm not sure which action would seem to them more suicidal in a major covert op. Us surfacing and for certain ruining our stealth, or not surfacing to maybe bluff them into going away? They'd figure that if our secrecy were paramount we'd go for the bluff. And they'd be right. So maybe they'll think we *are* here."

"If we do surface," Jeffrey said, "we compromise our mission and by doing so we compromise *Carter.* So *we* know we need to stay down. But the Russians presumably can't know that our mission is in fact directed against them somehow, not the Germans."

"We're between a rock and a hard place, cornered against these spires. For all we know they'll send divers down to take a look-see in person." Crewmen cringed as they listened to this mounting debate between captain and commodore.

"We just have to chance it. I've never heard of that being in their standard antisubmarine doctrine, using divers in shallow water. And Russians aren't noted for personal initiative."

"Sirs," Sessions said, "we have our own safety divers, and some of the Seabees might be dive-qualified. We could send men out to kill any Russian divers who do show up."

"The Russians would be missed," Jeffrey said tersely.

"They could chalk it up to a diving accident, sir."

"They'd send more divers to investigate. . . . No, we buy this diver-to-diver combat, it just prolongs the inevitable. We do nothing, stay quiet, wait for them to get bored and go away."

Challenger was pounded by an eruption with such bruising punch it was felt more than heard, the sharp vibrations painfully shaking Jeffrey's bones inside his body.

"Depth charge!" a sonarman shouted. "Within five hundred yards!" Men who'd been knocked off their feet recovered, checked themselves for injuries, then held onto something solid. They glanced apprehensively upward, thinking of what could come next.

"They'll work the area systematically now," Bell warned, "until we're all dead."

"Do nothing. That's a direct order."

"Sir, based on what reasoning? Intuition? A *hunch*?"

Jeffrey held his tongue. The silence that lingered was heavy with feelings of rage and betrayal from Bell, who'd wanted all along to run the strait on the U.S. side. The men, sensing this conflict, by now were confused and scared. The implied accusation from Bell was unmistakable: their new commodore was too clever for everyone's good.

There was another dreadful eruption. The control room darkened as red fluorescent bulbs shook loose in their sockets; consoles jiggled against their shock-absorbing mounts.

Jeffrey's teeth were jarred so badly they hurt; his feet ached.

"Depth charge! Within three hundred yards!"

Bell glared at Jeffrey. "It isn't too late to surface!"

"It's too early! You don't have a single flooding report!"

"I—"

"Aspect change on the Grisha-V," came from Chief O'Hanlon. "Grisha-V is . . . turning away! . . . Udaloy turning away!"

"Sir," Sessions said, "helicopters have ceased orbiting, are on intercept course with the Udaloy."

"See, Captain," Jeffrey chided gently. "They decided there was nothing here. They left." Happy crewmen traded high fives, or shot thumbs-up to their buddies. COB reached and gave Patel an approving jab in the shoulder.

"Why the depth charges, then?" Bell demanded. "It could still be a trick."

"One depth charge from each ship, it wasn't a trick. It was two bored Russian surface-ship skippers, using a good excuse to liven up their day with some fireworks on the Kremlin's dime."

CHAPTER 6

O nce the patrolling Russian forces departed, *Challenger* wormed her way north through the strait and entered the Chukchi Sea, where for hundreds of miles the bottom was less than two hundred feet deep. With Meltzer's assistance, Bell chose a course slightly west of north. This led toward a canyon in the continental shelf, giving a little more depth to play with. The canyon would pass safely east of craggy Wrangel Island—more properly, Ostrov Vrangelya, since it was Russian territory.

Tension of a different sort started to increase in the control room, and throughout the ship. If *Challenger* encountered the edge of the ice cap while the water was still very shallow, broken slabs projecting down by many feet, called bummocks, could block her path frustratingly. There was also real danger that she could hit a massive bummock head-on, doing damage where the ice above precluded any emergency blow to the surface. Crippled or sinking, with no way up or out, *Challenger* might be stranded, or lost with all hands. Advance intel showed this probably wouldn't happen, because global warming from natural and man-made factors, combined with normal random year-to-year fluctuations, had pushed the start of the solid pack ice in the Chukchi Sea more northward than usual. The ship had sonars specifically designed to warn of inadequate clearance between the bottom and the irregular ice. But using these systems meant radiating, which, as before, compromised stealth, so Jeffrey had forbidden it. This time, Bell didn't argue with him.

The gravimeter, though excellent for pinpoint navigation under the ice, by orienteering against finely detailed charts of the Arctic Ocean floor, unfortunately couldn't distinguish between sea water and the ice cap. Their densities were too similar; this was why ninety percent of an iceberg floated beneath the surface.

Jeffrey knew he was taking a serious risk, proceeding toward the hard roof of treacherous ice with all active sonars secured. But the data he'd been given, and the urgency of his mission, told his gut that the risk was worth it, even necessary.

Satisfied that Meltzer and Finch and their men were working in good order under Bell's leadership, Jeffrey went to his office to reread his orders. He also wanted to practice his Russian in private, using language tapes in the ship's huge e-book library, accessible through the LAN. He wasn't at it long when someone knocked.

"Come on in."

It was Bell. He shut the door behind him.

"Good afternoon, Commodore," Bell said gravely.

"Why the sudden formality, Captain?"

"I wanted to apologize."

"For what?"

"I was out of line, in the control room back there."

"How so?" Jeffrey knew, but wanted to hear Bell say it. He knew Bell needed to get it off his chest.

"I argued with you about tactics, in front of the rest of the crew. I feel . . . well . . . it undermined discipline and might have verged on insubordination." Bell exhaled deeply.

Jeffrey sat back. "Yeah, I admit it's different, with you being captain of *Challenger*. We had our knockdown, drag-outs often enough in the heat of battle, when it was us sitting at the command console, side by side. The dynamics have changed, that's for sure. . . . But it's *still* your job, in part, to advise me, backstop me—and don't forget filling in for me if I keel over from a stroke. You're my flagship captain, for God's sake."

"Still, I don't feel right about how I handled it."

Jeffrey flashed Bell a friendly grin. "I didn't exactly win any prizes myself."

Bell smiled for the first time in hours.

"Look," Jeffrey told him, "you and I, and this whole crew for that matter, have been through a hell of a lot in this war. We were a *team* in every engagement we fought. The winningest team in the whole submarine fleet. I don't want to lose that."

"Readjustments *are* necessary, sir. We can't deny the blunt fact."

"Yup. Can't deny it. Especially once we hook up with *Carter*. Then Commander Harley joins the equation. I don't know much about him, personally."

"I met him once or twice. I'd have to say that you and he are opposites."

"Opposites can be good, if they complement each other. If they fill gaps in the other guy's outlook."

"All true." Bell's tone hinted at more.

"What?"

"I'm not so sure he's quite the type of opposite you mean."

"I'll handle all that in due course." Jeffrey tapped one of his silver eagle collar tabs, to emphasize that he outranked Harley. "Commander Nyurba seems quite loyal to him."

"Yes, Commodore. I didn't mean to be prejudicial. It's

not my business, really. My impression of Harley was passing, brief, months ago, when he'd just been under huge stress."

"Not to worry."

But Bell still seemed pensive, hesitant.

"Finished with the preliminaries, then?"

"Am I that transparent, sir?"

"To me, after five combat missions together in barely six months, yes."

"Okay." Bell took a deep breath and let it out slowly. "I keep asking myself what I would've done when we were pinned down by those Russians, if you hadn't been there, hadn't been aboard."

"Without me to teach and challenge you, without me to do the final deciding?"

Bell nodded.

"Well, you got the big question out. So, answer it. What do you think you'd've done, if everything had rested on your head alone? And forget about *Carter,* leave that part aside."

"I'd have done whatever I thought you would have done in my place, sir. I mean followed your example, imagining you were the captain."

"Not a bad policy at all, I must say. But you have to find your own tactical style, whatever that might be, since you and I are also different people."

"Granted."

"So what specific answer comes up? What actions would you have taken? Issued what orders?"

"I know one thing. There's no way I'd have let a bunch of stinking Russkies force *me* to the surface until the very last extreme."

"Meaning what, in practical terms?"

"I'd have sat there, motionless, and gutted it out as long as possible. I'd have let their own doubts work against them, and waited for them to give up and leave. . . . Just like you did."

"And if they'd opened fire in earnest?"

"I can think of a few ways to freak them out nonlethally, and use our potent repertoire to defeat any inbound torpedoes. Then I'd hightail it back to U.S. waters, doing flank speed way shallow on purpose, to let them eat my dust, with my propulsor wake boiling behind as a dare for them to cross to my side of the treaty line."

"Freak out just how?"

"Launch a decoy or two programmed to sound like ADCAPs. Lob a few Polyphems, unarmed, to fall short of the May but give her aircrew the general idea."

"Four-oh, Captain." A perfect grade. "If I'd still been captain myself, and the depth charges had really come too close, or Sonar called a torpedo in the water, that's exactly what I would've done. Used our mobility to clear out of there, fast. Let them know from our tonals whom they were dealing with, and invited them to take on our eight widebodied torpedo tubes where our ROEs let us shoot back."

"Thanks, Commodore. For everything."

Jeffrey glanced at his wristwatch. "Well, I don't know about you, but with all that excitement back there, I worked up an appetite. Let's hit the wardroom together, shall we? Tuck in with gusto, side by side, leisurely like. No better way to show your officers, in very certain terms, that you and I are still on the same page."

———————

Eventually the water got much deeper, past the continental shelf, over the Chukchi Abyssal Plain. On Bell's orders, *Challenger* began maintaining a depth of nine hundred feet, and resumed a silent speed of twenty knots.

Along the way, submerged through the Chukchi Sea, *Challenger* began to pass more and more chunky icebergs, and flatter floes, bobbing and tumbling noisily on the ocean surface above. Then she crossed beneath the edge of the 2012 summertime Arctic ice cap. The boundary zone was extremely noisy, with wind and wind-driven wave action making broken ice chunks grind against one another and the outer margin of the solid cap. What marine mammals were heard now, on sonar, changed from whales—who rarely went under the ice cap since they needed to surface often to breathe—to amphibious creatures: seals and walruses, who ate the many Arctic fish. The seal and walrus adults and pups would enter and leave the water through open areas called polynyas or leads, which existed even in winter, but became more common and larger in summer. Teeming flocks of sea birds also lived off fish they caught in these polynyas.

Jeffrey reminded himself that polar bears walked around on the ice and snow up there. They hunted the seals and walruses. Inuit walked around, or paddled kayaks, or drove dog sleds or rode on snowmobiles, too. They also hunted walruses and seals, and sometimes had confrontations with the polar bears—which were edible, but just barely.

Challenger turned east, entering the Beaufort Sea north of Alaska, and began to steam across the Canada Abyssal Plain, in water nine to twelve thousand feet deep. Three and a half days after transiting the Bering Strait, well up under the ice cap, *Challenger* neared her rendezvous with USS *Jimmy Carter*.

Commander Dashiyn Nyurba was impressed by the food on *Challenger*. Whether breakfast, lunch, dinner, or midrats, the ingredients were the highest quality, the cooking the most skilled and imaginative, that he'd ever experienced in his fifteen years as a naval officer. And he'd traveled far and wide, ashore and on many surface ships, before being tapped for the Air Force Special Operations Squadron joint-service outfit that he was second in command of now.

The dinner dishes had been cleared a while ago. Nyurba's people were in the wardroom with Commodore Fuller, playing their last poker game before they transferred to *Carter*. While the card-playing helped to kill time—the Seabees had a lot to spare as they rode along on *Challenger*—the rounds weren't friendly. Everyone, including the commodore, spoke only in Russian. Since gambling was forbidden by Navy regs, the stakes were toothpicks and ego, especially the latter, which made the play extremely competitive. Nyurba thought that the commodore was getting noticeably better at both his poker face and his language fluency. His accent was atrocious, but that part didn't matter. Unlike the special ops team, Fuller wasn't supposed to disguise his nationality. No, his duty would be to emphasize it.

Through hooded eyes Nyurba looked the commodore over one last time. Soon enough, he knew, Fuller would find out for himself what his orders were in total. Nyurba had known his squadron's purpose for most of a year, though he'd beseeched the Lord that this mission never be put into effect. He expected that when they all went over to *Carter* in *Challenger*'s minisub for a major briefing and planning session, and the commodore opened his inner orders pouch when he got there, he'd be appalled.

As well he should be. What Fuller was being asked to do was truly appalling, but Nyurba had been told that it was the least of all the evils left for America to choose between. And at one point, Captain Jeffrey Fuller, United States Navy, would have to personally pull off the biggest, most important bluff ever conceived in military history.

The mere idea of it sent shivers up Nyurba's spine, and Nyurba was a very hard man.

A messenger knocked and entered the wardroom. "Commodore, the Captain's respects, and he requests your presence in Control."

"Da, spasiba," Fuller responded. Yes, thank you. He glanced at Nyurba. *"Pazhalsta."* Excuse me.

"Nichevo," Nyurba said. No problem.

"Sir?" The skinny, pimply complexioned young messenger was confused.

"Sorry," Fuller said, reverting to English. "I'll be right there."

The messenger left.

The round of betting wasn't finished. Fuller placed his cards facedown, and stood. Nyurba saw him covetously eye the big pile of toothpicks in the middle of the table—the pot.

"A shame. I had a full house. Jacks high."

"Let me see that." Nyurba reached across the table. He turned over the cards. "Liar. You got crap."

"But I had you thinking." Fuller smirked, then left the wardroom.

Nyurba viewed Fuller with a mix of admiration and pity.

He knew that together they'd soon pull the tail of the dragon of Armageddon as hard as anyone could. The odds were discouraging that many or any of the squadron's men would return from the land phase of the mission alive.

It will be a major miracle if Commodore Fuller succeeds at all the things his strike group must achieve like clockwork from here forward. If he fails, his name will be cursed for centuries by whatever is left of the human race.

From what Nyurba had seen and heard the past few days, he believed that Jeffrey Fuller was the right man to attempt what seemed forbiddingly impossible. Commander, U.S. Strategic Command, and the President of the United States above him, had chosen well.

CHAPTER 7

Jeffrey, Bell, and the sonar officer, Finch, stood side by side in the aisle behind sonar supervisor Senior Chief O'Hanlon's seat. Contact would be made with *Jimmy Carter,* and identities verified, using a secure undersea digital acoustic link. This system sent verbal or text messages in code, in a frequency band around one thousand kilohertz—fifty times above the range of human hearing. Each transmission's frequency jumped thousands of times per second, and the beam could be tightly focused toward the intended recipient, making it almost impossible for an enemy sonar to notice, even at close range.

"You think we'll hear *Carter* hailing us before we detect her broadband or tonals?" Bell asked Finch and O'Hanlon.

Lieutenant (j.g.) Allan Finch was in his mid-twenties, short and thin, with a serious personality. A naval officer generalist assigned to sonar only for now, he was sensible enough to know that on matters of real-world operations, Senior Chief O'Hanlon—with ten years' more experience and a permanent rating as sonar tech—could run rings around him.

"Let's hope so, Skipper," O'Hanlon replied. "Arctic acoustic conditions are way too tricky this time of year. The nominal range of our comms is about the same as the maximum range of our ADCAPS." Around thirty miles. "Getting *Carter* on the phone would ease my mind about a friendly fire embarrassment."

Two hours later, close to the rendezvous point, Bell went to silent battle stations as a precaution. Jeffrey sat at his borrowed console in the rear of the control room. Making the meeting with *Carter* even trickier was that a gale had blown in from the west, with winds that Sonar estimated as topping thirty knots. They got this figure by analyzing wave action in the larger polynyas under which *Challenger* passed every five or six miles. Bell ordered the sonar speakers turned on.

Background noise rose substantially with the storm. Sleet and freezing rain pelted the polynyas, causing hissing and drumming sounds. The wind made the summer ice cap, which averaged less than ten feet thick, bend and flex due to forces that ranged from sea swells carrying their up-and-down energy far under the edge of the ice, to the wind itself pressing against ice ridges that stuck up from the cap. The prevailing surface current, from the opposite direction, east, gained purchase against many downward bummocks, straining the ice even more.

The cap moaned and creaked continually. Sometimes, nearby or in the distance, it would emit a sudden loud *crack,* echoing off bummocks everywhere like rolling thunder, as multiple stresses fractured the cap and two adjacent sections either relentlessly squeezed together, piling up and fracturing more, or separated, making a lead of brand-new open water. *Challenger*'s sensors indicated that, with this gale, colder air was moving in, polynyas were freezing to slush, and the water temperature at shallow depth was dropping. Sonar conditions deteriorated.

"Sir," O'Hanlon called out, "intermittent contact on broadband, man-made, bearing is roughly zero-nine-zero, range ten thousand or twenty thousand yards." East, five or ten miles.

"That's near the rendezvous point," Sessions told Bell.

"Any acoustic link contact, XO?"

"Negative, sir." Sending messages back and forth to *Carter,* composed by Jeffrey or Bell, would be part of Sessions's job.

O'Hanlon frowned. "What we're hearing doesn't make sense."

"Explain," Bell said. Finch moved in and peered over O'Hanlon's shoulder, then moved down the aisle and looked at the different sonarmen's screens.

"Broadband signal intensity is stronger than it should be," O'Hanlon said. "*Carter* is supposed to hold her position, while we approach."

"Maybe she's running late," Jeffrey said.

"If I didn't know better," O'Hanlon responded, "I'd say there were two distinct broadband signatures, overlaid."

The ice gave off another loud *crack,* and again the noise reverberated like thunder.

"Sir, that was a torpedo warhead detonating."

"What?"

"We're getting . . . Rapid bearing rates on both broadband signatures, *not* consistent with any known under-ice sound propagation effects! . . . Assess signatures are a sub-on-sub dogfight!" Bearing rate meant the contact was turning through the water compared to *Challenger*'s steady course.

There was another sudden loud noise. This time, cued in, Jeffrey could tell that it had a rumbling, throaty quality, very unlike the natural sounds from the ice cap.

"Loud explosion bearing zero nine zero!" a sonarman

called. "Range approximately fifteen thousand yards. Assess as a high-explosive torpedo warhead detonating!"

"This shouldn't be happening," Bell said. He hesitated, for only a moment. "Sonar, can you estimate the speed at which those submarines are moving?"

"Not yet," Finch reported, "but from the intense broadband we're getting they have to be doing flank speed." All out, as fast as a vessel could go.

"Contact on acoustic intercept!" a different sonarman called. Acoustic intercept was used to warn of another submarine's sonar going active. "Assess as melee pinging by one of the vessels involved in combat!" Melee pinging was used to find the adversary and get an accurate target range while both subs made wild maneuvers.

"Identify active sonar system," Sessions ordered in his role as fire control coordinator.

"Impossible, sir," Finch told him after O'Hanlon shook his head. "System frequency unknown due to unknown target speed and Doppler shift."

"Very well, Sonar," Sessions said. "Captain, we need a more reliable acoustic path to understand what's going on."

"Concur," Bell said. "If they're doing flank speed their passive sonars will be almost deaf from flow noise. . . . So . . . Chief of the Watch, rig ship for deep submergence."

"Deep submergence, aye."

"Helm, make your course zero nine zero. Ahead full, make turns for thirty-five knots. Thirty degrees down-bubble, make your depth eight thousand feet."

Patel acknowledged, far more self-confident now.

Challenger's bow nosed steeply down, so steeply that Jeffrey's seat tilted back uncomfortably as he sat facing toward the stern. His inner ears' sense of balance told him that straight up meant not the overhead but the top screen of his console.

"Nav," Bell ordered, bracing himself against his console as it and he tilted forward, "tell me when we've covered five nautical miles along the bottom."

"Aye-aye, Captain." Meltzer was gripping a handhold on the overhead, standing sideways with his legs splayed wide, as the deck beneath his feet turned into a hillside.

Challenger went deeper and deeper. "Hull popping," O'Hanlon called out. With *Challenger*'s ceramic-composite hull, it sounded more like a crunch. The ship was being squeezed inward by the pressure of the ocean, but this was what she'd been designed to do: achieve total waterspace dominance by seizing the low ground near the ocean floor and then exploit her tactical superiority.

She began to level off. "Sir," Patel reported, "my depth is eight thousand feet." The outside pressure was more than three and a half thousand pounds per square inch—almost two hundred fifty times atmospheric pressure at sea level.

"Sir," Meltzer called out, "own ship has moved five miles."

"Very well, Nav. Helm, all stop."

"All stop, aye, sir. . . . Maneuvering answers, all stop."

"Helm, back full until our way comes off." *Challenger* still had considerable momentum; she'd halt much faster this way.

"Sonar and Fire Control Coordinator, tell me what's happening up there."

"Insufficient data," Sessions responded.

"Request put ship on heading due north," Finch said, "to present starboard wide-aperture array for optimal analysis."

"Helm, on auxiliary maneuvering thrusters, rotate your heading to due north."

Patel acknowledged and worked a joystick.

The wide-aperture arrays, one along each side of the ship, consisted of three widely spaced rectangular hydrophone complexes attached to the hull. Because they were big in two dimensions, and were held rigidly in three dimensions by the stiffness of *Challenger*'s hull, they could perform extremely detailed analyses of sounds to either side of the ship, in signal processing modes not possible with even the latest towed arrays.

"My heading is due north, sir."

"V'r'well, Helm," Bell said.

Sonarmen and fire-control technicians conferred and worked their keyboards. A tactical plot began to form on Sessions's main console screen, repeated on other displays around Control.

"Two ships in combat, Captain," Sessions stated. "Both appear to have flank speed of approximately twenty-five knots."

Jeffrey was surprised. *Slow by modern standards. Unless—*

"Getting definite tonals," O'Hanlon said. "Both ships nuclear-powered." Sound was traveling directly down from the dogfight, immune to the confusing effects at shallower depth.

"What classes?" Bell demanded. Knowing this was essential. It would tell him who fought whom.

"Torpedoes in the water," a sonarman called. "Engine noises indicate ADCAPs." An electric-like screaming came over the sonar speakers. "Noisemakers and acoustic scramblers in the water!"

Hissing, gurgling, and undulating siren noises intensified—Jeffrey realized he'd been hearing them already, almost drowned out by the noise of twisting and turning submarines with their propulsion plants going at maximum power.

"Sonar, turning own-ship east," Bell cued Finch and O'Hanlon. "Helm, make your course zero-nine-zero. Ahead one third, make turns for eighteen knots." Bell wanted to sneak closer, get right underneath the other two subs.

Patel acknowledged, this time it seemed with true relish.

Bell ordered him to stop and rotate north again.

"One contact is an Amethyste-Two," O'Hanlon stated. A modern, refurbished French sub, captured and crewed by

Germans. The Amethystes were slow and small, but maneuverable and deadly.

She's not supposed to be able to get here. So much for intel about the Allies' North Atlantic anti-U-boat blockades.

"Two more torpedoes in the water. F-Seventeen Mod-Twos." French-made, they could go forty knots, slow for an antisubmarine weapon, but more than adequate for a twenty-five-knot target.

The other submarine had to be American if it was firing Mark 48 ADCAPs. The latest version could go over sixty knots.

"Second submerged contact appears to be a newer *Ohio*-class SSBN. Possibly *Nebraska* or *Wyoming*." The *Ohio*-class boomers were built for maximum stealth, not speed. They only carried a dozen torpedoes and decoys, for self-defense. Their main weapons were the strategic deterrence of two dozen ballistic missiles tipped with multiple hydrogen bombs.

Jeffrey told himself this didn't make sense. All boomers were assigned specific patrol areas and transit routes, large but not infinite. Higher commanders would never send a boomer toward where two American fast-attacks were set to rendezvous.

There were more blasts, deafening to Jeffrey's ears with this closer range and direct acoustic path, as torpedoes exploded against noisemakers or decoys or ice bummocks. The throb and whine and hiss of submarines trying to kill each other continued.

O'Hanlon said something to Finch while pointing at one of his displays. Finch studied it, and nodded. "Captain," O'Hanlon called for Bell. "Am getting additional tonals, intermittent traces, weak, suggesting an S-Six-W reactor aboard the American sub. Not an S-Eight-G."

"What?" Bell was incredulous.

"Confirmed! Conjecture American vessel is *Seawolf* class, emitting false tonals to disguise her identity!"

Jeffrey stood up. *"How big is she?"*

"Acoustic shadow profile against noise of ice cap suggests approximately four hundred fifty feet."

Carter. It had to be. *Seawolf* was the same length as *Challenger*, about three hundred fifty feet. Real boomers were more like five hundred fifty feet. All three classes had the same beam—width—forty or forty-two feet.

"American submarine tentatively identified as USS *Jimmy Carter*," Sessions announced.

"There's nothing tentative about it," Bell snapped.

"Harley's been ambushed," Jeffrey said. "He's obeying his orders to not let *Carter* be detected. At least not detected as *Carter*." There were two melee pings in fast succession, one much deeper in tone than the other.

"Active systems confirmed as one French, one probable *Ohio* class!" Even Harley's sonar was mimicking a boomer.

In seconds, there were more torpedoes in the water, F-17s and ADCAPs screaming toward each other, their pitches shifting up and down from Doppler as their weapons techs steered them after moving targets—thus altering the speed at which they seemed to approach or move away from *Challenger* far below.

Both sides' ROEs let them go tactical nuclear when more than two hundred miles from land. But the dueling subs were too close together for that in this melee—their own warheads would sink them right along with their opponent.

Bell turned to stare at Jeffrey. "If Harley limits himself to half his real flank speed, and acts like he only has four torpedo tubes instead of eight, and doesn't dive deeper than an *Ohio* can, he's terribly handicapped."

"I know. What are the chances the Amethyste-Two might get off a report if we put a Mark Eighty-eight up her ass?"

The ultra-heavyweight Mark 88 fish were custom-made for *Challenger,* able to function as deep as the parent ship's crush depth. With a diameter of twenty-six and a half inches, to entirely fill her extra-wide torpedo tubes, they came in both high-explosive and tactical atomic versions; twenty-one-inch-diameter ADCAPs could carry either type of warhead but would implode at about three thousand feet.

The noise of submarines got louder than ever, as the tactical plot showed each vessel spawning a twin.

"Assess both contacts have launched decoys!" a sonarman yelled. F-17s and ADCAPS continued to scream.

The ocean was shattered by more torpedo detonations. Echoes and reverb pounded and roared. Jeffrey heard broken-off bummocks grinding against the underside of the ice, as buoyant shards were tousled by the newly made turbulence. The thin ice cap itself was blown sky-high in chunks; the heavy pieces showered back down, smashing and splashing.

O'Hanlon said that both real subs were still in the fight. *But how much longer can Harley hold out?*

"Mark Eighty-eight engine tonals are distinctive, Commodore," Bell warned. "If the Germans hear them, they'll know right away it's us who did the shooting."

"She may eventually realize that *Carter* is really *Carter,* whatever tricks Harley pulls. The way he's fighting, *Carter*'s too evenly matched with the German. We need to tip the scales."

"There are open polynyas within a few miles," Bell stated. "The German could float delayed-action radio buoys through one, sir, timed for when their polar-orbit comms satellite makes its next pass. Report both us and *Carter* as identified in company."

"You know we can't possibly let that happen."

"Unless we really smash the Amethyste-Two, she might reach the surface herself, for long enough to bounce a shortwave transmission from here to Berlin."

"Then let's smash her real good, and quick. *Two* high-explosive Mark Eighty-eights."

"From this depth they'll take more than a minute just to get up to target depth."

"We have to chance it."

"Understood." Bell cleared his throat. "Attention in Control. Fire Control Coordinator, remove ADCAPs from tubes one and two, reload with high-explosive Mark Eighty-eights."

Sessions relayed commands. Torelli and his people got very busy. Down in the torpedo room, the men and the hydraulic autoloader gear went to work, shifting weapons.

Up above, the dogfight continued to rage.

"Mark Eighty-eights loaded in tubes one and two!" Sessions shouted ferociously. These would be his first-ever warshots as *Challenger*'s XO.

"Very well, Fire Control," Bell said clearly and deliberately. "Make tubes one and two ready in all respects including opening outer doors."

Sessions issued more commands. Jeffrey watched on his weapons status display, copied into a window on his console's lower screen. The tubes were flooded and equalized to the outside water pressure, and the outer tube doors opened.

Torelli ordered parameter presets to define search strategies for the homing weapons, in case the weapon guidance wires broke—and to protect *Carter* from friendly fire. The presets were sent electronically to the computers in each fish.

Both tube icons turned green on Jeffrey's display, ready to fire.

"Ship ready. Weapons ready. Solution ready," Torelli recited coolly.

"Firing point procedures," Bell ordered, "tubes one and two. Target is the Amethyste-Two. Match sonar bearings and *shoot*."

"Set. . . . Stand by. . . . Tube one, *fire!* . . . Tube two, *fire!* . . . Tubes one and two fired electrically!"

Both Mark 88 units swam out silently under their own power, to avoid making a launch transient that the Amethyste-II might detect. Quickly they went to attack speed, while weapons systems technicians controlled each unit through their wires, spreading them apart by a hundred yards.

"Both units running normally," O'Hanlon confirmed.

Their engines were very loud on the sonar speakers, adding to the tumult from above, diminishing as they climbed, neck-and-neck, covering the distance to the target.

The Amethyste-II's captain and control room crew, fixated on their battle with what they thought was a valuable prize—a U.S. Navy boomer—suddenly noticed the Mark 88s coming at them from below. Each bore a warhead that weighed over a ton, three times the size of an ADCAP's. The Amethyste launched noisemakers, acoustic scramblers, and decoys, and started violent evasive maneuvers. These were standard defensive measures. None confused Torelli's people, with a perfect, upside-down bird's-eye view letting them track the target amid all distractions.

But the German captain's true intent became clear.

"Sir," Sessions said to Bell, "target is steering for this large polynya." Sonar had previously mapped the open water in the area, using the noises of rain and sleet. Sessions moved his cursor with his trackmarble; an arrow moved in unison on Jeffrey's screen. Jeffrey saw the Amethyste-II racing for the polynya, pursued at more than twice her speed by the twin Mark 88s. Though the map was changing fast now with the gale, and becoming garbled, that big polynya stood wide and clear.

Bell read his console data. "It's touch and go if she'll reach there before the Mark Eighty-eights reach her." Both of the units went active, their homing sonars making loud *tings* at distinct frequencies, to not interfere with each other. The two-toned ringing happened faster and faster as they closed in.

Jeffrey continued to watch the attack unfold on his display screens. Harley was wisely holding *Carter* back, so as not to block the Mark 88s or cut their guidance wires.

"Sir," Sessions warned, "target has increased her stand-off distance from *Challenger* and from *Carter*!"

Crewmen reacted as if they'd been hit by cattle prods.

Bell was stunned. "She's going nuclear on both of us!"

That clever bastard, Jeffrey told himself. *He* wanted *us to think his goal was to get off a sighting report. He faked us out. His real goal was to safely get off nukes.*

A tremendous double blast sounded over the sonar speakers, echoing off bummocks, bouncing back and forth between the ice cap and the bottom—sound traveled through water at almost one mile per second, so the vertical echoes came in rapid succession, and *Challenger* was right in their path. More than just sound, they were shock waves. The ship was battered again and again.

"Units from tubes one and two have detonated!" Sessions yelled. "Assess both as direct hits on the Amethyste!"

Above the cacophony came another, more horrible sound, a metallic rebounding *pshew*—the implosion of a sinking submarine's hull as it fell through its crush depth. The Amethyste shattered into thousands of pieces, in all different sizes and shapes. The remains of vessel and crew fell to the bottom in a cloud of wreckage whose chaotic flow noise was the loudest thing on the sonar speakers now—with spent noisemakers gurgling weakly, and now-irrelevant decoys receding rapidly, in the background above. There were no torpedo engine sounds—the Germans didn't get off a nuclear shot. *Carter* had ceased her fake *Ohio*-class flank speed noise emissions, and was inaudible.

Soon the Amethyste's pieces began to impact the bottom, with dull thuds, heavy crunches, and a pattering like pebbles tossed against a tin roof. The sounds went on for a very long time. The triumph felt aboard *Challenger* was tempered by dismay over the death of fellow submariners, even if they were the enemy.

"Contact on acoustic link," Sessions broke the collective, heavy human silence in Control. He interrupted the last of the noise of this terrible war's latest sea-floor debris-field forming—including the remnants of a nuclear reactor core, if the foot-thick alloy-steel containment had been breached.

"*Carter* has given valid recognition signal, acknowledges receipt of signal from us. Captain Harley sends, 'Good shooting and much thanks. Commence rendezvous procedures at your convenience.'"

"Commodore?" Bell awaited instructions.

"Oh, er, tell Captain Harley, 'Excellent defensive subterfuge tactics against the Amethyste-Two. Our minisub will dock with *Carter* shortly.'" Jeffrey had been preoccupied, mulling over everything until Bell grabbed his attention.

Sessions typed on his keyboard and sent the message through the link. In a moment he said, "*Carter* acknowledges, sir."

"Wait," Jeffrey said. "Make signal to *Carter*, 'What is local direction of surface wind?'"

The response, which took a minute, was read out by Sessions. "'Gale has veered to west-northwest.'"

"Very well. Make signal, 'Docking to be delayed. Maintain battle stations. Strike group steer in company, course west-northwest, speed twenty knots, depth eight hundred feet.'"

Sessions reported that *Carter* acknowledged.

"Sir?" Bell asked. "Your intentions?"

"I'm changing the place for the docking. This brew-up could draw other predators, and I don't mean polar bears. We steam into the heart of the gale and use its bad under-ice acoustic effects as perfect concealment."

"Understood." Bell issued helm orders. Patel acknowledged, impressively calm in the aftermath of the battle. He'd found his combat sea legs, as every crewman had to in their own way.

Jeffrey pondered. What was a German submarine doing at the rendezvous point? The meet had been scheduled for when no Axis or Russian spy satellites passed overhead. Canada's armed forces kept enemies from planting underwater listening devices anywhere near this part of the cap. Harley and *Carter* were too good to have been trailed all the way from New London. Was the German assigned on a barrier patrol, to catch U.S. subs moving between the Atlantic and the Pacific, and simply got lucky? . . . Or had someone told the Germans that *Carter,* or *Challenger*—or both—would be at this location at this time? The Arctic Ocean was far too big, and sonar detection ranges too short, for it to have been a coincidence, *Carter* meeting the Amethyste-II like this.

CHAPTER 8

Rear Admiral Elmar Meredov, sitting in his squeaky high-backed wooden swivel chair, decided to take a break from the endless paperwork that came with his job in the Russian Federation's *Voyenno Morskoy Flot*—the Russian Navy. A dowdy antique clock ticking on one of his bookcases told him it was nearing the end of the regular workday. So did the particular way the rosy, horizon-hugging Arctic sun streamed through the tall windows, with curtains drawn, of his spacious, high-ceilinged corner office. He got up from behind his massive mahogany desk; it was so old he imagined it must date to Stalin's era, perhaps once used by a succession of gulag commissars in Magadan or Yakutsk—real cities, and former labor camp centers, far to the south.

Meredov stretched, then considered asking his secretary to bring him another hot tea. His secure telephone rang. The caller ID said it was one of his favorite subordinates, a captain, first rank at a base two hours away by helicopter—the only way to get anywhere quickly in this rugged part of Siberia.

He picked up the phone. "And how are you, Aleksei, on this fine afternoon?"

"I'm well, thank you, sir. . . . I'm afraid I'll be late with the month-end aircraft maintenance reports."

"How late?"

"I might need as much as a week, unless you want me to just fake some numbers to get it all in on time."

"The last thing I desire is to see us slipping back into habits of the bad old days. There's enough of that going on around us. You know precision and honesty please me most, Aleksei. Always. I'm simply curious, why the delay?"

"Too many engine refits, and not nearly enough qualified mechanics. Delegation wasn't working, and leadership does little good with sullen, raw conscripts who don't want to be led. I had to become directly involved, scramble for spare parts everywhere, then get my hands dirty out on the flight line. Took me away from admin. I've fallen way behind. You know how it is, sir."

Meredov could sense the younger man shrug in semidefeat over the phone. The scourge of AIDS—spread by a lack of clean needles even in hospitals, intensified by the easing of Soviet-era travel restrictions—made it hard to find willing, healthy recruits. Other chronic diseases made the pool of viable draft-age manpower shrink even more, causing constant problems for Meredov as throughout Russian national defense.

"What's your regiment's operational availability?"

"Sixty percent, sir. Unlikely to improve."

"That's quite excellent, under the circumstances you so aptly describe, especially with the weather we've been having." A strong gale had blown through, leaving clear skies in its wake, but disrupting air and ground operations at more than just the base from which this subordinate's maritime patrol bombers flew. As regiment commander, he was telling Meredov that sixty percent of his bombers were airworthy on short notice—meaning the other forty percent were not. By some standards, forty percent out of action would be dreadful, but this was Russia.

"Thank you, sir."

"Was there anything else?"

"No, sir."

"Then send me your end-of-June forms filled out as soon as you reasonably can. If Vladivostok complains about timeliness, which I seriously doubt, I'll handle those supreme bureaucrats my way." Meredov's double meaning, supreme bureaucrats, was intentional. The commanders at Pacific Fleet headquarters in Vladivostok were very senior, and maddeningly hidebound to go with their exalted ranks and advanced ages. Meredov was grateful that his immediate boss spent all his time down there, fifteen hundred kilometers away. "You just keep your airplanes ready, Aleksei, and your pilots sober . . . and the rest of the aircrews more-or-less sober." Meredov chuckled.

"Easier said than done, sir. It's tough on them, being stationed here."

"Remind them there's a war on. They're supposed to be protecting the sacred Motherland!" He lowered his voice. "Even if we are in theory neutral in this one."

"Yes, sir."

"Tell them, if you have to, that they should be grateful the risks they face come from storms and their own carelessness, not combat with the Americans." *At least, not yet.*

"Understood, sir."

"And inform me at once if your July aviation fuel allocations aren't delivered when due."

"Of course, sir."

"Very well, Aleksei." Meredov hung up.

For a moment he listened to the steady hiss of the ancient steam radiators, from which the dirty white paint was peeling in scabs. He wore his winter formal uniform, dark navy-blue wool with a double-breasted jacket, mostly to help stay warm—the temperature outside was well above freezing, but his office was drafty with the winter shutters taken down. The windows were double-glazed, but their frames were warped and loose. His jacket cuff edges were shiny from wear, and so was the seat of his pants, which he thought, as with the radiator and the ragged carpet, was symbolic: *threadbare, not pretty, but effective enough to get by, like Russia herself.* The numerous medals on his jacket swayed and clinked whenever he moved. These seemed symbolic, too, since he'd never been in battle, never had to fight a shooting war. Even so, Meredov was proud of the medals and ribbons. He'd earned them for various outstanding achievements, including vital peacetime ballistic missile submarine deterrent patrols. Yet he also felt the decorations emblematic of a wider national culture based on puffery and bluff, deception and disinformation, as much as on any true substance. He glanced at the photos, models, and other memorabilia decorating his office walls and desk; the experiences and relationships behind these were quite genuine.

Twenty-five years of service to my country. My sad, despairing, tormented country.

He went to the windows, taking in the view of the snow-capped Cherskiy Mountain Range on his left, southwest, and the uninterrupted vista to his right, northward, as the land fell away toward boggy lowlands and the desolate permafrost tundra. In the foreground, silver birches soared, hardy shrubs clung to the moist and mossy taiga soil, and wildflowers bloomed in open fields that teemed with migratory birds; though six months from now the temperature would be brutally, killingly cold, at the peak of summer's heat in August a person would sweat standing still in the shade. In the distance, scattered smoke plumes rose from wood-pulping paper factories, from coal-fired power plants, and from smelters busy purifying valuable metals from ores.

Eventually, in that same direction, north, too far to see

from where he stood, mainland Russia ended, where frigid waves from the Laptev Sea and the East Siberian Sea broke against the shore. In winter, he knew from experience, those waves froze to solid ice. Now both seas were sprinkled with icebergs, and their farther sides bordered the polar cap itself. Past the New Siberian Islands was no more dry land until well beyond the North Pole, in an alien place called Canada—not much more distant from Meredov in one direction than Vladivostok was in the other.

He gazed thoughtfully to the north. Out there lay his area of responsibility. Rear Admiral Elmar Meredov commanded all shore-based and surface naval forces that defended the northeastern part of the Siberian coast against amphibious assault, and protected nearby home waters from incursion by foreign submarines. *What an absurd military arrangement.* Three thousand kilometers of coastline in his jurisdiction, not counting the islands, and he had no control over army troops, air force fighter jets, or any major fleet formations or Russian submarines. His own assets—smaller ships, long-endurance patrol planes, his undersea hydrophone nets, and even his headquarters building itself—depended for their own defense on other departments, directorates, and branches of the armed forces, between which cooperation, even in these turbulent times, was conspicuous by its nonexistence.

Meredov was very used to such things. In a way, he'd started out his career as a product of the Soviet state at its best. The son of poor factory workers in Leningrad, with no Party affiliations at all, he'd excelled in mathematics in school. After he won a regional math contest against stiff competition, the communist system sent him to college at Moscow State University, where he received a superb education in the mid-1980s. As graduation day approached he was invited to join the navy, by a regime whose invitations could not be refused. Trained as a junior officer, his technical talents and resilient, even-tempered personality led him to an assignment in submarines.

The Berlin Wall fell, the Soviet Union collapsed, and Russia deteriorated into an era of experiments with democracy and capitalism—experiments that tragically failed. The Russian military dwindled, pay became increasingly irregular, but at least there was food and clean clothes. This was a lot better than most civilians had, including his parents, whom he was forced to scramble to support. He'd married a woman he met at university, a linguistics major of great inner character strength and no great beauty. But Elmar Meredov was neither charming nor handsome himself—and he knew it. In real life, love and passion had nothing to do with good looks; the marriage thrived and they raised three wonderful, bright, athletic sons. His wife's language skills won her plenty of work as a translator, and the extended family, with her unemployed parents too, got by.

Meredov rose further in the Russian Navy based on his evident merit and persistent hard work, plus an increasingly shrewd sense of how to play the ridiculous system. He became the assistant captain of one of Russia's handful of Project 941 subs. NATO called them Typhoons. Weighing almost as much as a World War II battleship, carrying twenty long-range missiles that each bore ten hydrogen bomb warheads, a Typhoon was immense and almost indestructible. Meredov earned another promotion, but there were too few submarines still in commission for him to get to command one. Instead, he was put in charge of a sector of Russia's equivalent of the American SOSUS underwater sound surveillance system. The ever-adaptable Meredov adjusted quickly, making the most of his prior experience as a qualified submariner, and became a leading expert in antisubmarine warfare instead.

Russia turned autocratic again, just as tremendous oil and natural gas reserves began to be efficiently exploited—and exported—to the full. The resurgent Kremlin wanted a strong defense and suddenly had the hard currency to pay for it. Meredov made rear admiral, much higher than he ever thought he'd go. It was a symptom of his continuing lack of insider connections that he was posted to the portion of Siberia which, even for Siberia, was truly the middle of nowhere.

Someone knocked on his office door.

"Yes!"

His senior aide and deputy chief of staff came in, a captain, second rank—equivalent to a commander in the U.S. Navy. "Sir, is there anything else you'll be needing?"

Meredov made eye contact. The woman, like him, was a Slav, the main ethnic group within the heart of western Russia. She had a heavy frame and stocky build, with open, expressive, but rather plain features. She carried herself with surprising grace, considering her ample girth.

"No, Irina, I think we're having another quiet day. You needn't remain at the office."

Irina Malenkova perked up. She wanted to get home to her family, in the cheap but sturdy housing provided for married base personnel; reliable day care was part of this package. She turned to leave.

The secure phone rang again. Meredov pursed his lips. The caller ID said it was his counterpart in Anadyr, on the Bering Sea, responsible for the coast to the east and then south of his own jurisdiction—including the Bering Strait. Anadyr had a sheltered harbor and an airport. Using icebreakers when needed, it was navigable most of the year.

He picked up the phone. "Meredov speaking."

"Have you seen the new intelligence report?" Rear Admiral Balakirev said without preamble or pleasantries.

"I see many reports," Meredov answered, sounding as blasé as he could. Balakirev, a peer, was also a rival, and could be annoying on purpose; the physical resemblance that made some people mistake them for brothers only egged Balakirev on. The two were not brotherly. "Which report?"

"The one about the new German strategy."

"What new German strategy?" Meredov knew that Russia's spy services were active in Berlin and Johannesburg, not trusting the regimes there even while Moscow supported them.

Irina overheard this, and halted in midstride.

Balakirev gave the communiqué's number and priority code. It was sent via the Defense Council, the highest authority over the Russian military. "You're on the distribution list. We both have a need to know. It could affect our operational areas and our readiness state."

"Hold on." Meredov muted the phone. He asked Irina if they'd gotten this communiqué.

"Sir, you know I would have told you at once."

"Check again."

She hurried out. Meredov unmuted the phone. "We're searching for our copy."

Balakirev grunted, sounding bored and superior.

He didn't call just to make conversation. He never does.

Malenkova returned and shook her head.

"Ours must have been misrouted," Meredov told Balakirev. Important messages being lost was a longstanding feature of the Russian military. Meredov hadn't forgotten how, back in 1995, Norway fired a science rocket toward the pole, after more than a week's prior notice to Russia. The notice got lost somewhere in Moscow's Defense Ministry, Russian radars thought it was an incoming American ICBM—and before the mix-up was clarified, President Yeltsin had opened the briefcase with the retaliation launch codes. "Not the first time things were delayed or misplaced, and certainly won't be the last."

"My, but you're the cynical one. You should be more careful how you talk. Even secure lines can be monitored by *them.*"

Meredov did have to be careful. While he wasn't really frightened of any thought police from the FSB—successor to the old KGB—curiosity and original ideas at the rear-admiral level weren't encouraged or appreciated by more senior admirals and the Kremlin. The Russian military was run purely from the upper echelons down. Going by the book, following standard doctrine and rigid procedures, was paramount. Centralized control was cherished, maintained by a haughty divide-and-conquer attitude. It often had the effect of making even flag officers, including Balakirev, act like competitive adolescents.

"What does the message say?"

"The Germans want to step up their psychological pressure on the Americans, to get them to finally crack and agree to an armistice. More scare tactics. Their High Command has decided to try to sink one or two American ballistic missile submarines, their *Ohio*-class, the so-called boomers."

"They can *try*. I seriously doubt they'd ever succeed."

"Being *seen* by the U.S. to attempt it would be enough, don't you think?"

The U.S. would confront that classic dilemma whenever a deterrent force suffers attrition: Use it before you lose it. The implicit balance of terror's unspoken arrangement between Allies and Axis was, no H-bombs unleashed or endangered. Now Meredov was deeply concerned. He knew the fragile thermonuclear threshold had almost been breached more than once. *With each new Axis thrust in the war, Berlin and Johannesberg become increasingly reckless.* "It changes the entire outlook of the conflict," Meredov said half to himself.

"And not for the better," Balakirev answered.

"What measures are we supposed to take?"

"There's nothing specific in this bulletin."

No specifics meant no accountability, either, for cooperative action or lack thereof. *Typical.*

"Other than making sure I sleep badly tonight, was there some other reason you called?"

"I have a problem. Of less strategic importance, I think, but it strikes much closer to home. I need your help."

"What help?" Meredov was instinctively suspicious.

"Four days ago a few of my forces prosecuted a submerged contact, in the strait on a northerly course. At least the sensors on the barrier fence did indicate a valid contact heading north. They dropped sonobuoys, signal grenades, then depth charges, but there wasn't anything there."

"How sure are you of the lack of an actual hostile?"

Balakirev summarized the maneuvers and tactics used, emphasizing the very constricted geography and shallow water. "No submarine could have possibly escaped."

"False positives are common in antisubmarine operations."

"This one was different. It all went on under the Americans' noses. They reacted."

"How? Did they fire any warning shots?"

"Worse. They filed a diplomatic note with Moscow, protesting an unannounced live-ammunition exercise. As they put it, 'provocatively close to the treaty line, in a narrow international commercial waterway.'"

"How did Moscow answer?"

"They didn't. Why would they? The decision was made that we owe the Americans nothing."

"So what's your problem?"

"The Ministry of Defense passed heat to our mutual boss." A dour vice admiral in Vladivostok. "He's taking it out on me."

"Taking what out?"

"They're saying that men under my command showed ill discipline, and incompetence, attacking ghosts and letting the American surveillance and signals intercept positions observe Russian forces acting on a full combat footing from point-blank range. Thus betraying vital secrets in a manner that borders on treasonous. On my watch."

"Sounds like someone's really out to get you."

"I responded that the data from the barrier fence are on record, showing definite indications that an unidentified submarine was there."

Meredov thought this over. The military and internal political considerations were intertwined, as usual. "I see your dilemma. The bureau who designed the fence and sensors, and the commander who maintains them and interprets any signals, refuse to concede that a flaw in their setup could lead to a strongly convincing false-positive contact."

"Combined, they outnumber me, and they also have better Kremlin connections."

"From their selfish perspective, the fault has to be yours."

"Yes."

"Now I see your difficulty. . . . But I think it's even worse than you realize."

Balakirev paused. Meredov sensed him hesitating. "Explain," Balakirev said curtly, but defensively.

"One of two things happened. The fence gave a false alarm, and by responding to it your field personnel revealed procedures and electronic warfare intelligence to the Americans. Or . . ."

"Or what?" Balakirev was definitely uncomfortable now. He knew Meredov was much smarter than him. Balakirev had risen as far as rear admiral by attending the Naval Academy—a special pedigree, a door-opener—and from then on he brown-nosed shamelessly. His background was in guided missile cruisers, though the one he'd been captain of seldom left its pier. He knew little about submarines and antisubmarine warfare.

"Or, there really was a submarine there that was somehow able to outwit your forces." *In ASW work, one can never be too paranoid.*

"I was afraid you were going to say something like that. It's the real reason I phoned."

Now came the time for the understated negotiating games, the manipulation and countermanipulation that often occurred when two Russian officers spoke.

"What do you expect me to do to assist you?"

"I'd rather be censured for what our boss wants to think already happened, than be shot later on if the incident was just the opening act of something larger."

"You have my sympathies." Meredov didn't like being

sarcastic, but it was normal to toy with someone else when the situation implied any chance for advantage.

"You're clearly objective. You have the technical skills for it, and I wouldn't know where to begin. If I send you all the data from the engagement, from the fence spires, the sonobuoys, the Il-Thirty-Eight, the surface-ship sonars, can your staff take an independent look? Do a peer review, so to speak."

"I see what you're trying to do. Drag me in as a second voice of rank equal to yours on which no blame has fallen so far. Together we jump on the question of whether the fence's false alarm wasn't false. If an unknown submarine did somehow evade your Bering Strait forces, and my surveillance hydrophone-net center's supercomputer can prove it, you get the fence people off your case, bravely raise the alarm to our boss to preempt severer punishment later, and maybe keep your career on track by publicly demoting a couple of ship commanders under you for lack of sufficient diligence. . . . And if I can prove that there was indeed nothing there even though the spire sensors said there was, you shove back against the pro-fence contingent's self-serving allegations, make them the scapegoats while your unit's rash actions right under American eyes appear instead to be reasonably justified. . . . Did that capture all of it?"

"Yes."

"Just one question. Why should I help you?"

"I know we have our differences, but look at the larger picture. Normal American submarine transits going by the Arctic Sea route to the Atlantic would surely use their side of the strait. Right? And we know the Axis have no submarines at all in the Pacific."

By now Meredov was thinking out loud as much as he was talking to Balakirev. "If the fence detected a sub that was really there, then it's certainly up to no good."

"And presumably it would be, or could be, heading right for your area of responsibility. With something sinister planned."

Meredov frowned. Balakirev was doing a good job of forcing his involvement. "I need to do two things, then. Have my people start crunching your numbers under my supervision and guidance, but also bring my forces to a heightened state of alert."

"Yes."

"Hold on a minute." Meredov muted the phone. He looked at Irina, standing in the doorway. "You're following this?"

"Mostly, Admiral."

"I'm afraid it's going to be a late night for both of us. Tell the computer center to expect a very large data file from Anadyr soon, via the secure fiber optic line. I'll issue instructions on what to do with it once I get a better feel for what sort of data we have."

"Yes, Admiral."

"Get in touch with my chief of staff." Malenkova's direct superior. "My deputy too." Meredov's second in command. Both men—captains, first rank—were traveling at far-flung bases. "Have them establish a higher alert for an undersea intrusion."

"Yes, sir."

He unmuted the phone again. "If there's nothing new or useful embedded in the data," he told Balakirev, "you're really going to owe me for this."

"If the fence needs recalibration, you get the credit for proving it, and for bolstering our defenses in a vital naval choke point. But if an unidentified sub turns out to have snuck through our side of the strait, and you can show that, again you look good but also protect the Motherland from what might well be a dangerous threat."

"A very dangerous threat, if this hypothetical sub can really do what you seem to want me to think it can do."

"I know."

And by calling me now on the record, instead of just keeping your mouth shut, you save your ass later if worse does come to worst. "A submarine that was detected by our underwater barrier, and even so defied careful investigation from immediately above its head, must be one extremely sophisticated vessel. With an extremely steely-nerved captain. . . . Send me the data." *It's been slow here.* "I do always welcome this sort of challenge."

An hour later, Malenkova knocked and entered Meredov's office, holding a file of papers and computer printouts. "Initial summaries from the data center, Admiral." She handed him the materials.

"Sit, Irina, while I take a quick look through these."

"Yes, Admiral." She settled into one of the overstuffed guest chairs. He could tell that she was troubled.

"What's the matter?"

"This Germany strategy change that Rear Admiral Balakirev told you about. . . . It makes the future seem very volatile, sir. The chance of a nuclear holocaust now . . ."

Meredov put down the papers. "Irina, listen. For fifteen centuries, since Eastern Slavs first settled along the Dnipro River, when has the Motherland's future not been murky, and her present not fraught with strife? Viking overlords, Tatar hordes, the Poles, the Swedes, the Turks, Napoleon's Grand Army. The Crimean War, the Turks again, the Japanese, the kaiser. The foreign Interventionists meddling in Lenin's Revolution. Oppression by the tsars. Oppression by the communists. The Cold War. Afghanistan, Chernobyl, Chechnya. . . . My parents, as children, survived the siege of Leningrad, you know. For nine hundred days Hitler's Wehrmacht attacked and our forebears fought them off without flinching. A million people died of starvation. I saw the mass graves in the cemetery north of the city as I grew up. The Great Patriotic War taught my parents to face the present and future with courage, not fear. And they taught me. Individuals count but little. Mother Russia is eternal. Mother Russia has already lasted far longer than ancient Rome."

Irina glanced thoughtfully at her hands, folded neatly in her lap; Leningrad, or Petrograd under the tsars, was called St. Petersburg now, and still had fewer cats and dogs than other Russian cities—pets became human food in the siege.

"Courage," Meredov told her. "Not fear."

CHAPTER 9

Jeffrey sat in *Challenger*'s control room. The compartment was hushed as technicians intently watched their displays. Noises from the gale-wracked ice cap kept coming over the sonar speakers. The 3-D surround-sound gave the vivid sensation of moving beneath an almost solid yet frenetically dynamic roof extending forever in all directions above his head.

"Captain? Commodore?" Meltzer called from the navigation plotting table.

Jeffrey and Bell turned to face Meltzer, from opposite directions, Bell seated in front of him and Jeffrey behind.

"Sirs, five minutes to revised rendezvous point."

"Very well, Nav," Bell acknowledged. "Commodore, shall we get ready?"

"Affirmative," Jeffrey said with a smile. This would be the first full coming together of his strike group's key people.

A junior officer relieved Meltzer at the navigation plot. Bell made Bud Torelli, Weps, command duty officer, acting captain. Torelli told one of his own lieutenants (j.g.) to take the fire control coordinator's seat that Sessions vacated.

COB told Lieutenant Torelli that *Challenger*'s pressure-proof hangar's water, surrounding the minisub's hull, was equalized to the ocean outside at present depth, eight hundred fifty feet. COB would activate the silent hydraulics to open the hangar doors when Meltzer told him via intercom that he was ready to depart.

Jeffrey, Bell, Sessions, Meltzer, and Finch walked aft.

"I'll catch up in one minute," Jeffrey told them, ducking into the stateroom he shared with Sessions. The others continued down the red-lit passageway, only wide enough to go single file, toward the airlock trunk that connected to *Challenger*'s minisub. The high-test hydrogen-peroxide-powered mini, housed in the in-hull hangar amidships, was German and had been captured in a battle six months earlier. Using it instead of a standard battery-powered U.S.-made Advanced SEAL Delivery System minisub had proved to be a valuable subterfuge more than once. Meltzer was very adept as its pilot. The co-pilot, a chief from what was now Meltzer's navigating department, was already up in the mini, going through prelaunch checklists. Commander Nyurba and his four men had also boarded and taken seats in the transport compartment, aft of the mini's multi-diver lock-in/lockout hyperbaric chamber.

Alone in *Challenger*'s XO state room, Jeffrey opened the safe. He removed the orders pouch that he wasn't supposed to read until he'd boarded USS *Jimmy Carter*. With the thick pouch under an arm, he headed aft.

The mini was eight feet high on the outside and had no sail. Because it was so crowded, Jeffrey crammed behind Meltzer in the two-seat control compartment, forward of the central diver-sortie chamber that doubled as a personnel entry and exit vestibule. The forward compartment resembled a tiny version of *Challenger*'s control room, with high-definition flat-screen displays on the bulkheads, joysticks, and keyboards, but no periscope; a photonics mast and antenna mast folded flat on top of the mini.

The ride from *Challenger* to *Carter* was short. The mini-sub docked onto the mating hatch and lockdown clamps behind *Carter*'s sail, while both full-size submarines, at all stop, drifted with the gentle under-ice current. Look-down photonics sensors in passive image-intensification mode helped keep the docking safe but stealthy; tiny lights on *Carter*'s hull showed where to aim, and let Meltzer judge his angle and rate of approach.

Since *Carter*'s special in-hull garage space—for oversized weapons and off-board probes—wasn't designed for a sixty-foot-long minisub, *Carter* hadn't brought one of her own. Jeffrey knew that she might easily have carried one on her back as she snuck out of port on the U.S. East Coast, but the external load would have caused much louder flow noise than usual, compromising her stealth. Bearing an outside mini would also have forced *Carter* to keep to speeds far below the optimal for her five-thousand-mile transit from New London to Alaska: otherwise, the water drag of a mini load, streamlined as it was, would have torn it from its fastenings and hurled it sternward, smashing *Carter*'s rudder or sternplanes or pump-jet propulsor—or all three.

But Jeffrey couldn't help wondering how eighty Special Operations Squadron commandos and all their gear were going to get ashore quickly, clandestinely, with only one mini available. The north coast of eastern Russia had the widest, shallowest continental shelf in the world. Almost everywhere, the water didn't reach a depth of even one hundred feet until more than a hundred miles offshore. A single round trip in the German mini at such range would take an entire day and run the fuel tanks dry; *Challenger* carried no refill of the extremely corrosive, explosive peroxide. The only exceptions to this unhelpful seabed geography led right toward heavily protected Russian naval bases.

———————

Captain Charles Harley, tall, slim, clean-shaven, with piercing blue eyes and neatly combed blond hair, was waiting at the bottom of *Carter*'s airlock trunk as the minisub's passengers climbed down the ladder. "Welcome aboard, Commodore Fuller," Harley said. They shook hands; Harley had a firm, confident grip. He struck Jeffrey as rather handsome, even debonair, but stiff and distant. Other introductions were quickly done.

First things first. "I need to use your XO's stateroom."

Harley noticed the pouch under Jeffrey's arm. "Come this way. The rest of us will be in the special ops battle management center. When you're ready, a messenger can show you how to get there on the first try. The *Seawolf* boats were a bit of a rabbit warren even before *Carter*'s extra hull section was added."

Jeffrey followed Harley forward through red-lit passageways, indicating modified battle stations for the lengthy rendezvous.

"Care for a quick look at our control room?"

"By all means." Jeffrey couldn't be an inconsiderate guest to one of his captains. This was also a chance to begin assessing Harley and his crew.

"Let's take the longer way, stretch our legs, and you can see more of my ship."

Jeffrey noted that Harley conducted himself as if giving a tour to a visitor—not being inspected by his boss. He led Jeffrey down a ladder, walked on, then climbed up another ladder. They entered *Carter*'s control room from forward, facing aft. Harley lowered his voice. "This part must seem old-fashioned."

"The four-man ship control station," Jeffrey stated.

"Yep. Enlisted ratings at helm and sternplanes, diving officer, chief of the watch. Separate sonar room. Periscope tubes." Both were retracted, deep into their wells within the ship, but their bulky tubes and hydraulic piping, and the big red-and-white overhead rings for raising and lowering them, were visible and took up room. "No vertical launching system for Tomahawks, either. Have to shoot 'em through our torpedo tubes."

Jeffrey peeked at console readouts. This required standing behind technicians and looking over their shoulders; there were no widescreen vertical bulkhead displays here, as on *Challenger*.

His strike group maintained their rendezvous formation using occasional gentle pushes from their auxiliary maneuvering thrusters; the acoustic link was working well; no threats had been detected; the gale was stronger.

Done with the instrumentation, Jeffrey took in the people themselves while they interacted by issuing and acknowledging orders or status reports. Harley's officers and enlisted men reflected his own personality, as was typically the situation on any well-run submarine. They were formal, polished, disciplined, and competent—not exactly unfriendly, but lacking the chummy swagger of *Challenger*'s crew. As a group, they seemed well trained and cohesive. Jeffrey liked what he saw.

"Right in here." Harley left Jeffrey alone and went aft.

Jeffrey locked the stateroom's doors to the corridor, and to the head that was shared with the captain's stateroom. He sat at the little desk, cleared the XO's odds and ends to one side, and switched on the reading lamp. He disarmed the security device on the inner sealed pouch, removing his mission orders.

They took more than two hours just to gain a broad overview. By the time he got that far, he felt he'd aged ten years.

CHAPTER 10

Jeffrey grabbed the intercom handset next to *Carter*'s XO's desk. He wasn't sure how to reach the Special Operations briefing space, so he called the control room.

"Messenger of the Watch, sir."

"This is Commodore Fuller."

"Yes, sir. Captain Harley asked me about ten minutes ago if I knew how much longer you'd be, but then he said I shouldn't disturb you."

"Have Captain Bell and Lieutenant Meltzer see me now."

"In the XO's stateroom, sir?"

"Yes. Inform Captain Harley that I'll be needing him here, too, in private. I can't say when yet, so give him my compliments and ask him to please continue waiting."

"Understood, Commodore."

Soon someone knocked on the door. Jeffrey got up and unlocked it, letting Bell and Meltzer in.

Jeffrey sat, Bell took the one guest seat, and Meltzer stood politely.

He studied the two of them, his flagship captain and his part-time executive assistant. He sized them up, measuring for himself whether they could handle the difficulties that Jeffrey now knew lay ahead.

"I'm not sure quite where to begin." He tiredly rubbed the bridge of his nose. "There's a major counterespionage effort going on back home that's all too relevant to us. There's an Axis mole *somewhere* in undersea warfare planning. . . . A remark Commander Nyurba made to me, that *Carter*'s mission to Norway had been compromised in advance, resonated strongly with a cautionary warning in my orders here."

"Why do we need to know about this?" Meltzer asked.

"There's danger of undetermined degree that our present mission was also leaked by the mole."

Bell opened his mouth to say something; Jeffrey held up a hand to not interrupt.

"That's why our current tasking has been organized and coordinated by a group of senior people selected by the President. Extraordinary compartmentalization was used to implement each detail. Even more than usual, those outside the President's closed group have only very tiny pieces of the puzzle, with elaborate cover stories to justify activity they saw going on, those same cover stories spun so as to hide the special security measures. This gives only partial reassurance, as we proceed, that we haven't been compromised. . . . My strike group has been provided with a cover story to use ourselves, explaining why we'll be where we'll be once we get there."

"In case we're detected, sir?" Bell asked.

"This is where it goes byzantine. Part of *Challenger*'s job, but not *Carter*'s, is to be detected. More than just detected."

"Sir?" Meltzer blurted out.

"Patience. I want Captain Harley involved for that part. One difficulty is the battle with the Amethyste-Two. The Amethyste being there to begin with might have been the work of the mole. Let's pray that compartmentalization kept the actual reason for the rendezvous, and the specific identity of our two ships, hidden from the Axis. If so, but *only* if so, our sinking the Amethyste, and surviving, have largely negated the work of the mole. Pray I'm right on that. If I'm wrong, and our adversary knows the actual reason why we're coming, we're heading into a terrible trap."

Jeffrey reached for the intercom. "Tell your captain I'm ready for him."

In two minutes Harley knocked and came in. Meltzer scrunched to make room; the compartment was packed. Bell offered Harley the guest chair. He shook his head. He stood instead, in a proprietary manner, arms folded, leaning against the bulkhead. Jeffrey sensed he was feeling slightly violated—from his angle, a close-knit clique from *Challenger* had been caucusing alone, in a subordinate's stateroom on *his* ship. Harley could tell that the caucus had not been fun.

"Everybody listen up," Jeffrey said, "and listen good. The President wants our mission to be accomplished in a hurry because we have to forestall the next major German move, whatever that might be, and our own forces globally are becoming too worn out. In particular, the delivery of the next Eight-six-eight-U nuclear sub from Russia to Germany is scheduled very soon, and from what we know of its capabilities we *must* forestall that delivery."

"We sink it?" Harley asked. "Blockade it?" He seemed game for the fight.

"It's far more complicated, I'm afraid, because far more is at stake. There's the unlimited supply of oil and natural gas, aircraft, tanks, other arms of all different kinds that Russia keeps supplying to the Axis. . . . Our assignment is probably the single most important and dicey mission ever attempted in this war or any shooting war. It's a last-ditch chance to halt the brinkmanship once and for all, before humanity incinerates itself. . . . We need to squelch our ethical reservations, we dare not flinch, because an objective observer could easily argue that what we've been ordered to do is a war crime."

"Huh?" Harley's guard was down now, so Jeffrey eyed Bell and Meltzer, then began to hit the three with the conclusion he'd been leading to.

"We'll go into details with Lieutenant Colonel Kurzin and Commander Nyurba and their people in a few minutes. I want to set this up by asking you a question first, Captain Harley. It isn't a trick question."

"Go ahead, sir. Commodore."

"How do you think this war will end?"

"With Allied victory, I hope."

"Even though the Axis has nuked several populated islands, including Diego Garcia, very painfully for us? Even though they attempted to get two South American countries embroiled in tactical atomic combat with each other, *on land,* while trying to make it look like the U.S. was to blame? And even though, failing in that by a fraction of an inch, they then launched an offensive in the Middle East that could easily have unleashed Israel's nuclear arsenal? With staggeringly catastrophic consequences if that had happened, which it very nearly did?"

"The oligarchy in Berlin are desperate dictators."

"With no intention whatsoever of surrendering to avoid an apocalypse. They've proven that time and again. Like desperate dictators everywhere, they care nothing for the lives of their own citizens. Their intention all along has been to *use* the threat of apocalypse to get the U.S. to back down."

"Would we do that? Back down? Ever?"

"If events continue as they have, voters may force Congress to offer an armistice. Let the Axis have Europe and Africa. Let the United Kingdom fend for themselves and go under. That's exactly what Berlin and Johannesburg have been gunning for all along. Their envoys in Sweden prod ours, then they talk to the international media when we refuse, make Washington look like the heavies, the ones who drag out the war. Put enough pressure on the American public, that pressure gets passed to Capitol Hill. They'd override the President's veto, we'd have peace of a sort, with our war leader gone from the White House in disgrace. Forget Election Day 2012. Armistice means impeachment. Escapist pacifism quickly takes firm hold."

"That's a grim picture."

"Especially since the Axis wouldn't be satisfied to just keep what they got. They'd use that lopsided peace to squash the U.S. economically, flush our remaining prestige down the toilet, put a noose of diplomatic isolation around our neck, build up their military might, and eventually have another major stab at the parts of the world they don't yet control."

Harley scratched his jaw. "Agreeing to an armistice is a snare, an illusion? It only delays the inevitable?"

"Very much so. Thorough wargame simulations have been performed in the past few months, to see where things could possibly go from here." Jeffrey tapped the thick hardcopy orders on the desk. "Several independent sets of players and computer models were used, including at the Naval War College. I was assigned to their simulations department before I wangled a transfer to *Challenger*. I can testify that those folks do objective, reliable, conclusive work. They're the best."

"I know. They have a world-class reputation."

"Other war colleges, private think tanks, consulting firms, were also involved. They all came up with similar results."

"Which were? . . ."

"Suppose we continue the war, with the aim to unseat the Axis leadership. How do we do it, and what happens when we try? A D-day-like assault across the English Channel, after a big buildup in Great Britain, is out of the question with tactical nukes in play. Ditto for an amphibious push from North Africa using the Med. And a land-route invasion of Germany, through the Middle East or Asia, will certainly cause the German regime to introduce widespread tactical nuclear weapons on land to defeat our oncoming offensive, no matter how broad the front along which we and our allies attack, and no matter how severe the collateral damage and civilian deaths."

"Lord."

"Worse. Following a period of armistice with America if one is indeed arranged, their second wave of aggression would be just as murderous. The juiciest prizes left for grabs, with Russia continuing as Germany's pseudo-neutral friend, would be the big countries in the Middle East and Asia. With a whole different lineup of targets and objectives then, cross-ocean sea lanes wouldn't have today's significance. Tactical nuclear weapons would come into use offensively and defensively, unlimited, on land. . . . In either of the two potential scenarios, continuing to prosecute the war or granting an armistice, according to our planners the ultimate outcome remains the same. With so many countries getting involved and so much destruction and slaughter in main population centers, the conflict is certain to escalate into wholesale thermonuclear war. The U.S., Russia, China, Israel, Japan, everybody else. Hundreds of millions dead right away, maybe billions, and billions more not long after that if there's a nuclear winter. The end of modern civilization, maybe the end of humanity." Jeffrey tapped his orders again to emphasize the reality of what he'd been told in such harsh terms in writing.

"So what do we do?" Harley asked. "Why doesn't the Pentagon glass Germany right now? Preempt?"

"Because Russia brought Germany under her own thermonuclear umbrella. Even if Russia broke *that* promise and held her fire, us glassing Germany would kill tens of millions of innocents outside German borders from fallout alone. Because Russia's command-and-control systems are so gimpy, they might think our missiles were coming at *them,* and launch a massive retaliatory strike . . . at America. Because Germany has cruise missiles with fission warheads hiding at sea, which would come in low and fast and nuke the whole U.S. East Coast, and Gulf Coast, and reach inland past the Mississippi. Tens of millions more dead."

"So what do we do?" Bell repeated Harley's question.

"We perform our mission. There *is* a third scenario. One and only one alternative to Apocalypse Soon or Apocalypse Later. We take Kurzin and his men to Siberia, where they pretend to be Germans pretending to be Russians, infiltrate a missile silo field, take control of several brand-new SS-Twenty-seven ICBMs with one-megaton warheads, and launch them at the United States."

CHAPTER 11

Bell and Harley were horrified. *"What?"* Meltzer blurted.

"I have documentation, Captains Harley and Bell, which you can authenticate with your own emergency-action-message codes. This way you can satisfy yourselves that these are valid, legal orders from our commander in chief. . . . The goal is to appear to try to start a nuclear exchange between Russia and the U.S., and leave ironclad forensic clues that German operatives, disguised as Russian extremists, did it."

Harley fidgeted nervously. Bell squirmed in his seat. Meltzer chewed his lip so hard that Jeffrey thought his teeth might break the skin.

"There's finely reasoned method in this madness. If the commando squadron, and I, succeed in our assigned roles, and *Carter*'s stealth holds up, the missiles that take off from Siberian silos, fully armed by technicians from Kurzin's team, will detonate long before they actually land on American soil. Instead, the warheads will be set to go off outside the atmosphere over Russia. The radiation from the blasts will dissipate into the already-radioactive Van Allen belts surrounding our planet, and from there be blown by the solar wind safely away into deep space. The Greater Moscow area will be blanketed by a nonlethal but extremely damaging electromagnetic pulse. This much we know from tests performed in the late nineteen-fifties and early sixties. . . . Russia, hurting, panic-stricken at the thought of American vengeance and outraged at German treachery, will at a minimum withdraw all support from the Axis, and she might well, of sheer necessity, join the Allied side. That would leave Berlin isolated, cut off from strategic sustenance. On the ropes, with the Boers withering on the vine at the far southern tip of Africa. The Axis leaders, knowing that they're not at fault but being unable to prove to Russia that we so cold-bloodedly framed them, would also have been sent a stinging message. One with plausible deniability, but unmistakable, about what ruthless risk-takers Americans are once sufficiently provoked, thus destroying the Axis sense of control and undermining their power. An amnesty, if the oligarchs step down at that juncture, could neatly wrap up the war."

Harley sputtered. "Would we give those sons of bitches an *amnesty* after all this? Let them *walk,* after starting a premeditated tactical nuclear war?"

Jeffrey smiled sweetly. "Oh, I suppose the amnesty might be broken eventually, maybe by hit squads from Israel's Mossad."

"I like that part," Meltzer said.

"For one stage I'll need to go to a base in Siberia, as a back-door emissary to convey America's extreme displeasure by making certain deadly threats, and also pretend to test Russia's good faith, since most of Moscow will be knocked out of the loop by the EMP, including our somewhat ineffective diplomats stationed there. By then the President will be on the Hot Line to Russia's president, assuming the Hot Line isn't knocked out too. And if it is still working, Washington will cause temporary outages at crucial times, for 'technical reasons,' to help underscore my discussions and suitably tweak and tune the psychological chaos likely in the Kremlin by then. Part of my job will also be to quickly get inside Moscow's reaction and decision time scale, to keep them from doing something precipitate, something irrevocably disastrous for the world."

"And if you can't?" Harley demanded.

"If things backfire? If Kurzin's team can't sneak and fight their way into a highly restricted area, then bypass booby traps and override software safeguards properly, or their and our strike group's subterfuges are seen through or my bluffs are called, or we get sunk and identified, then Russia will surely become a wholehearted member of the Axis. Our commandos might even by accident nuke a few U.S. or Russian cities for real."

"But—" Bell tried to object.

"Then the only way out of apocalypse isn't even a negotiated armistice, it's fast and abject Allied surrender. We kiss good-bye to the American way of life, confront enslavement instead, and learn to speak German or Russian or Afrikaans. That's if we're lucky. If we're unlucky, the missiles Kurzin launches are only the first of many, and then more, and more, from Russia, the U.S., and other places. You could call that outcome, the worst-case mission failure result, Apocalypse Now."

Jeffrey knew how his subordinates felt, because his own head was swirling with unanswered questions and troubling what-ifs. "Captain Harley, I think we ought to be getting to the briefing session." Bell stood, and Meltzer let his seniors precede him.

Harley, not so crisp and detached as when Jeffrey first met him, led the way, around sharp corners and down steep ladders, then through a long, straight corridor. He said, with pride, that this was the wasp waist in *Carter*'s Multi-Mission Platform. The pressure hull narrowed to eighteen feet, creating ample garage space inside the forty-two-foot-diameter outer hull.

They came to the full-width aft part of this specially added pressure hull section. Some doors here held security warnings, and were protected by electronic and mechanical combination locks. They went up a ladder and came to another door, open. Inside was a briefing room. Jeffrey did a double take.

Except for officers and chiefs from *Challenger* and *Carter*, who wore khakis or jumpsuit blue, several dozen men were dressed in Russian Army uniforms—mostly urban- or forest-pattern camouflage fatigues—and they talked in small groups in fluent Russian. Their short haircuts, the set of their features, the ways they moved, were subtly foreign, not American. Some had shirtsleeves rolled above elbows, and even their forearm tattoos—the motifs, the colors, the alphabet used for the words—bore an alien look. Jeffrey also saw battle scars, from shrapnel, bayonets, or bullets.

Their mean and emotionless faces gave the appearance of street gang members, ones who'd had the individuality beaten out of them by a merciless mental and physical thrashing that left these, the survivors, tougher and more ruthless for it. What distinguished each were their ethnic features, body types, and hair color, blond or brown or frizzy red or glossy jet black.

One man at the front of the room stood up. Jeffrey thought he bore a close resemblance, in bearing and attitude as well as in his build and appearance, to a youngish Leonid Brezhnev, the reactionary Communist Party General Secretary who led the USSR during its violent repression of Czechoslovakia in 1968 and the genocidal invasion of Afghanistan in 1979.

"Sergey Kurzin," this strange apparition said to Jeffrey,

shaking his hand. "A pleasure to meet you, Commodore." His English was unaccented. He said he grew up in Chicago.

Jeffrey glanced around the briefing room. "You have quite an outfit here, Colonel." Then Jeffrey saw Commander Nyurba approaching. He too looked different, like he really was a serving officer in the Russian Federation's armed forces.

"Don't mind us, Commodore," Nyurba said. "We need to stay in character."

"Where are the rest of your team?"

"I decided to send them by squads to eat," Kurzin stated, "or to use our exercise equipment, since you were even longer than I expected reading your orders."

"Can we get started now?"

"After I talk to you and Commander Nyurba in private."

Jeffrey eyed Bell, Harley, and Meltzer. "Introduce yourselves around to . . . to our new friends in the meantime."

"Boy, this is weird," Meltzer said under his breath.

"I know it," Bell responded. "These guys look like Spetsnaz or something." Spetsnaz were Soviet-era special forces sabotage and assassination troops, which continued to exist under the Russian Federation with different roles. "Like they'd slit our throats if we gave them half a chance."

"They would do so quickly and silently, I assure you," Kurzin said. He wasn't smiling.

He led Jeffrey and Nyurba past the battle management center, full of mission-planning and communications consoles, some of them manned, and over to a compartment whose watertight hatch said "SMALL ARMS LOCKER. CAUTION: EXPLOSIVES AND PYROTECHNICS." Kurzin undogged the heavy hatch and flipped on a light switch, and they went inside. A narrow aisle led down the center. The compartment was filled with safes, locked storage cabinets, and racks on both sides of the aisle holding many dozens of wicked-looking Russian assault rifles—each shrink-wrapped in clear plastic. Kurzin shut the hatch behind them.

He saw Jeffrey's curiosity. "Nikonov AN-Ninety-fours. Nicknamed Abakans. Successor to the AK-Forty-sevens and AK-Seventy-fours. Russian elite units use them. Beside the usual one-shot and full-auto selector modes, they fire special two-round bursts at a cyclic rate of eighteen hundred rounds per minute. That's almost three times as fast as an M-Sixteen. More accurate, too, trust me. These have time-shifted recoil action, so the user doesn't even feel the gun go off until after the pair of bullets leave the barrel. Both slugs hit the same spot at a hundred yards or more, one a thirtieth of a second behind the other. Great way to tear through body armor. Extreme lethality."

"These are real? I mean, made in Russia?" They were all a solid gun-metal gray, including the fiberglass-polymer folding stock and fore-grip—Jeffrey saw none of the wooden or brown-colored plastic parts as on the venerable AK-47.

"We have ways of obtaining the genuine article."

"What about ammo?"

"Caliber is five-point-four-five millimeters, slightly narrower than the NATO standard five-point-five-six bullet. They take sixty-round box magazines, short but thick, rounds stacked four in a row. Those, we have foreign-made."

"Won't that be a giveaway?"

"A metallurgical analysis will show that the bullets and shells were produced at a munitions plant in Germany."

"So that the raiders will seem to have come from there. Okay, I follow that, but how did you get the ammunition from Germany?"

"You don't need to know. You don't want to."

Kurzin switched into rapid-fire Russian, bombarding Jeffrey with it, catching him off guard.

Jeffrey tried to keep up, stammering.

Kurzin cursed in Russian, then turned, enraged, to Nyurba.

" *'Vy skazaki chto on byl gotovy!'* " You said he was ready!

"Grazhdanin, ya dumal chto on byl gotovy." Sir, I thought he was ready.

Kurzin reverted to English. "Forget it. This is hopeless. You'll need to go back to *Challenger* until the next rendezvous, and work with Commodore Fuller much more."

"Yes, sir," Nyurba said.

"What's the problem here?" Jeffrey asked, trying to reassert his authority.

"Commodore, don't pull rank on me," Kurzin said in a sharp, nasty way. His eyes showed cold fury. "Have you any *idea* what you'll be up against?" He didn't let Jeffrey answer. "For purposes of this mission, Commander Nyurba and I are your training officers. Your rank means nothing. Nothing. Your *readiness* is all that matters. *All.* Your Russian stinks, you'll have to do a lot better than that. And I saw you blink, you were flustered. *Unacceptable!"*

"But—"

"Do *not* talk back to me. If you let on just once during this mission about what you really think inside, how you really feel, you've screwed the pooch big-time. My men will have risked their lives, *given* their lives, for nothing."

"Now wait a minute, Colonel."

"No, *you* wait a minute." Kurzin moved in close and loomed over Jeffrey. "What did I just tell you?" he said in a loud, angry voice.

"That I'm in training."

"Christ Almighty, don't you realize the Russians will be recording every word you say? Running it through stress analyzers? They'll have hidden video cameras *everywhere.* Every facial inflection, the way you inhale, the way you fidget, they'll be watched again and again by a team of the FSB's best experts!"

"Why can't I just bring a translator?"

"Because the whole act hinges on your personal command presence, your prestige, your image as Axis nemesis, your tactical nuclear warrior's worldwide fame. An aide, an assistant, a translator, in this context they'd dilute your impact. You *must* go alone. The President made that decision."

"Won't the Russians have translators?"

"Of course, you fool! Do you think that for one moment you can trust *them*? Who will they be loyal to?"

"The Russians."

"Whom you're supposed to confront as an enemy, correct?"

"Yes."

"Whom you're *supposed* to think have just tried to nuke the United States, *correct*?"

"Yes."

"Role-play it out. You're nowhere there yet. Thank *God* you've got ten days more to work on your part."

"All right," Jeffrey conceded. "Lay it on as thick as you need to."

"Don't worry, I will, and I *don't* need your permission."

Jeffrey was starting to think that he was in boot camp, lower than dirt—in some bizarre through-the-looking-glass netherworld of lies embedded in other lies. *That's an accurate summary.*

The rows of AN-94s all around him gave the compartment, and the discussion, a surreal quality. Added to the browbeating by this Kurzin-cum-Brezhnev persona confronting him, Jeffrey started to feel disoriented.

Kurzin came so close that Jeffrey smelled the onions lingering on his breath. "Be glad, be *very* glad, that it'll probably be the Russians who feel defensive, conciliatory. Your job is to convey wrath and resolve, not merely your own but your nation's, and your nation's commander in chief's. A commander in chief who by then will have full power to push the button. *Use* that."

"Uh, right."

"And leave your moral qualms out of it altogether. Deception and bluff in a war situation aren't lies, they're necessary tools, and part of your duty!" Kurzin jabbed Jeffrey in the chest with his index finger, so forcefully it hurt. "Have you ever *not* done your duty?"

"No."

"Then don't start botching."

Jeffrey decided it was time for a counterattack—he had to get in the spirit of things as much as Kurzin was. "Let me know when you're finished, Colonel. Or should I say, *Podpolkovnik.*" Lieutenant Colonel in Russian. "Your histrionics grow tiresome to me." Jeffrey faked a yawn as best he could.

Kurzin didn't react in the least. "Good, I'm getting through to you."

"Speaking of moral qualms, I have some questions about how this whole thing is supposed to work."

"Upstairs. *Now.* It's undignified to stand in a closet."

Jeffrey didn't point out that this cozy chat in the closet was Kurzin's idea to begin with.

Kurzin stroked one of the AN-94s lovingly, as if he looked forward to using it soon against live, human targets. He undogged the door and stalked out.

Jeffrey turned to Nyurba. "Is he always like that?"

"You haven't seen him in combat."

CHAPTER 12

The assembled strike group's first mission briefing began. After a while Kurzin announced a pause for
questions. Everyone deferred to Jeffrey.

"I'll ask what I think are my easier questions first and
save the toughest one of all for last."

"Please proceed," Kurzin told him with supreme confidence.

"The easiest one, I believe I've answered for myself, but
I want to make sure."

"Yes?"

"Why aren't you aiming the ICBMs at Germany?"

"A natural query. What do you think is the reason?"

"Given Berlin's mentality these days, it'd immediately
provoke a nuclear exchange between them and Russia.
Which could spread. Armageddon could break out."

"It could. An undesirable outcome."

*Kurzin's talent for deadpan understatements is remark-
able.* "Aiming the missiles *away* from Germany," Jeffrey
said, "toward the U.S. instead, in a much more sophisti-

cated gambit, is as effective for us in the end but safer . . . at least in theory."

"Correct. We hurt Berlin by indirection, deal them what we hope is a staggering geopolitical blow, by the total ruination of their friendly terms with Russia. But we must not tempt them to escalate, to retaliate against the Kremlin, or against Washington, in an irrational fit of rage when they already have tactical nuclear weapons in play. Rather, in actual real life, Washington as the imaginary supposed target understands why the missiles took off, and knows from the start that they were programmed to explode outside the atmosphere. These factors lead to moderation in U.S. behavior, and this visible moderation from the very first moments will be greatly calming to Moscow. Berlin, though angered by a purely statecraft defeat, will see the same moderation and calm and thus be dissuaded from acting so rashly as to launch an atomic first strike against anyone's homeland—which if they did would mean their own instant and utter destruction at Russian or American hands. There's vastly more to it that we'll walk through step by step. Next question?"

"You're supposed to be German commandos of Russian ancestry, disguised as Russian Federation extremists—"

"Ethnic Russian *Kampfschwimmer* as loyal to their adoptive country as we are to America!" *Kampfschwimmer* were German Navy combat swimmers, the equivalent of U.S. Navy SEALs.

"Okay. Okay. What if the Russians don't see through the disguise, and they think the raid and the missile launch were done by their own people? Chechens, or ultra-hardline neocommies, or anarchists, or whomever?"

Nyurba answered; Jeffrey had thought him a hard-to-read sort, but that was before he met Kurzin. In comparison to the colonel, Nyurba seemed like a really nice guy.

"Commodore," Nyurba said, "the people who planned this out had a number of Blue Teams and Red Teams go through all the possible permutations of partial success, partial or total failure, and potential misunderstandings, with a healthy respect for Murphy's Law. The U.S. view, the Russian view and response, they even had a Tiger Team behaving as the Germans might, both as planners of the raid and as the party later accused of it while knowing their lack of involvement. . . . If the Russians don't see through the disguise, then most likely two things would happen. First, our mission will fail because there'd be no rancor created between Russia and Germany. The Kremlin would be very apologetic to Washington, sure, and would make some token concessions, but it's unlikely their logistical support of Germany would be swayed. Second, there'd be a brutal crackdown against whichever faction Russia concludes was responsible."

"Which means you're setting up an innocent group for a pogrom, a purge. Persecution and extermination."

"We'll leave enough hard evidence so the Russians quickly figure out that the team did come from Germany."

"Such as the metallurgy in the ammo expended?"

"And our flesh and blood. We expect to take losses. Getting into a Russian missile silo field will not be a cakewalk, even with all of our cleverest preparations. Wounded men will bleed. Men killed in action will be left behind, of necessity, as abhorrent as that sounds."

"How would that help?"

"For some time, all the medications we've been taking, to protect us as much as possible against diseases and toxins in the areas we'll cross, are of German manufacture."

"Prewar?"

"No. They've developed some interesting pharmaceuticals since the start of the war. We have an adequate supply for our purposes. Don't ask me how we got them. You don't need to know."

"American-manufactured copies?"

"The original German formularies."

Kurzin broke in. "The key was to plan and execute this mission the way the Germans would. They'd rely a lot on technology. Their mistakes would be very subtle. But they would make mistakes."

"What if they didn't? Don't?"

"Hah!" Kurzin pounced. "You're getting so caught up in this, you're thinking the Germans are doing the raid!"

"Woops. I did have myself going for a minute there."

"Good. Get as deep into this as you can. And stay deep."

"The point is, sir," Nyurba continued, "*we* control the parameters of physical outcomes. The Germans, if they did perform this raid, would have no compunctions framing some ethnic group or splinter political faction in Russia. Outwardly, that's how *we* make it look. . . . That's why our ammo propellant is Russian. To use German powder would be too obvious an error."

"With the chaos you induce, who's to make these complex lab analyses of bullets and blood? And where do the baseline comparison samples come from for the forensics match?"

"Vladivostok will be unaffected by the raid. They own state-of-the-art facilities to study the metals and blood chemistry. They'll have a potent need to do so, to find out and prove to the U.S. who perpetrated it, since Russia's president will know it wasn't something he authorized himself. . . . The Kremlin's elite appointees take these fancy German drugs, too. They know their own medical system and public health stink. Rank-and-file troops, even Spetsnaz, don't get them. . . . Russia buys spare parts made from the same Polish sheet metal and rod stock that were used to make our ammo. . . . If they don't put it all together on their own, you can nudge them."

"Then what about DNA, speaking of matching and blood? And fingerprints. You're all in the Pentagon databases." He was referring to stored information used for identifying remains of men and women killed in action. "The Germans could hack their way in, then prove that you're all U.S. military."

Nyurba smiled. "Our records were quietly changed. Genome profiles that fit our outward body characteristics, to avoid drawing suspicion from any overambitious moles. But the data's made up. It won't correspond to real people, living or dead."

"All right. Let's step way back. One much harder question is, what's Berlin's motivation for this raid supposed to be?"

"You mean, for breaking into a Russian missile-silo control bunker and shooting off a handful of ICBMs at America?"

"Yeah."

"Keep in mind from the start that this is purely hypothetical, the German rationales and points of view."

"It still needs to make sense, to me and to the Russians."

"Granted. Then consider this. Few live warheads would get through the U.S. terminal defenses out of the very small number launched. They'll be aimed at military targets in sparsely populated areas, but significant targets. Nuclear theorists call that a limited counterforce strike."

"I know."

"America would be damaged using Russian missiles as proxies, frightening the U.S. public half to death, which directly helps the Germans. America would not be damaged fatally, by any means, except in an extremely powerful emotional sense, which fits perfectly with Berlin's psychological-warfare grand strategy."

"Keep going."

"The U.S. government would then have to decide how to react, respond. The worst case that's deemed likely by think-tank thinkers is called *lex talionis,* a tooth for a tooth. Speaking again hypothetically, this is what planners in Berlin would wargame. The U.S. retaliates against Russia in kind, tit for tat, despite Moscow's profuse apologies and instant denial of government culpability. This retaliation hurts Russia, but if the exchange is proportional, say three live H-bomb warheads launched in return for the three that get launched out of Russia, then Russia isn't harmed fatally either. It's weakened, presenting less of a future threat to German world supremacy, but Russia would still be able to provide a lot of natural resources and arms support to Germany. A deep wedge would have been driven between Moscow and Washington, irrecoverably. Good insurance for Berlin. After that, Russia would never, ever join the Allies and could conceivably be driven straight into the Axis camp."

"What if things do escalate, and more and more missiles start flying back and forth?"

"Germany would assume that those in charge in Moscow and Washington would not be so insane."

"That sounds awfully risky, from Germany's point of view."

"They know that the concept that nuclear war could never stay limited is not valid military science but a myth planted in many civilian minds. A myth, by the way, that traces its roots to Soviet propaganda and KGB agitators in the nineteen-fifties, when their atomic arsenal was weak compared to ours."

"I'm aware of that. Still. Myths sometimes come true."

"Returning to the hypothetical, specifically German concern about escalation, this is exactly the sort of risk that we, and Russia, have seen them take in different ways repeatedly."

"So your presumption is that if the Germans really did what you're going to pretend they do, then they wouldn't target Washington, or some other major city, or U.S. strategic command-and-control, to make sure that what's limited stays limited? Avoid mass deaths, not go for a leadership decapitation strike?"

"Not unless the Germans were insane, which they aren't. They're extreme risk-takers, yes, but the calculated risks always make sense, and the consequences of losing are never fatal to them. The proof of this being that even though their gambles collapsed upon them several times, they're still very much in the war. That's why we need to perform this mission, take back the global initiative. And that's why it's plausible that the Germans would push the envelope even more, hit America by using Russian weaponry, exploit the Kremlin as patsies, and set up an innocent Russia to take all the blame."

"Lord," Jeffrey said, "this gets complicated."

"It certainly does," Kurzin said. "Concentrate on the view from sixty thousand feet for now. Just get a basic sense of all the moving parts and how they interact. See for yourself the rigor of the logic that went into this. If you start to feel overwhelmed today, just stick to the highlights. Greater clarity will come, with time and with the unfolding of events."

Jeffrey nodded. "So these alleged Russian separatists, or warmongers, or whatever . . . The Germans would have gamed out this part too. . . . What's the motivation of the supposed Russian perpetrators that the *Kampfschwimmer* go disguised as? . . . Before, that is, your men masquerading as pseudo-Russian *Kampfschwimmer* get unmasked by our deceptions as being genuine Germans. We hope."

Nyurba answered that one. "The faked perps' motivation is to discredit the regime in charge in the Kremlin, because it's too repressive or because it's not repressive enough. Or because it's too neutral toward the U.S., or not in alliance enough with Germany. Sacrifice some American and Russian lives for the good of the Motherland, at least as the made-up fanatics see it. These imaginary rebels would want to force Russia to take a firmer side in the Allies-versus-Axis conflict, or force a regime change in Moscow, or even both."

"They're internal terrorists?"

"Not in their own minds," Kurzin said. "They'd be heroes, martyrs. They'd see the mainstream Russian government as the terrorists, and maybe the U.S. too. Their actions against both would be justifiable retribution. Or, they'd see the Moscow crowd in office now as being much too moderate. . . . Chechens, modern anarchists, pro-German

Russian FSB agents, or military megahawks, we want to leave ambiguity in Kremlin heads as to who were the bad actors, in the first few crucial minutes after the SS-Twenty-sevens launch. Ambiguity *you* will play off of, Commodore, as and when suspicion starts getting cast on Germany."

"But—"

"The team that gamed out the German approach said they'd want ambiguity too, leave Moscow confused and unfocused so they're more likely to come over and cling to Berlin in the face of American ire while the handful of mushroom clouds bloomed on two continents. Even our Red and Blue Teams concluded that real rogues, if they existed, wouldn't claim credit initially, to sow more seeds of doubt and then surge into the power vacuum."

Jeffrey fiddled with his ear. "I don't know about this."

"Sir," Nyurba told him, "there's important precedent. It's what gave our commander in chief the idea to begin with."

"Continue. Please."

"The Golf-class diesel boat that sank in the Pacific in nineteen-sixty-eight? The one that Howard Hughes with CIA backing tried to salvage off the ocean floor with the *Glomar Explorer*?"

"Aw, not that boondoggle."

"Sir, it's been in the open literature since the late nineteen-nineties that the U.S. concluded almost immediately that it was virtually certain the Golf sank because a rogue faction in her crew took over the ship and tried to nuke Hawaii with one of the three ballistic missiles in their vertical launch tubes at the rear of the conning tower."

Jeffrey nodded. "I read about that. Nixon used it behind the scenes to threaten, blackmail Russia. It's how he forced Brezhnev to come to the arms reduction table at some summit meeting. Then Nixon took credit for terrific statesmanship. What a charade. I forget the details."

"But this *is* real-life stuff, Commodore. And it *was* declassified, or leaked, or whatever, in documents, books, available to the public since before the Global War on Terror began. And Russia and Germany know it too."

"Granted."

The motivation of those rogues in 1968 was to trigger nuclear war between the USSR and the U.S., perhaps because they felt the Kremlin at that time wasn't hawkish enough. It couldn't be known positively, since they all died. The U.S. was pretty sure they died because they failed to bypass all the range-safety devices—the booby traps installed to prevent an unauthorized launch. American intelligence did know that Moscow was often more afraid of an in-country splinter group hijacking a missile and aiming it their way than they were ever afraid of a sneak attack by America. The liquid fuel in one of those ballistic missiles exploded thanks to the booby traps, and the Golf sank with all hands in three-plus miles of the Pacific Ocean, with a big hole gaping in her side.

"Some of this is beginning to come together for me," Jeffrey said. "The Russians are aware they had a rogue faction attempt a nuclear launch once before."

"At least once before that we know of," Kurzin interjected.

"There might have been *others*?"

"Our intelligence services have their suspicions. Some of the Soviet accidents with rockets, that blew up on the launchpad or went off course and were self-destructed or crashed. Traces of plutonium that might have come from a nuke warhead destroyed on the ground or in midair."

What other Cold War secret history has yet to be revealed? "So the plan is that the Kremlin will believe it plausible that some other rogue faction tries the same thing now, except with a land-based silo missile instead of using a submarine."

"Precisely, sir," Nyurba said. "And the Germans are aware of all these things, so a scenario of them using their commandos to launch missiles and blame it on Russian rogues is also plausible. Russian governmental and military insiders are most likely to have the knowledge and resources to plan and then conduct the raid. They're far more obvious culprits than Chechens or anarchists."

Jeffrey held his head for a minute. "God, who dreamed this stuff up?"

"Some of our best and brightest, Commodore," Kurzin said.

Jeffrey turned to Bell and Harley. "What do both of you make of this?"

Bell deferred to Harley. "It's as we discussed among ourselves before, sir," Harley said. "Our country has three choices. Apocalypse Soon, Apocalypse Later, and this mission if we can pull it off."

"Which is still one hell of an 'if,' " Jeffrey said. "Let me get to the other part that's bothering me. Or *an* other part, because all sorts of things are bothering me. This bluff mentioned in my orders about a next-generation missile shield. Using supposed stealth satellites, ones that the Russians don't know about and also can't detect, so they have no way to judge their capabilities."

"Stealth satellites are nothing new, sir," Nyurba said. "The idea, and their actual existence, got leaked to the press ten years ago. Leaked, or officially announced."

Jeffrey stared at the overhead, talking to himself. "A magical, mystical missile shield that can detonate an armed nuclear warhead outside the atmosphere, over the country that launched the ICBM. That part sounds great. I wish we really had something like that. But you and whoever planned this mission know damned well that we don't. I want to go over again how we get the Russians to believe it."

"We'll program the warheads to go off exoatmospherically, over the European part of Russia. With trajectory mechanics as they are, given the Earth's rotation and the Coriolis force and all of that, it's why we need to launch from one of their new bases in Siberia. It puts the missiles beyond effective reach of the old ABM system that still rings Moscow, so the Russians can't shoot their own rogue missiles down." Nyurba was referring to the antiballistic missile system allowed by a 1970s treaty.

"And the exoatmospheric detonation is what causes the massive electromagnetic pulse that does a lot of damage between Moscow and the Urals. That part I get. Russia is really hurting, and it looks like she's been deservedly punished for trying to nuke the U.S. Punished by this magical, mystical, mysterious missile shield. I remain extremely skeptical."

"Remember, sir," Nyurba answered, "the shield doesn't need to exist. The Russians simply need to believe, or be convinced, that it exists."

"But it has to be plausible. I can guarantee you, no matter how badly computers and communications are degraded in western Russia, there'll be enough engineers and academicians in fine shape in other places to put together whatever the Russians call a tiger team. They'll look really hard at how anything could make two or three separate SS-Twenty-seven warheads all go off simultaneously after third-stage booster separation, in the vacuum of space. Assuming you even manage to get the missiles to launch properly, with the proper programming. If you, like those Russkie rogues back in sixty-eight, goof and a booby trap goes off, this mission is a flop. What if you do manage somehow to actually achieve an unauthorized launch of several armed ICBMs, but your reprogramming is flawed and they *do,* for real, target the U.S. homeland?"

"In real life this launch won't be a surprise. Commander, U.S. Strategic Command will be expecting it. He'll know exactly where and when the missiles will launch, and he'll be very well prepared to target and destroy them using our conventional ground- and sea-based missile shields."

"Assuming they work reliably at the time."

"Yes. But they only have to work if our reprogramming of the live warheads doesn't work."

"That's one hell of a 'but'!"

"That's why we're only launching three missiles."

"That's one hell of an 'only'!"

"Allow me to address your other concern or question," Kurzin interrupted. "Achieving successful launch of Russian ICBMs at all. Without going into details that you don't need to know, suffice it to say that we have both human and electronic intelligence that provides us with a good deal of critical information about the SS-Twenty-seven missile and warhead-bus design. Including methods of arming the warhead and triggering detonation, and of bypassing range-safety devices."

"Sorry, Colonel, I *do* need to know. If I'm not convinced this whole thing from A to Z makes total sense, there's no way I'll ever convince the Russians in a no-holds-barred confrontation somewhere in Siberia while *they* have every home-field advantage."

Nyurba looked to Kurzin for direction. Kurzin reluctantly nodded, and Nyurba responded for both of them.

"It's no secret that the U.S. recovered intact nuclear ballistic missiles from a Soviet Yankee-class SSBN that sank in the Atlantic a few hundred miles from Bermuda in nineteen-eighty-six."

"I know. *K-Two-nineteen.*"

"Specialists, aware of the earlier loss of the Golf-class, dissected the range safety devices carefully."

"That's twenty-five-year-old technology!"

"And the basis for all further Soviet and Russian thinking."

"They know we grabbed some missiles. They'll have changed everything!"

"Seeing how they thought at one time gives hints at what they'd change and how they'd change it. And we know that, to save money, some parts in the SS-Twenty-sevens are identical to those in earlier land-based missiles which because of arms reduction treaties were dismantled and destroyed in public. For many of these parts we gained illicit actual samples, or very good intel about their specs."

"That's still too much of a stretch."

"On its own, yes. But we also have expatriate Russian missile engineers and nuclear scientists who worked on their weapons programs more recently. They emigrated to the U.S. over the years after the Berlin Wall fell. They were discreetly interviewed."

"They might have been sleeper agents, giving you disinformation. That's a favorite Russian gimmick."

"Which of course the CIA and the Pentagon realize. There were methods to cross-validate what they told us."

"Such as?"

"Other Russians with similar expertise, after the USSR collapsed and they found themselves unemployed, were less enthralled at the prospects of coming to America to wash dishes or drive a taxi. They put themselves up for grabs on the world underground arms market. During the Global War on Terror, some of them were captured. Let's just say they were thoroughly interrogated."

"This part, I truly don't want to know."

"You see, Commodore, we're not entirely in the dark on what we'll be trying to do. And before you ask, in this context it's perfectly believable that the raiders were sent by Berlin. Germany had its own ample share of arrested rogue weapons scientists, and honest Russian emigrés too, especially ones with key technical skills. Germany was Russia's largest import-export partner even before this war. Since the communist state imploded two decades ago, many Russians having the ways and means abandoned the dreary place with lasting bitterness. Some moved to Germany. Some are German citizens now. As we already covered once, immigrants can be passionately patriotic to their new homes." Kurzin's men nodded.

"Fine," Jeffrey said. "But there'll be computer passwords, now, today. Ones that are frequently altered, if their procedures are anything like ours. You won't have those passwords, will you?"

"Some things we can sort of hotwire," Nyurba said, "if

we can't intercept the couriers or overhear the new passwords as they're conveyed by electronic means."

"You're taking far too much for granted."

"No we aren't," Kurzin stepped in firmly. "If any set of circuitry requires a certain password to unlock any protective device in real time, that circuitry itself must know the password. Correct?"

"Uh, yeah."

"If the password is anywhere in such circuitry, and that circuitry falls into our hands on this raid, we have ways to force it to reveal the password to us."

"Who's this 'we'?"

"Among my squadron officers are experts who were stationed in American missile silos, and others who have great talents at computer hacking. We brought with us devices, designed in the U.S., mimicking German high-end hacker styles, and constructed using Russian and German or neutral components and tools, which will assist us in attempting to crack the codes."

"You said 'attempting.'"

"Total success is never guaranteed."

"All right, let's be optimists on that for now. I have a good cover story for why *Challenger* is where she is when the warheads go off. I'm on my way to blockade the next Eight-six-eight-U-class submarine that the Russians are selling to Germany. And *Carter* will emit the acoustic signature of a German Amethyste-Two if she faces any risk of detection. Those parts work for me, in and of themselves. But how do you get into a silo bunker to begin with? They're hardened against attack by nuclear bombs."

"The bunkers and silos are hardened, but their locations are permanently fixed. We know exactly where they are, which is a significant plus. Russia's road-mobile nuclear missiles are far too elusive to preplan a hijacking with any surety. Their carrier vehicles can move much faster than we'd ever be able to keep up with on foot. Their crews, out in the open, if they see they're losing an ambush, can sabotage their own ICBMs too easily. Ditto for rail-mobile units. The same is *not* the case for missiles in silos. And *yes,* the control bunkers are hardened, but the people on duty inside them are not. The humans must rotate in and out periodically, for recreation and rest, the same as U.S. Air Force silo crews. This is their Achilles' heel."

"Which they'll take severe precautions to protect."

"Once *Carter* drops us off where we'll sneak ashore through toxic coastal waters, our five-day overland hike will be timed to reach a particular missile base just before a regular silo personnel shift change. We intend to commandeer the approaching trucks bringing in replacement crews, and penetrate the installation that way. We'll then take over the control bunkers for half a dozen ICBMs."

"Horribly chancy."

"We anticipate that our silo entry phase may become extremely violent. We are fully prepared for this."

Jeffrey glanced around the room at Kurzin's commando force. Their faces were blank, inscrutable. "You're telling me you're going on a one-way mission."

"We understand the meaning of service and sacrifice."

"Come back to how we're supposed to make Russian latest-generation warheads go off prematurely."

"That part is in the script included in your orders."

"If I'd tried to learn the whole script in one sitting, I'd've been in that stateroom for forty-eight hours or more."

"That's why you still have a week-plus to memorize everything," Nyurba said.

"What I did see, or skim, I'm not so sure about. Gammaray lasers and microwave lasers and proton particle beams in the vacuum of space, plus radar spoofers tuned perfectly, all making a nuclear warhead think it's reentered the atmosphere, that it feels the heat and the rising air pressure and the deceleration, and its radar altimeter, if it has one, detects the ground coming up. Zapping timers and blinding celestial-navigation sensors, without ruining the warheads altogether. . . . You're counting on too many things going just right."

"Again," Kurzin told him, "you're so caught up you forget that this is all bluff. It does not actually have to exist, let alone work correctly. The Russians just have to believe that it's plausible, and see the evidence with their own eyes that tells them it's real and it did work."

"The exoatmospheric blasts."

"Yes."

"Which fry so many satellites and ground systems instantly that the Russians have no telemetry to prove that there never was a gamma-ray laser firing, a particle beam gun discharging, a radar spoofer radar broadcasting. All deployed from supposed nuclear-powered stealth satellites that they can't detect, not because they're too stealthy to detect, but because in fact they never existed."

"An excellent summary, Commodore. Remember, it's the President's job, on the Hot Line, to convey all this to the Kremlin. A deep-black DARPA project, now unveiled. You wouldn't have known about something so secret in advance. You know what you do know, supposedly, because of a radio message received only after the warheads explode. The same long message that orders you to Siberia as your commander in chief's personal, on-site, back-channel mouthpiece. Your role in this part of the act is a supporting one. You merely need to believe what you were told."

"Which brings us back full circle, to one main thing that still is bugging me. What if the Russians think it's all too pat? *Challenger* appearing at just the right time and place by sheer happenstance, and this magical, mystical missile shield idea being swallowed whole by the Kremlin, *and* them not seeing that *we* had strong motive to have done the nasty deed ourselves to frame Berlin and reap large benefits. Expecting that all of this comes together and Moscow never questions our package of lie after lie after lie . . . It's too much like tempting fate."

"They can't call our bluff on this next-generation missile shield," Kurzin said. "The only way would be to launch a live ICBM at the U.S. Suppose they do. Then you posit that the shield has imperfections, that it can leak. Since there's no way for the Russians to self-destruct an ICBM once it's in flight, the whole idea of ICBMs as deterrents being that they can't be recalled after launch, we'd either shoot it down in our end zone along its trajectory with what conventional missile defenses we do have, or it'd detonate over or on U.S. soil. Either way their launch would be an intentional act of war, and we'd certainly retaliate, quite possibly by targeting the Kremlin. Because, remember, we'd still be acting as if we were entirely innocent of anything except protecting ourselves against a Russian preemptive attack, using the nonexistent mystery shield to inflict electromagnetic-pulse damage, which is more or less nonlethal, on the Kremlin environs. . . . Therefore the only way to call the bluff amounts to an act of suicide for Moscow."

"I follow the nonlethal aspect of the punishment from this made-up missile shield. I like it as an idea, I said that before, and I wish someday we could field such a system for real. But the Russians don't have to actually *test* the shield to doubt its existence. They can simply conclude on their own that it's just theoretical concepts and double-talk."

"This is where your faked rage and bluster onshore in Siberia come in. The analogy to magic is more apt than you may recognize, Commodore. It's a psychological sleight of hand. Your dire accusations and threats as champion atomic warrior, to a senior Russian Navy officer who'll know exactly who you are. *Challenger* lurking with her tactical nuclear cruise missiles in case they mistreat you. Very *useable* weapons, you'll say, since they don't breach the barrier to hydrogen bombs. This will all divert Russian thinking away from the U.S. being to blame. *Challenger* herself becomes a sleight of hand as well, distracting the Russians from thinking that another American sub is present."

"*Only* if I can bring it off. Face to face, on camera, hour after hour. Alone in Siberia, among Russians who become our mortal enemy if I make even the slightest misstep. Russia's romance with Germany sours *only* if I can bring it all off."

"Yes." Kurzin was unemotional. "Only if you bring it off."

"What if Russia sees through the bluffs and hand-waving and phony biblical wrath, despite even our president over the Hot Line reinforcing me? The Kremlin would strike back in kind, shooting a missile to go off high above America, to inflict an electromagnetic pulse and fry the entire U.S. homeland. For exoatmospheric EMP, a higher detonation is better, it pancakes a larger area. They fling a warhead where our best real defenses can't possibly reach. We lose the war in a millisecond."

"That is, unfortunately, true."

"Russia arrests me, and *I'm* the one who's the international terrorist. I'm perfectly placed to be our commander in chief's sacrificial lamb, the scapegoat in this giant fiasco, to placate the Russians. I can picture the show trial in Moscow on *that*. The Germans will love every minute. The ending is a bullet in the back of my neck. Unless the Kremlin decides to cremate me alive, feet-first as was the KGB's custom, so it lasts longer."

"Inarguably that is one scenario. Two, if you consider each method of execution as a separate scenario."

"Suppose that Russia buys into everything, and buys it all too well. How do we stop them from glassing Germany with ground-hugging cruise missiles immune to our magical space-based shield?"

"Aside from the fact that doing so would bring them into wholesale nuclear war with Germany? Which neither will want?"

"Aside from that. The Kremlin does have true megahawks."

"That's why our president sends you to Siberia. Charm, guile, warnings, wordplay, it's a crucial part of your job."

Boarding the mini for *Challenger,* everyone was exhausted and glum. The trip was a mob: six experts who needed to transfer from *Carter* added to the passenger load. Jeffrey and Nyurba took the two seats in the last row of the transport compartment.

"You know," Nyurba said, "in the more remote parts of Siberia, there are still some practicing shamans."

Jeffrey hesitated, but sensed that Nyurba, who seemed subdued, felt the need to talk. "Is that your religion?"

"My family is Russian Orthodox. But the old creation myths are kept alive. Many peoples equate the North Star with a bear."

"You mean, like constellations?"

"The star Arcturus, in some Lapp and Finn and Siberian groups, is called Favtna. The hunter. The Big Dipper is supposed to be his bow."

"I thought it was a plow, or something."

"The ancient prophecy is that someday Favtna will shoot an arrow at the bear. And the North Star, around which the heavens turn each night, is known also as the pillar of the world."

"Makes sense." Jeffrey wondered where Nyurba was leading. He'd heard that Russians, including Siberians, could be moody.

"When Favtna's arrow strikes home, at the bear, the North Star, the pillar of the world, the prophecy goes something like this: 'The sky will plummet down, and then the earth will be smashed, and the world will burst into fire and smoke, and it will be the end of everything.'"

"That's pretty morbid stuff."

Nyurba stared into space. "Sometimes, with this mission, I think I'm Favtna. The bear is Russia, the arrow is an ICBM, and when I shoot the missile the prophecy will literally come true."

CHAPTER 13

Right after the rendezvous, Jeffrey had his strike group begin to proceed by a devious route under the ice cap, to eventually worm into position north of Siberia. The route had been chosen consulting with Meltzer and *Carter*'s navigator, while Bell and Harley offered advice. No one past the two ships' hulls could possibly know which dog-leg courses and zigzags Jeffrey intended to take—including that mole in DC.

Soon after he first returned to *Challenger*, Jeffrey handed a packet from his orders pouch to Bell, for the ship's systems administrator, a rather cerebral senior chief with a master's degree in computer science.

"What's this?" Bell asked.

"Disks with special software. We'll need it running later. Intel-gathering, to support our endeavor. . . . And message code phrases we'll receive to formally confirm or cancel our mission. . . . Operating specs and installation info are in there."

To take a breather, Jeffrey went to his office, *Challeng-er*'s XO's stateroom. He sat in one of the guest chairs, putting his feet up on the other. He stared into empty space, at a spot that seemed miles beyond the bulkhead only inches from his shoes. He tried to make sense of all that was going on.

His orders said that Commander, U.S. Strategic Command and the President would be waiting, and the start of Kurzin's assault on the ICBM complex would be observed from orbit by American spy satellites. To explain the lack of initial reaction to these events on the ground in Siberia, U.S. commanders could always claim they assumed this activity was a Russian security drill, with mock invaders firing blank rounds, and chicken blood used for realism. Missile launches would be detectable by other satellites—the SBIRS-High system—that watched for the distinctive infrared heat signature of rocket engines; these satellites hovered over Russia constantly, in geosynchronous orbit a tenth of the way to the moon.

When Kurzin's men were seen to move to attack, Jeffrey would receive an ELF message to come to periscope depth in a polynya, and raise his photonic masts and antennas to act as the U.S. President's eyes and ears. This was needed because satellites that didn't shut down would be blinded, and some would be destroyed, by the H-bomb blasts and resulting persistent energetic particles in space. If the SS-27 missiles did take off, and did detonate hundreds of miles outside the atmosphere over Moscow, Jeffrey would see the visual and electromagnetic effects. *Challenger* would be far enough away, her masts and antennas shielded and hardened, so as not to suffer from the EMP.

The President of the United States would know when to pick up the phone to the Kremlin, and what to say, if the President of Russia didn't grab the phone and call him first in panic. From SS-27 liftoff to warhead detonation would take less than two minutes—as opposed to the half-hour a warhead needed to strike the U.S. Neither America nor Russia would have time to bring their strategic nuclear missile forces up to immediate launching status. This was one major advantage of using the SS-27: the missile's more powerful engines shortened the boost phase significantly compared to earlier-generation Russian ICBMs. The dust would settle, reason would prevail, and common sense would kick in, well before a wholesale thermonuclear exchange came close to occurring. Or so it was intended in the mission plan.

But that would all come days from now, and the train of events is fraught with imponderables and uncertainties.

In the meantime, it was vital that Allied command and control give no hint whatsoever, through unusual physical or signals activity, that anything out of the ordinary was on the verge of happening. For a while yet Jeffrey and his strike group were entirely on their own. He'd always preferred to work like this, unsupervised and with lots of opportunity for initiative. But later in Siberia himself, coordinating via conference call with his President on the Hot Line in real time while potentially hostile Russians joined in—both face to face and from Moscow—would be a completely new experience for him.

He had mixed feelings on many levels. There was no one in whom to confide. The loneliness of strike group command tasted vile. He decided, once and for all, to repress his emotions and follow an inner, amoral, task-oriented autopilot.

Yet he could tell that his deepest self was becoming worn down. He knew that following orders, though they formed his sworn and inescapable duty, would be no excuse on a higher plane or in a court of law. Violating Russian sovereignty, in the premeditated way he would do it, was an act of aggressive war. He'd snuck onto neutral or Allied soil before, but never like this. The ultimate mission goal amounted to a crime against humanity, if viewed in isolation from its benefits. The necessity and the benefits were pure theory, based on wargame simulations only, no matter how credible that modeling effort might be. The pressure on Jeffrey, and the corrosive effect on his soul, felt immense.

*Nyurba's morbid mood, probably just standard prein-
sertion heebie-jeebies, must be contagious. . . . Yes, it's just
the usual doubts and fears before any fresh mission gets
rolling.*

Jeffrey liked this rationalization, conveniently invented
though it was. The notion—delusion?—of normal prebattle
stage fright fit well with his newfound get-the-job-done
amoral compass. The inner compass was a survival tool,
for which he expected he'd sooner or later pay a heavy
price. But that would come afterward, when he could afford
to let his conscience return and try to reconcile his actions
with his own value system, his ethics, his religious beliefs.
He'd find out then, the hard way, here or in the afterlife, if
reconciliation was even possible. In the meantime he
needed to shake these too-distracting ideas off.

It occurred to him that boomer captains and crews must
have gone through the same sort of agonizing issues often,
wondering how they'd feel if they got an order to fire their
missiles. But those orders never came, whereas Jeffrey's orders sat on the desk, in writing. Though there truly was no
precedent for what he and his people had to do, thinking
like a boomer captain could help a little for Jeffrey to
cope.

And while he might be lonely, he didn't need to be alone.
He went into *Challenger*'s crowded control room, with men
at every console, and icons dancing on the displays. As
Challenger and *Carter* steamed in company away from the
rendezvous point, secured from battle stations but maintaining ultraquiet, Jeffrey began to feel mentally restored.
The human company, the active motion of his strike group,
the collective sense of purpose, were excellent tonics. He
quickly returned to his normal self, the driven warrior. The
surest sign of this was that another important tactical insight sparked within his brain.

He asked Bell for a moment with him in the captain's
stateroom; it was larger than his office, and he welcomed
the slightest change of scenery. They went inside.

"Sir?" After all that had been discussed on *Carter,* Bell wondered what Jeffrey could possibly want to go over now.

"For a while the most immediate threat is blundering into a Russian sub, at random, point blank."

Acoustic conditions under the ice were as bad as ever. All active sonars remained secured, except for the covert comms link—no enemy could detect its energy buried in the pack-ice noise.

"Concur, sir," Bell answered. "My worst fear would be a Russkie boomer using their favorite under-ice tactic." Hovering stationary, hugging a thin spot in the cap from below, and masked to the sides by ice keels. "Killing time, nearly dead silent, prepared in the event that a missile launch order comes through." Low-frequency radio signals traveled well through Arctic ice.

"We might not hear them on passive sonar until we ran right under one. And he hears us too, from above and in our baffles. Raw survival instincts kick in, he greets us with a snap shot up our ass. *Carter* returns the favor from behind us in self-defense. World War Three is on, a bit prematurely, by accident."

"Not appetizing."

"So I want you to establish a special gravimeter watch."

"Commodore?"

"At short range our gravimeter should be able to pick up the density discontinuity of a motionless nuclear sub's reactor compartment, or compartments." The thick shielding, the massive containment vessel, the heavy uranium core; some Russian submarine classes had two separate nuclear reactors.

Bell nodded, seeing what Jeffrey was getting at now. "If the other sub isn't moving, it's the only way to get very much advance warning that he's there. . . . We can signal *Carter* and maneuver to avoid, and maybe not lose our stealth."

"That's what I was thinking. Make sense, Captain?"

"Absolutely. I'll talk to my XO. . . . I like that. A special under-ice lookup gravimeter watch."

"I'll be in my office. Don't hesitate to disturb me."

Bell went into *Challenger*'s control room, to speak with Sessions. Jeffrey went the other way through the corridor, the few steps aft to the XO's stateroom. He opened out the VIP rack above the one that Sessions used, climbed up and fully dressed except for his shoes, got comfortable, and grabbed some badly overdue sleep. He slept like a rock, dreamlessly and peacefully.

───────────

The sneaky approach toward Siberia took five days and covered almost two thousand nautical miles. They never did encounter another submarine. A message from Commander, U.S. Strategic Command came through, via extremely low-frequency radio that could penetrate deep seawater. The cipher said the mission was confirmed, a definite "go."

Jeffrey received the news with no little trepidation. It made him admit to himself that, unconsciously, he'd been hoping the scheme would be canceled and the strike group would be recalled.

No such luck.

With this final mental barrier toward the reality of his duty now broken down, he put the remaining transit time to good use. Data disks in his inner orders pouch, opened while on *Carter,* included scripts to study to prepare for the role it would soon be his burden to play. Since Colonel Kurzin had told Nyurba and his four men to return to *Challenger* and work with Jeffrey on his Russian language skills and acting ability, he modified those original orders; lone mental rehearsals weren't his preferred style. *Challenger*'s crew included a RuLing—a Russian linguist—but that chief wasn't cleared for crucial portions of the mission.

Instead, the SERT Seabees and Jeffrey talked through versions of the script out loud. They assumed different parts, ranging from the Russian and American presidents to hypothetical hawkish Kremlin advisors, outraged German diplomats, and the senior person in Siberia whom Jeffrey expected to meet with—his back-channel contact, one Rear Admiral Elmar Meredov. Jeffrey's orders included an intelligence file devoted just to Meredov—his personal biography, a copy of his service record, and an assessment of his psychology by a CIA profiler.

By the end of the five days of rigorous practice and no-holds-barred critiques, Jeffrey felt as ready as he'd ever be.

"It's time," Nyurba told him. "We part ways, you and I, until whenever." Before Jeffrey could say something maudlin or gloopy, Nyurba cut him off. "There's a serious risk you'll come across to the Russians as overrehearsed."

Jeffrey was taken aback. "You mean, too smooth? Too glib?"

"You're supposed to be responding to all these horrible goings-on as if they're completely new to you."

"I love how you put that."

Nyurba, who still reminded Jeffrey of a latter-day Genghis Khan, placed one big and powerful hand on Jeffrey's shoulder.

"Remember what I told you. Real life doesn't follow a script. These runthroughs were only to give you a basic idea."

"Yup. An idea."

"When you're there, don't rush your thought processes. Don't let the other side rush you, either. Set a deliberate, gradual pace from the start. Then stick to it."

"Steady, unhurried, not rushed." Jeffrey repeated the words, mostly to himself, as if they were a mantra.

A messenger arrived to say the minisub was ready for boarding. Jeffrey wordlessly escorted the Seabees aft to the hangar airlock trunk. He shook hands with Nyurba and his team; he wouldn't be going with them to *Carter*. The second, final rendezvous had a very different purpose.

CHAPTER 14

Jeffrey went into *Challenger*'s control room to oversee the ticklish activity about to begin. The personnel transfer to *Carter* was the least of it.

Instead of using his console at the rear of the compartment, he stood in the aisle next to Meltzer at the navigation plot. All the data he needed were easily visible either there or on the various widescreen displays on the bulkheads. And now was not the time to sit with his back to people.

Challenger and *Carter* were still under the Arctic ice cap, at the edge of the east Siberian continental shelf, where the water's depth dropped steeply from very shallow to six thousand feet. The terrain that interested Jeffrey most was a short distance ahead on his intended track, due south. Tiny Genrietty and Zannetty together represented the extreme tip of the Novosibirskie Ostrova—the New Siberian Islands. Both were frozen into the ice cap year round. They were the northernmost dry land in this part of Russia, occupied by military surveillance and communication posts. Jeffrey thought of them as like the outer part of a set of *matryoshka* dolls, those nested wooden egg-shaped figures, a popular image of Russian culture.

Penetrating Russian defenses will be a lot like cracking open a locked set of these dolls-within-dolls.

On Jeffrey's order, the strike group went to silent battle stations. "Proceed with minisub release for *Carter* docking."

Bell issued the orders, COB worked his console touch screens, *Challenger*'s hangar doors opened, and the mini began to move. It was being piloted by a chief from *Carter*'s crew, and co-piloted by another chief, a Navy SEAL by background, from Kurzin's commando group. Both men, already fully qualified in the American ASDS minisub design, had come over to *Challenger* at the end of the previous rendezvous. Since then they'd been thoroughly checked out in operating the German mini, by Meltzer and COB. This intense extra preparation was needed, Jeffrey knew, because the German mini, vital to the mission in more ways than one, would never return to *Challenger* again.

The mini began to cover the modest distance across to *Carter*. The two full-size nuclear subs used Jeffrey's preferred rendezvous formation. *Challenger*'s heading was north, and *Carter*'s was south, with neither ship making forward motion; each bow sphere sonar covered the other ship's baffles, since no towed arrays were deployed. They kept just enough horizontal and vertical separation to avoid any collision hazard, and not block each other's wide-aperture arrays on the sides where they faced. Jeffrey liked to think of this as circling the wagons.

In a split second, all calm evaporated.

"New passive sonar contact on the starboard wide-aperture array!" Chief O'Hanlon called out. "Broadband contact, submerged, intermittent, contact bearing is . . . zero-five-zero! Acoustic sea state too high for meaningful ranging!" Noise from the ice cap was interfering with one of the wide-aperture array's most important functions: instantly finding the range to another submarine. "Contact not close," O'Hanlon added after a pause to study sound-path data. "I designate the contact Master One."

Bell acknowledged, surprised and concerned. "Fire Control, commence a target motion analysis on Master One."

Sessions spoke with Torelli. A tracking party got busy. With enough passage of time—and if the contact wasn't lost—Master One's range, course, and speed could be estimated by computer analysis based solely on the way in which the bearing to the contact slowly changed.

"Sir," Sessions reported, "*Carter* signals, 'New sonar contact.'" Sessions read off the rest of the acoustic-link message, which made it clear that they'd detected the same vessel, Master One. "*Carter* asks whether to proceed with minisub docking while contact is held."

Bell turned to Jeffrey. "Commodore?"

Jeffrey was forced to make a very difficult choice. "Anything yet on Master One's range or speed?"

"Negative, sir," O'Hanlon stated. "And no tonals."

"Nothing here yet either, sir," Torelli replied.

"He's moving and we're not," Jeffrey said. "That gives us a sonar advantage."

"Only if we put the docking on hold," Bell warned. "Master One might pick up mechanical transients otherwise, sir."

"If we shift the strike group's position, and have the minisub follow along, we'll waste its fuel and we can't get a refill. We aren't ready to climb up on the continental shelf, to hide from this guy that way. Deploying off-board probes to scout ahead on the shallow bottom will make mechanical transients too."

"Hug the slope at the edge of the shelf, and wait for him to go by?" Bell asked.

"Sir," Sessions interrupted Jeffrey's train of thought, "*Carter* signals, 'Minisub requesting clearance to dock. What are your instructions?'" The mini's acoustic-link system was too weak for it to have overheard the very low power messages between *Challenger* and *Carter*. Its passive sonars were much too unsophisticated to have detected Master One on their own. The pair of chiefs in its control compartment were unaware that a third, unfriendly, nuclear submarine was so nearby.

"Master One signal strength increasing slightly," O'Hanlon said. This suggested it was coming closer.

"Weps?" Bell asked. "Anything?"

"Bearing has shifted left, sir. Worst case is that Master One is approaching, will cross in front of our bow."

"Can you say when?" Jeffrey asked.

"Could be twenty minutes, could be two hours."

Sessions spoke up again. "*Carter* has repeated her signal."

Jeffrey was in a real bind. None of the tactical alternatives were good.

"*Carter* signals, 'Unknown submerged contact will cross my baffles within one hour.'"

The words were matter-of-fact, but the implied tone was insistent. A serious threat was approaching, and soon would enter the baffles zone in which *Carter* was totally blind.

Bell, Sessions, and Torelli kept glancing at Jeffrey, waiting for him to tell them, Harley, and the minisub what to do.

If you don't have any good choices, pick the one which seems least bad. . . . And the sooner the better. That threat gets closer every second.

"Signal *Carter*, 'Designate contact Master One in further messages. Warn minisub of unidentified vessel's presence, then proceed with caution but make docking smartly. Signal flagship soonest when docking complete.'"

"Yes, Commodore," Sessions typed. Though the danger hadn't diminished, the decision to do something made the men around Jeffrey feel better. Harley acknowledged Jeffrey's message.

"Sonar," Jeffrey said to Finch, "monitor the mini docking for transients' duration and signal strength. I want to know in a heartbeat if Master One could have heard anything."

Finch turned to Chief O'Hanlon, and they conferred.

A sonarman with headphones on, assigned to monitor the minisub, visibly cringed.

"Thump and scraping," O'Hanlon reported. "Assess as docking attempt aborted. Detection likelihood by Master One unknown."

Jeffrey cursed to himself. The two chiefs on the mini were handling the little craft clumsily.

"Signal *Carter,* 'Put docking on hold. Will match your depth to shield you acoustically from approaching contact.'"

Sessions sent the message; Harley acknowledged.

"Captain," Jeffrey told Bell, "rise on autohover, make your depth seven-three-zero feet, smartly."

Bell gave the helm order; Patel acknowledged and tapped at his keyboard and touch screen.

Jeffrey watched *Challenger*'s depth decrease from eight hundred fifty feet until her bulk stood between the upper part of *Carter*'s hull and Master One. "Signal *Carter,* 'Resume docking.'"

Once more Sessions typed, and Harley acknowledged.

The sonarman cringed again.

"Thud and clunks," O'Hanlon said. "Assess as mating collar lineup, and lockdown clamps engaging."

Carter signaled that the docking had succeeded.

"Detection likelihood by Master One undetermined," O'Hanlon said. Without knowing what class of submarine Master One was—what quality of passive sonars it carried—plus still lacking any useable data on distance, O'Hanlon and Finch had no way to calculate an enemy detection threshold for the noises just made.

Jeffrey had another idea. "Could we and *Carter* somehow triangulate a range to the contact?"

"Negative, sir," O'Hanlon said. "We're too close together. Otherwise I'd've suggested it."

"Very well, Sonar Supervisor."

"Master One still approaching. No further data."

"Very well."

He'd fallen behind the curve of unfolding events, thrown off guard by Master One's appearance when his strike group was at its most vulnerable—in the middle of a mini-sub rendezvous next to unfavorable terrain. He pushed to get back ahead of the curve.

"Signal *Carter*, 'Strike group maintain formation and continue to track Master One. Secure all unnecessary machinery for maximum silencing.'"

Once more Sessions typed, then announced *Carter*'s acknowledgment. Bell issued orders to COB, including to secure the ventilation fans. O'Hanlon said that Master One continued coming closer. Torelli said his people thought the contact was now about ten miles away, and might come within four miles before passing and going off into the distance. Given the uncertainty in these figures, this was much too close for comfort.

"Sir," Sessions called, "*Carter* signals, 'My pump jet is exposed to Master One's probable track near closest point of approach. Will be unable to suppress echo if Master One goes active.'" The rotary slats at the back of a pump jet had no effective anechoic protection.

Jeffrey examined the navigation plot and the gravimeter. He faced the same problem as before. The nearby slope from the continental shelf down into deep water showed clearly on the gravimeter. The strike group was pinned against that slope. The shelf itself was only two hundred feet deep here, and for *Carter* to rise that high on autohover from her present formation depth of seven hundred fifty feet might cause her steel hull to pop—a dead giveaway to the ever-approaching Master One. And there were unknown dangers up on that shelf, including maybe antisubmarine mines or sensors, or both.

"Captain," Jeffrey told Bell, "on auxiliary maneuvering

units, translate own-ship sideways one hundred yards due east."

Bell gave the new helm order; Patel acknowledged and worked his console to put it into effect.

"Signal *Carter*," Jeffrey said, " 'Am increasing separation. Prepare to pivot your ship on auxiliary maneuvering units to heading due north.' "

Patel reported when he'd completed the eastward lateral shifting of *Challenger*. That gave *Carter* enough room to safely rotate her bow from south to north.

Jeffrey signaled Harley to pivot his ship. Now both ships' baffles, and their pump jets, were protected by facing the slope of the shelf. This was the best that Jeffrey could do. If Master One was also hugging the edge of the shelf, bad things would happen quickly. Depending on that other sub's depth, a collision wasn't impossible, even if she didn't open fire. The strike group was in international waters, but not by much. Genrietty Island wasn't very far away.

"Your intentions, Commodore?" Bell asked.

"Sit here and wait."

"I'm not sure I can agree with that, sir."

"Why not?"

"The shelf floor seems to be safer than the steep open side of the slope. We know Master One is a submarine, and it's approaching. We don't know for sure there are any sensors planted on the shelf. That makes Master One the greater threat, the one to maneuver smartly to avoid."

"Negative. The known threat is not the greater threat. The greater threat is the unknown floor of the shelf."

Bell frowned. "At least rotate both ships so we're facing Master One head on, show our smallest profiles, and point our torpedo tubes right at her."

"Sorry, but no. I don't want to lose the contact we hold on the wide-aperture array, then risk not regaining it soon enough on the bow sphere. Turning now would show our largest acoustic profiles at Master One's closest point of approach instead, which is more dangerous." A sub typically emitted greater acoustic energy from her sides than in the direction of dead ahead. And twirling both subs in place with their auxiliary maneuvering units, to keep their noses pointing at Master One, was too noisy and too complicated. "We can't open fire first, our ROEs don't allow it here. Besides, if we do have to shoot when shot at, I'd rather save the best setup for when Master One is nearest us. Our tubes will be aimed right at her then, with hers aimed away from us. . . . We stay put."

Bell frowned again. "Understood."

As always when the fans were stopped, the control room was getting stuffy. This latest tactics dispute between Bell and Jeffrey had heightened the already existing tension among the crew. People tried to settle in for another uncomfortable wait.

"Signal *Carter,* 'Acknowledge this message and then secure acoustic link except for extreme emergency. I will signal if evasive maneuvers required, or when I deem Master One is out of counterdetection range against strike group.' "

Jeffrey watched the tactical plot as Master One changed from a large, multicolored blob, showing a broad area of uncertainty, into a point: O'Hanlon and Torelli at last had better data.

Yikes. The closest point of approach would be within two miles, not four, in ten minutes. Master One was on a course due west at fourteen knots, at a depth of six hundred sixty feet—two hundred meters to her captain, who'd be thinking metric. *Very close.* She was an Akula-II, identified by quirks in her signature as *K-335,* commissioned in 2001 and upgraded since then.

O'Hanlon's initial detection had been a fluke, showing how unpredictable sound propagation could truly be under the ice cap. Akula-IIs were extremely quiet.

"Sir," Bell said in an undertone, "the Akula-Twos have very good nonacoustic ASW detectors."

He knew Bell meant magnetic anomaly sensors, wake turbulence measuring devices, and chemical sniffers.

Jeffrey wasn't worried about magnetic or turbulence detection. Even the revised closest point of approach was too far away for *Carter*'s steel hull to be detected above the magnetic field noise caused by the proximity of the North Magnetic Pole, over in northwestern Canada. Turbulence wasn't an issue since Jeffrey's strike group was drifting with the current. The real problem was the current, which ran from west to east: from the strike group toward the Akula-II.

Every submarine gave off traces of lubricants and hydraulic fluid into the surrounding sea. Fuel oil for the backup emergency diesel engine, even sewage from the waste-holding tanks, might also leak in small amounts. *Carter* had just come from six months in dry dock. How well was she repaired? Battle damage was known to greatly increase the rate of chemical leakage. If *Carter* was leaving a big and strong enough plume, *K-335* would notice.

Despite the warmth in Control, Jeffrey's hands began to feel morbidly cold. There was a burning sensation in his stomach. But all he could do, as he'd already told Bell, was wait.

Oh crap.

Jeffrey walked up the aisle to Bell. He bent over to talk into his ear. "Akula-Twos have gravimeters."

Bell's jaw clenched immediately. He remembered what Jeffrey had said days ago, about setting a special gravimeter watch. If *Challenger* could spot a stationary submarine's reactor compartment, the same thing would work in reverse.

"What's our speed over the ground?" Jeffrey asked.

Bell pointed at his console display. The window indicated 0.3 knots. They were moving with the current, but not by much.

"Is that fast enough?"

"To not be detected, sir?"

Jeffrey nodded.

"With Russian equipment? I'm not aware of intel on that. With U.S. equipment, it'd be touch and go. Two miles, resolution is sharp. They might see us both. At best we'd have one heck of a lot of explaining to do. At worst . . ." Bell didn't need to say it aloud. The mission would be doomed before it began.

"Have *Challenger* put on one-half knot of speed translating downcurrent on auxiliary maneuvering units. Break acoustic-link silence and instruct *Carter* how to mimic our movements."

Bell told Patel what actions to take at the helm. Sessions, distressed, typed gingerly, as if the sonarmen on *K-335* might hear him touching the keys.

The motion put on to hide from gravimeter detection meant mechanical transients, flow noise, and turbulence. They'd be subtle, minimal, but this was an extremely high-risk situation.

Patel sounded nervous acknowledging Bell's commands. When Sessions reported that *Carter* acknowledged, he sounded nervous.

K-335 was almost at her closest point of approach. Thinking of her out there gave Jeffrey the creeps. He locked his eyes on the sonarmen. If the Russian detected the strike group and reacted, they'd be first to know, by hearing telltale noise.

Noise from tubes flooding, or if she's patrolling with weapons wet, then noise from torpedoes in the water. If that happens I go down fighting, to give Carter *a chance to escape.*

"Range to Master One increasing," O'Hanlon murmured. *K-335* had crossed *Challenger*'s and *Carter*'s bows, and was continuing on course, west. But no one relaxed. It might take time for *K-335*'s computers to process fresh incoming data. There could be a lag before her captain realized he'd passed so near two intruding submarines. The uncomfortable wait continued. People began to squirm and sweat. *K-335* receded, at a rate a bit under five hundred yards per minute—faster than a gold-medal Olympic marathon runner, but in *Challenger*'s control room it felt like a leaden crawl.

At last O'Hanlon reported that he'd definitely lost the contact. Jeffrey knew the crewmen around him wished that they could cheer.

"Signal *Carter*," Jeffrey ordered, " 'Rise on autohover, five-zero feet per minute, make your depth one-six-five feet. Make your heading one-eight-zero.' " Due south.

The slow rise should help avoid hull popping.

"Captain Bell, ditto for *Challenger*." Nonstandard terminology, but Jeffrey was feeling something like glee after outwitting *K-335*. It gave him a new level of confidence, to have tested his strike group's stealth at such close quarters against a first-class opponent.

Both ships finished rotating to face south, and *Carter* put herself behind Jeffrey and off *Challenger*'s starboard side. They rose vertically, toward the ice cap looming above. On the gravimeter, the continental slope—showing missing chunks and fissures such as scars from old earthquakes—slid progressively beneath them, until the shelf itself stretched out in front. The water ahead was sandwiched between the ice cap and the shelf. Clearance between, two hundred feet maximum, was tight.

Conspicuous on the gravimeter display, as two small lumps on an otherwise featureless plain, were Genrietty Island, fifteen miles off, and, thirty miles further southwest, at the extreme range of the gravimeter's field of view, Zannetty Island. Both jutted barely one hundred fifty feet above the sea.

It was time to deploy remote-controlled unmanned vehicles from *Challenger* and *Carter*. Harley's were larger and more capable, because his garage space sported arrangements to hold and release several Seahorse IIIs. Bell had to make do with smaller, older probes that were launched and retrieved through *Challenger*'s torpedo tubes.

The seemingly bland plain of Siberia's silty continental shelf, and the hard lid of the ice cap so close above it, held unknown man-made hazards as well as ice keels that could endanger the strike group and ruin the mission. But the continental shelf also held an invaluable, indispensable prize. Jeffrey opened his mouth to issue an order.

"New passive contact on the starboard wide-aperture array!" O'Hanlon broke in. *"Broadband contact, submerged, bearing two-seven-five!"* Just north of due west. "Range uncertain! Designate the contact Master Two."

"Sir," Torelli told Bell, "timing is not inconsistent with *K-335* having turned back this way."

"Range? *Estimate?*" Jeffrey demanded.

"Insufficient data," O'Hanlon said flatly.

"Suppose Master Two is Master One," Jeffrey said. "Suppose it's the same situation but he's coming at us from the other direction. What can *anyone* tell me?"

"He's further away from the shelf," Torelli said, "by a couple of miles. Conjecture he's following an oval track, a possible barrier patrol."

"A barrier patrol against *what*?" Jeffrey snapped.

"Protecting the islands, sir?" Jeffrey could hear a shrug implied in how Torelli answered.

"Protecting them from *what?* From *us*?"

For a minute no one said anything, cowed by their strike group commander's raw anger. Jeffrey made himself cool down. "Or are we looking at it backwards, assuming the world revolves around our mission when it doesn't yet?"

"Sir?" Bell was confused.

"A Russian boomer bastion. I bet they have one north of us, in the Wrangel Abyssal Plain. Think about it."

Bell nodded. "*K-335* isn't protecting the islands. The islands are outposts to help protect the bastion."

"Sir," Sessions said, "*Carter* holds new submerged passive sonar contact, west. They conjecture *K-335* is reexamining this area after finding signs of us in their sensor data."

What if I'm wrong and Harley's right? His mind-set, his intuition, perspective, judgment, would be different from Jeffrey's—and possibly better. He'd gotten clobbered on his previous mission, whereas Jeffrey didn't know firsthand what that was like: he might become a victim of his own prior unbroken successes, by making the incorrect call.

"Sonar, Weps, what's *K-335*'s speed now?"

"No data," O'Hanlon repeated in frustration, edgy, irritable, taking his wrestling match with the bad local acoustic conditions very personally.

"No reason from bearing rate to believe speed has changed," Torelli said. "But I can't say for sure that speed hasn't changed, either, sir."

"What's the contact's CPA?" The closest point of approach.

"Four miles, sir. Maybe."

"You said that last pass, and it was only two."

"Understood, sir." Torelli sounded as if he felt he was letting his commodore down. The tactical plot showed a wide error zone in Master Two's position.

"If he were after us," Jeffrey said, "I *think* he'd either go noticeably faster or slower than before." *Shit.* "We don't have time to deploy our probes and scout ahead enough that we can get safely up onto the continental shelf and out of his way."

"Same tactics?" Bell asked tentatively.

"Affirmative. Bows north, translate east a half-knot faster than the current, keep real quiet, wait for the threat to go by."

Things were out of Jeffrey's hands. *K-335* knew they were there, or she didn't. If she didn't, she'd detect them on this pass, or not. If she opened fire she opened fire. If *K-335* did shoot, Jeffrey knew what to do: draw the weapons away from *Carter,* and stop *K-335* from launching more or reporting *Carter*'s presence. But in sub-on-sub combat, the first well-aimed shots were usually fatal; at this short range the duel would be savage, over quickly—and *Challenger* might easily lose.

If that did happen, Harley would escape on his own, then somehow regain stealth, and carry on as best he could. The struggling Allied cause just didn't have the months it would take to abort the mission and start it again from scratch when the diplomatic, military, and intelligence flurry over an undersea firefight in Russian home waters subsided. Harley would have to hope that Jeffrey's sudden death at the hands of *K-335*'s captain didn't too badly handicap the President negotiating with Moscow over the Hot Line. All involved could only pray that *Challenger,* if sunk so close to Genrietty Island, didn't shatter Kurzin's pseudo-German frame-up subterfuge.

Fat chance. The risks might have looked acceptable at the Pentagon or the White House, as paper studies in conference rooms with tired people sitting amid big piles of empty coffee cups. Standing in the control room, with an Akula-II so close that Jeffrey could practically reach out and touch it, tore away the academic tone of the simulations. What was going on right now, right here, was much too real.

He seriously considered opening fire first. This would utterly violate his rules of engagement, and with Russian hydrophone nets in range the action could surely be reconstructed accurately. Ambushing *K-335* to save his mission, in the short term, would start the very Russian-versus-American war he was supposed to help permanently avoid in the long term. Jeffrey was handcuffed from every direction. He hated not holding the initiative. He had to regain it, period, if necessary by sheer force of will. He ran through all that had happened so far. He saw that he needed to pick between being an optimist and a pessimist . . .

K-335 won't shoot. He hasn't seen us yet, and he won't.

"New plan," Jeffrey announced theatrically to dispel the tension and gloom. "This guy's just what the doctor ordered."

"Commodore?" Bell was mystified.

"These waters are awfully polluted. I doubt he pays his chemo-sniffer readings any mind. So we continue drifting, and do nothing until after he comes back once again from the east. Russian command and control are rigid. I expect his oval patrol track and his speed are fixed, dictated by superiors. I want to know this guy's schedule. When *we're* ready, he'll be the perfect key to unlock the outermost shell of the *matryoshka* doll."

CHAPTER 15

Challenger and *Carter* waited for *K-335* to return. In the meantime, Jeffrey ordered the strike group to secure—stand down—from battle stations, so people could eat, rest, and use the heads. He took a much-needed nap himself, then a refreshing hot shower, grabbed a bite in the wardroom, and dosed himself with every submariner's drug of choice: caffeine. He filled a travel mug with more strong coffee and went to Control.

Apprehension there mounted. There was no guarantee that *K-335* would come back. Another ELF message came through from Commander, U.S. Strategic Command, reconfirming that the mission was still on. This time, Jeffrey was secretly glad. He was too far in, too mentally engaged and emotionally committed, to welcome any idea of withdrawing.

His adrenaline surged when contact on *K-335* was regained, ten hours after she'd disappeared east.

Satisfied that he understood her schedule, Jeffrey issued orders for *Challenger* and *Carter* to release their off-board probes. They'd use them to scout several miles ahead before following at the same speed the probes were making, seven knots.

The tension thickened as the vessels moved onto the continental shelf. Jeffrey told Bell to turn on the sonar speakers. With the strike group sandwiched so narrowly between the ice cap and the bottom, groans and creeks and crackling from the pack ice were louder than ever. Jeffrey also heard constant *splish-splashes,* and barks and yips and different kinds of cries.

"Biologics are raising the acoustic sea state," O'Hanlon reported. Closer to land and the edge of the summertime ice cap, seals and sea birds swarmed. Crewmen jumped when an agonized animal scream filled the air. It died off abruptly.

"A polar bear just caught lunch," O'Hanlon said. The sonarman sitting next to him seemed squeamish. "Enjoy the extreme ecotourism, me boy."

Bell's two probes, shaped like torpedoes, battery-powered, loaded with sophisticated sensors, searched a narrow path on the shelf for anything emplaced by the Russians that might give *Challenger*'s or *Carter*'s presence away. Data and imagery from the probes filled several screens in the control room, coming through their fiber-optic tethers as Torelli's men directed them with joysticks. Captain Harley had deployed three Seahorse III unmanned undersea vehicles. Much wider and heavier then *Challenger*'s probes, and thus better equipped as robotic investigators, they helped check the seafloor and the underside of the ice.

The Seahorses gave much earlier warning of polynyas than the strike group's passive sonars could. Jeffrey wanted to stay clear of such open water almost as badly as he craved avoiding a crash into an ice keel. He thought of each hole in the ice as a window through which his ships might be seen and attacked.

One value of the probes was that their small size and silent propulsion made them essentially invisible. Near Genrietty they located man-made objects in a line along the bottom, and in a more uneven line above, attached to the underside of the ice.

Carter signaled again: "Unknown if objects are mines or ASW sensors or both. Classification requires high-frequency Seahorse sonars go active."

"Captain?" Bell asked.

"Doesn't matter what they are. Regardless, we need to find a way past. . . . Fire Control, signal *Carter,* 'Active sonars to remain secured, repeat, secured. Commence passive search for access route trending south.' "

Technicians on *Challenger* and *Carter* sent their probes swerving in a coordinated pattern, to find a gap broad enough for *Challenger,* and then *Carter* following behind, to squeeze through at three knots. One of Torelli's probes won this friendly competition. Jeffrey ordered Sessions to relay the information to *Carter.*

When safely beyond the Russian picket line of sensors or mines or whatever they were, both ships went back to seven knots.

"Commodore," Sessions soon called, "*Carter* signals, 'Permission to commence active search for cable?' "

Tapping this buried undersea fiber-optic communications cable was the next vital part of the mission plan. One of the Seahorses had a narrow-beam, low-frequency, look-down active sonar. Its purpose was to penetrate the ocean floor and find buried objects. By moving slowly just above the bottom, the bulk of the Seahorse was supposed to mask the returning echoes from prying enemy ears. At such close vertical range, if an object wasn't too deep into the silt or sand or gravel covering different parts of the shelf, a long-wavelength search beam could seek incongruous materials and shapes a few yards down.

Blood pressures started rising in *Challenger*'s control room. Going active was an iffy tactic in such confined and hostile waters. As the navigation plot and the gravimeter proved, the strike group was pinched between Genrietty and Zannetty Islands. Satellite surveillance had shown that both were occupied by garrisons of naval infantry troops. Facilities for living year-round had been dug deep into the rock of the islands. Radar domes, and radio antennas, were conspicuous in the picture files provided in Jeffrey's orders pouch. Both islands had helicopter landing pads, and helos. These could shuttle southwest, to the much larger parts of the New Siberian Island landmasses, or could fly due south to the mainland, three hundred nautical miles away.

The helos didn't just rotate troops and bring in supplies. They patrolled aggressively, dropping dipping sonars and LIDAR projectors through the polynyas. And the troops, on skis or using snowmobiles, patrolled the surface of the cap, moving back and forth between Genrietty and Zannetty, watching for commandos who might think there were easy pickings here. Jeffrey assumed the naval infantry followed routes mapped out by the helos across the uneven, ever-changing, treacherous ice.

Which is why I picked this area for infiltration and eavesdropping. It's the last place they'd expect a pair of American nuclear subs to actually be.

And since the islands were plugged into the regional communications net, the trunk cable Jeffrey wanted to find was likely to run very near them.

Except the Russian mind is infamously difficult to read. Maybe, to them, this is precisely *where spy subs would come, into the teeth of their defenses and right under their sentries' feet.*

Once Harley's probe went active, the Seahorse might instead set off a buried acoustic-intercept intruder alarm, or even detonate a mine. The Seahorse was expendable, but the unmistakable blast would bring alerted forces from everywhere, and the strike group would be surrounded with nowhere to run or hide. If the mine was an RMT-1, similar to the American CAPTOR but more lethal, it would release a torpedo that rose from the mud and homed on the nicest target within the considerable range of its seekers—which meant *Challenger* or *Carter*.

The senior control room teams on both ships knew there was no way around this. The strike group simply *had* to locate the cable. Jeffrey was taking his biggest gamble yet. He granted Harley permission to go active with his probe.

Fatalistically, Jeffrey waited for *Carter*'s Seahorse to produce results. Whether the next thing to happen would be Harley's signal of success, or the eruption of a mine going off, or the whine of a torpedo inbound, only time would tell. The acid burning in Jeffrey's stomach acted up again. From the jittery movements of people sitting or standing around him, he knew he wasn't alone in this torturous stress.

The solid resistance to perpetual pack-ice drift, caused by the two small immovable islands, was an added factor making the cap here unusually dynamic, constantly splitting and piling up and grinding. Those noisy 3-D quadraphonic effects on the sonar speakers, giving spatial cues for the violent natural goings-on so close above, made Jeffrey feel oppressively hemmed in.

"*Carter* signals," Sessions finally announced, " 'Have located buried cable. Ice above it is thick, solid, and jagged. No polynyas are near. Permission to commence cable tapping?' "

"Signal *Carter,* 'Permission granted, commence cable tap operations. At will, inform flagship ideal position assume for massive parallel data processing.' "

Harley's ship took the lead. *Carter* and *Challenger* converged on the Seahorse III that was hovering over the buried military fiber-optic cable.

CHAPTER 16

For the next phase, Nyurba's duties and status as second-in-command of Kurzin's squadron meant that his proper place was in USS *Jimmy Carter*'s battle management center, within her Multi-Mission Platform. To Nyurba, the space's layout and the feel of its people at work resembled *Challenger*'s control room, except most of the staff were nonsubmariners—passengers aboard *Carter* who formed a support-and-liaison section that wouldn't go into Siberia with the Air Force Special Ops Squadron. But instead of having a ship control station, the command center had stations for controlling off-board probes. Other consoles were being used to operate diver airlocks and the hangar space's ocean interface—through which unmanned vehicles departed or returned covertly. Near the forward end of the space, the bulkheads angled inward; *Carter*'s wasp waist began to taper there, at the front of the battle management center.

The data and imagery on the console screens and bulkhead displays consisted of everything relevant to the commandos completing their mission. A tactical plot aided team situational awareness: *Challenger* was two hundred yards away, ahead and to starboard. The commodore had two of the three Seahorses, and both LMRS probes, deployed five miles off in different directions, as early-warning trip wires.

Colonel Kurzin stood impatiently, in overall charge, while an Air Force major handled minute-to-minute decisions and orders as leader of the mission-support section. Activity here was so classified that not even Captain Harley could enter without Kurzin's permission while espionage divers worked on the bottom, as they were right now. Several intercom systems and dedicated sound-powered phones, as well as fiber-optic data buses, let the control room and the special ops center stay in constant touch. From these it was clear that Harley and his people had their hands full, making *Carter* hover as if glued in place.

Nyurba watched for progress, or problems, while a display screen showed six Navy SEALs, in closed-circuit mixed gas rebreather gear, carefully digging into the bottom muck to unearth the buried fiber-optic cable. The rebreathers had much longer endurance than open-circuit scuba, with the added benefit of not releasing bubbles that rose to the surface to increase the risk of being detected. The mixed gas was necessary at a depth of two hundred feet, where compressed air's oxygen could cause convulsions, nitrogen would induce the pleasant but often fatal rapture of the deep, and it also increased risk of barotrauma—the bends—even if the divers were returned to normal atmospheric pressure gradually.

The widescreen display was windowed to show the divers from several perspectives at once. The pictures were sharp, because now that the immediate area had been thoroughly scoured for threats, Commodore Fuller ordered active laser line-scan cameras to be used. One feed came from the Seahorse III that had found the cable, and hovered nearby. Other feeds came from photonic sensors mounted along *Carter*'s keel, and from a hand-held camera used by one of the divers. His camera had a fiber-optic tether of its own, and a SEAL chief at one console in the special ops center, wearing headphones and a lip mike, was in continual voice contact with him through that tether.

The divers all wore harnesses connected to lifelines fastened to fittings on *Carter*'s keel. This was a standard safety precaution.

One diver spent almost all his time looking up. This was for safety, too. He was watching *Carter*'s hull for depth change or drift. The ship's rounded underside was only fifteen feet directly above the divers' heads. A sharp drop and she could squash them. A quick rise and the lifelines would yank the SEALs up shallow too fast, to hideous deaths.

Carter was being held in position laterally by her auxiliary maneuvering units, her bow facing into the current—which near the bottom set to the east at one-quarter knot. This was enough to cause noticeable drag against someone standing upright. The divers had to be cautious to keep their footing and not kick up silt; their buoyancy-compensation vests were deflated to make them heavy—they stepped softly and slowly in their extra-large-sized combat swimmer fins. As they dug, using titanium shovels meant for the purpose, they deposited the muck downcurrent, so they could see what they were doing. Nyurba understood all these things because he was a qualified Seabee diver himself, although he'd mostly used compressed air or pure oxygen and rarely gone below thirty feet. His focus, as a construction engineer, had been on assessing underwater repairs—for bridge abutments and water mains—or planning submerged obstacle-removal demolitions.

The SEALs hadn't yet exposed the cable. Their trench looked about three feet deep. From what the Seahorse's sonar had shown, they wouldn't need to go down much farther.

Nyurba glanced at another bulkhead display, a large-scale map. He knew from prior briefings how to interpret it at a glance. Icons, and color-coded ribbony bands that reminded him of party streamers, explained why the trunk fiber-optic cable was here, why Commodore Fuller had decided to tap it here, and why Kurzin and Nyurba would lead their men ashore on the mainland Siberian coast nearest to here.

The central part of the Russian Federation consisted of a wilderness with virtually no east-west transportation infrastructure. Other than aircraft flights, or plodding cargo ships taking the Northern Sea Route in the brief Arctic summer, the only way from Moscow to Vladivostok—even today—was the Trans-Siberian Railroad. The trip in one direction took a week. To lessen the chance that secret messages would be intercepted, and to increase protection against an electromagnetic pulse attack—which might be nuclear or nonnuclear—fiber-optic cables were used as an alternative to satellite communications and shortwave radio. Fiber-optic cables covering long distances could either be laid underwater, or on land. Moscow years ago chose some of both. This provided redundancy, in case one cable broke down, as sometimes happened. It also saved money, because even with the need for icebreakers or commercial submarines to help lay a fiber-optic trunk line along the whole north coast of Russia, this was still far cheaper than stringing or burying lines across the heartland anywhere except along the Trans-Siberian Railroad's right of way. The railroad ran through the southernmost part of Siberia, more than a thousand miles from the Arctic coast. And between the two, north-south, were dozens of Russian military installations of all kinds.

Intermediate lines branched off the Arctic undersea cable, to reach into Siberia like fingers. Most of these branch lines existed due to the major rivers flowing north, draining into the different seas that fringed the Arctic Ocean itself. These rivers formed the primary transportation and heavy logistics arteries in that whole part of Russia. In winter the rivers froze solid, becoming ice highways for trucks. In spring and summer, when the waters, due to snow-thaw

runoff, drained millions of square miles of Siberian interior, the biggest rivers were navigable. Then cargo ships
would use them, serving small, seasonal ports up to hundreds of miles inland.

One of these rivers, the Lena, supported the western edge
of the jurisdiction of the rear admiral with whom Commodore Fuller would try to meet. Another, the Indigirka, led to
very near that admiral's central base. A third, the Kolyma,
near the eastern edge of the admiral's turf, was the logistical route to the ICBM field that was Kurzin's and Nyurba's
target, and was also their planned route of egress if all went
well. A smaller river, the Alazeja, on the Siberian mainland
coast at the spot that was closest to Genrietty and Zannetty,
happened to cut diagonally southeast—down and to the
right on the map—from near the Indigirka's delta toward
the Kolyma near the missile field. The missiles were three
hundred miles in a straight line from the admiral's office,
but that route on the ground was impassable.

The Alazeja's mouth was where Kurzin, Nyurba, and
their men would sneak out of the water. Nyurba dreaded
this part. The Alazeja was one of the most polluted rivers in
the world. The continental shelf near its mouth was a major
Russian nuclear-waste dumping ground.

Which is exactly why that's where we plan to sneak in.

"They've got it," Kurzin said tightly.

Nyurba turned back to the bulkhead screen showing the
divers. And there it was, a cable as thick as his wrist, unearthed. Pairs of SEALs, dive buddies, went to work at
each of the opposite ends of the trench they'd dug, exposing
more of the cable, while the cameraman and the safety
monitor watched. They signaled they were ready, then all
stepped well away, upcurrent, using the play available on
their lifeline tethers.

"Hyperbaric work chamber pressurized to depth at the

keel, one-eight-zero feet," the SEAL chief in the command center reported. "Atmosphere gas mix correct. Chamber is ready."

Kurzin acknowledged. He went to a different console. Nyurba joined him there. The technician sitting at the console accessed the look-down imagery on one of his displays. He activated a low-power blue-green laser range finder. An aiming reticule appeared on his other console screen. He began to manipulate his trackmarble and joystick. A grapnel lowered itself from a big open hatch in *Carter*'s underbelly, gradually reaching toward the cable. He squeezed the red button on top of his joystick, and grabbed the cable on the first try. He worked more controls and the grapnel arm slowly retracted, drawing up a length of cable with it, so that the cable ran from the grapnel down to the two ends of the trench, where it disappeared in the bottom sediments.

On camera, the SEAL safety monitor made an okay sign with one hand. The technician continued lifting, until the grapnel, holding the cable, withdrew back inside the Multi-Mission Platform's outer hull.

"Cable now in place in hyperbaric work chamber," the SEAL in the command center stated. The chamber was a pressure-proof compartment in *Carter*'s garage space.

"Recall the divers," Kurzin ordered.

The SEAL chief spoke into his lip mike. The SEAL on the bottom made hand signals to the others. They double-checked that all their tools were still attached to their lanyards. They made sure that their lifelines weren't tangled. They swam up toward the look-down cameras, and disappeared through the hatch into the work chamber.

The SEAL chief activated different cameras. These showed the work chamber. It was in there that the SEALs would begin the highly classified steps, first developed by the National Security Agency, that were needed to tap an undersea fiber-optic cable. The cable now was locked in place on what resembled a surgical operating table. The SEALs removed their scuba and dry suits, no longer needed since they were in a shirtsleeves environment, where the atmosphere was safe to breathe at a depth of one hundred eighty feet—five and half times sea-level air pressure, enough to hold back the ocean below.

They unreeled a rubber hose connected to *Carter*'s holding tank of extremely pure distilled water, usually used for topping up the nuclear reactor's primary coolant loop. With the hose, they thoroughly washed a portion of the muddy cable about a yard long. Then they rinsed away, down into the open bottom hatch, any other traces of mud and of highly conductive seawater, making sure to douse themselves in this manner, too.

"Chamber high-speed fans are on."

The SEALs opened small lockers in a bulkhead of the work chamber, removing new tools and supplies. They dried everything using special lint-free absorbent cloths, and donned disposable white garments, including hats and masks, like the outfits worn in a technological clean room. The high-speed fans scrubbed the atmosphere, purging it of lint and dust and even shed skin cells. The men put on long rubber insulation gloves and rubber boots, and stood on thick rubber mats. Once done with their complex task, Nyurba reminded himself, they'd begin a lengthy decompression in a different chamber, ready to rejoin the full commando squadron only as *Carter* reached Kurzin's final dropoff point.

The SEALs began to cut away the cable's outer armored sheath, which gave the cable its structural strength. Then they peeled back the softer waterproofing layer under the armor, revealing the working innards of the cable. The most dangerous part of the process now, from the perspective of the SEALs, was avoiding the power cable that ran beside the eight cladded fiber-optic strands. The power cable carried thousands of volts, needed to power the signal amplifiers that a trunk fiber-optic cable required every few miles. Nyurba knew that fiber optics weren't superconductors— they did suffer signal loss with distance. Whether the trunk cable was strung underwater or on land, automated amplifiers had to be part of the system. Electricity to run the optical amplifiers needed to come from somewhere. Land lines could use local power suppliers along their routes. Undersea cables brought that power with them.

Slowly and carefully, they separated the eight cladded fiber-optic strands, to be able to work on them individually. Inside every strand, through a thread of glass the thickness of a human hair, a stream of coherent laser light carried information at a rate of about twenty billion bytes per second.

With devices resembling instruments for microsurgery, they painstakingly inserted the ends of even smaller glass threads of their own into each of the Russian ones. These threads, Nyurba had been told, drew off the signal without reducing its strength enough for the Russians to notice. The delicate threads were connected to optical amplifiers, and the output of those amplifiers was fed to *Carter*'s onboard supercomputer.

"Commodore," Sessions said, "*Carter* signals, 'Ready to send across fiber-optic lead for *Challenger* supercomputer.'"

Jeffrey was expecting this. "Phone Talker, inform Systems Administrator that *Carter* is preparing to connect fiber-optic feed from cable tap." The System Administrator's station was on the deck below the control room.

"Fire Control, signal *Carter,* 'Ready to receive fiber-optic lead.'"

Bell told COB to put the hull-mounted photonic sensor imagery onto one of the main vertical display screens.

They watched as a pair of divers from *Carter* emerged out of the murk, swimming with a reel of cable carried between them. They connected the end of the cable to a fitting inside a small hatch in the port side of *Challenger*'s sail.

"Sir," the phone talker reported, "Systems Administrator

confirms good connection with the cable, handshake between supercomputers successful. Data feed from tap appears to be nominal."

Jeffrey went below to visit the Systems Administrator. Bell remained in Control in case a threat was identified while the strike group was glued to the undersea cable like flypaper.

"How's it going?" Jeffrey asked.

The Systems Administrator's office was the size of a broom closet, just large enough to hold the equipment he needed to control the ship's local area network performance and manage the status of different computers and software.

"Artificial intelligence routines are mapping out the contents of the cable strands right now, sir. Methods called expert systems and genetic algorithms. Pretty neat stuff."

"What's the map showing?"

"Well, the cables transmit a mixture of voice and data and video. Each strand handles several thousand separate message streams at once. But they all follow known formats and protocols, so step one is figuring out what's where. The next step will be monitoring the information flow and finding which channels have the specific traffic we want to listen in on."

Jeffrey nodded, and smiled. Supercomputers were very expensive, but they didn't take up much space. What they did need was a very clean environment, a lot of electricity, and facilities to take away the immense waste heat they created. But with a reactor and turbogenerators—to drive air-conditioning and refrigeration equipment, which fed ventilation ducts and chilled-water pipes that already ran all over the ship to keep the combat-system electronics cool—a nuclear sub was the ideal place to install the most advanced available supercomputer. Rapid warnings to the CIA or the

Pentagon could be sent with tight-beam laser or radio buoys, talking to dedicated submarine communication satellites.

And by the link between his ships, Jeffrey was using two supercomputers at once—massive parallel processing. Four NSA experts, who'd come from *Carter* in the German mini at the end of the first rendezvous, were in *Challenger*'s electronic support measures room; four more NSA men were in *Carter*'s. They'd guide the automated interpretive work done via hardware and software.

"OK, sir," the systems administrator said. "The uh, the channel maps are completed. The sifting through to locate the stuff we care about is starting."

"How long should that take?"

"I'm guessing about two hours, sir."

"I'll be in my office. You can reach me there if you have any problems. Otherwise, call me when we're ready to stir up the hornet's nest."

CHAPTER 17

Jeffrey was back in *Challenger*'s control room. The system administrator had called him a few minutes ago. *Carter* confirmed through the acoustic link that they were ready, too.

As prearranged during the mission briefing days before, *Carter* positioned two of her Seahorses in polynyas spaced widely apart, with their signals intercept and electronic support measures antennas raised out of the water. These were coated with a white radar-absorbing material, for camouflage and stealth. They would capture radio and radar transmissions across the entire frequency spectrum, and by direction-finding triangulate on each transmitter's position. The computers would produce a map of any facility that emitted anything at all. This map would be extremely wide-ranging, because surface ducting from side lobes, of even spaceward-focused satellite relay ground stations, could be picked up and amplified billions of times from hundreds of miles away. Side lobes were unavoidable leakage from any radiating antenna, in directions other than where the antenna was aimed. Ducting was an effect where a layer of air at ground or ocean level trapped and held radio and radar waves, minimizing signal-strength loss over vast distances, and bending them along the curve of the earth. Surface ducting was especially effective in mist and fog—and just such weather prevailed in the seas near *Challenger* this time of year, because differences between air and water temperatures caused heavy moisture condensation.

The computers and analysts on *Challenger* and *Carter* were ready to capture transmissions through the air and through the cable tap. To gather intelligence vital for completing the strike group's mission, it was now necessary to get both the Siberian coastal defense forces, and Russia's Strategic Rocket Forces, very excited very suddenly.

Jeffrey knew exactly how he would do this.

"Captain Bell, load a Mark Three brilliant decoy in tube eight." The new Mark III design was a programmable decoy that, unlike the Mark IIs, could operate down to *Challenger*'s crush depth. Thus it could mimic the ship in every respect. Mark IIs would implode at about three thousand feet—much too shallow.

Bell issued orders to Torelli.

Jeffrey leaned against the side of Bell's console. "Call up the large-scale tactical plot and let's look at the predicted track of *K-Three-three-five.*"

Jeffrey began to issue instructions. "I want you to have the Mark Three programmed to sound and act like *Challenger*. You can work out the details on course waypoints and timing with the Nav. But basically this is what I want it to do."

Jeffrey pointed with his index finger as he spoke. "Have the decoy proceed at stealth speed off of the continental shelf and on an intercept course with *K-Three-three-five*'s projected position over the Polar Abyssal Plain. Run it at a depth of eight thousand feet, to avoid any risk of collision and give a clearer acoustic path. When within six thousand yards of where we think the Akula-Two will be, have the decoy accelerate to fifty knots and turn sharply north. One of the Akula's passive arrays should pick up the contact. *Here,* have the decoy go quiet, veer west, and gently bury itself in the bottom. It'll have outrun and outdived *K-Three-three-five* before she can even get off a shot. We'll put the Akula's captain in a tizzy that he detected USS *Challenger* dashing into the middle of their boomer bastion at a speed and depth that only this ship can make."

Bell broke into a grin. "You'll light up every radar from here to Anadyr, and every switchboard from here to Polyarny."

"And, I hope, once the Akula's laser-buoy report hits the Kremlin via Russian Navy headquarters in Moscow, we also trigger a higher alert by their ground-based Strategic Rocket Forces."

"How does that last part help us, sir?" Sessions asked. "It sounds destabilizing."

"They'll un-destabilize, for a while, when they see they lost contact with *Challenger* and nothing bad occurred to their boomers. Before then, we listen to them freak out over the fiber-optic cable. If we're lucky, some important things will come through in plain text, or an encryption clerk will make a mistake and we'll read a useful message in code we can break. This will hopefully aid Kurzin's people to do their job. When I surface as *Challenger*'s captain in a different place, they'll figure I used a decoy to evade one of their fast-attacks while on my way to blockade the Eight-six-eight-U. God willing, they won't realize I'm playing a game on a much, much higher level."

Bell's people programmed and launched the Mark III decoy.

In ninety minutes, things did begin to happen. First, a higher-level naval antisubmarine alert was sounded. All sorts of radars and radios, on ships, on planes, at bases, and on satellites, that weren't already radiating gave themselves and their technical specifications away. An invaluable charting of threats and spoofing strategies and gaps in Russian defensive coverage resulted. Several previously unidentified coastal supersonic antiship cruise missile installations were also plotted; these might have turned out to be fatal traps, given the way Harley intended to bring *Carter* close inshore.

Messages at the local Russian Navy level were caught and translated from the fiber-optic cable tap. The organization chart of units, tactical boundaries, and lines of authority—previously almost opaque to Allied intelligence—revealed itself in crisp detail. The coding-decoding abilities in this military district were swamped by the clarion call from *K-Three-three-five*, and some people talked in the clear.

Amazingly, Jeffrey was able to hear Rear Admiral Elmar Meredov telling the leader of a regiment of maritime patrol bombers to get everything that could fly airborne. Meredov sounded confident, not cocky, fierce and direct, and on excellent personal terms with his subordinate. Then came an even bigger, unpleasant surprise.

"Remember my cardinal rule of sub hunting. Aircrews must assume that the first antisubmarine contact they make will not be the last. If one contact is actually held, you need to allocate forces between harassing that American sub and searching for another."

"Understood, sir," the regimental commander said.

"Don't forget to have them look in the least likely places, Aleksei, including our continental shelf and especially the noisy water near the islands."

This was useful to know for future reference, but Jeffrey grew extremely concerned. Meredov was, and would be, a formidable adversary, one who left nothing to chance and who knew that as far back as the Cold War, U.S. spy subs did sometimes work in pairs in Russian waters. *If* Carter *is exposed . . .*

Jeffrey intended to listen to the recording over and over, sifting and absorbing every syllable and nuance.

It took longer to see how the Russian strategic rocket forces reacted. Jeffrey, and everyone else in his strike group who understood what was happening, hated every minute ticking by. O'Hanlon kept reporting sniffs of snowmobiles and helos, fading in and out of his passive sonar detection range. So far as Torelli could figure, they were quartering the area between and around their pair of small islands. It also seemed as if they were examining the route of the undersea cable, wherever polynyas or flat-enough ice made the route practical to reach. If the two Seahorses still assigned to signals-intercept duty heard on their own passive sonars that someone was coming too close, they'd have to dip down beneath the ice and the task group would lose their vital electronic surveillance at the worst possible time.

Jeffrey gritted his teeth as a maritime reconnaissance aircraft roared overhead nearby, its slow speed of two hundred knots showing that it was on active patrol. It sounded different from previous ones, more of a throbbing whine than a growl. O'Hanlon said the engines were turbofans, making it a militarized version of the Tupolev-204, Russia's newest, most numerous model of antisubmarine plane.

Besides magnetic anomaly detection, with a mental jolt Jeffrey saw a whole other reason to worry: His two ships had been in one place long enough that the warmed seawater exiting their steam condensor cooling pipes might be noticeable on infrared scanners aimed at polynyas downcurrent from the cable tapping site—where *Challenger* and *Carter* had no choice but to loiter, motionless, hooked up to the fiber-optic lines.

His heart missed a beat at an even worse thought.

An airborne gravimetric gradiometer, at close enough

range, would see our reactor compartments, dead to rights.

Such airborne gravimeters did exist, used by civilian geologists. Jeffrey hoped that the Tupolev's speed, its engine vibrations, and air turbulence near the sea would impair the resolution if the aircraft actually carried one. Again Jeffrey felt like a fly stuck to flypaper. He was annoyed at himself for not realizing these dangers sooner, but there was nothing he could do to avoid them anyway.

The Tu-204 went away and nothing unpleasant happened.

But after ten hours of waiting on excruciating tenterhooks, it became obvious that the Strategic Rocket Forces never would react to Jeffrey's scheme with the Mark III decoy. The generals in charge, apparently, didn't see what an American fast-attack by the North Pole near some missile subs had to do with their ICBM silos far inland. They were too smart—or too paranoid—to generate extra signals traffic, only to have it intercepted somehow, somewhere, by spies. Jeffrey, disappointed beyond words, couldn't argue with their logic. In retrospect, this aspect of the intel grab was a long shot from the start.

Via the fiber-optic link between *Challenger* and *Carter,* he and Bell held a conference call with Harley and Kurzin. The decision they made was the only one they could make. Patch, release, and rebury the cable, smooth over any signs that the bottom had been disturbed, then press on with the mission. Maybe if *Carter* continued her radio surveillance while on the move with her Seahorses, something might still turn up. Kurzin stated darkly that there were other ways, once near the silo field, to gain the information he needed to help get inside.

Jeffrey already knew that Nyurba didn't like good-byes, and Kurzin certainly wasn't the type. He wrapped up simply. "Good luck. See you someday in a better place."

The two ships parted, *Challenger* going west and *Carter*

east. *Challenger* needed to keep up the cover that she was after the 868U at the furthest end of Russia. *Carter* had to put Kurzin's squadron ashore in close coordination with Jeffrey's schedule, or the double-teaming plan against the Russians would come unglued.

CHAPTER 18

As soon as he'd transferred to *Carter* again at the start of the second rendezvous, Dashiyn Nyurba had given a high priority to exercise. The rule of thumb for commandos in transit submerged on a submarine was to work out hard six hours a day. On *Challenger* this had been difficult, because her provisions for physical fitness were rudimentary. *Carter*'s Multi-Mission Platform, in contrast, included a superbly equipped PT room with two dozen of the latest workout machines—like a top-of-the-line health club without any windows, with rather Spartan decor, and with extra vibration damping and noise suppression engineered in. *She also has an expanded sickbay, with two experienced combat trauma surgeons aboard, to treat incoming wounded from my squadron.*

Nyurba could tell that he and his four SERT Seabees had lost conditioning during their unexpected, extended rehearsals with Commodore Fuller, when Kurzin had needed to send them back to *Challenger* at the end of the first rendezvous. By dint of effort and copious sweat, with Nyurba egging the others on, in the few days still available they built back toward the peak of strength and endurance they'd need in Siberia.

Tougher training now could mean less bleeding later.

As Nyurba climbed up the sail-trunk ladder and stood on the open grating at the top, the first things that struck him were the fresh, tangy salt air, the feel of the bracing wind on his face, and the immensity of the twilit sky above, a deep electric aquamarine. He drew in delicious lungfuls. He blinked to help his eye muscles focus, for the first time in weeks, at actual infinity instead of optical illusions within a virtual-reality helmet. He experienced, by the sudden lack of it, how claustrophobically confined he'd been inside *Challenger* and *Carter* and the minisub. Then, despite the extreme-weather clothing that he wore against the Arctic chill, he felt starkly naked as he stood in the tiny cockpit on *Carter*'s sail.

All parts of the submarine that he could see from outside, with the ship on the surface now, were coated bluish-white. This included the sail itself, plus her entire long rounded hull—and even the top of the rudder sticking out of the water, aft of where the teardrop-shaped hull tapered into the very cold sea. The radar-absorbent tinting, the first of its kind on a nuclear sub, had been applied when the ship was in dry dock; though the yard workers made jokes about it, the paint job didn't seem funny to Nyurba at present. It was a matter of life and death.

What was missing was the minisub, no longer carried on *Carter*'s back. Since it couldn't be deployed while *Carter* was surfaced—it weighed almost sixty tons, sitting high and dry—it had already been released and was waiting submerged with its two-man crew, away to port.

Above Nyurba, on the sail roof, two crewmen in white camouflage smocks—lookouts—peered through image-stabilized binoculars, their urgency and concern infectious.

Carter's photonics masts were both raised, though only by inches, their sensor heads spinning and bobbing as they scanned in every direction for threats on visual and infrared. The electronic support measures antennas atop both heads were steadily feeding data for analysis below; airborne surface-search radars were the ESM technicians' main worry. The depth here was less than ninety feet, and too soon *Carter* wouldn't be able to dive at all if she'd wanted to.

Nyurba didn't bother with binocs; he didn't need them. Flat ice floes, the occasional jutting berg, smashed-up bergy bits, and slush were all around. So were birds and seals— resting on the floes and bergs, or flying or slipping into and out of the water. Their noises were familiar; they'd been coming over the sonar speakers in *Carter*'s control room the whole time she worked her way southeast to the edge of the solid cap and onward into the marginal ice zone. Then she'd blown her main ballast tanks in spurts while the crew hoped the sounds, if detected by the Russians, would be mistaken for whales cavorting.

What was unfamiliar to Nyurba was this sensation of being so terribly exposed. Every minute counted. But this was the only way to get the German minisub into practical range of the mainland, almost a hundred miles further south through the increasingly less ice-choked and ever more shallow East Siberian Sea. From here the mini's fuel load was just enough to make the trip there and back only once, even at slow speed, and this would never do for shuttling eighty commandos with all their equipment to the beach. The idea of towing the mini once released had been rejected early on: *Carter* wasn't designed for it, improvised tow cables would foul her sternplanes or rudder, and any pitching in rough seas would whipsaw the minisub violently. It had been known for months that, as part of the overall mission concept, *Carter* would need to surface and serve as a special operations taxi until the distance to Russian soil became much shorter.

Captain Harley stood shoulder to shoulder with Nyurba,

in the cockpit that was officially called the ship's bridge. *Carter* was stopped, dead in the water. She rolled and pitched in the moderate swell, the same swell that made the chunks of ice in all directions bob rhythmically, almost hypnotically. A phone talker was next up through the sail trunk. He squeezed in beside Nyurba, but Harley already had an intercom headset on and was plugged into the bridge connection. He was frowning, his thin lips pursed, his blue eyes darting everywhere with a power of perception that impressed Nyurba. His own instincts from prior land combat screamed to crouch low, keeping his head down, but Harley stood extra erect, setting an example that all those with him were quickly inspired to follow. He took evident pride, even relish, in steering his ship and leading his crew into harm's way on his country's most vital strategic business.

"Control, Bridge," Harley said, "tell Colonel Kurzin we are ready."

Nyurba's job was to help supervise from the bridge—the highest available vantage point—and to interface with Captain Harley on any sudden tactical emergencies.

Thick round hatches on the hull swung open against their massive, hydraulically damped hinges. Men began to climb out quickly, also garbed in white. At the same time, three other men clambered up the bridge trunk inside the sail, wordlessly squeezing past Nyurba and Harley. One carried a scoped sniper rifle, wrapped in white tape to break up its outline. The other two each lugged a shoulder-fired antiaircraft missile launcher, with outer parts dappled in white. Nyurba helped the threesome reach the roof of the sail, where they took up positions and clipped on safety harnesses—also white, instead of red-orange.

The sniper's job was to scare off or kill any polar bears that came too close. Polar bears were good swimmers; they negotiated the gaps between grinding floes with ease, and tended to be attracted to any surfaced submarine. The missiles would protect *Carter* in a different way, from attack by aircraft, but only as a last resort if the Russians opened fire first.

Carter's topside, fore and aft, grew crowded with men from Kurzin's team. They opened locker doors faired smoothly into her superstructure—a low, free-flooding casing that ran for much of her length just above the actual pressure hull. With coordination born of constant practice during training, the men hurriedly removed and laid out heavy scrolls—like baseball field ground cloths, only colored bluish-white. Divers were lowered on lifelines, and they fastened one edge of the cloths to *Carter*'s port side below her waterline. Other men threw grapnels, attached to thick manila ropes, past the ship's starboard side, grabbing at the border of a large floe that drifted beyond a gap of fifteen yards of sea; the old-fashioned manila was needed because it wouldn't stretch like modern nylon. Still other men lowered cylinder-shaped bumpers, attached to nylon lines, into the watery gap on the starboard side. They each played out some twenty feet of line, placing the bumpers to protect the widest part of *Carter*'s hull, then fastened the free ends to light-duty cleats that unfolded from the superstructure.

Nyurba could hear Kurzin shouting angrily for his men to work faster. Two from the commando team, Seabees under Nyurba, came up through the sail trunk, standing on upper rungs of the vertical ladder, with more rolled cloths across their shoulders.

Harley noticed them, inspected the other frenzied activity, gestured for them to come up, and then used his lip mike. "Helm, Bridge, on auxiliary maneuvering units, translate ship to starboard until physical contact is made with floe. Make your rate of closing one-tenth knot." He sounded, if anything, jaunty, as if he were at a yacht club event—Harley seemed the type who'd belong to one, too.

The Seabees squeezed awkwardly into the overcrowded cockpit. They began to unfold the sheets they carried and lowered their edges over the sides of the sail, a twenty-five-foot drop into the hands of men waiting below on the hull; Nyurba's chief almost poked him hard in the eye with his elbow. The lookouts, the missileers, and the sniper led one cloth aft on the sail roof, making sure it lined up with holes meant for *Carter*'s masts, then wriggled out from underneath. They tossed the cloth's free end down at the back of the sail, then stood on the cloth and resumed their vigils. The Seabees fastened it to the other cloth, now draped over the front part of the sail. This cloth piece had a square hole cut for the cockpit, so Nyurba and Harley could see.

Captain Harley would speak into his lip mike now and then, saying things like, "Very well, Sonar," or "ESM, Bridge, Aye," or "On the acoustic link, signal minisub, 'Understood.'" His vessel was at battle stations, and he had the deck and the conn. Two Seahorse III probes were on station, wide apart, miles ahead of the ship, their stealthy antennas raised, passing live signals intercepts back through the tethers to the NSA specialists and *Carter*'s supercomputer. There was still a chance, or so Nyurba hoped, that they'd pick up something useful to Kurzin later.

Nyurba felt a bump and saw a sloshing of greenish water, as *Carter* eased alongside and touched the floe. Harley had made very sure that her horizontal sternplanes would be far enough aft past the end of the floe to not be endangered by the invisible, hard, unyielding underwater part of this gigantic slab of ice.

Men handling the grapnel lines ceased taking in the slack. Keeping them taut, they wrapped their ends of the manila ropes around large unfolding cleats, ones big enough to hold against immense strain.

The divers, back up on the hull, swam across and climbed onto the floe. The whole thing projected barely a couple of feet out of the water, on average. Its sides were a wet, translucent blue; swells would slap against it, and seawater sloshed and sluiced in puddles and rivulets near its fringes. Its middle, almost as big as two football fields joined end to end, was featureless and flat. Dry parts of the top were covered with what looked to Nyurba like white detergent power—recent sleet or granular snow.

Carter was made fast to the floe, whose smooth bottom extended twenty feet beneath the waves. The third Seahorse probe had checked, and Kurzin and Harley had agreed that, from the several floes they'd examined while staying submerged, this one would do best. Camouflage-cloth edges were passed across to the floe, and were firmly fastened using ceramic-composite spikes.

Kurzin, on the hull near where the minisub had been carried, shouted something. In a moment the phone talker spoke. "Colonel Kurzin asks, How do we look?"

Nyurba inspected their handiwork. *Carter,* draped in a tenting of camouflage cloth that extended over the water and onto the ice, would pass well enough for a medium-tall hummock at one side of a flat floe, a not uncommon shape for something broken off the edge of the pack ice. The cloth suppressed any heat signature and gave off a radar reflection similar to ice.

"What do you think, sir?" Nyurba asked Harley.

Harley smiled. "Perfect."

"I agree." Nyurba told the phone talker to ask Kurzin if they were ready to test the mooring lines yet.

"All men are off the floe and out of the water on deck, sir," the phone talker said.

As the hubbub of manual labors subsided, sea birds began to alight on the floe, and even on portions of *Carter.*

"Good," Harley said. "An illusion of normalcy."

"Agree, sir. Can't hurt."

Harley used his intercom mike, sounding as always brisk and precise. "Helm, Bridge, ahead one-third, maintain present ship's heading, using rudder as required. Make turns for three knots, inform maneuvering room that steam throttle will need to be opened wider due to drag of large moored load."

Harley listened on his headset, and seemed satisfied. "Very well, Helm."

Water churned aft of *Carter*'s rudder. The mooring lines creaked and seawater squirted from between their strands as they drew extra tight, but they held. *Carter* and the floe began to move, slightly crabwise until the helmsman found the rudder deflection that kept the lash-up on a straight course.

"Sir," the phone talker said, "Colonel Kurzin reports special topside watch is set to monitor for gaps in cloth and possible problems with mooring."

Harley made eye contact with Nyurba. He wasn't smiling now.

"Let's hope the Russians don't notice we aren't moving quite like the rest of the sea ice. . . . And that we don't get in someone's way in the Northern Sea Route shipping lane, so an icebreaker comes pay a visit to shove us aside."

Nyurba just nodded. He could think of other things that might go wrong. When the sea ice around them now began to dwindle, as they eased their way toward the Alazeja River mouth, they'd appear more and more like an errant floe with a peculiar mind of its own. Given the restricting bottom contours and extremely shallow depth in this whole area, *Carter* would have to follow a course that bucked the trend of normal floe drift. At least the prevailing wind and surface current were mostly in their favor.

"Phone Talker," Harley said crisply, "inform Colonel Kurzin that nonessential personnel may go below."

"Colonel Kurzin acknowledges, sir."

"Very well," Harley said. "Helm, Bridge. Right five degrees additional rudder, use auxiliary maneuvering units to aid the course change, make your course one-five-five. Make turns for four knots."

The helmsman acknowledged. Nyurba glanced aft. The white rudder shifted slightly, ropes creaked and ice groaned, and the floe began to rotate compared to those around it. Their heading steadied, south-southeast.

"We're leaving a bit of a wake," Nyurba said to Harley.

"Pump jet's cavitating too. Can't be helped. It'll die down somewhat when the floe gets up to speed."

"Understood, Captain. But what if an aircraft comes close?"

"I'll order all stop till it's gone. If a wake-anomaly ASW satellite's watching, even if they can pick us out from all this environmental clutter, they might think they're seeing turbulence from a misshapen part of an ice keel. Right now my biggest worry is the sea ice gets too crowded and we hit something big, or need to nudge our way through with force to keep going."

"Would the mooring lines hold if that happened?"

"Depends. We hit too much warm air, the mooring spikes could melt free on their own."

Nyurba grunted. There wasn't much he could say. He just hoped that this stunt was so reckless and offbeat that the Russians would never guess at the truth. In a few hours at four knots, with *Carter*'s surfaced draft displacing over thirty feet, her keel would almost be brushing the bottom. Even if the Russian Navy drove them off by nonlethal means, the mission would end in embarrassing failure—raising questions in Kremlin minds that would preclude a similar mission attempt in the future. The catastrophic result, Nyurba knew, as Commodore Fuller had put it succinctly, would be Apocalypse Soon or Apocalypse Later.

CHAPTER 19

"Weps, Bridge," Harley said blandly, "deploy Sea-horse III unit from tube six to examine our pro-jected track for obstructions or mines." This was the probe that had studied the undersides of floes, while the units from tubes seven and eight listened in for Russian signals. Harley waited a beat. "Very well, Weps." He turned to Nyurba. "Mines are doubtful in these parts, I think, but you never know. And an uncharted wreck could ruin our whole day."

"Yep."

"You can stay up here or not, Commander," Harley said. "Your choice, but please don't feel you have to keep up with me. You need your sleep before we make landfall. I rather doubt I'll get much myself for a while. ESM room says we're being tickled by Bear-F radars, now and again. So far, just intermittent routine search sweeps, but it could get exciting later."

"Captain, is that your way of telling me to sleep well?"

Harley grinned broadly, enjoying himself. "Take a nice nap. We'll be fine."

Nyurba turned away.

"ESM, Bridge, aye," he heard Harley say into his lip mike. "ESM, Bridge, wait one."

The change in Harley's tone caught Nyurba's attention.

"Commander, the NSA boys say they have something for you."

"What?"

"Here. Talk to them." Harley handed Nyurba his headset.

"Where's Colonel Kurzin?" Nyurba asked the phone talker.

The young crewman used his microphone. "Sir, Colonel Kurzin is topside, aft."

Nyurba pulled the headset on, and spoke to one of the NSA signals analysts. The Seahorses had overheard what was encoded as a routine administrative supply requisition, but the context—once flagged and decoded by the super-computer—revealed the schedule of the next shift change for the silo crews at the missile field that was the special ops squadron's ultimate destination and target. The analyst gave Nyurba the information.

"Captain," Nyurba asked with sudden impatience, "can the phone talker by the colonel be patched into this intercom?"

"Negative. The circuits are incompatible."

"Phone Talker," Nyurba said, "inform Colonel Kurzin that . . ." He tried to choose how to phrase it. Intel reports had amply confirmed that silo crews rotated every three days. But because of deception tactics such as dummy activity at Russian missile fields, no one could be positive when real shift changes took place. Satellite imagery analysts in the U.S. had, with care, formulated a best estimate. Now, too late, it was realized they'd been wrong. "Next shift change is in four to six hours."

The phone talker repeated this stark fact into his mike, verbatim, then waited for an answer.

"Colonel Kurzin says, excuse me, sir, he says 'Shit.' "

"Your boss is nothing if not pithy," Harley said.

"I need your rig," Nyurba told the phone talker. He returned Harley's intercom headset and donned the sound-powered phones. "This is Commander Nyurba," he told the crewman at the other end. "Have Colonel Kurzin put on your rig." He waited.

"Kurzin."

"Nyurba here, sir."

"If the next change is in only two days, then the one after that is in five days, not six like we were told."

"I know, sir," Nyurba said. "It's either that or wait for the following one, in eight days."

"We can't afford to loiter or dawdle! I won't add three extra days in-country, with thirty times the risk! We'd destroy our coordination with *Challenger* too!"

"Then we have to make the approach march over four days, sir, not five. The men will arrive exhausted, going straight into the assault."

"*Don't you think I know that?* We have no choice. . . . All right. So be it. At least now we know what we needed to know." Kurzin sighed. "Meet me in the command center in ten minutes. . . . We've got to rework our entire schedule and the whole damn duty roster among eighty men. Find different route waypoints and encampments, change everybody's man-packed loads, less food and more ammo. Christ."

"Sir, we have almost a full day before we reach shore."

"We'll need every minute of it." He paused as if he wanted to say something else, but didn't. "Out," Kurzin ended testily.

Nyurba gave back the sound-powered rig.

"More time pressure?" Harley asked.

"To put it mildly, Captain."

Before going below, Nyurba looked around one last time, at the austere yet beautiful scenery. Local time was midnight. But the sun, a misshapen golden orb softened by mist and fog in the distance, kissed the horizon in full view, glinting off intervening spots of open water. Kurzin for a moment felt disoriented and slightly depressed, in the same way he'd get from extreme jet lag. Something was wrong, something that made the vista seem like a landscape on an alien planet. Then he put his finger on it: the sun was due north. For days yet, until summer aged more past the solstice, the sun at this latitude would circle round and round the entire horizon and never set.

It seemed unnatural, although he understood astronomically why it happened. He took his leave of Captain Harley, and climbed down the ladder. As he reached the second of the two open watertight hatches in *Carter*'s sail trunk, he had a disturbing thought. All too soon, if things went as planned, he'd be unleashing new suns that were horribly more unnatural.

For a day, the strange little flotilla moved south. *Carter* steamed at four knots, moored to the ice floe. The minisub, small enough to stay submerged even in such shallows, followed beside, getting good fuel economy at such a low cruising speed. The Seahorse IIIs probed ahead and to both flanks, checking the bottom and airwaves for threats or new information. The special ops squadron leadership cadre, Kurzin and Nyurba especially, used the Multi-Mission Platform's command center nonstop, to revise their logistics and land-travel arrangements, since the NSA experts' signals intercept told them they'd lost a valuable day. The stay-behind support section, and the eighty commandos who'd go on the raid, ate and slept when they could, which was rarely.

The changes didn't just involve computer and console work. Most of over a hundred hermetically sealed heavy backpacks and equipment bags, already combat-loaded in the U.S., had to be opened, spread out, reloaded with a different mix of contents, and checked and sealed again, one by one. This needed to be performed in the cable-tapping clean-room chamber, under antiseptic conditions, to avoid leaving the slightest forensic trace—particulates, lubricants, lint—that would reveal that the packs and bags had ever been aboard a U.S. Navy submarine. The process was an annoying, exhausting chore.

Twice near the start of the passage south through the East Siberian Sea, men in dry suits had to cross to the floe, hiding under the tented camouflage cloth, and emplace new mooring spikes as previous ones came loose. Other men, in parkas and ski pants, stationed on *Carter*'s hull, often needed to take up the slack on the lines while the floe slowly shrank from melting, as by the hour both air and sea grew ever slightly warmer. Nyurba and Kurzin took turns overseeing this work. When free, Nyurba would climb down a hatch and go into the command center, to note the broader situation status on the displays.

Coastal sea surveillance radars swept over *Carter* wearing her disguise. Their signal strengths were gradually rising, coming from directions that—thanks to Commodore Fuller's trick with his decoy and *K-335*—presented few surprises and so far posed no risk of counterdetection as anything other than an ice floe. But Nyurba was experienced enough at combat to understand how radars would play cat-and-mouse. Some were mobile, driving quickly elsewhere after they'd given themselves away, to peek again from a bearing and range that might be a lot more dangerous. Not all installations would radiate during a single alert, to be able to electronically bushwhack the enemy later. That steadily approaching hostile shore held many unknown risks.

Nyurba increasingly felt as if Rear Admiral Meredov was watching for him and his team in a personal way.

Patrol boats with antiship cruise missiles more than once crossed *Carter*'s path. Were these patrols routine, or were they sneaking into position to get *Carter* surrounded where they knew she couldn't possibly dive? Three times *Carter*'s lookouts saw merchant ships go by much closer than the horizon; their navigation radars, once detected, could be tracked, and Harley made very sure that none were collision dangers. But the Russians sometimes used merchant ships for spying or counterespionage. Did these have concealed sonar rooms and passive arrays below their waterlines, recording every whiff of tonals and broadband that *Carter* gave off?

The closer the floe drifted toward the nuclear-waste dumping ground—with *Carter* surreptitiously pushing—the less Russian forces of any type came within visual range. The continental shelf continued rising. When the bottom of his ship got too near the bottom of the sea, Harley ordered that several variable ballast tanks be pumped dry, to raise *Carter*'s hull slightly higher out of the water. Soon, Nyurba knew, even that wouldn't be enough.

Kurzin told Nyurba to go forward into *Carter*'s control room, to liaise there with Captain Harley during the next step needed to get the commandos toward shore.

When Nyurba got there Harley greeted him, pointing at the tactical plot. "We're already in the bay, Commander." The Ularovskaya Guba. "See? The nav chart and the gravimeter show you the Indigirka delta, and the Alazeja mouth." Harley tapped keys on his command console, and the gravimeter changed from its bird's-eye-view display mode into look-forward mode.

Now the arrangement of seafloor and coastal geography appeared to Nyurba as if he were seeing through the windshield of a car. He noted the big navigable channels into the Indigirka River, and, to his left on the screen, the two much smaller channels where the Alazeja River forked five miles before its outlet, creating a thin, low-lying island in midstream. The tactical plot showed the island was unoccupied—Nyurba knew it was totally lifeless.

"Now we can't avoid some noise," Harley said. "I'm counting on chaotic thermal updrafts from heat sources on the bottom, and turbulent river outflows, to keep anybody from noticing."

"Understood, Captain." Nyurba shuddered to think of what made that heat.

"Sir," the control room phone talker said, "Colonel Kurzin reports men are in position on superstructure."

"Very well. Helm, all stop."

They waited for the ship's and the floe's momentum to come off. This didn't take long—the front of the floe made a lot of water resistance, like a barge.

"Phone Talker, tell Colonel Kurzin to stand by to adjust mooring lines as needed."

"Colonel Kurzin acknowledges, sir."

"Chief of the Watch, blow more air into all main ballast tank groups as needed to reduce ship's draft by three feet."

"More air, all groups, as needed, reduce draft by three feet, aye, sir," *Carter*'s chief of the boat answered. Lanky and dour, he was quite a contrast to *Challenger*'s COB in both build and personality, Nyurba thought to himself.

He heard the hiss of high-pressure air. He knew that submarines could adjust their depth at the keel this way, to some extent; being surfaced wasn't an all-or-nothing proposition. But the more their hulls were lifted up, especially at the stern, the more their propulsors would cavitate—a distinctive hissing sound—or even throb, called blade-rate. If the COB wasn't careful and deft, extra air might leak out through the open bottoms of the ballast tanks, bubbling to the surface alongside the hull, the worst acoustic giveaway of all.

Harley's previous jauntiness up on the bridge had deserted him. With the added effort of pushing the ice floe, starting from a dead stop could make *Carter*'s pump jet, bordering on the ocean-to-atmosphere interface, suck vacuum. The propulsion shaft would race, potentially causing permanent damage. The noise transient—a new one for the typical Russian sonar technician—would be impossible to miss. All the effort to convince Meredov that the floe was just a floe—by pushing it to the last place anyone in their right mind would want to approach—could be squandered in five seconds flat.

And no matter how quiet *Carter* could be, her ruse might not hold up forever. She still faced a long trip surfaced like this, as Nyurba and Harley well knew. After the commando dropoff, *Carter* and the floe would make their way back to the marginal ice zone—it having looked then like the floe had drifted in a giant U that trended from west to east with the prevailing current and the variable winds. Harley's men would take in the camouflage cover, detach from the floe, and submerge. *Carter* would then begin a whole new series of difficult actions to get ready to pick up the surviving squadron members with maximum stealth, several days hence.

Carter had eased in as close to the beach as she could. It was time for the commando team to switch to a smaller taxi. They were in a location meant to be the seemingly least likely point of covert entry that mission planners could possibly conceive of. Self-preservation alone should discourage Russian forces from searching this place. Satellite surveillance had appeared to confirm the fact. But that didn't mean that Kurzin and his followers were safe—not by any stretch of the imagination.

Nyurba would lead the first ten-man group in their short underwater crossing to the minisub. From swim fins and scuba rebreathers, to dry suits and dive masks and weapons and everything else, what they wore or used or carried was

Russian-made. Russia's borders were porous, and a brisk underground bazaar of military equipment was constantly active. Nyurba knew that sometimes corrupt supply non-coms, or disaffected and demoralized soldier-draftees, often heroin addicts, would sell anything for hard cash, even to their enemies—especially on the steadily smoldering Chechen front, or along Russia's newly tense border with China.

The group, tethered in dive-buddy pairs, did final checks inside the jam-packed airlock chamber in *Carter*'s Multi-Mission Platform. Constituted temporarily as a point element for the squadron, they were by background a mix of Navy SEAL or Seabee, Marine Recon, Army Ranger or Green Beret or Delta Force, and Air Force Special Operations Squadron shadow warriors. From here they would put into practice armed forces jointness to the full, as they had in training for most of a year. They were part of a hand-picked elite from within the elites, and they knew it. Nyurba was proud to be leading them.

They each, in their own way, showed the mix of eagerness and fear that he himself was feeling, the indescribable high that always preceded mission insertion. They placed their rebreather mouthpieces between their teeth, verified that their oxygen supplies were good, and made "okay" hand signs to Nyurba.

"Don radiation suits and watertight hoods," he ordered tersely. "Fins over the suit booties."

The radiation suits were thick and heavy. The hoods had Plexiglas window plates. Everyone helped their buddy use Velcro strips to bind the suits as snugly as they could to their bodies and gear, working from the legs upward. This was to squeeze out air pockets that might otherwise make them too buoyant—they'd pop to the surface like beach balls, helpless. If they forgot to exhale rapidly, an uncontrolled ascent could burst their lungs.

Once the hoods were fastened on, the scuba rebreathers became the men's self-contained respirators.

They put on uninflated buoyancy-compensation vests—adjustable life jackets—over the suits. They strapped titanium dive knives to their left arms; these were survival tools, not weapons. Special weight belts went on last, so they could come off first if anyone did get into trouble.

Nyurba signaled to the command center that the chamber was ready to be equalized. Air hissed in, increasingly, to match the pressure of the sea outside. Everyone swallowed to clear their eardrums. The pressure, for scuba divers, was mild, less than double the norm at sea level. It squeezed their suits and pressed hood windows against the dive masks covering their faces.

A SEAL chief opened the bottom hatch. In pairs, with Nyurba and his dive buddy going last, they sat on the edge of the hatch, holding in their laps their seawater-proof backpacks and equipment bags, which were tethered to their waists. These had floatation bladders, to make them neutrally buoyant. They slipped into the pitch-black water, and disappeared.

Carter's chemo-sensors had already thoroughly tested this area for toxins.

You would not want to swim in this water without a radiation suit.

<hr />

Nyurba and his buddy—a Marine Recon gunnery sergeant—slid into the water. They fell a very short distance and landed feet-first on hard sand. On foot, in slow motion because of water drag, they moved out from under *Carter*'s hull and her shadow as fast as they could; they had to crouch because the clearance was so small. Pockets of less salty water, thanks to the freshwater rivers, provided less lift to any object compared to regular seawater; if such a pocket drifted under *Carter* they'd be squashed like insects—the ship, even with ballast tanks blown empty, weighed more than ten thousand tons. From the surface swells alone the hull heaved up and down enough to make the diver lockout evolution be one hair-raising experience.

Nyurba heard moaning and popping sounds from the floe attached to *Carter*'s other side, but such effects from any big floe were typical. He opened a tiny cover on the ship's hull and rotated a handle, to signal to the command center that the chamber was ready for its next load of men, in case the chamber's video cameras failed.

Nyurba's dry suit, layered inside his radiation suit, helped keep him warm. Even so, he felt a chill go up his spine. The water here was clear enough to see the edge of the dumping ground. The surface of the bay overhead, an undulating sheet of green discolored with hazy brown, gave uneven but adequate light that shone in rippling streaks—distorted sunbeams. The water was utterly lifeless, not a fish or eel or even a stalk of seaweed in sight.

What caught his eyes were eerie blue glows, where fresh spent fuel rods from nuclear reactors had been discarded carelessly. He also saw dozens of barrels, some of them rusted through and leaking, in haphazard piles. What gave him the willies, most of all, was the huge cylinder lying on the bottom, so big that its top must extend near the surface, so long that both ends were lost in the murk to Nyurba's right and left. It was a derelict Russian sub, scuttled here, probably after being used for a while as a mobile nuclear power plant. Nyurba thought that this idea in itself was clever of the Kremlin, since Siberia, supercharged with rampant resource extraction, had an insatiable demand for electrical power. Vessels afloat that the Russian Navy couldn't afford to keep battleworthy were still able to produce many valuable megawatt-hours. The casual discarding of the vessel once her reactor core was aged out, in contrast, he found abhorrent. She lay with her keel toward Nyurba, masking her sail and superstructure; he had no idea what class of sub she might be. But there were cracks in her hull, through which seawater circulated freely— maybe these fractures resulted from her scuttling, or afterward from storms and winter punishment by bergs. He wondered how many other subs had been dumped here, and how much of the waste in this area had been accepted from foreign countries in exchange for hefty fees. He glanced at his portable radiation instruments. The readings were more than sufficient to hurry him along.

He knew that uranium or plutonium inhaled in tiny amounts caused cancer—symptoms took years or decades to show, and the cancer might be curable. But lighter radio-active isotopes, by-products of nuclear fission that built up by the tons in spent reactor cores, gave off vastly higher rems per hour—acute radiation sickness would kill within days. Outside his suit he was being bathed in offal from dead cores. The slightest leak and a hellish cocktail of strontium, cesium, barium, and yttrium would envelop his flesh and penetrate bodily orifices. He'd never live to reach the missile site, let alone launch armed ICBMs.

Doing this is insanity.

Nyurba tried to steady his respiration rate. The rebreathers had an endurance of about ten hours for a physically fit man exerting himself. Oxygen from a small pressurized tank would be added to the air Nyurba exhaled, while chemicals would scrub it of carbon dioxide, releasing more oxygen—and he'd breathe it again. He and his dive buddy trudged along the seafloor to the hovering minisub. They handed their equipment bags to men already inside, then with their help climbed up through the open bottom hatch, into the mini's hyperbaric chamber. Nyurba reached for and lifted the bottom hatch until it shut, then turned the wheel to make it watertight.

The two-man crew in the forward compartment reduced the chamber's air pressure to one atmosphere. Nyurba and his dive buddy went into the transport compartment. They took seats, fully garbed like the others, still using their respirators. The crew in front kept the pressure-proof hatch to the control compartment dogged, and Nyurba knew why. Everything in the minisub aft of that hatch was badly contaminated by poisons the dripping-wet point team had unavoidably carried aboard.

And there'll be seven more shuttle trips like this before the entire squadron's ashore.

The eight-foot-high minisub brought Nyurba and his people as close to the beach as it could. The water was twelve feet deep, and the surf zone was a mile away.

The men climbed down through the open bottom hatch, crawling into the narrow space between the mini's hull and the seafloor, much as they'd done under *Carter* herself twenty minutes ago.

The water here was unspeakably filthy, and almost completely opaque. The men all tethered themselves together, in single file, by feel, using lanyards.

Nyurba led the way, guided by a glow-in-the-dark miniature inertial navigation system strapped to his wrist. He also held a waterproof mine detector, using it to check the mud and stones on the bottom in front of him. He wondered how well it would work in these conditions. Stray bits of metal debris, scattered on the bottom, forced him and the parade of divers behind to sidestep often—nothing they walked on exploded.

It took more than an hour of this, underwater, to get close to shore. As nonchalantly as they could, they proceeded along the bottom until, one by one, their heads and then their torsos broke the surface. They wiped their hood faceplates as clean as they could; Nyurba's view was streaked by oil and worse.

Nyurba looked around, catching his first glimpse of his ancestral homeland—now to him foreign soil whose sovereignty he was violating in direct contravention of international law. After they dressed in Russian Army Spetsnaz uniforms, having come here to commit acts of war, if captured he and his men could—according to the Geneva Conventions as Moscow might choose to interpret them—be summarily executed by firing squad.

Terrific. Welcome to the old country.

The looming threat didn't really bother Nyurba. He and his men had arrived to kill or be killed. His rules of engagement said that lethal force was authorized to preserve the security of the operation, and no one could let themselves be taken alive. Each squadron member had a cyanide pill and a pistol; the medics were bringing enough morphine syrettes to—if need be—put all of them to sleep forever. He knew that real Spetsnaz in wartime worked the same way.

The terrain to Nyurba's front was barren and flat, the Arctic tundra on the fringe of the Kolyma Lowland. The sound of the surf was muted by his antiradiation hood. The wind was strong, maybe fifteen knots, and blew in his face, off the land.

They pressed on, plodding through the thigh-high breaking waves that shoved and tugged at their bodies, and onto a strip of gravel that crunched beneath their swim fins and Kevlar combat bootie heels. The mine detector still hadn't found any mines. The tidal range was modest, but the high-water line was well inland because the beach slope was so gradual. The high-water line was discolored with scum and goo in livid green, sickly pink, and clotted black. Dead fish and dead birds floated among the waves or lay decomposing on the gravel; others had been reduced by hardy bacteria to skeletons, or to nothing but scattered bleached bones and bits of feathers. Nyurba was very glad that his suit and respirator kept out the smells. He saw no sign whatsoever of seals or polar bears, and wasn't surprised.

The team made no attempt at concealment. They didn't remove their firearms from the waterproof equipment bags—not yet. Their radiation suits were colored blaze orange, for maximum visibility. From now on only Russian would be spoken. The intention was to hide in plain sight.

Their cover story for this mission phase, in the unlikely case that someone came along the beach and asked, was straightforward: They were Navy Spetsnaz troops on a training operation, infiltrating a simulated nuclear battlefield. *And it isn't so "simulated."* They'd locked out of a secret compartment below the waterline of a passing merchant ship beyond the horizon, then used undersea scooters to get close to shore. They were part of a larger unit that was following, who would climb out of the waves soon to join up.

None of the men carried papers or any ID, since Spetsnaz wouldn't do so on a practice or full-blown op—nor would rogues or terrorists, or German *Kampfschwimmer* pretending to be Russian rogues or terrorists.

Nyurba reached for his respirator mouthpiece, and grabbed it with his gloved hand through the flexible material of his hood—this way he could speak. He told the nine guys with him to rest while they had the opportunity, then inserted the respirator back between his teeth. They put down their backpacks and bags, unfastened their tethers and lanyards, and removed the Velcro straps—no longer needed—from around their suits, so they could move about more freely. Even so, their walking was slower than normal, ponderous and deliberate; out of the water, the radiation suits and respirators inside were heavy.

Nyurba glanced out to sea. He examined the lonely floe and its hummock, only four miles away. From here, the camouflage was convincing. The birds that had roosted on it earlier were gone. The horizon in that direction was hazy from mist. The sun was to his right as he gazed at the water, low in the sky, northeast. It provided a glaring, diffuse light through thin overcast.

It occurred to Nyurba that today was the Fourth of July. *Happy birthday, America. The big fireworks haven't started.*

Nyurba used his instruments to make and record more measurements of the water, the air, and the grit between the larger pieces of gravel. He used a sample kit to collect small portions of the different-colored goos. This information would be of great importance soon, and later.

Not only would he study it to advise the squadron on which decontamination techniques to follow, and what German-made detoxifying medications to take. Eventually, if they returned from the mission, the data would be invaluable to environmental scientists in the U.S. already planning the postwar global cleanup effort. Secretly quantifying in detail the chemical and radioactive mess in this particular climate, at this high latitude, would fill in crucial blanks, extending available data from nearer the equator, thereby bracketing the latitude range of Europe—still a potential tactical nuclear battleground. Far more realistic, efficient, and cost-effective methods could then be devised to help heal the war-maimed worldwide ecology.

He'd already heard rumors of wonderful things, such as genetically engineered pumpkins and thistles that grew in harsh climates, absorbed and retained uranium and plutonium, and were unpalatable to animals. Harvesting these plants, and disposing of them properly, cleaned the soil and made it fertile again.

Nyurba would continue his data collection, in different ways and for different reasons, throughout the squadron's march to the missile field, their assault, the unauthorized launch of Russian ICBMs, and their attempted escape back to the water many miles away from here. As second-in-command under Kurzin, it was standard for him to be the unit's decontamination specialist. As a Seabee Engineer Recon Team veteran, he had the expertise to assess this pollution meaningfully in the context of coastal and inland topography, soil drainage, and other factors.

I'm thinking too far ahead. First we need to launch the missiles and get ourselves home alive. As a Navy Civil Engineer Corps officer with an advanced degree in structural design, he understood how hardened bunkers and silos were built—and how they could be penetrated without destroying their contents.

He noticed a sign posted near the beach, with its back to him. Using the mine detector as a precaution, he went up the gravel toward the sign. As he got closer he saw it was made of corroded sheet metal, nailed to a weathered gray wood post. Rust from the nail heads streaked down the front of the sign. The post stood at a cockeyed angle.

He laughed out loud, almost madly, when he realized what the sign said. It was ridiculous, but it had been placed here by a government, a system that subsequent history showed was transcendentally hypocritical and outrageously absurd.

The sign, so faded and stained it was barely legible, warned labor camp escapees that the swim from here to Alaska was two thousand kilometers. It said that their labor belonged to the Soviet State. They should go back to camp and turn themselves in and they wouldn't be punished.

He wondered what incredible idiot had ever thought to put such a notice here. He wondered if anyone it was meant for had ever, once, been by to see it. It was an emblem of personal tragedies, tens of millions of them, most of which would go forever untold.

Shaking his head in a mix of regret and disgust, he returned to his men.

Four hours after he'd first emerged by this beach in northern Siberia, the last of the eighty commandos came into sight. Nyurba knew instantly, just from the arrogant way in which the suit hood moved, and the bullish manner in which he walked through the surf, that his superior, Lieutenant Colonel Kurzin, had arrived. Kurzin immediately barked orders, muffled through his suit but clear enough.

Nyurba also issued orders. The squadron formed up into four infantry platoons, each of two squads. They moved out, crossing the beach at an angle, aiming for the nearest branch of the Alazeja's mouth. Nyurba stayed with the lead platoon, acting as Kurzin's deputy and monitoring for toxins from in front. Other platoons deployed to cover both flanks. Kurzin, with the headquarters platoon, brought up the rear as he had in the water.

The beach petered out. They stepped onto the Arctic tundra proper. Beneath their feet the permafrost was spongy; six feet down it became as hard as concrete, and stayed that way year-round. A mixture of compacted snow, sand, gravel, and larger stones, it was a leftover from the last ice age—excavations sometimes unearthed the remains of woolly mammoths. Permafrost's remarkable seasonal properties dominated, even defined, the whole look and feel of the different environmental belts of Siberia, before man's interference. In some places it reached two thousand feet deep. Elsewhere it was shallower, often overlying coal and gold seams, oil and natural gas deposits, or diamond chimneys and valuable ores. Tundra topsoil was arid and thin.

Nyurba and Kurzin set a grueling pace. It would be miles, and hours, before they advanced alongside the river far enough to get safely away from the offshore nuclear dumping ground. Then they hoped to find fresh water clean enough to wash the lethal sludge of radioactive isotopes off their outer suits and equipment bags, so they could remove the suits to bury them and their scuba gear in the appallingly polluted Alazeja's never-visited banks. *If the water isn't clean enough, we'll have to wash in it anyway. Otherwise we'll all suffocate when our respirators run out of breathable air.* The choice between severe radiation, and exposure to chemicals including arsenic, lead, dioxin, mercury, PCBs, and DDT, was unpleasant to have to make. But the clock was ticking in more ways than one, and not just on their air supply and the dosimeters under their suits.

They didn't expect to need their burdensome suits and scuba gear later. If the raid's plan came to fruition, the men not killed or severely wounded would make their escape at a much cleaner place, down the mighty Kolyma riding a commandeered high-speed boat, still acting as legitimate Russian Spetsnaz.

CHAPTER 20

The village of Logaskino near the Alazeja's mouth was a ghost town. Decades-old shacks and rotting log cabins tilted crazily, half-sunk as if being swallowed by the earth. Dreary Krushchev-era cinderblock apartment buildings, each a standard five stories tall, stood crumbling and cracking on concrete stilts dug into the permafrost. Without these stilts, which Nyurba knew were common in much of Siberia, structures heated in wintertime would melt into the ground; even sewer lines had to be laid on stilts above the permafrost or they'd twist and rupture.

With mineral wealth and fishing near here tapped out or killed off years ago, the occupants had abandoned Logaskino and moved on. The commando team gave the place, with its mountainous slag heaps and forlorn piles of rusting machinery, a very wide berth. Siberia was full of ghost towns, each a monument to broken dreams and once-close, now scattered and lost communities.

They intended to use the Alazeja's bed to navigate. For a three-day forced march, the river would lead them southeast. At the spot where it suddenly turned sharply west, the men intended to aim in the opposite direction, east. Another day's cross-country slog should bring them to the foothills of the Oloy Range—and the densely forested taiga where the missile silos hid. Because the silo crew-change timing was tighter by twenty-four hours compared to what they'd been led to expect, they hadn't a moment to waste.

Out of their radiation suits and dry suits and respirators, the men would, of necessity, cover more than fifty miles a day. Now they wore Army Spetsnaz camouflage fatigues and ceramic battle helmets, waterproof boots, and backpacks weighing nearly one hundred pounds; the mild weather and steady exertion ruled out parkas or thick pants. The fatigues were specially treated to be impervious to chemical weapons and also repellent to insects; the trouser bottoms were tucked into their boots.

Other equipment festooned their belts, bulged in their cargo pockets, or hung from load-bearing vests on the front of their torsos. Most carried their AN-94 Abakan assault rifles by the sling, over a shoulder. A hand at any one time gripped their Abakans, ready for instant use. The bayonets were in scabbards attached to their belts. Fighting knives—each man chose his favorite—were slipped in the top of their boots. Spetsnaz PRI pistols in holsters were strapped to their upper thighs. Across their bellies, in slots of the load-bearing vests, each man bore a dozen sixty-round box magazines for the AN-94s. Under these vests they wore state-of-the-art, nonconstricting lightweight body armor. In each squad two men had grenade launchers clipped under the barrels of their Abakans. The squadron was well supplied with shoulder-fired antitank and antiaircraft missile launchers too. Several men carried SVD sniper rifles instead of Abakans—long-barreled, futuristic, and deadly accurate out to almost three thousand yards.

Before long everyone was sweating, their lower backs were sore, and their legs burned from the steady exertion. Since it never got totally dark, they would march sixteen to eighteen hours a day, with short stops to eat from their rations and drink, or rest and drink, then pause to make camp and get four or five hours sleep before starting the next day's trek.

———

As they moved away from the sea the first day, it grew warmer and warmer. Perspiration dripped off Nyurba's chin and soaked his fatigues. Unlike its wintertime moonscape of white, of snow drifts and blinding blizzards, in summer the tundra got hot. The permafrost was covered with moss and lichen in rich shades of green. Trees were uncommon, and stunted, just now budding halfheartedly, because their shallow roots gained little nourishment. Bushes and scrub, bearing red berries, gave the only variety to an open and endless plain in which each mile seemed the same as the last. Wolves, lemmings, and Arctic foxes populated the tundra in summer, but Nyurba never caught sight of one, or their burrows or droppings or tracks.

The team, following the river, saw a band of native tribespeople on the horizon, going northeast toward a healthier section of coast. His binoculars showed some were armed with shotguns or hunting rifles.

"Yakut," Nyurba said, "from the looks of them." They wore furs despite the warmth, driving a herd of reindeer. The men rode sturdy horses. So did some of the women and older kids, while others sat on sledges drawn by pairs of reindeer. The creatures were big, almost the size of moose, but their antlers were different, much thinner than moose antlers, and very long. "Heading for the seaside summer grazing grounds."

Reindeer did well on a diet of moss, lichen, and berries. The cold ocean breezes there would hold down mosquitoes and horseflies, which were starting to swarm voraciously and would only get worse to the south, and which drove the animals crazy—sometimes even killing them by sucking too much blood. The reindeer were bred for meat, which Nyurba had heard was low-fat and was said to be delicious. He knew the Yakuts liked to eat horsemeat too. They ignored Kurzin and Nyurba and their men, not a glance or a wave. Relations between native tribespeople and Russia's military were strained. These Yakuts clung to an old way of life, but the army still drafted their sons, who'd come back two years later sick or wounded, if they came back at all.

Nyurba guessed that the reindeer herd totaled about a thousand. It took an hour for the two groups to pass, the Yakut families with their livestock and the phony Spetsnaz company.

The contrast appealed to Nyurba's sense of cynicism. This part of Siberia was in the governmental *oblast*— region—called Yakutia, one of eighty-nine that made up the Russian Federation. When the USSR folded, Yakutia was renamed the Autonomous Republic of Sakha, but there was nothing autonomous about it; the new name fell from use during the strongman crackdown after the 1990s experiment with democracy failed. The regional governor, in the oblast capital of Yakutsk—a real city a thousand miles southwest—was appointed by the Kremlin. Representatives from Yakutia to Russia's parliament in Moscow, the Federation Council upper house and the Duma lower house, were hand-picked for their loyalty to centralized control. Local legislative elections were also corrupted, rigged, the majority of the winners always compliant to Moscow's will.

Sometimes, alas, democracy is only a phase on a pendulum that swings.

———

Nyurba woke up on the morning of the third day feeling stiff and drained and thirsty. The air buzzed steadily with clouds of insects. Despite his gloves, and the face net draped over his helmet, while he slept he'd been bitten. The mosquito bites itched and bled, and the horsefly bites stung annoyingly. He got up off his ground cloth—used more as protection from ticks than for comfort. He carefully reached into his pack for cream to prevent infection and reduce discomfort from the bites. His hand brushed past safed grenades and blocks of explosive.

Around him dozens of other men stirred, on their own or when their squad leaders prodded them. They made their morning preparations; an expedient field latrine had been laid out the evening before. The biggest problem was potable water, but the team had come ready for this with reverse-osmosis filtration systems in their packs. Powered by compressed air replenished by a foot pump, the modularized units slowly forced water through a molecular sieve. The water itself, obtained from rivers, rain puddles, swamps, or even permafrost melted by body heat, passed through the sieve, but everything from bacteria and viruses to dissolved chemicals was caught and held behind. Each individual system could make a few gallons a day, in smaller batches ready every few hours. A concentrated sludge, by-product of the filtration, was discarded. The filters would eventually get saturated and clogged, but they'd last long enough for the mission. *Drinking water from these filters isn't exactly what I'd call healthy, but it's much better than what went in. And it sure beats death by dehydration.*

In warm weather, special ops forces never made cooking fires, an unnecessary luxury whose smoke and odor could compromise stealth. All around Nyurba, men ate cold high-calorie breakfasts out of their Russian field-ration pouches. With medics supervising, they gulped down pills to prevent diseases common in Siberia, strains of which were vaccine-resistant: hepatitis, dysentery, cholera, malaria, and a long list of dreadful parasites. As Kurzin watched, they also swallowed tablets picked from a menu that Nyurba prepared, after he'd taken updated measurements of the environment. These German-made drugs included chelation agents to reduce heavy-metal poisoning, and other pharmaceuticals that suppressed the neurological and genetic damage caused by some components in the pollution.

Nyurba made a face as he drank—the filtered water tasted awful. It wasn't any better when he added a packet of instant coffee, stirring it with a spoon from his mess kit. Like the others, he had to lift his face net, resembling ones that beekeepers wore, each time he ingested something. Aside from being bitten again, it was hard to keep from swallowing bugs, or inhaling them.

"I'd almost rather just go without," he said to Kurzin as he stared at the bottom of his empty drinking cup.

"Nonsense. We all need to keep up our strength. There's nothing like a rousing jolt of caffeine when you've slept in the field." Kurzin smacked his lips pointedly, but Nyurba knew this was more from the need to try to clear the persisting, bitter aftertaste of the water than it was from any sincere delectation.

Done with his morning chores, Nyurba surveyed their encampment and its surroundings. Sentries had been posted while their teammates slept, and they were relieved by others to maintain perimeter security. Up to now this was mostly a precaution—while they'd walked all day and most of the night they'd met no one but the Yakut herdsmen, and no aircraft had come within miles. But each day brought them closer to their target, which they knew would be heavily guarded, the area around it patrolled. Squadron discipline could not be relaxed.

Their camp was on a type of terrain feature peculiar to this part of the tundra, called a pingo by native Siberians. It was a sort of blister in the permafrost, a conical hill rising a hundred feet about their surroundings. Pingos at this time of year were covered with coarse yellow sedge grass. Their slopes provided good drainage, so their footing was firm and dry. They also made excellent lookout points.

It was 3 A.M. local time, and the sun shone, dull red,

above another pingo to the northeast. Aside from the whine of insects and the occasional chirp of a bird, the loudest natural sound came from the river, a steady rushing and gurgling; the commandos themselves were virtually silent. Patches of morning mist, on lower ground, drifted in the slight breeze. Rising much higher above the tundra was a layer of smoggy haze. Wispy clouds floated slowly in the sky way overhead, but it was too light and too hazy to see any stars between the clouds. Nyurba took a deep breath. The smell of damp earth combined with something else that irritated and clung to the back of his throat. There was a smell in the air like burning wood and burning rubber combined with chlorine and ammonia. His instruments had confirmed what his nose was telling him, and had also picked up traces of formaldehyde, nitrous oxide, sulfur dioxide, and phenol—an industrial solvent—and coal-tar aerosol—yet one more toxic pollutant. The smog came from factory complexes many miles off.

The team geared up and set out on their route march once again. Now they wore pressure spreaders attached to their boots, based on a traditional local design of short and wide work ski, but plastic with upturned edges—like a pair of small snowboards-cum-water-skis. They were needed to cross the tundra, which was becoming increasingly soggy. The Alazeja's banks often gave way to stagnant marshes, which the men had to skirt. This area on their maps was marked *"Mnogo ozyor."* Many lakes.

"Many" doesn't begin to describe it. There are tens of thousands of bodies of open water in this part of Siberia alone.

Nyurba trudged with the point squad, as they tried to pick their way between the mushiest patches of ground, to find spots where the footing was better. It was wearying, monotonous work, conducted always under harassment by relentless, bloodthirsty, giant mosquitoes and big horseflies. The work, the perspiration, and the insistent buzz of the insects went on all day.

Some of the puddles they passed gave off a rainbow sheen, tainted by raw petroleum or refinery spills. Other puddles, miles later, were colored bright red from iron oxide runoff.

They began to encounter another type of terrain feature unique to the tundra and taiga. Year after year of wintertime frost heave created oval-shaped ponds and bogs, each surrounded by a ring of stones and boulders. Fungi grew on these rocks, giving them a silvery or orange tint. Mushrooms sprouted around the ovals' edges. The commandos wove between the ponds and bogs.

At some points the best route took them toward and then right along the Alazeja. Nyurba saw big logs, one after another after another, caught in pockets worn into the banks, or washed up in hordes on gravel beds at riverbends, or stranded midstream on rocks that formed small rapids. The logs obviously resulted from lumbering somewhere upriver—their ends were sliced by chainsaws and their branches had been lopped off. As the third day wore on, he must have seen thousands of these pieces of felled trees, from further south in the taiga belt. It was a sign of the chronic wastefulness of Russian fast resource extraction that they'd lose such quantities of valuable timber to begin with, and then not care.

Samples of the river showed it heavily laced with coliform germs—a marker of raw sewage—plus fertilizers, pesticides, and defoliants, even cyanide. The silt content was very high. Agricultural mismanagement on a monumental scale had putrefied millions of acres of once-fertile farm fields, turning them into poisonous dust to be washed away by thaw and rain, or blown away by the wind. Out-of-control clear-cutting made the erosion problem much worse. Nyurba detected traces of radioactive waste. He knew that underground tests had been conducted in Siberia, some military and some civilian, and fission by-products were leaching into the groundwater. The civilian tests had been for such mad purposes as mining natural gas cheaply, or digging canals. *Only in the Soviet Union.* Then there were the secret nuclear weapons plants, some still in operation, including underground nuclear reactors to make plutonium for warheads.

At the end of the third day, extremely thirsty and tired but on schedule, they reached their next waypoint, where the Alazeja turned west. Here they made camp on the slopes of another pingo.

Nyurba took more air measurements, and soil and water samples; coal dust and kerosene were problems. He chose a pond where the water was least bad, though acidity readings shocked him. The men drank from their filtered supplies, ate, and took more drugs. They reloaded the reverse-osmosis modules from the pond, working the foot pumps to raise the air pressure that made the things go, so they'd have more drinking water in the morning.

After he and Kurzin checked that the field latrine was properly established, that the first sentry watch was posted, and that the men were settling in with no problems that platoon leaders or medics had to report, Nyurba unrolled his ground cloth. He laid out the thin sleeping bag that provided him modest shielding from the ever-present flying, hopping, and crawling insects. He got into the bag, with his AN-94 outside on the ground cloth—keeping it clean and dry but within easy reach. He smeared his face and neck, even his hair, with insect repellent, arranging the insect net to protect his head.

He fell asleep immediately.

In the morning, everyone attached the low-power optical scopes that were a standard part of the AN-94, clipping them onto brackets to the left of the iron sights. By squad, they took turns zeroing in on the sights, firing at targets improvised from tied tufts of sedge grass. The tufts would shiver and dance when they got hit. The rifle reports were loud, but the noise here was acceptable because they were still in the middle of nowhere.

The stench of bullet propellant mingled with the natural odors and the smog. The smog was thicker than the day before, and had a different mix of chemicals; the particulate content was higher—soot from coal and fuel oil smoke from furnaces and boilers, and diesel exhaust. The men were stingy in their use of ammunition, as disciplined troops always were.

They collected all the spent brass. Then, squatting on their ground cloths, wearing gloves from now on so as not to leave fingerprints, they field-stripped and cleaned the firearms, including their pistols. The gloves were tight-fitting, flame-retardant and puncture-proof. Morale improved despite the increase in tension. Nyurba thought that using their weapons had helped to liven things up. The gunsmoke in his nostrils certainly gave him a surge of adrenaline, and of anticipation.

Kurzin addressed the squadron, in his usual curt and taciturn way. "One more day, men, fifty more miles. Then a few hours sleep, and we put in action what we've practiced for a year. *So let's get moving!*"

The team set out, heading east. The land began to rise. The ground was drier; the men could remove their snowboard boot attachments. The swarming insects never let up. If anything, they were thicker than ever as the men neared the tree line, where the bleak tundra yielded to the heavily forested taiga.

They began to see the first tangible indications of settlement. Cloth streamers were fastened to bushes, flapping in the breeze. Wooden and metal wind chimes hung from dwarfish spruces, making tinging and clunking sounds. *Tokens of worship . . . Animism, and Buddhism.*

By noon the land in front of them rose out of the haze, as blue-gray hills. They worked harder, gaining altitude with their weighty loads. The topsoil now was richer. They walked by jagged, crumbling outcrops of weathered slate and shale. Hummocks weren't permafrost pingos any-more—they were granite.

At 4 P.M. the squadron climbed a last slope into the pine forest. The trees blocked the light and the sky. Their trunks interrupted lines of sight, which previously, on the tundra, had been wide open. The shadiest spots even sheltered clumps of snow. The men acclimatized to these new conditions, spreading out into a tactical formation, more alert.

Some of the tall trees leaned against their neighbors, as if they were drunk. The men were still walking on permafrost, just a few feet down. Tree roots couldn't get much purchase before they hit the frozen-solid layer beneath the soil. Storms, or the tree's own weight, would make the weaker root systems fail.

They came to a clearing of dozens of acres, and passed what at first appeared to be a meadow covered by wildflowers. Butterflies and bees enjoyed the nectar. But then Nyurba began to notice clues to something else. Among the wildflowers were ramshackle lines of fenceposts, half rotted. Attached to the posts were rusted, broken strands of thick barbed wire. He explored more and came to a disorderly pile of weatherbeaten planks, with what looked like old telephone poles, lying on their side by the planks. Most of the planks were splintered and loose, but some, he realized, were still nailed to a frame, like a platform or a flat roof. Finally it dawned on him. He was looking at the remains of a collapsed guard tower. This field had once been a forced-labor camp.

There were no signs of any buildings. The inmates and guards alike had to have lived in tents year-round.

A death camp, pure and simple. Winters here, with the windchill, can reach eighty below. . . . Gulag executioners were often executed themselves. Dead guards meant no witnesses.

Kurzin walked up to him. "The corpses would've been buried, or dumped, or left where they fell, right around here someplace. We're standing on a cemetery."

"Siberia is one giant cemetery," Nyurba said.

"The direction the Kremlin's been going in lately, things like this could recur."

Nyurba just nodded, knowing Kurzin was right, and feeling angry.

"Take strength from this," Kurzin told him. "It embodies the reason we came. Tyranny, pure evil, the forces of darkness, they aren't a myth."

Nyurba gazed at the meadow. "I keep telling myself our job is to help stop things like this from spreading, from happening again."

"That is our job. A job, a cause, worth dying for."

CHAPTER 21

Too exhausted to be kept awake by last-minute fear or excitement, that night the commandos slept as soundly as hibernating bears. Very early the next morning, they prepared to advance from their clandestine bivouac to the final recon position.

"A good day for a firefight," Kurzin told Nyurba after gulping down his pills with cold instant coffee. He gave orders to safe and charge their rifles and move out. Metallic *clicks* and *snaps* and *snicks* sounded everywhere.

Nyurba flipped the plastic covers off of his optical sight. He checked the end of his AN-94's barrel for dirt—Abakans were made with an unusual figure-eight-shape combined recoil brake and flash suppressor, which was very effective. A bulky sixty-round box magazine was already inserted, from the night before. The safety, on safe now, was inside the trigger guard. Nyurba pulled back the right-handed charging handle and released it to chamber a round. The separate firing mode selector was on the weapon's left side; he chose the special two-round-burst time-shifted option, instead of single shot or full auto.

The air at higher altitude was cooler, enough to keep down mosquitoes. The sky that Nyurba could see between the leafy crowns overhead was cloudless. Worming between the tree trunks, scouts preceded the main formation with mine detectors, but found no mines, tripwires, or motion sensors. They saw no sign of Russian foot patrols—neither humans nor guard dogs—as they eased closer and closer to their target, but they did see scat left by wolves. Then, on Kurzin's command, everyone went to ground and formed a defensive perimeter where the trees began to give way to a big man-made clearing. Four snipers inched forward with their weapons to pre-chosen vantage points, now wearing billowy burlap camouflage suits they'd custom-made for the terrain and foliage colors they'd been briefed that they would encounter. The snipers were far more than superb sharpshooters, Nyurba knew. They were men of infinite patience, masters of self-concealment under the eyes of alerted foes, and with observation skills honed to an astonishing degree.

According to the signals intercept by the NSA experts on *Carter,* the supply shipment and the missile silo crew rotations were scheduled to occur at 8 A.M. local time. Nyurba expected that, unlike many things in Russia, these events would be very prompt. Hiding among the firs and larches, he surveyed the silo complex through binoculars. It was surrounded by a swath of open taiga a full kilometer wide; every tree had been cut down and the stumps removed. This no-man's-land was empty except for dead short grass and plant shoots, all a telltale orange-brown—sprayed by military defoliants. Then, within the huge rectangle of triple twelve-foot-high electrified fences—posted with warnings that the area between them was mined—there wasn't much to see unless you understood what to look for.

A concrete guard tower in each corner, plus pylons for high-voltage wire, many poles for floodlights—turned off now—and various radio antennas rose from what might almost have been an empty parking lot; the area surrounded by the fencing was flat. A metal guard shack inside the gate through the fence barrier was surrounded by sandbags as if to stop bullets or shell fragments. A chimney and an air vent in the roof of the shack suggested it was heated in winter, and contained a bathroom for the guards. Several guards stood in a circle, talking and smoking outside the shack, their AK-74s slung casually over their shoulders. Near the shack was a small sandbag emplacement, which Nyurba assumed was protection for a tripod-mounted heavy machine gun. Aside from two worn khaki-colored UAZik Russian jeeps near the guard shack, the enclosure held no vehicles. The guts of this installation, Nyurba reminded himself, were underground, dug into the living granite bedrock.

It looked new—it *was* new.

Within the triple fence, a scattering of squat gray concrete structures, with sloping sides to deflect airborne nuclear shock waves, rose only a couple of feet above the surfacing of black asphalt. These structures were the tops of the entryways to the silo control bunkers, protected inside by interlocking double blast doors. Nyurba also saw concrete roads, branching from the main gate like veins, ending in hard-stand areas for parking heavily laden flatbed trucks and mobile cranes. Most of the hard-stands were next to what looked like gigantic round pot lids, painted glossy white to reflect heat. Each of these was the top of an SS-27 missile silo. The hinged lids made of alloy steel—three meters thick and seven meters in diameter—could be raised hydraulically in seconds, just before a missile was fired. Each lid weighed eight hundred tons. There were nine domed lids altogether, as he'd expected from high-resolution satellite photos. Each was flanked by two openings, missile engine exhaust ducts—somewhere for the flames and gas to go when the first-stage booster fired. These were sealed by reinforced-concrete slabs designed to slide open sideways on rollers when the time came. Other, smaller projections were hardened inlets and outlets for primary air supplies for the missile crews and for the diesel generators that drove backup electric and hydraulic systems; some bumps were TV surveillance camera pods, or armored shutters for spare antennas. Nyurba could see the bulk of EMP shielding where every high-tension wire or antenna or camera feed entered the ground.

Three separate control bunkers were spaced hundreds of yards apart, each responsible for three missiles in their silos. Together this constituted an independent regiment of SS-27 ICBMs.

A wide concrete access road, raised well above the surrounding terrain for good drainage and less snow buildup, led to Nyurba's left from the gates and disappeared into the forest. The power lines followed a cutting through the pines, paralleling this road. Both led toward the regimental support base, ten miles away near the town of Srednekolymsk, on the Kolyma River. The support base, in a secure cantonment of its own, had staff offices and barracks, maintenance and storage facilities, and an underground command bunker. Srednekolymsk boasted all the creature comforts and vices—including sordid fleshpots—that a Siberian river harbor town typically offered.

Kurzin crawled up next to Nyurba. "The sniper-observers have seen no signs of life in any guard towers. They think they're unoccupied."

"Not surprising," Nyurba said, "considering the attitude of the guards at the gate."

"I expect they'll act more conscientious when the relief crews and supply trucks get here."

Nyurba glanced at his wristwatch, wiped of fingerprints and worn over his left glove. It was almost 6 A.M. "Pull back and establish our phony roadblock?"

At this roadblock, posing as beefed-up security, we intercept at least one silo relief crew. The team would learn from these Russians correct crew changeover procedures, and get whatever essential items and knowledge they carried in with them, such as one-time-use launch-order validation codes, new launch-key safe combinations, updated passwords, and valid IDs. Some of Kurzin's men would either impersonate a relief crew or force a real one to help specialists from the teams get into a control bunker. Their interrogation and manipulation would be greatly aided by fast-acting intravenous drugs the team had brought, made in Germany, the modern equivalent of truth serums and hypnotics.

It was the Nazis, after all, who invented sodium pentathol.

"Tell the snipers to stay in place," Kurzin said. "Have everyone else assemble on my HQ." Kurzin's headquarters was a hollow in an especially thick stand of trees.

Over his miniaturized tactical radio, Nyurba issued orders to the platoon leaders. He wore the radio's lightweight headset under his helmet. The radio was Russian special forces equipment, copied from American technology. The squadron's radios used a method to avoid detection or jamming that was similar to the undersea acoustic links of the subs they'd ridden to get here. Voice messages were encrypted and turned into digital pulses. These were transmitted on frequencies that jumped around thousands of times per second. The frequency band they used was normally meant for radar. As a result, the transmissions penetrated undergrowth and bounced around structures, to give better reception than regular radios could.

Except the team's Russian equipment had been changed. The battlefield encryption-decryption routine was German, one recently broken by the NSA. The frequency-agile specifications programmed into the radios were also German. Even real Russian Spetsnaz, with the same type of radio sets, wouldn't be able to monitor the team—which was vital to mission security.

And when some of the radios were left behind during the raid, their altered software would be one more piece of evidence incriminating Germany.

An hour later, Kurzin's squadron was set up in the trees that lined the access road, three miles away from the gate into the silo complex. The road curved slightly to avoid granite outcroppings, and took a steep grade down toward the support base near the town by the river, so this spot didn't have a view of either the base or the missile site—and vice versa.

Nyurba switched his lip mike to voice-activated mode. "Snipers, Nyurba, radio check, over."

One by one the four men confirmed that they could hear him. He responded that he could hear them, too. He requested a status report from the missile complex. The sniper-observers, hiding in the dead undergrowth in the defoliated zone around the fences, each reported that nothing significant had occurred since the main body of the squadron had maneuvered off through the woods. Nyurba acknowledged, and left his mike open so they and the rest of the team could get from him a running commentary on any developments.

Eight A.M. came and went, but nothing happened on the road.

Nyurba began to worry. "Sir, you think they did the shift change all by helicopter?" If so, leapfrogging any roadblocks by air, the squadron's task had just become infinitely more difficult.

Kurzin shook his head. "It's not that far. We'd've heard."

The team continued to wait, and wait.

By 2 P.M., Nyurba grew very concerned. "Sir, what if our NSA guys made a mistake? Or the Russians changed the schedule?"

"What if?" Kurzin asked sarcastically. By now he'd also

set his radio to open-microphone mode. "We could be here for days."

Around him, Nyurba sensed the other commandos reacting to having heard this, and he could feel their morale start to drop like an almost physical thing.

"Adopt the contingency plan?"

Kurzin turned to look at Nyurba. He opened his mouth to say something when they both heard a sound in the distance, from Srednekolymsk or the support base.

All four snipers called in at once, pandemonium in Nyurba's headset.

"Radio discipline!" Kurzin snapped.

The confusion on the circuit stopped. The seniormost sniper-observer reported, more calmly. "A guard in the shack got a phone call. Then he ran out and yelled to the others. They took off in every direction. . . . The guard towers and machine gun nest are manned. Tripod-mounted machine guns are now visible in each of the towers. Estimate them as seven point six two millimeter." Thirty-caliber antipersonnel weapons.

"Acknowledged. Report any changes. Kurzin out."

That sound Nyurba had heard was getting much louder.

Suddenly two Mi-24 Hind-F attack helicopters came around a bend in the road and zoomed by, almost brushing the treetops. Nyurba was lashed by the downdraft from their five main rotor blades; he saw tree branches sway. Each Mi-24's sides had stub wings bristling with rocket pods and missiles. There was a thirty-millimeter tank-buster gun on a turret under their chins, a Gatling cannon that distinguished Hind-Fs from earlier versions. F-models carried no passengers, just the gunner plus a pilot seated above and behind him. Both Mi-24s were colored a mottled matte green-brown, which made them seem businesslike and merciless.

No silo crews on those *lethal machines.*

"Kurzin, Sniper One," an edgy voice called.

"One," Kurzin responded, "go."

"An Mi-Twenty-four-F is circling the complex. A second is searching the woods."

"Kurzin, roger, out." The air now stank of sickly sweet helicopter turbine exhaust.

"Extra precautions for the shift change?" Nyurba asked.

"Not a favorable development. Satellites never saw this sort of thing tied in to crew rotations."

Nyurba heard another engine sound, different in quality. Heavy vehicles were climbing the road from the base to the complex—the only paved route in the area.

"That's our cue," Kurzin said tightly. Nyurba's heart began to pound. They and eight men stepped out into the middle of the road, their special forces equipment and Spetsnaz insignia conspicuous. Some wore cloth shoulder patches, others large enameled-metal breast badges; the main feature on the insignia was a pack of vicious wolves. Kurzin and Nyurba were both dressed as lieutenant colonels—hefty rank.

Instead of a UAZik jeep, or supply trucks, a BTR-70 eight-wheeled armored car tore around the curve at fifty miles per hour, top speed, painted dark green with black patches. Behind it immediately followed another, identical BTR-70. The front of each as it came on was a steeply sloping wave deflector; the BTRs were amphibious. On the roof, just behind the driving compartment, was a small conical turret with a thick machine gun barrel. Nyurba knew this was a 14.5 millimeter weapon—bigger than .50 caliber, it could tear right through engine blocks of soft-skinned vehicles, even disable other armored cars. The twin gasoline engines of each BTR strained hard.

He and Kurzin stood their ground and raised an arm for them to stop. *Since when do they change silo crews using armored cars?* The first BTR's driver saw them and blew his air horn. He wasn't slowing.

"Back!" Kurzin shouted. Both drivers swerved to get out of their way. Each nimble BTR-70 had a triangular-shaped door in its side through which infantry could dismount. As the armored cars roared past, Nyurba had time to see rifle barrels sticking from the gun ports in their passenger compartments.

Before Kurzin could order his men to take cover, the BTRs were gone, around a bend, their engines still roaring as they raced toward the missile complex, leaving trails of sooty, pungent smoke.

"They're in one hell of a hurry," Kurzin said.

"At least they didn't shoot at us," Nyurba said.

"Of course not. They think we're friendlies."

"What do we do?"

"See what happens next. Sniper One, Kurzin, do you copy?"

"Kurzin, Sniper One, affirmative."

"Situation report."

"Helicopters behaving as before."

"Any sign they've seen you?" The four snipers were out in the open. Effectively invisible to other men on the ground who weren't too close, they might still be noticed from the air if their camouflage wasn't perfect, or they cast eye-catching shadows from the low sun.

"Negative. . . . Wait one. Two BTR-Seventies now arriving."

"Confirmed. They passed us. What are they doing?"

"Wait one. . . . They've pulled up at the gate to the complex. . . . The gate system is opening. . . . One BTR has moved through the gate. It appears to be starting a roving patrol inside the complex. Six troops have dismounted from the other. . . . They've walked through the gate, and they appear to be reinforcing the guards."

"What's that BTR doing?"

"It's. . . . Oh crap. It's starting a roving patrol of the defoliated strip."

"Sniper One, can all observers withdraw to the treeline?"

"Er, negative. If we move we'll be seen from the air."

"If you don't move you'll get run over."

"We could trust to luck that the BTR misses us. The cleared zone is half a kilometer wide. Visibility from within that type of vehicle isn't terrific."

"Do you see silo crews being rotated?"

"Negative. No indication that new silo crews have arrived."

"Wait one. Kurzin out."

"Maybe they're prepping the area," Nyurba said, "and the fresh silo crews will come next. We can still set up our roadblock and waylay the crews and interrogate them."

"Kurzin, Sniper One!"

"Sniper One, I said wait one."

"Negative, negative. More troops have dismounted from BTR outside of gates. Troops are walking with vehicle as it proceeds. Troops are prodding underbrush with AK-Seventy-fours with fixed bayonets."

"Shit."

"Concur, sir," Sniper One answered.

Kurzin turned to Nyurba. "Ideas?"

"It depends on what's going on."

"They're searching for us is what's going on."

"Maybe not, sir. It could be Commodore Fuller's trick with his decoy finally made its way through the Strategic Rocket Forces bureaucracy. They might be reacting to *that,* regionwide, not to specific information on *us,* here, now."

"Days later?"

"It's Russia, sir. Or maybe they just found *Carter*'s ice floe with the scars from spikes and mooring ropes."

"Or spotted our tracks in the tundra, and all *real* units are accounted for." Noise from the Hind-Fs emphasized his remark.

Nyurba blanched. "I don't think new silo crews will come soon." The on-duty crews, inside the bunkers, had food and water for thirty days. Time was definitely on the Russians' side.

"All snipers, Kurzin, are any of you likely to be detected within one hour if you hold your present positions?"

"Kurzin, Sniper One, not sure."

"Kurzin, Two, very risky, Colonel."

"Kurzin, Three, one hour is touch and go."

"Kurzin, Four, iffy, sir."

"What should they do if they're caught?" Nyurba asked. "Try to claim they're part of the heightened security?"

Kurzin was fuming. "On their own? Suspicious Russians won't buy it. *Where* did they come from? *What* unit and where's the rest of it? *Who's* their commander? *Why* were they there from well before this alert got sounded? If they're guarding the complex, why are they all facing *toward* the complex? They *can't* reveal themselves. And we *need* them to support our assault!"

"Understood, sir."

"Kurzin, Sniper Three," came over the headset in a barely audible whisper. "They just passed me. One guy's bayonet missed my nose by an inch. They're using a widening-box search pattern. Next go-round, they have me for sure."

"All snipers, sit tight. We'll take the pressure off you." Kurzin shouted for the entire squadron to come out on the road. "Fix bayonets!" He told the men with grenade launchers clipped to their rifles to load dual-purpose high-explosive fragmentation grenades; unlike older AKs, the bayonet lug was to the right side of the Abakan's muzzle, not underneath, so that bayonets and grenade launchers could be used at the same time.

"Uphill! Route-march formation! To the complex, now, *run!*"

Seventy-six commandos with their heavy packs and weapons began to charge up the road in a column, four abreast.

"Look sharp, for God's sake," Kurzin bellowed. "You're supposed to be an elite! I want to see some *arrogance!*"

"Sir," Nyurba gasped between heavy breaths at the head of the column, "what are your intentions?"

"We're more reinforcements. Spetsnaz. For the complex."

"On foot?"

"Our trucks broke down."

"What trucks?"

"Let's pray the Russians don't ask until it's too late."

"What if a helicopter"—pant—"or a BTR"—pant—"goes looking for broken-down trucks?"

"What do *you* think?"

"They won't know to"—pant—"before we arrive."

"Therefore?"

"When we arrive"—pant—"we stop them from looking."

"Good." Kurzin halted abruptly, but waved for his men to keep going. "Squadron, Kurzin, contingency plan Khah is now in effect as rehearsed." Khah was the Cyrillic letter X. "We lie and cheat and fight and blast our way in as best we can. Follow my lead and take cues from your officers. Out." He ran faster than ever, then turned to Nyurba. "Issue your orders!"

Nyurba ran more slowly, to let each platoon pass him by, to address and steady them separately, and also to catch his breath. The men were younger than him, in better shape. Their boots thudded on the pavement; equipment jangled; backpacks bounced.

"Antitank rocketeers, *up*!" Nyurba shouted. "Antiaircraft missileers, *up*!" The preassigned men shouldered their AN-94s by the slings. They pulled long tubes from their packs, with aiming and trigger gear attached. Some had protruding, bulbous shaped-charge rocket warheads—reloadable RPG-27 Tavulgas. Other tubes had protective caps—disposable supersonic SA-16 Gimlets. They held these as their primary weapons, and blended in with the rest of the company rushing up the road.

The headquarters platoon, with the Air Force missile technicians and computer hacker specialists, came next to last for better protection—they were the least expendable men. The last platoon was rear guard. Nyurba double-checked that he could hear no engine sounds from the direction of the support base, and the Hind-Fs weren't coming.

"Antitank mines across the road, right here, from shoulder to shoulder! Same thing in the cutting for the power lines!"

One squad of ten men broke off from the rear platoon, then split in half. A group darted into the forest, the short distance to the lane cut by the Russians for their high-tension towers. The group on the road emptied their packs of mines—flat, round, menacing things. They lay them in a zigzag across the road, armed them, and carefully armed the antitamper booby traps. Camouflaged a concrete color, and put down just past a bend in the road, they'd be hard to see and easy to hit.

The other group would do this in the weeds by the power lines—that lane through the pines was the only alternate route, for tracked vehicles, up to the silos. It was easier to block off, since the pylons themselves made good obstacles.

Nyurba, satisfied, ran ahead. The miners would reunite as quickly as possible on the road. Their backpacks lightened, they ought to catch up during the three miles to the missile complex. In the meantime, they'd seem to any witnesses like the stragglers inevitable on a military training run.

With the mines emplaced, no more BTRs or troop trucks or tanks would get through for a little while.

CHAPTER 22

The fake Spetsnaz company dashed within sight of the missile complex's guard towers, with Kurzin in the lead and Nyurba running with the headquarters platoon; Nyurba and the SERT Seabees were among the nonexpendable specialists now. The security troops in the nearest guard towers trained their machine guns. Kurzin waved, then pointed at his shoulder patch and held up his AN-94—a distinctive-looking weapon used almost exclusively by Spetsnaz. Then he ran even faster toward the gate. Nyurba could see the high-voltage wires strung on ceramic insulators along the sides of each chain-link fence; their tops were festooned with razor wire. The mines between them—probably a mix of antipersonnel and antitank—were buried in the earth. The BTR-70 within the complex drove nearer and began to pace Kurzin's people as they ran along the road. Its turret machine gun, and the rifles sticking through ports in the passenger compartment, aimed their way; the other BTR was on the far side of the complex, continuing to patrol the defoliated strip where Kurzin's snipers desperately hoped to stay hidden.

One of the Hind-Fs flew overhead and noisily buzzed the commandos. The roving chin-mounted cannon's muzzle never once left Kurzin's column. Nyurba waited to see that threatening cannon begin to spit flame, but the helicopter kept circling as if to herd and corner the strangers, from warily inside the minimum arming range of antiaircraft missiles. The other Hind-F examined the site's outer border, the big square treeline.

The guards inside the gate looked very sharp now. The machine gun in the sandbags trained back and forth along the ragged formation of breathless, sweating commandos.

A sergeant among the guards confronted Kurzin through the three fence gates that sealed the complex from the road. He saw Kurzin's rank and insignia. Nyurba thought the man was suspicious, surprised, and impressed all at once.

"Kto vy?" the sergeant shouted above the noise of the helicopters. Who are you?

"Armiya Spetsnaz. Vy slenoy?" Army Spetsnaz. Are you blind?

"We're on alert, sir. We can't let you in." Relations between the Russian Army and Strategic Rocket Forces varied from jealous to apathetic, but any lieutenant colonel was hard to ignore.

"We know about the alert!" Kurzin barked. "We're on a field training exercise. We were ordered to come as reinforcements." The two services' radios were incompatible, so this claim was safe to make.

"The support base never heard of you." The man must have already phoned.

Kurzin sputtered in disbelief at such defiance of his authority. "They wouldn't have, would they? Use your head!"

"I suppose not, Colonel." The sergeant shrugged.

"Is your alert for real or a drill?"

"They never say it's a drill before it's over, sir."

A lieutenant came out of the guard shack. The sergeant was visibly glad to pass the buck.

"What do you want, sir?" the lieutenant asked.

"I already told your sergeant. We were ordered here as reinforcements."

"Where's the rest of your unit?" Eighty men was small for an Army Spetsnaz company. One hundred thirty-five was the official size.

"We're understrength," Kurzin said. "Like everybody else." He pointed around at the site defenses. "Seems to me you're understrength too."

The lieutenant looked insulted.

"What's the scenario for this alert?" Kurzin demanded.

The lieutenant didn't want to give out free information. "What were *you* told, sir?"

Nyurba knew that Kurzin needed to take a shot in the dark, and take real risk. What he said next had to sound genuine, but it could instead make the guards more cautious and distrusting.

"Raiders or rogues reported in the area. Intentions unknown, but this base is one obvious target."

"Of course it would be."

"We double-timed it to get here. If there's a coup going on, don't you think they'd start by seizing control of ICBMs?"

"What coup?"

"Look. Your defenses are flimsy. Where's your antitank and antiaircraft weaponry?"

The lieutenant gestured at the two BTRs and the Hinds. The helicopters carried antiaircraft missiles among their mix of armaments. The men inside the BTRs might have antitank guided missiles—the BTRs' roofs had launch rails for them, but Nyurba hadn't seen any missiles on the rails. The Hinds did have their antitank rockets and cannon.

"Like I said, Lieutenant, flimsy. Your armored cars and guard towers need much more infantry support than you've got. Two helicopters are trying to do too much at once already. I've brought eighty men with all their weapons and tactical expertise. With all due respect, you're garrison troops. We understand maneuver warfare. So will anyone attacking the base. And I don't like standing here bunched up in the open."

The lieutenant knew Kurzin made serious points. "We have our own reinforcements. At the support base."

"How long before they show up? Our own trucks broke down. How many of theirs will even start?"

"Well . . ."

"We're here *now*. And we have to assume this alert is real, correct?"

"Correct. So how do I know you aren't part of this coup? With respect, sir, you Spetsnaz people are capable of anything."

Everyone jumped at the sound of a sharp detonation. It came from the direction of the support base. Dark smoke began to rise above the trees. A vehicle had hit one of the mines—something coming up from the support base, as Kurzin and Nyurba had expected and intended. Guard troops and fake Spetsnaz stared. Flames shot high, above the treetops. There was another big eruption. The ground shook. A tank turret soared into the air, tumbling end over end, its long gun pointing wildly as the turret—itself belching flame and leaving an arc of smoke along its trajectory—crashed down in the woods.

"An ambush!" Kurzin shouted. "*We* didn't do that, we've been standing right here in front of you wasting time. For the love of Mary, let us in so we can deploy!"

The lieutenant nodded to the sergeant, who told a private to open the gates. Electric motors hummed, gears whined, and the chain-link gates swung inward.

The two Hind-Fs flew off toward the ambush site.

Kurzin ordered his men into the complex. Then the guards closed the gate. The men dressed in Spetsnaz uniforms began to fan out to cover sectors of the perimeter—getting closer to the guard towers and the missile control bunker entrances.

A radio in the guard shack crackled. The lieutenant rushed in to answer it.

Nyurba heard his end of the short conversation. "What? *Mines?*"

The lieutenant turned to Kurzin. "You—"

Kurzin shot him in the face. The report of the AN-94 was loud. The pair of high-velocity bullets made the lieutenant's head explode.

Kurzin opening fire was the signal for contingency plan Khah to roll into action. Men far enough into the complex for their rockets to cover the minimum arming distance in flight spun around, knelt, and fired RPG-27s at the guard shack and the machine gun nest. Nyurba and the headquarters company with him threw themselves flat. Each warhead had a pair of shaped charges, one behind the other, designed to get through the heaviest tanks equipped with external reactive armor—which blasted outward to break up the Mach-thirty jet of molten metal and superheated gases created by an antitank shaped charge. The first warhead charge sacrificed itself setting off such reactive armor; the second charge then penetrated the main armor underneath.

Shaped charge detonations created explosive force in all directions. The guard shack was blown into tiny pieces. The machine gun nest burst from within—burning fragments of sandbags flew everywhere. Nyurba, still lying flat, for a moment stunned and disembodied, felt himself being pelted with hot sand.

Assault rifles and machine guns fired in every direction with rising intensity.

BTR-70 armor was plain steel less than one inch thick. An RPG-27 rocket warhead roared at the one by the gate, hitting the vehicle's front dead-on. The double armor-piercing jets burned their way completely through and out the back. Gas tanks ignited instantly. The armored car shuddered as ammo inside cooked off. The triangular side doors blew open. Flames shot out, not troops. Pools of fiery gasoline spread under and around the vehicle. It sagged and threw off gouts of impenetrable black smoke as all eight tires began to burn.

The ringing in Nyurba's ears cleared. He was dimly aware of Kurzin's voice on his radio headset, shouting something.

Nyurba looked around and saw killed and wounded, from both sides in the battle, lying everywhere, whole or in pieces.

He was pelted again, by chips of asphalt and concrete. The machine guns in the guard towers, and the heavier gun on the surviving BTR-70, were spraying the area, taking a toll on their friends and Kurzin's attackers alike.

Their job is to protect the silos at all costs. Their own troops are being sacrificed to pin us down and decimate us.

Nyurba heard Kurzin's voice again, more clearly. He was using the burning BTR as a smokescreen, leading a platoon to get in RPG-27 range of the other armored car. But that BTR was almost a kilometer away, five times the effective range of the RPG rockets. His men fired smoke grenades to enhance their concealment as they ran across the wide-open asphalt. Each produced a cloud of white smoke, contrasting with the black from the BTR.

The snipers and other commandos were dueling with the machine guns in the four guard towers. Those machine guns fired repetitive short bursts. The squadron, all contained inside the fence line except for the snipers, was caught in enfilade—deadly fire from several directions at once. Suppressive fire from the men's AN-94s was having little effect. The guard towers held the high ground and their walls were made of solid concrete.

Then one guard tower, overlooking the gate area, shifted its fire, dueling with a sniper. He began to pick off the machine gun crew one by one. Fire from that tower stopped. Men with grenade launchers under their rifles were trying to land grenades inside the other tower near the gate, but their grenades kept hitting the roof or the outside of the tower, or missed and landed on the ground. Each grenade went off with a bright flash, making a dull concussion that

Nyurba could feel in his gut. Grenade fumes created a gray haze around the guard tower, but not enough to make its fire ineffective. Two RPG rockets streaked by the tower, one aimed too high and the other too low; both went off in the dead grass and started small fires.

"Antiaircraft missileers," Kurzin yelled in Nyurba's headphones. "Watch for the Mi-24s to come back. Expect them to approach from any bearing."

No sooner had he said that than the two helicopters appeared above the trees. The BTR crew, confused about who was fighting whom, aimed its turret at the helicopters and began to spit tracer rounds.

"Missileers hold fire!" Kurzin ordered.

The Mi-24 crews, equally confused, launched antitank rockets at the BTR. The Mi-24s were armored, very tough targets, hard to shoot down. Green heavy machine gun tracer rounds and bright yellow antitank rocket motors darted in opposite directions, leaving trails of criss-crossing smoke. The BTR, its rounds moving much faster, scored a kill. Pieces flew off an Mi-24's fuselage. A big chunk of a main rotor came off. The helicopter spun wildly and landed on its side in the defoliated strip, and its fuel exploded. A split second later a salvo of Mi-24 antitank rockets detonated all around and on the BTR. Flames came out of holes in its armor, through its shattered windshield, and from past the edges of the shut passenger doors.

Rockets and missiles on the downed Hind-F began to cook off from the heat of the fuel fire, exploding in place or launching themselves erratically. Some ran along the ground, setting more dead weeds on fire. Some took off skyward and disappeared in the distance.

The other Hind-F crew, enraged, began to pulverize all the men it could see on the ground.

"Missiles free!" Kurzin shouted. "Knock the goddamned thing down!"

Commandos knelt and fired their SA-16s at the helicop-

ter. Each missile went faster than Mach 2, and used a combined infrared and ultraviolet target homing seeker to ignore
heat flares the Hind began to launch in self-defense.

Missiles hit the helicopter, their warheads detonating. But
the warhead charges weighed only four pounds, not enough
to get through its armor. The helicopter zigged and zagged
but kept flying; its chin-mounted tank-killer cannon kept
firing.

Soldiers and snipers, on the ground or in guard towers,
continued shooting at each other too. Nyurba looked up
from where he and the headquarters platoon were still
pinned down in the open. The pit of his stomach felt empty.
The commando assault had lost its momentum. Russians
still controlled the high ground in the remaining guard towers, they had the advantage of air power with that Hind-F,
and time had always been on their side. The mission had
reached dire straits, and was in imminent danger of failing
at the start.

Nyurba saw a figure in the distance stand, with an SA-16
on his shoulder and another in his left hand. It was unmis-
takably Kurzin.

"Get down, sir!" Nyurba yelled into his lip mike.

Kurzin ignored him. He launched one missile at the helicopter, which did it no damage. He placed the other missile
launcher on his shoulder, and just stayed there brazenly
amid the drifting smoke and flying debris.

Kurzin achieved his goal. The Mi-24 turned to face him,
to present its narrowest target profile, even as the Gatling
cannon swiveled to bring him into its sights.

The gunner walked his fire toward the latest threat. Asphalt chunks and concrete dust churned, amid bright flashes
and zinging bits of white-hot, razor-sharp fragments from
the cannon shells. Kurzin staggered, as if he'd been hit by
some of the shrapnel. But he never flinched. Nor did he fire.
Cannon shells drew closer.

Missileers near Nyurba seized their chance. The whole
right flank of the Mi-24 was exposed to them, and the heli-

copter's weapons were all pointing the wrong way—a perfect setup.

Nyurba saw Kurzin disintegrate. His missile never launched.

The SA-16s near Nyurba launched. Three of them struck the Mi-24 at once, around the machine's transmission at the base of its rotor shaft. It couldn't take such concentrated punishment. The shaft snapped. The rotors continued to spin in midair. The body of the Mi-24 dropped like a stone, inside the complex.

Other men, furious that their commander had had to sacrifice himself, fired RPG-27s at the downed Mi-24. They intentionally aimed at the pilot and gunner compartments. Nyurba could see both men frantically trying to get out of their stricken aircraft. The RPG warheads struck, hitting below the cockpit windows. When the flashes and smoke of their detonations cleared, Nyurba watched both crewmen burn alive.

The commando group was still spread out in disorder, pinned down—and now leaderless. Nyurba was second in command.

"Rocketeers!" he ordered. "Hyperbaric rounds, target the nearest guard tower. Snipers, concentrate on the more distant towers." Only two of the snipers acknowledged. *The other two must be dead.* "Missileers, watch for additional aircraft!"

Two men had reloaded their RPG-27 launchers with the new fuel-air explosive hyperbaric rounds. These were designed for troops in foxholes with overhead cover. The commandos fired them at the guard tower.

The rockets soared away from Nyurba toward the tower. His perspective foreshortened, he could see their exhaust flames and smoke trails from behind as if in slow motion. But by now there was smoke and flame everywhere, and wafts of other trails from missiles and rockets and tracers filled the sky.

The hyperbaric warheads impacted the front of the concrete guard tower, below the lip from which the machine gun was shooting. They dispersed their fuel aerosol into a cloud, and a split second later the igniters set off the cloud. The guard tower was engulfed in a blinding red flash that created an overpressure so strong Nyurba felt as if he'd been hit by a hundred-pound bomb. When he pulled himself together, his ears hurt worse than ever and the guard tower was a wreck, chunks of concrete and bodies landing and bouncing on the torn-up asphalt.

Other hyperbaric rounds took out the remaining guard towers.

Suddenly, all firing stopped. The commando team had no targets. Medics were busy treating the wounded.

Secondary explosions from the Hinds and armored cars continued as more ammunition cooked off. Above them, Nyurba heard a deep *thud* in the distance. Smoke and flame rose anew, this time near the mines in the lane through the trees for the power pylons. More forces from the support base or the town of Srednekolymsk were probing this way.

Air began to whistle as it was sucked into bunker ventilator shafts. Filtered for contaminants, that air was feeding emergency diesel generators down below. The mine going off by the power lines toppled a pylon, shorting out or snapping the cables—main power to the base complex was dead. The proof was that seconds later, gray smoke belched out of the diesel exhaust shafts. This vividly reminded Nyurba that there were Russians, and SS-27 ICBMs, alive and intact in the underground chambers.

He stood, examining the battlefield. About a third of his men were killed or wounded, and another ten or twelve were occupied helping those who were hurt.

I've got barely forty effective combatants.

Timing was critical. Russian reinforcements would get here soon. The crews inside the silo bunkers probably heard and felt nothing of the assault, because they were behind such strong shock hardening and acoustic-vibration damping insulation. But the camera pods on the surface, aimed at the silo lids, fed into the bunkers so the crews could monitor each missile launch. They would have caught some glimpses of the fighting. And hardened, buried communications lines came in from the regimental command bunker at the support base. The silo crews would have been warned of a security alert hours earlier, since their normal rotation out had been postponed. Nyurba had no idea what the support base had told them since then, if anything, because he had no idea what the support base itself yet understood about what was going on amid the silo field.

Nyurba made a difficult choice. In this situation, he had to divide his forces. The only underground cover inside the entire fenced-in complex was the entryways to the three control bunkers. Occupying all three entries meant the company could give each other covering cross-fire against the impending Russian counterattack. The team had brought enough specialists to go after two bunkers at once; such redundancy was built in from the very start of planning, in case some Air Force missile experts or SERT Seabees were wounded or killed. But headquarters-platoon casualties so far were unexpectedly light; its role had been to take cover and save ammo, not draw fire. Going after two bunkers simultaneously gave the highest likelihood of achieving the ultimate goal—liftoff of at least two properly armed ICBMs.

"Let's go, let's go, *let's go!*" Nyurba shouted into his lip mike, projecting his voice so the nearest men could hear him directly. "First headquarters squad, take control bunker one! Second headquarters squad, go for control bunker two! Medics, use control bunker three entryway as a dugout to shelter the wounded! . . . Snipers, remain in position and feed me situation reports on the surface! . . . Everyone else, take ammo and explosive charges from the wounded and dead with you, and form up at bunkers one and two! Even number squads take two! Odd numbered squads head for bunker one! Five men closest to bunker three, proceed there to defend the wounded! *Forward!*"

CHAPTER 23

Nyurba, leading a squad of men, stooped under the concrete overhang that sheltered the entrance to control bunker one. The entryway was deserted, emphasizing the eerie lull in the aftermath of the violent open-air firefight. He quickly took the stairway down, and followed it as four long flights made sharp right-angle turns. He knew these turns were designed to help weaken surface blast overpressures and stop flying debris; he was almost one hundred feet underground. The next turn led to a flat area, not stairs. After a quick check for enemy microphones, he quietly verified on his special ops radio that the commandos going after bunker two could hear him. They responded, five-by-five. He told them to listen on his open mike, and follow the deception gambits he would use.

The man in charge of that group, a Marine Recon major, acknowledged the order. He was now second-in-command of the company, and would take over from Nyurba if necessary—the same way Nyurba took over when Kurzin died.

Nyurba had one of his men, a Delta Force sergeant, use a

tiny mirror to peek around the final corner. There was a surveillance camera, in a vestibule, all as expected.

Nyurba whispered his deception plan, parts rehearsed for most of a year and parts made up as he went.

His Seabee chief and a SERT petty officer pretended to be loyal defenders, retreating before an overwhelming assault. They removed their packs, then backed down the steps until they were visible to the camera, with their weapons aimed up the stairway. Someone near the top of the stairs, part of the entryway's rear guard, fired into the air, in case the camera had a microphone. To the echoing sound of these shots, Nyurba's men flopped over dramatically, facedown, as if they were dead.

The men guarding the top of the stairs fired several more rounds. Two Delta Force corporals fell into the vestibule—more supposedly loyal Spetsnaz, giving their lives protecting the Motherland's missiles. They landed faceup, writhing in agony from mortal wounds. In reality, they were unhurt, busy inspecting for a second, hidden camera or microphone.

There was none.

The sergeant reached his arm around the corner and shot out the camera with his pistol. The bullet ricocheted, but he'd aimed so the spent slug was unlikely to hit the men on the floor.

Soon all the commandos with Nyurba were inside the vestibule at the bottom of the stairs. The slain Spetsnaz came back to life and got up to join their comrades.

The stark and stuffy vestibule was lit by bare fluorescents hung on springs. In front of them loomed the outer steel blast door, the first of two that protected and led into the control bunker. It was painted an ugly military-institutional shade of dark green. Signs on the walls gave security warnings and instructions about radioactive decontamination. Just in case, Nyurba took measurements. He found no leakage coming from the H-bombs in the silos. In a full-scale thermonuclear war, these decontamination instructions would take on significance, but he wondered who might be alive out here to read them. He reminded himself that his mission, if something went wrong, might itself be the cause of that war.

Nyurba harnessed the ugly mixture of angst and determination these thoughts brought up, to bring more power into his acting performance. He started to put into play the next moves in an intricate, preplanned con job, one that he'd never have needed if they'd been able to properly waylay fresh silo crews at their intended roadblock this morning after all. He figured enough time had gone by for an imaginary counterattack by nonexistent additional loyal troops to have trapped and slain the pretend traitors—the ones who'd "killed" four Spetsnaz in front of the camera and then shown an arm with a pistol from around the corner of the stairs. He picked up the intercom handset that hung on the wall, so he could speak to the men in the bunker. The intercom undoubtedly was used for crew changeover procedures, but he had something else in mind. The crew still on duty would not be gullible. He needed to trick them, but what he said had to sound unquestionably true.

"Hello!" he said into the handset. "Hello!"

Someone answered, the junior officer who led the crew. *"Kto eto? Tcho takoye?"* Who is this? What's going on? The voice was husky, under stress. The accent suggested its owner was an ethnic Russian who'd spent his youth in what was now Ukraine, before moving to Russia proper after the Soviet Union collapsed.

"Slyshi khorosho." Listen carefully. "This is Lieutenant Colonel Nyurba, Army Spetsnaz counterterror. A nationwide coup is occurring." He felt safe using his real last name. It was common enough, and he didn't expect this silo crew to survive.

"A coup?" The young man sounded worried, but not surprised—there'd been failed reactionary coups against Gorbachev in 1991, and Yeltsin in 1993.

"Yes. Listen to me. Rebel forces have taken over the support base, and penetrated the command bunker there. We were able to overpower them here, so the missile complex itself remains in friendly hands."

"Was that what went on just now in the vestibule, sir?"

"Four good men died. My men. I feel responsible."

"What do you want us to do?"

"The rebels in the command bunker will try to convince you to make an unauthorized launch, or, much worse, use their electronic link to the silos to permanently disable the missiles. That would leave Russia defenseless against a nuclear attack."

"Mother of God."

"Yes. The situation is that serious. So you must do three things immediately."

"Tell us what they are, Colonel."

"Sever all fiber optics from the command bunker."

"We can't, sir. They're hardened."

"Don't you have tools for maintenance? For firefighting? Axes, metal saws, so on?"

"Yes."

"Use them. But first send men through the tunnels into each silo. Protect the missiles from interference by the rebels at the support base the same way you defend your control bunker systems. Cut all connections from the command bunker simultaneously. *Simultaneously.* Do you understand?"

"Yes, sir!"

"Second, ignore any radio messages you receive about either harming *or* launching the missiles, even if they're in valid codes and have the proper passwords."

"Ignore them?" ICBM bunkers had multiple communication backups, to assure absolute and constant control by the Kremlin.

"Do *not* use any radios or telephones, or intercoms other than this one, and do *not* respond to any calls other than mine. We don't know how far the coup's infiltration extends. Hurry!"

"You said there were three things, sir?"

It was time for Nyurba to build more credibility, to support the big lies about isolating the bunker from the support base and higher officials. He had to keep the junior officer from thinking too much, calling the support base to see what they said, or talking things over with the rest of his silo crew or the men in the other two bunkers.

"On no account let anyone into your bunker. We will defend the entrance from out here. More rebel forces will arrive soon. Stay where you are, you'll be safe. You can hold out for weeks if you have to, longer if you ration your food and parcel using electricity. When the rebellion is suppressed, the government will find some way to give you an unambiguous all-clear."

"What about you, sir?"

"We're Spetsnaz! Oo-rah for the Motherland!" He hung up.

Echoing down the concrete steps, above the roaring and crackling of the burning Mi-24s and armored cars, Nyurba could hear the heavy beating of more military helicopters.

"Missileers up," he ordered, to those with him and over the radio. Assigned men rushed up the stairs and opened the three dozen backpacks arrayed there—some of which had belonged to the wounded or dead. They went through this improvised ammo dump until their arms cradled bundles of SA-16s. Situations like this were why they'd worked out six hours a day while on *Carter*; each loaded missile launcher weighed twenty-five pounds, and the staircase was ten stories high.

Nyurba told his two SERT Seabees and three of the Delta Force to stay with him, and sent the rest of the men up the stairs; two SERT Seabees and their Delta Force teammates were with the group assigned to enter bunker two. The remainder of the commandos, he'd decided, were most valuable for defense against the superior forces about to arrive. The ICBM launch specialists would crouch halfway up the staircase for now.

Several men, minor wounds bandaged, darted from bunker three to strengthen the teams at each of the other two entryways. As this was reported by radio, Nyurba felt proud of their devotion, but knew full well how vital every man with a weapon would be very soon. Listening on his radio, seeing his commandos on the stairs or in the vestibule, he sensed their fidgety hyperalertness as they awaited the next phase of combat.

His own immediate task was getting inside bunker one—whose crew he'd just told to admit nobody whatsoever.

The outer blast door measured about eight feet on a side. It would be several feet thick, weighing tons. It opened outward, so that the overpressure from a nuclear blast would shut it more tightly against the massive steel and reinforced concrete frame. As a result, the door hinges had to be on the outside.

This was the whole design's weakness. Proof against the widely distributed force of a nuclear blast, those hinges could be attacked by a pinpoint placement of custom-shaped charges. There were four hinges from top to bottom; the armored steel of each was a foot wide and four inches thick.

"What do you think?" Nyurba asked the Delta Force sergeant, an expert in forced entry and hostage rescue.

"Three or four charges in sequence per hinge, sir. We need to chip away at stuff this thick."

The SERT Seabee chief, experienced at sizing up and taking apart all sorts of structures, eyed the hinges and agreed.

"Let's get to it," Nyurba told them.

They discussed the weight of C-4 plastic explosive to use in each charge. Too much at once would be wasteful, and dangerous.

They molded the first set of charges to the hinges. They carefully inserted blasting caps to obtain the optimal cutting effect and connected the caps with wires so that they'd go off at the same instant. They led a master wire and a backup through the vestibule, well into the staircase. The sergeant connected these to a detonator control box. Nyurba opened his mouth, covered his ears, and braced himself. The sharp, hard *vroom* that came up the stairs was deafening. The concussive force of it punished his insides. Dust and fumes drifted up the stairs.

"Time for gas masks," Nyurba ordered. Everyone pulled theirs on before running back down the stairs. The hinges had grooves cut partway in. They cooled the red-hot metal with water from their canteens, so they could install more C-4 quickly. Then they began the methodical process of molding and placing another set of shaped charges, inserting all the blasting caps, and connecting all the wires.

Three more times, they ran up the stairs, set off the charges, and ran back down.

The last time, the echoing explosion felt and sounded different. When they reentered the vestibule, the hinges at last were severed through. Lacking their support, the multi-ton door had come off the retractable pins, on the side opposite the hinges, that held it locked closed. It lay flat on the floor in the vestibule. The sergeant eased around the edge of the vestibule and used his mirror to look into the gap where the door had been. He fired his pistol, taking out another TV camera.

Nyurba and the other explosives handlers moved in. Beyond the now-empty door frame was the inside of the blast interlock, and at its far end was another, identical door. A mechanism made sure that, without special steps to override it—such as for installing large pieces of new equipment—the outer and inner door were never open at the same time. On the walls and ceiling of the interlock were shower heads, hoses, and other items needed for decontamination. Nyurba ignored these, and his crew went to work on the inner blast door.

"Nyurba, Sniper Two," crackled in his headphones, now worn over his gas mask and under his Russian-style helmet.

"Sniper Two, Nyurba."

"Mi-Twenty-six transport helicopters are landing on the road near the complex. Two Mi-Twenty-four Hind-Ds are approaching the complex."

Nyurba acknowledged. He needed to hurry up.

The Mi-26s could carry dozens of soldiers with full battle gear. The Hind-D version of the Mi-24 lacked the Gatling cannon, but still carried rockets and missiles—and the fuselage had a passenger compartment for squads of air-mobile troops.

Soon, from up the stairwell, he heard shouting and shooting. Russian reinforcements had arrived; his men were engaging them.

His team repeated their painstaking actions with C-4, placed on the inner door hinges. They once again laid wire and worked their way far up the stairs.

A very real Russian counterattack was in full swing. Nyurba's men in each of the three bunker entryways had their hands full, firing hyperbaric grenades, antiarmor grenades, and antiaircraft missiles, and expending magazine after magazine of AN-94 rounds. The steps around Nyurba's boots were littered more and more with bouncing spent brass and discarded grenade packaging, and he noticed backpacks and bloody load-bearing vests emptied of every bit of ammo of any kind. Fumes from bullet propellant and rocket propellant grew thicker and thicker near the top of the stairs, obscuring visibility through his gas mask.

A roaring noise outside rose to a booming crescendo—a rippling salvo of helicopter rockets impacted near the entryway. Nyurba saw the flashes and felt the heat, an instant before he was almost knocked backward down the stairs by the blasts.

Incoming bullets smacked into concrete, or screeched as they ricocheted.

The SEAL chief worked the detonator box. A blast of a different sort pounded Nyurba from underground.

He and his demolition team rushed down. The decontamination showers were damaged, the hoses were torn to shreds, and water poured from broken mains in the ceiling. They refilled their empty canteens and used them to cool the sizzling-hot hinges, to be able to set the next charges.

This time when they withdrew up the stairs, two commandos lay dead for real, at the bottom of gleaming, dripping blood trails; they weren't faking anything for hidden TV cameras. Over his radio Nyurba issued more orders, and received status reports. All contact had been lost with the sniper-observers. The men in bunker two had also reached the inner blast door. The medics in the vestibule of bunker three were doing what they could for the wounded, but two of their patients had already died. All three bunker entryways were receiving heavy fire from a coordinated Russian assault, and the men there were taking losses.

Nyurba was forced to rethink his plan. It was looking like too slow a job to blow open the bunker blast doors, and the Russian counterattack was gaining momentum too quickly. Advancing hostile troops were going to trap the commandos against the inner door. Even if they did have time to break open the door, they'd be caught between fire from a forewarned silo crew and Russian soldiers. If they overcame the silo crew, the bunker without any blast doors would be an undefendable cul de sac.

Clustered like this in underground chambers, the risk of Russian ordnance knocking men out to be captured alive was high, but the mission doctrine stated that that outcome was unacceptable. Nyurba realized he needed to do something drastic, fast, to preserve the inner door as an armored barrier yet also get behind it somehow. Otherwise he'd have to issue the final, most hideous order of all—mass self-murder, to avoid incriminating the U.S. His family's adopted homeland would be left at square one, facing Apocalypse Soon or Apocalypse Later.

He grabbed the intercom handset on the wall of the interlock chamber. It had been knocked off its hook by the shaped charge explosion and was dangling by its cord. He hoped it worked.

"Hello! Hello! This is Colonel Nyurba!" He was breathless and hoarse and worn out—that part wasn't faked.

"Colonel," the same junior officer answered, "what's going on? We did what you said, but now the cameras show more combat on the surface, and we heard our inner door being blasted."

Everything depended on what he said and how the other man reacted. Instead of toothpicks and ego with Commodore Fuller, Nyurba was playing poker for the highest stakes imaginable.

Half-truths are the best way to lie.

"Listen to me. The battle is seesawing. It's like Stalingrad out here! Rebels forced their way down and almost penetrated the interlock. My men wiped out the traitors, but now more rebels have arrived in greater strength. We're being overwhelmed. You need to open the inner door and let us in so we can help protect your bunker in the last extreme."

"But you said to let no one in."

"The situation has changed! My men are dying, we can't hold out much longer. The outer blast door's completely down. We need to shelter inside the bunker and defend it."

"We have our own weapons."

"What weapons do you have? *Pistols?*"

"Yes."

"We have grenade launchers and assault rifles!"

"How do I know I can trust you?"

"You saw us shed our blood to protect you! You saw it right on the fucking TV!"

"Er, yes."

"Now you must help protect us, and let us help protect you further, or else they'll blow open this inner door and kill you all and take the bunker."

"I don't know, sir. Maybe we should just smash the launch consoles and hope for the best."

"And leave the Motherland defenseless? You'll be shot

for treason yourselves if you destroy the launching computers! Now override the interlock and *let us in!*"

"We need a minute to work the mechanism."

"Do it!" Nyurba hung up and ran up the stairs.

He told his men defending the entryway that they might
need to fight a rearguard action, slowly withdrawing down
the stairs, using each right-angle turn as a strongpoint until
forced further back. He explained that he'd convinced the
silo crew to open the inner door to let the Spetsnaz in, on
the belief that they, not the Russians busy counterattacking,
were the genuine loyalists.

By monitoring Nyurba over his open mike, the men infiltrating bunker two had known to use his same logic and lies
to get that bunker's silo crew to open their inner door.

Once the commandos seized control of bunker one and
bunker two, and closed the inner blast doors while they •
worked to launch the missiles, the rear guards on the stairs
could keep in touch via the interlock chambers' intercoms—their radios wouldn't penetrate the EMP-shielded
doors. A wounded man would be stationed by each intercom, as a phone talker.

Nyurba ordered his men in bunker three's entryway to
hold out as long as they could. He reminded the medics that
nobody in the squadron could be taken alive. *Over the open
mike, every one of my people heard that.* He hated this, but
it wouldn't be long before other Russian rapid-response
shock troops reached the scene, even genuine Spetsnaz
units who'd fight ferociously.

He collected the experts he'd need once they got into the
bunker. He told the ICBM specialists to hide around the
corner of the vestibule. He and the bunker entry team—
Delta Force and SERT Seabees—took up positions, with
military tear-gas grenades in their hands, and nonlethal
rubber bullets in the grenade launchers clipped to their rifles. All were close-combat veterans; the Seabees could instinctively grasp the arrangement of an industrial-like
installation with an unknown floor plan.

Everyone was ready. The mounting noises of battle on the surface urged them on. Nyurba picked up the intercom, telling the Russian junior officer to open the inner door. It began to swing outward slowly toward them. The entry team hid behind it.

As soon as the door was open by one meter, the Seabee chief reached around and placed a titanium bar in the gap to prevent the bunker crew from closing the door too soon. The others rushed inside, tossing gas grenades in every direction and knocking down every man they saw with rubber bullets.

Some of the silo crew tried to don their gas masks. Others reached for their pistols. None succeeded. Nyurba saw one officer begin to swallow something. When he aimed his weapon at the man, the Russian raised his hands in surrender; dangling on a lanyard from one hand was one of the launch keys.

The Russians were gasping and choking; their eyes teared so badly they were practically blind. Two were doubled over in pain, where rubber bullets at short range had hit their abdomens.

The entry team quickly disarmed everyone they saw and secured them with duct tape, gagging their mouths and binding them hand and foot, a total of four prisoners—two officers and two senior enlisteds. But this was only the on-duty half of the crew. These men stood twelve-hour shifts in every three-day work rotation. Half of them would be on the lower level, where they slept and ate and relaxed during their twelve hours off.

A metal stairway led below. The entry team dashed down, preceded by more gas grenades, their weapons reloaded.

Nyurba was confronted by a man holding a pistol. He shot the man in the stomach with a rubber bullet. He fell onto his backside but raised the pistol again. Nyurba shot him with the AN-94, a two-round burst to the head.

Another off-duty officer, when he saw how heavily armed

the commandos were, including their bulletproof vests, committed suicide with his own pistol, to not be captured. The remaining two on the accommodation level, enlisted men, were less brave or less stupid. Already in gas masks, they put up their hands. The entry team disarmed and secured them with duct tape. Nyurba dragged both Russians upstairs. He dumped them next to the first four prisoners, then removed their gags before the men could suffocate as their noses ran with mucus from the gas. Beneath him, part of the entry team was searching the utility spaces in the bunker's lowest levels, for anyone cowering there, and for any signs of sabotage—or bombs emplaced by higher command to kill rogues. A Delta Force commando and a Seabee worked together at this, pooling their knowledge of booby traps and machinery.

"Find the blowers," Nyurba shouted through his mask. "Clear the air." He was gasping from exertion, and wearing the mask didn't help. He saw a Russian junior officer involuntarily glance at an equipment console on a wall. Nyurba pointed to it. "See if that's the environmental control."

A Seabee read the panel labels, flipped switches, and the tear gas quickly cleared. The team removed their masks.

"Get back outside and firm up the rear guard," Nyurba told them. "Get the launch specialists in here." He rethought. "Chief," he said to one Seabee, "don't leave." Nyurba was a SERT Seabee officer himself, but because Kurzin was dead, he was too busy leading the entire effort to be able to apply that expertise. He needed someone on hand who could figure out repairs that might be called for of electrics and hydraulics.

One group of commandos stepped out, through the blast door standing ajar. Different men came in. The last removed the titanium bar and sealed the blast door shut, as others took seats at the consoles, or riffled through technical manuals sitting in piles, or began to inject the silo crewmen with truth drugs.

CHAPTER 24

Jeffrey Fuller awoke groggily from a sleep so deep he didn't remember dreaming.

"Commodore!"

Jeffrey recognized Bell's voice. That was what had woken him. "Yes. Yes. I'm awake."

Bell switched on *Challenger*'s XO stateroom's light. Jeffrey squinted until his puffy, bleary eyes could adjust. Sessions, asleep in his own rack under the VIP rack, began to stir.

Lord, he was out cold even more than me. Jeffrey wondered for a moment whether he himself had slept well due to peace of mind about the mission, resulting from his newfound amoral coping mechanism. Or were internal conflicts and ethical qualms so repressed for now that they'd destroy his mental health later?

He brushed this troubling thought aside and glanced at his watch. All peace of mind vanished. "What's wrong?" He wasn't supposed to be woken for another three hours. And he should have been woken by a messenger, normal procedure, not by Captain Bell.

"We got the code-letter group by ELF, sir. Colonel Kurzin has begun the attack on the silo complex near Srednekolymsk, as observed and confirmed by surveillance satellite. We're to proceed to periscope depth, smartly, and monitor further events per our previous orders."

"*Now?* Are you *sure*?"

"The message was repeated, sir. I checked the decryption myself."

"But it's a day early."

"Something must have sped up their plans."

Jeffrey climbed out of bed, standing barefoot in his skivvies. He ran a hand over his face.

"I guess something did. . . . All right. . . . Give me five minutes to use the head and get dressed. Have a messenger meet me in Control with coffee. You better prepare the ship for coming to periscope depth and raising the masts."

"Yes, sir. I'll have Meltzer start to calculate the relative bearing to watch for missiles rising above our horizon." Bell turned to leave.

"Wait." Jeffrey's thoughts were racing. "Do we know how the attack is going?"

"They wouldn't send us a code for that, due to overall mission security, sir, assuming even Washington knows."

"Oh, yeah, right. Sorry, my mind's still fuzzy."

"No problem, Commodore."

Jeffrey read the XO stateroom situation display. Sonar held no threats, neither submerged nor on the surface nor airborne. He called up a navigational chart, as Sessions, also in his boxer shorts and undershirt, looked on. The ship was heading northwest, in the middle of the Laptev Sea, on a course to skirt north of the Svernaya Zemlya islands. The nearest land was Cape Dika, about one hundred fifty nautical miles southwest. The nearest naval base in Rear Admiral Meredov's area of command was almost due south by three hundred miles: the port of Tiksu, on one edge of the Lena River's huge delta. *Challenger* was under the pack ice, near the marginal ice zone, using the noise there to hide acoustically at Bell's favorite depth, nine hundred feet, moving at a stealthy twelve knots. They were in six thousand feet of water—the continental shelf here dropped off much closer inshore than it did by the New Siberian Islands, far astern.

Jeffrey started to figure the distances and timings.

"Sir," Bell said, smiling at his superior's typical obsession with work. "Take care of your business first. There's a polynya ideal for our purposes only three miles off."

With the blast door closed, it was oddly quiet in control bunker one. Nyurba realized he missed the constant pounding and vibrations that the surface battle had been causing through the air and through the ground. Given the tidy, high-tech appearance of the launch consoles—computer screens and keyboards, rows of switches and knobs and dozens of indicator lights, all labeled with strange abbreviations and acronyms—the bunker seemed surreal. Safes, electronic and power supply cabinets, communications and decoding equipment, printers, and storage lockers lined the walls in the low-ceilinged enclosure. It was antiseptic—a stark contrast to the absolute mess outside.

The lack of any sensations from the violent life-and-death struggle being fought so close above his head brought home what he already knew as a civil engineer: the bunker he was standing in rode on a system of massive springs and torsion bars, powerful shock absorbers and vibration dampers, and suspension rods with high-friction universal joints. Such components surrounded the entryway blast interlock, the control bunker, the blast interlocks at both ends of the tunnels leading to each of the three missile silos, those long tunnels, and the missile silos themselves. Each of these major underground structures was a separate module made of steel and reinforced concrete, with massive rubber bumpers at the joints between them, so the whole system could flex and twist as independent pieces—and thus not build up added stresses or destructive harmonic resonances. Most of the shock-modulation components were installed in a "rattle space" between excavated bedrock and the exterior of the modules; that space was accessible through maintenance hatches. The modular design, including multiple blast interlocks, meant that if one section did fail, those around it would be isolated from any propagating fracture or collapse. American land-based ICBMs, the Upgraded Minuteman IIIs, were housed in a similar way. But the newer SS-27 complexes were built to withstand greater dynamic shear, strain, compression, torque, and shaking than were their older, lifetime-extended U.S. counterparts. Nyurba sent his Seabee chief to gather all the intel he could on the Russian construction methods and specs, using one of the Japanese digital cameras the team had brought to make permanent records. The espionage opportunities were priceless.

"We have intercom communications with bunker two," the Air Force major said. His name was Akhmed Ildarov, born in Russia's restive Muslim region of Dagestan. Ildarov was stocky and swarthy, all business at all times; he'd been naturalized as a U.S. citizen during his childhood. "Our people have seized control in bunker two, sir. They report proceeding to obtain information and items required for armed missile launches."

"Very well," Nyurba acknowledged. "Activate all surface TV cameras."

"Yes, sir."

The silo crewmen must have turned them off because they found the combat scenes too disturbing.

Display screens lit up to show views, in full color, from aboveground; the pictures weren't very sharp, and the cameras had no zoom lenses. As the major's men hurried around doing their jobs, Nyurba mostly studied these screens. Some of the cameras had failed even though they were armored—these, like the radio antennas, were expected to be lost in an attack, and reserve units hid behind armored shutters. Nyurba decided to save those cameras for right before bunker one's missiles launched—assuming they ever did.

The cameras that were working showed that the fight for the bunker entryways, so vicious while Nyurba was in the stairwell, had reached a stalemate. Before, he'd only been able to see what a pounding his men were taking. Now, he could see what they'd dished out.

New funeral pyres of aircraft and vehicles threw flames and smoke into the sky. Dead Russians lay contorted where they fell. Charred corpses smoldered. Wounded crawled or clutched at entrails or raised their arms in pleading for help. Some of the figures that burned were moving, either because limbs drew into outreaching postures as muscles and tendons were cooked—or because they were still alive.

The Russians had suffered heavy losses from the squadron's supersonic SA-16 missiles, the shaped-charge and hyperbaric warheads of the RPG-27s, and the grenade launchers and flak-vest-piercing AN-94s. Surviving helicopters and armored cars and troops in the open were mostly keeping their distance. Individuals fired back and forth sporadically, but at longer range the AN-94 was much more accurate than the AK-47 or the AK-74. The camera displays showed that the triple chain-link fences had been knocked down in a number of spots, but the area between them still held many unexploded mines. It was difficult to defuse these mines while under fire from the commandos—this was one factor working to the squadron's advantage. It held the Russians at bay, even as it trapped the commandos.

On one screen, Nyurba saw man-sized lumps moving on the ground by a gap in the fence. *Russian minefield-clearing teams?*

The earth around them leaped into the air in many small clods. *Hits from AN-94 rounds?*

Some lumps jerked or rolled over and stopped moving. The others kept advancing. There was a sudden bright flash on the screen, weird because the picture had no sound. Lumps, and parts of lumps, cartwheeled through the air and landed heavily.

Scratch one more mine-clearing team.

But small units, whether Mi-24s of different varieties, or BTR-70s—or the newer, diesel-powered BTR-80s that had shown up—or squads of soldiers, would make lunges and feints to get the commandos to waste their ammo. Realizing this, the commandos in the entryway dugouts held their fire, playing possum, until the lunges got too close for their weapons to miss. Then they'd fire a missile or a grenade, causing further Russian losses—but expending further ammo, and sometimes taking killed and wounded themselves.

Nyurba saw another lunge, this one by a squad of twelve infantrymen each holding an RPG-27 or similar grenade launcher. They spread out wide to make harder targets, and ran right into the minefield through holes in the fence. Three of them set off mines, and grabbed for legs that weren't there until they set off more mines and lay dead. Nine men never broke stride, and now were on the asphalt. They were charging straight toward bunker two, from the direction facing its entryway. They obviously wanted to get within the two-hundred-yard range of their warheads and use them as bunker-buster grenades. They wore extra-thick body armor; sometimes they hesitated or staggered as if they'd been hit, but then kept coming. One man was hit in a leg—Nyurba saw a puff of pink vapor come out the back of his thigh. He hopped forward on the other leg. A commando in bunker two fired at one Russian using the grenade launcher under his rifle, but its range in a high lob from the launcher was no better than that of the RPG rockets with their flatter flights. A flash and a puff of smoke showed that the commando's grenade fell short. That soldier broke ranks, knelt, and fired back. A rocket streaked toward the bunker, and a ball of fire above the asphalt showed that it too fell short—a hyperbaric warhead. The other Russian soldiers were still coming on. One by one they were picked off with shots to the head or neck, or crippling shots to the lower abdomen and groin—or raking full-auto fire that shredded their thighs or their calves. Nyurba was transfixed by this amazing show of courage. Only one Russian had to get within effective grenade range, out of the dozen who had started this death charge, to take out everyone on the stairs of bunker two.

One last man got close enough.

He knelt and aimed his rocket launcher.

A shower of grenades landed all around him. Nyurba was impressed—the commandos had fired in advance as a group, anticipating where he'd be before he got there, so the arcing pop flies of their grenades impacted before he could shoot. Amid the flashes and smoke engulfing the Russian, there was a brighter, more prolonged eruption—a grenade fragment had set off the rocket warhead and its fuel while still in the barrel. All that was left were burning pieces of flesh.

After this the battle went into another lull. It had become a slow and grinding attrition fight: each side wore the other down, bit by bit. The winner, at least of this phase of the larger contest, would be whoever ran out of resources last. The Russians could run low on aircraft and armored cars—or troops could run out of the willingness to advance in the next probe or feint, only to die horribly like those who'd gone before. The commandos could run out of men or ammunition. Based on the numbers on both sides, as Nyurba judged from the camera views and from reports he got over the intercom in the interlock—from which the bunkers' defending squads were all within radio contact—the commandos would eventually lose. The real question was whether they'd be able to launch some SS-27s before Russian troops broke into bunker one and bunker two and stopped them. The Russians didn't seem in any major hurry now, which implied that their commanders didn't think the attackers—whoever they actually were—would be able to launch an ICBM.

Are they underestimating the preparedness and skill of my squadron, or are we underestimating their preventives against an unauthorized launch?

Do they realize we're already inside two control bunkers?

Nyurba tore his eyes from the screens and watched as the ten men with him continued their assigned tasks systematically and speedily. Some were digesting the normal launch procedures, using the manuals that provided explicit details and checklists. Others were busy hacking the computer systems, to learn the current arming and targeting passwords, and find out how to set the desired flight coordinates and detonation parameters.

Two men kept bombarding their prisoners with questions. The six Russian silo crewmen had been blindfolded, then divided into two groups held out of earshot of each other, one in a corner on the upper level and one on the level below. By cross-examining the men, now deeply under the influence of truth serums, and then comparing answers to the same questions asked of both groups, the interrogators could confirm information and weed out any lies. The chemicals flooding their brain cells made it very hard for the Russians to lie. But these rigorously selected silo crewmen had a strong sense of duty—as two had shown right at the start, they'd rather die than help rogues launch armed nukes.

For all they knew, Nyurba was targeting Moscow.

One of the very first questions was about bunker voice or video recorders. These were located and smashed.

What simplified the main work was that Nyurba didn't care about procedures to verify that an incoming launch order was valid. This was a large part of silo crew training in any country, but today's purpose was achieving unauthorized launch. A valid order would include directions for safing the complex's antirogue traps—the team had to assume that all radio messages now were tricks meant to disable or destroy the ICBMs.

A pair of warhead-bus and missile-system experts were in one silo, to complete an overall inspection making sure there'd been no gross damage done, and to verify that the electronic links to the support base command bunker had indeed been severed by the crewmen as Nyurba asked. Everything looked good on that front, so far. Nyurba hoped, as a result, that all passwords and codes in the launch console software matched those in the missiles and warheads—and that no instructions had been inserted secretly, deep within millions of lines of computer programming, to abort the launches or self-destruct the missiles or de-enable the warheads.

A pair of men, Air Force Special Ops Squadron commandos by original background, were included in each bunker team as explosive ordnance detection-and-disposal experts. The warhead and missile specialists worked closely with them, searching with electronic sniffers, and their eyes, for any range-safety devices that amounted to hidden bombs or incendiaries. Their task was badly complicated by the fact that missiles did include explosive bolts and cords as part of their normal design, to assure separation of each booster stage, and to release the aerodynamic nose cone from over the missile bus—which had its own small liquid-fueled maneuvering rocket. The thermonuclear hydrogen-fusion warhead included high-explosives too, to set off its plutonium implosion-fission trigger.

The two different types of experts were working hard to sanitize the first silo, making slow progress. When done with that, they'd go on to check the second and third silos as well; retractable platforms surrounding the missiles gave them access to maintenance hatches, but there were so many things that needed to be examined thoroughly.

The special ops ordnance men, with surgical precision, had already blown open control-bunker safes whose combinations were unknown to the crews; to prevent an unauthorized launch, the combinations would arrive only with a valid launch order. The Kremlin's premise was that with eight men in each control bunker crew, one or two who went berserk and tried to use brute force or guile would be stopped by the others—if the regimental command bunker didn't stop everything first by remote control. And since one part of normal oncoming crew rotation procedures was a close bodily inspection of the new men for explosives, burglar tools, and other improper equipment or materials, what the commandos were about to do could supposedly never be done by regular crews.

Via the intercom system, the major in charge of the efforts in bunker one kept tabs and compared notes with his counterpart in bunker two. A friendly competition had started. So far, bunker two was making slightly faster progress. This was fine by Nyurba. Competition brought better results, and he personally didn't care which bunker launched the three desired missiles. The winning team, if they survived, could have all the bragging rights they wanted— though permanent security restrictions meant there was no one they could brag to afterward.

The intercom from the blast interlock to the entryway made a warbling noise. Nyurba answered.

"Sir," an Army Ranger told him over the intercom mike, bypassing the phone talker, "we heard many heavy transport choppers landing a few miles away, out of range of our missiles. We also saw fixed-wing aircraft drop sticks of paratroopers. From the number of chutes, I'm guessing in company strength." Company strength was a vague term, since many real Russian units were known to be undermanned, but it could mean two hundred paratroopers.

Nyurba looked at his watch. It was more than three hours since the commando's attack began. The Russians had had enough time to get organized. This military district's commanding general, or even the Kremlin, might inject new backbone into another, more powerful counterattack.

"Any heavy equipment with the paratroopers?"

"You mean, like field artillery, sir?"

"Yes, that's what I mean."

"Negative, sir. At least not yet."

"What about mortars?"

"We haven't taken mortar rounds yet either, sir."

"Inform me at once if you do."

"Understood."

"Nyurba, out." He replaced the handset.

The concrete overhang of the entryways should stop direct hits from mortar or artillery shells. But near misses would throw blast and shrapnel, increasing the rate of attrition for Nyurba's ever-dwindling squadron. His greatest dread was that Russian fighter-bombers might soon reach the scene, as distant as it was from any such bases, and drop napalm.

"Sir," Major Ildarov called Nyurba, "bunker two wants to speak to you. The guy sounds upset."

He grabbed the handset. "Nyurba."

"We missed a range-safety feature." The man rattled off technical specifications that were gibberish to Nyurba.

"Wait!" he shouted to the technicians around him, repeating the specifications. "They think they did something wrong. Do you understand what those specs mean?"

The major's people did. Now they knew one thing to *not* do, or an extra thing they *should* do . . . or something like that. Nyurba had to delegate the arcane technical work. But he grasped that this information was valuable. He told his men to keep working, then spoke into the intercom.

"What's the problem? You seem fine. Calm down."

"You don't understand, sir. The engines of all my missiles have ignited inside the silos."

"What?" Nyurba examined the camera displays. "But the lids are still closed. The exhaust covers haven't slid open."

"I know. The heat and pressure are building up inside. Two of my men were trapped, cremated."

"Jesus. . . . Okay. . . . Just stay where you are. You should be all right, with the blast interlocks between you and the silos."

"What about the men at the entryway?"

Nyurba glanced at the TV displays again. There was still no sign of any trouble from bunker two.

Then movement caught his eye.

The Russians were making a human-wave assault. Four hundred men on foot, six BTR-70s or 80s, and five Mi-24s were attacking all at once. Armored car machine guns, and rockets and cannon on the helicopters, blasted lanes through the minefields for the ground troops.

The troops were through the fence perimeter in overwhelming force. Their concentrated fire drove the teams back from the entryways to all three bunkers.

"I—"

Nyurba didn't have time to finish. In volcanic eruptions like nothing he'd ever seen before in his life, one after another of bunker two's SS-27 silo lids blew off.

They're hardened against attack from the outside, not tremendous overpressure and searing heat within.

Giant flaming chunks of solid missile fuel were flung into the air—each missile contained fifty tons of it. The shock waves from the lid eruptions were so powerful that Nyurba could see them as moving fronts of ghostly condensation spreading out at the speed of sound; he swayed on his feet, then realized it was the bunker that was swaying on its springs.

The shock waves mowed down the Russian troops as if they were blades of grass. Countless chunks of solid fuel, burning at thousands of degrees Fahrenheit, weighing anywhere from a pound to a ton, plunged out of the sky like rain from hell.

They landed everywhere, bright yellow, as blinding as pieces of the sun. Some of the surface cameras failed and their screens went blank. What Nyurba saw on the other screens was enough.

Helicopters were snapped in half in midair. Armored

cars tumbled end over end along the ground until they exploded. The dirty yellow fumes from the missile fuel swirled crazily.

"Bunker two, have your outside team take cover!"

"I've lost contact, sir. The intercom failed, or the men are all dead. I can't open the blast door for them anyway now."

"Stay put. I need to get off."

The intercom from the vestibule to his own bunker was warbling.

"Nyurba," he snapped. On the TV screens, flames continued to blast forth from each of bunker two's silos, like three blowtorches reaching hundreds of feet into the air. Near one camera, on a display, he saw a big chunk of burning fuel literally melt its way through solid concrete and the steel rebars underneath. Waves of heat rippled above the hole it made for itself, and more dirty yellow fumes belched out to mingle with the fog of fumes that was blanketing the complex. Then the chunk of fuel hit permafrost, and a gigantic steam explosion burst out of the hole. As more chunks burned through elsewhere, geyser after geyser of steam and scalding water and shattered concrete or asphalt was added to the flames and fumes. Even distorted hunks of metal from the missiles burned; magnesium flared a brilliant white. Nyurba felt as if he were watching a silent movie—except in color with modern special effects.

A horror movie. Dante's Inferno *has nothing on* this.

"Sir," someone gasped over the intercom, his voice so muffled by a gas mask that Nyurba couldn't tell who it was. "The fumes are getting through our masks. We need respirators. Let us inside or we'll die."

"Get hold of yourself! Wait one." Nyurba turned to Ildarov. "How many emergency respirators are in the bunker?"

Ildarov told the interrogators to find out, and learn where they were kept.

The answer came back: eight. One for each man in a silo crew.

Nyurba had an awful thought. Each incinerated missile

had carried a one-megaton nuclear warhead. Radioactive plutonium and tritium, and other deadly isotopes, were drifting amid the smoke and fumes. He looked at the TV screens. Lumps of fuel that had landed on asphalt set the asphalt on fire before melting through. Big swaths of the defoliated strip were also burning, sometimes cooking off mines among what was left of the fence barrier. Parts of the forest around the complex had caught fire.

Ildarov's men were carrying the eight respirator packs toward the door, that thick slab of steel which separated the bunker from the nightmarish scene outside. The Russian labeling said their pure oxygen supply was good for one hour. Then it would be back into gas masks, come what may, for the commandos on the surface—the respirators came with no spare tanks.

"Major, call bunker two and tell them to mimic our actions. Get their rear guard to contact bunker three's medics via radio. Medics are to barricade bunker three's stairs with backpacks and duct tape to keep out the fumes. Bunker three rear guard will have to make do with gas masks." The Russian silo crew in bunker three was still taking cover within, laying low, not interfering.

"Understood, sir." Ildarov called bunker two.

"Chief," Nyurba ordered. "The environmental controls. Raise air pressure in the bunker to one point two atmospheres."

The Seabee chief acknowledged. Nyurba's ears crackled. He gave thanks that the emergency backup diesel generator, in its hardened containment with its filtered air supply, continued functioning. He knew the bunker had a large battery bank that would last several days if the generator broke down and couldn't be fixed, or it ran out of fuel.

He spoke into the intercom. "Have your men come into the decontamination chamber. I'm going to give you all the respirators we have. Hold your breath before taking off your gas masks. Don't inhale until you have the respirators on. The air around you is radioactive. If there aren't enough of the packs to go around, you'll have to share them and buddy-breathe."

"Understood. We're going in."

"Call me on the intercom in there."

In a second the intercom warbled.

"Nyurba."

"We're all by the door."

"I'm going to crack the door and toss out the respirators, then reseal the door. Expect a gush of wind, I've overpressured the bunker to keep out contaminants. But I can't let you in. I need you to stand guard just in case any Russian soldiers are still alive and in a mood to fight up there."

"Understood. We'll be ready for them."

"Good man. Nyurba, out." He hung up. "Major, crack the door."

The gush of air almost sucked the respirators out on their own. Nyurba had to be careful not to be sucked out with them.

"Shut it!"

The door closed and locked.

"What's interior pressure now?"

"One point zero five bars, sir," the Seabee said. Bar was the metric equivalent of one atmosphere—all the Russian readouts were calibrated in the metric system.

"Keep it there, just in case. How's the environment in our missile silos?"

"Temperature, pressure, humidity are nominal."

"Major, how are the missiles?"

"Electronic checkouts of missiles and warheads all read as nominal," Ildarov said, "safed against arming and launch."

"How much longer until we'll be able to do that last part?"

"The missiles use ring-laser gyros so there's no time required to spool them up. A lot depends on what the silo inspection teams find, or don't find, or miss finding, while they're sanitizing the missiles and silo machinery. We have the targeting coordinates ready for the missile flight profiles we want, and we have the codes and procedures to set and prearm the warheads to go off exoatmospherically. We have both launch keys."

CHAPTER 25

Challenger hovered at periscope depth in an area of thin, flat annual ice that had begun to break up and melt. Both photonics masts were raised, one aimed toward where ICBMs from Srednekolymsk were expected to become visible if all went according to plan. Jeffrey stared at the screen display on his borrowed console in the rear of the control room. His concentration kept wandering, from worry and lack of results. The other photonics mast scanned constantly for airborne threats that might be maintaining radio and radar silence—Russian antisubmarine aircraft could rely on their observers alone, to seize the element of surprise by avoiding detection on an opponent's electronic support measures equipment. Jeffrey had enough respect for Rear Admiral Meredov by now to expect that his planes sometimes did this. But both photonic displays showed only featureless ice and empty sky.

The ESM heads on *Challenger*'s photonics masts did pick up occasional weak signals from Tupolev 204s in the distance, to the east and the west, but none so far were approaching this part of the cap in mid–Laptev Sea. It was only a matter of time, though, before their standard search patterns brought them much too near.

Challenger had deployed her trailing wire antennas, unreeling them in a line downcurrent to float up against the underside of the pack ice. Her sonar towed array wasn't deployed. When things started to happen, they'd happen fast—there'd be no time to retract the array, and Bell didn't want to have to jettison it. Jeffrey concurred. The antenna masts were also raised, to grab what information they could in the meantime, and not waste a moment when the big show began.

He felt awfully exposed to Russian sensors while keeping this lookout post, but his orders required it. Soon, satellites would have to shut down to avoid being fried, and Jeffrey needed to be available as his President's eyes and ears. World War III with Russia could break out if things went awry, and *Challenger* might well be the best, or only, operating early-warning platform America had.

If I see many more than three ICBMs, I'll know that Armageddon has started. I'll need to violate radio silence, so the U.S. knows what's on the way, for all the good that would do.

Jeffrey dearly missed the information from *Carter*'s previous tap of the fiber-optic cable. What the NSA teams in *Challenger*'s radio room and ESM room were catching via signals intercepts didn't tell him much. Meredov's forces were being surprisingly quiet, now that the furor over Jeffrey's decoy from days before had died down. Russia's reaction to the commando raid was hard to gauge. Main command channels transmitted constantly, random numbers or gibberish between genuine messages, to prevent eavesdroppers from noticing alterations in the amount of traffic. Indications of heightened activity or raised alert levels could only be gained if the codes used on those channels had been broken. Russia's Strategic Rocket Forces changed their codes often. History taught that any encryption system, if used too long, could be cracked.

Hours had gone by since the ELF message came in telling Jeffrey that the commandos' attack had started; the sun had moved a long way in its perpetual summertime waltz with the horizon since *Challenger* came shallow here. It now seemed probable, as intelligence analysts had predicted, that the Strategic Rocket Forces hadn't even informed the Russian Navy that something was amiss. And they were being cagy in every way with communications about any response to a ground attack against one of their SS-27 complexes—that complex was a thousand miles distant from *Challenger,* which made overhearing anything useful all the more difficult.

And if caught dwelling here suspiciously, too soon, before Kurzin's missiles took off, Jeffrey's cover story—about a German sub purchased from Russia, far away—would be shot to pieces. The whole game plan would totally unravel after that.

The intercom from the ESM room blinked. Bell answered. "Commodore, they want to speak to you."

Jeffrey's chest tightened. "ESM, Fuller, what is it?"

"Sir," the NSA technician said in a deep-South drawl, "we got peculiar traffic from our own spaceborne platforms, and neutrals. Huge fires raging at the complex near Srednekolymsk."

"What *sort* of fires?"

"Near as we can tell, heat signatures of three SS-27s but they're stationary, no launches. Assessing as in-silo explosions and ground-level burning of solid fuel."

Before Jeffrey could react to this news, which seemed to imply that Kurzin's team had failed disastrously, Bell called him again. "Sir, Radio wants you. I told them you were on the line with ESM, but my comms officer says he needs you, smartly."

"Wait one," Jeffrey told the ESM room. He switched circuits. "Radio, Fuller, what?"

"Sir, we just finished receiving an ELF three-letter block. Decoding confirmed as cipher for 'To Commodore, *Chal-*

lenger Strike Group, personal. Hot Line in use. Remain on station.'"

———

"Let's get this damn ball rolling!" Nyurba ordered. "We've got three missiles to launch!"

He fretted, because the time element was constantly becoming more and more critical. Every added hour that passed expanded by hundreds of miles the distance, and exponentially increased the area, from which stronger and stronger counterattacking forces could be staged, flown in, and ordered to make the next assault. Eventually the pieces of missile fuel from bunker two would burn themselves out, and the steam geysers they were causing would subside. The worst of the deadly fumes would disperse on the wind, and aircraft and airborne units wouldn't be deterred by moderate forest fires. The commandos definitely couldn't stand up to another, more massive counterattack.

The Air Force missile specialists did their thing, speaking in Russian terminology—as they'd been briefed by expatriates, and as they knew from the manuals and checklists.

Nyurba understood the basics from his own briefing materials. Explained in U.S. terminology, the launch crew had to first achieve a permissive action link unlock, enabling the nuclear warhead to be armed at a later date. Then they had to program into the missile and warhead electronics a correctly formatted safe-to-arm signal, which would be sent into the warhead just before the warhead bus separated from the third-stage booster. The signal would only be sent while in flight if the missile's self-contained computers decided that everything was functioning properly, and the missile was on course toward its designated target. Then came warhead arming. For an exoatmospheric blast immediately after third-stage booster separation, this was relatively simple. It tied in with the fourth major event, actual warhead fusing and detonation.

It would have been much more complicated, and more difficult to achieve without authorization, if the launch team really wanted to target a place on land in a foreign country. Those complexities were the various factors—deceleration, air pressure, altitude—related to the supposed spoofing ability of what Commodore Fuller had labeled the "magical, mystical, mystery missile shield." But they weren't the launch crew's concern now, in real life.

Nyurba listened with a mixture of awe and dread while Major Ildarov and his people ran through the various checklists. Lights on panels changed colors as they performed each step. They made status reports to each other, or issued orders.

By now, big antirogue bombs hidden in dehumidifier cabinets in the silos, adjoining the missiles' second-stage boosters, had been found and defused. Electronic booby traps, designed to erase essential files and scramble passwords, were bypassed. Circuit elements that had to be inserted manually, after being removed from safes with secret combinations, were inserted where they were supposed to go. Mechanical devices that needed to be put in place, or dismantled, were taken care of. Alarms blared again and again that were meant to warn the rest of the crew that things were being done to undertake launch procedures, and each time the commandos turned them off as irrelevant.

The silo inspection team was still at work in silo three. A specialist monitoring the bunker's radios and decryption gear, tuned to district command channels, reported that a two-battalion airborne assault, with air-dropped field artillery and light tanks, was on the way. Two battalions were over a thousand men.

"It's now or never, guys!" Nyurba said. They had to trigger liftoff immediately. After that any ambulatory squadron remnants would need to try to escape and evade through the horrific conditions above. Once the next counterattack formations reached the scene, escape would be totally hopeless.

Major Ildarov recalled the silo team. They came into the bunker from the interlock to the tunnel to silo three. They were drenched in sweat and smeared with grease and oil, their faces were pinched, and their stances showed utter exhaustion. They couldn't guarantee what would happen with the missiles.

———

Jeffrey still sat at his console. For the umpteenth time, seeking hidden meanings and any reassurance he could find, he examined a paraphrased transcript of a brief but pointed conversation the presidents of the U.S. and Russia had had, via the Hot Line, after three missile silos at Srednekolymsk blew up—and the complex became obscured from further detailed spaceborne recon by heat and smoke. The exchange had been encoded and relayed to Jeffrey by satellite, for his use as a heads-up and for situational orientation.

The trend of events was not reassuring. The American President was already compelled to improvise, off-script, with guesswork and hedging forced as to what scenario was really unfolding. The possibility that one isolated group of silos would explode, while Kurzin's men might still be working to achieve successful launches of another group, had never been considered in mission planning—an oversight, glaringly obvious only in retrospect. Jeffrey cursed the lack of more specific information from on scene, but the commando team were incommunicado and entirely on their own.

The text in his hands conveyed no inflections or tones of voice between the two heads of state. But both presidents played games, jabbing and blocking according to different agendas, their diplomatic choreography very much at cross-purposes. *In a potential nuclear crisis, doublespeak becomes perverse. . . .*

WASHINGTON: Why have three of your SS-27 silos exploded?

Moscow: An unfortunate maintenance accident while

blast interlocks were overridden. One missile set off the other two. It is not a concern, for us or for you.

That's lie number one, Jeffrey told himself.

WASHINGTON: How can I be sure this is not a subterfuge, a distraction, a prelude to a strategic first strike?

MOSCOW: You insult me. Your intelligence assets would give signs if we were preparing for such a mutually suicidal act.

WASHINGTON: Depending on your tactics and goals, you might not consider it suicidal. Do not attempt to manipulate me by your own view of American antinuke phobias.

MOSCOW: Our submarines are not surging! Our bomber fleets aren't mobilizing! It was only a maintenance accident.

WASHINGTON: Then am I to assume there will be no further accidents in the near future?

MOSCOW: Do not ask of me impossible promises. You had a Titan II explode during maintenance in Arkansas in 1980. It blew the lid off the silo and hurled the warhead through the air. Can you assure me that such a thing will not occur again in America?

WASHINGTON: Yes, we have had accidents. But never an attempted rogue attack like from your submarine in 1968.

MOSCOW: Do not harass me further with such ancient history!

WASHINGTON: Then you can assure me that no such unauthorized launch was attempted today? And no more attempts are in progress?

MOSCOW: [Long hesitation] Of course not! It was a maintenance accident!

Gotcha twice now. That "long hesitation" suggests Kurzin's team hasn't been wiped out yet . . . but the Russian president chooses to count on the fact that they will be.

WASHINGTON: We will monitor the situation carefully. I have nine SSBNs at sea. They alone give me a thousand warheads for a retaliatory strike. Each W-88 yields half a megaton.

Moscow: I will not be extorted by any such wholly unjustified insinuations or threats! . . . However, as a safety concession, we will hold our strategic thermonuclear assets below their maximum force readiness. We will not raise readiness if you do not go to your DEFCON One. Let us agree now to both avoid a launch-on-warning strategy.

Jeffrey knew that launch-on-warning meant "pushing the button" as soon as you received indication that the other guy's ICBMs were taking off. *The Russian president is nervous. . . . As well he should be. And he just telegraphed, to me and my commander in chief, that Kurzin does still have a chance.*

Washington: I agree to not follow a policy of launch-on-warning. The events in Srednekolymsk show us both how dangerous such tactics can be. Misinterpretation of vague or unconfirmed data can lead to disaster.

Moscow: I concur wholeheartedly.

Washington: I will keep my strategic thermonuclear forces at DEFCON Two, but giving me an equivalent assurance about your own strategic command-and-control is not enough. You must stay immediately available for further verbal consultation. And do not evacuate your leadership. Do not evacuate your civilians from cities. I would consider either as proof of impending aggression. In return, as a gesture of good faith, I will not leave the White House for the next forty-eight hours. I am sure you have assets that can verify my whereabouts.

Moscow: I give my word on these matters. I will remain in my suite in the Kremlin for two days.

Washington: Why did you not inform us in advance of your maintenance work in Srednekolymsk? By treaty you are required to, precisely to avoid confrontations like this.

Moscow: [Long hesitation] The announcement was issued. It may have been misplaced. We must all be more cautious in future.

Another bald-faced lie, and a cover-up too, Jeffrey thought.

WASHINGTON: You really need to shake the dust and deadwood from your bureaucracy. You misplace important messages too often. I sometimes suspect that you do it on purpose.

MOSCOW: This conversation is ended.

WASHINGTON: No it is not. I must insist on more. The tactical nuclear conflict with Germany is too destabilizing, and they will have their own theories about unfolding events at Srednekolymsk despite what you might tell them. The potential for misunderstanding or unintentional provocation between your country and mine is high, when additional thermal signatures from Srednekolymsk may not yet be ruled out, or others elsewhere may be misidentified. Human error and mechanical breakdown in any complex system are most likely, and most damaging, while under such stress.

MOSCOW: With that I agree. What do you want?

WASHINGTON: Issue an order to your high political and military commanders immediately, and insist on positive confirmation of receipt of the order by each.

MOSCOW: What order?

WASHINGTON: That if for some reason in the next two days their contact with you is temporarily lost, for instance due to an attempted coup or sudden illness, they are not to exercise independent initiative, or implement succession plans, going so far as launching any ICBMs themselves. Only during the next two days, as a cooling-off period for both our nations.

MOSCOW: [Pause, background murmurs audible, appears to consult with advisors] You are overreacting to nothing. However, that being the case, I see no harm in issuing such orders. Provided that you reciprocate, regarding your own chain of custody for thermonuclear forces. I will not be held hostage to American whims because of a minor maintenance accident!

WASHINGTON: I will reciprocate. Caution is not whimsy, with half the world already at war.

Moscow: This discussion is ended. [Terminates call.]

Jeffrey smiled to himself despite the uncertainties and dangers, and the trials that he knew lay ahead. The President of the United States had politely but firmly kicked ass, while skillfully putting in place arrangements to avoid inadvertent escalation by either side—setting things up for the bluff about a next-generation missile shield. And he'd caught the President of Russia, on the record, repeatedly telling blatant untruths. If Kurzin's team succeeded, those untruths would come back to haunt him—partly at Jeffrey's behest. But if Kurzin made the wrong mistakes, Jeffrey was the one who'd be haunted.

The U.S. had raised its H-bomb alert status to DEFCON 2 at the start of the war with the Berlin-Boer Axis. The last time this had happened was during the Cuban Missile Crisis.

I've had my doubts about this scheme all along, but it's way too late to back out now.

CHAPTER 26

As Nyurba watched, Ildarov's team switched each SS-27 over to internal battery power; indicator lights showed that operations continued to be nominal. By remote control they disconnected all physical and electronic links to the missiles, except for the launch umbilicals.

"We are ready to launch, sir," the major said. "I think."

"Deploy all reserve TV cameras. We need to see how the launches go, and what the Russians try next."

More display screens lit up. The inferno topside still raged furiously, but all three silo lids were clear of obstructions.

Nyurba couldn't afford to take any chances. The unbreakable mission doctrine, and circumstance, forced him to issue the most difficult order he ever imagined having to give.

"Major, contact bunker two and bunker three vestibules and all bunker entryway squads. Inform them to take cover, we're preparing to attempt missile launch." Too much hinged on that single important qualifier, *attempt*. But it got worse. Nyurba continued. "Men unfit to run for twenty miles without assistance are to be . . ." He struggled for the words. "Rendered permanently unavailable for hostile interrogation. This is a direct order. I accept full responsibility."

A dark pall came over the group of commandos in the bunker. Everyone knew this was coming, but repression and denial, and their own will to survive, had up to now kept them from accepting the brutal, raw fact.

"Each martyr today might be helping save hundreds of millions of lives later on. The calculus of war is abhorrent, but inescapable. May God forgive me."

I doubt He will. There's war fighting, and then there's murder. Nyurba had to blink back tears. The squadron had trained together for a year. Every man felt like a brother. Their bonding was stronger than family.

Ildarov needed to clear his throat twice to be able to speak. He relayed the orders.

"Bunker two acknowledges. . . . Medics in bunker three vestibule acknowledge. . . . Squads at entryways to all bunkers acknowledge." The major's voice was dead and flat.

"Very well," Nyurba said coldly. "Launch the missiles."

His heart had been pounding. Now he took a deep breath, his throat painfully constricted with grief, waiting for something to explode—or for everything to simply go dark and useless, inert, which would be just as bad.

The men used their controls to select the first missile. To initiate the final launch sequence, Ildarov and one of his men inserted and turned their keys. Other lights started flashing. A camera showed the lid of the silo rise open by its hydraulic jacks in less than twenty seconds—it tapered toward its bottom, like a cork, to seal the silo top against incoming nukes. Nyurba felt disembodied as he watched, and became fascinated by trivial details: the bottom of the lid was painted dark green.

I'm an executioner, not a warrior. And I'm the first person in history to launch a hydrogen bomb in anger, not in a test.

The flame-deflector exhaust duct covers slid open, pushing debris and bits of burning fuel aside. The first-stage booster engine ignited. On TV, towers of searing flame shot through the surface exhaust ducts. Nyurba saw the missile's nose cone emerge from the silo, followed by its sleek, silvery body. It seemed to barely move. Then the monster was out of the silo, seventy-five feet long and six feet in diameter, its engine nozzle giving off blinding yellow glare and a churning cloud of brownish smoke. The missile climbed faster and faster. Ildarov followed it with one camera, using a joystick. Soon the missile was too high to see anything but the incandescent glow from its engine, until that moved out of the camera's field of view, around the solid curvature of the Earth. Nyurba prayed that the warhead actually detonated, and prayed even harder that it went off only where it was supposed to, in outer space above Moscow.

The team repeated this with the second missile, and a guilt-wracked Nyurba repeated his fervent prayers.

Then they launched the third. As it began to leave its silo, a scattering of Russian troops, still alive amid the surface inferno and fumes, managed to rally and rouse themselves.

They found their last reserves of drive and energy, knowing what was unfolding before their eyes.

Nyurba grabbed for the intercom to the interlock, to warn his commandos to rush to defend the missile. But it was too late. As he watched on the TV display, Russian soldiers aimed their rifles at the missile and fired. The engine nozzle came out of the silo and roasted them.

Nyurba waited to see what damage they'd inflicted. The missile soared into the sky like the others, but it headed in a different direction. It was off-course, its trajectory all wrong. He had no idea what its warhead would do, and had no way to disarm or self-destruct it.

Nyurba felt that his last ounce of humanity was shredded by what the team under his orders had just made happen. "Major, have your men bag up as much intel materials as they can carry."

Ildarov was more than glad to hurry his specialists to this task. He knew what was coming, and welcomed distraction.

The mission doctrine saying "no prisoners" cuts both ways.

Nor could the commandos afford to leave any witnesses. They might have seen the team do subtle things revealing that they were Americans. Deceased, the silo crewmen's corpses would stop metabolizing those all-important, telltale German interrogation chemicals in their blood.

Nyurba drew his PRI and unemotionally shot each Russian silo crewman in the head; the small-caliber bullets made tiny holes and stayed inside their skulls. The pistol reports were deafening. Ejected shell casings bounced and clinked and rolled along the floor. The pistol slugs and the casings, under close forensic analysis, would be found to have been made in German-occupied Poland, not Russia.

"There it is!" one of *Challenger*'s fire control technicians shouted.

Jeffrey, startled from his reverie, saw it on his screen, a tiny yellow dot moving up in the dusky purple sky; it was after midnight, and the sun lay behind them to the north.

"Make a proper report," Bell snapped before Torelli or Sessions could. Everybody was understandably on edge.

"New visual contact, designate Victor One, assess as a Russian ICBM in flight."

"I concur with assessment," Torelli said.

"Very well, Weps," Bell acknowledged.

Jeffrey saw another dot, following the first.

"New visual contact! Designate Victor Two! Second Russian ICBM in flight."

The photonics head began tracking the missiles. The first one blinked out, then reappeared. "First-stage booster separation. Second-stage ignition." The spent first stage, already outside the atmosphere, would burn up on its way down.

"Maximum image magnification," Jeffrey ordered. The picture zoomed in and narrowed, like a twenty-four-power telescope. The technician kept shifting the head from Victor One to Victor Two and back again, since they didn't fit in the field of view at once now. Both were accelerating rapidly.

Victor Two seemed to blink for a moment. "Victor Two first-stage separation, second-stage booster ignition."

The second photonics mast was busy scanning the horizon to the south and east. *Missiles on other trajectories, or launched from other places, could mean a full-scale Russian preemptive first strike—despite everything the two presidents said.*

A third yellow dot appeared above the horizon, on a more northerly course. "New visual contact, designate Victor Three!"

Victor Three was definitely *not* behaving like the other two missiles. Who had launched it? From where? And why?

Jeffrey grabbed the handset for the radio room. He was so agitated he almost fumbled it the first time he tried to press the Talk button. "Radio, Commodore Fuller. Prepare to transmit on all available frequencies, warning of an unaccounted-for Russian missile in flight, targeting appears to be West Coast United States."

Victor Three suddenly began plunging back toward the Earth.

"What the—"

"Rig for nuclear depth charge!" Bell shouted. The missile appeared to be coming straight for them. Had the Russians detected *Challenger* after all, and uncovered Kurzin's disguise, and chosen a fitting method of revenge?

Victor Three burst into pieces. The scene reminded Jeffrey of the destruction of the space shuttle *Challenger*.

An unfortunate choice of namesake for this ship.

"Victor Three explosion is chemical," Sessions announced. Victor One and Two had already gone into second-stage booster separation and third-stage ignition. Even on maximum zoom with further computerized image enhancement, and one mast's sensor in infrared mode so the missiles would stand out better against the frigid backdrop of outer space, they were tiny dots receding just above the visual horizon, far to the east. Their speed would top out at Mach twenty-four—over fifteen thousand miles per hour.

"Victor Three wreckage includes a one-megaton warhead," Torelli cautioned. "Warhead status is unknown."

Debris was fluttering and falling through the sky, trailing smoke. The warhead reentry body, if intact, would be dense and aerodynamically streamlined. It could carry much farther than other wreckage. Its fusing might think it was nearing a target.

Challenger, so shallow and with masts raised, would not withstand the shock and EMP this close. But Jeffrey needed to keep observing for more Russian missile liftoffs. He couldn't order Bell to go deep. And Victor One and Two, assuming they were launched by Kurzin and not the Kremlin, might have faulty fusing—and could target the U.S. homeland for real.

"Victor One detonation!"

A violet-white flash lit up the entire sky. The brilliant flash was followed by a diffuse greenish glow that lasted about a second. When this faded, a warhead fireball of evanescent blue and red—excited gas molecules and superheated plasma—swelled in the vacuum of space, only a few degrees above the eastern horizon, but four hundred miles above the Earth.

"Victor Two detonation!"

Another bright flash, another green glow, another eerie expanding sphere.

"Bearings are correct to pancake the Moscow-to-Ural-Mountains area," Torelli reported by the weapons consoles.

"I concur," Meltzer said from the navigation plotting table.

On the photonics display screens, the whole sky turned blood red, in shimmering sheets and dancing curtains—an awesome aurora caused by the exoatmospheric nuclear blasts. As intended, *Challenger*'s location, and all of eastern Siberia, were outside the area hit by the powerful twin EMPs.

Jeffrey waited for reports from ESM and the Radio Room. He waited to see if more missiles took off. He waited to see if the warhead from Victor Three was live and still coming his way.

In the next few minutes, no nuke exploded from the third ICBM that had launched from Srednekolymsk. No more missiles launched anywhere, so far, that he was aware of. ESM and Radio tuned to local news broadcasts, which were being fed incomplete reports from the edges of the worst-affected zone. These helped confirm that—as expected—the electromagnetic pulses had pancaked cities ranging from Moscow to Magnitogorsk. They'd knocked out power and communications in a broad area of European Russia, sowing confusion and chaos, starting electrical fires in everything from large transformers to laptop computers. Rumors and speculation reported by Russian newscasters about the cause of all this varied from UFOs, to an asteroid hit, to nuclear war, to a new German or American secret weapon.

An ELF code group came through meaning Jeffrey should wait fifteen minutes and then commence the next mission phase, and put his script into action—ELF was immune to distant, prompt EMP effects. The wait was to make it look like he'd received and studied a longer message sent by low-frequency radio, with a much faster data rate than ELF.

Even a quarter-hour later, reception at higher, tactical frequencies was heavy with static—hissing and whistling and popping—but Radio managed to make line-of-sight contact with a Tupolev-204 to the east. Jeffrey used his best Russian.

"Tupolev, Tupolev, this is Captain Jeffrey Fuller of the United States Navy, on USS *Challenger* in international waters."

"American submarine, American submarine, this is Tupolev-Two-Zero-Four, call sign Sable Seven. What are your intentions?"

"Sable Seven, Sable Seven, I have been ordered by the President of the United States to meet in this emergency with your regional commanding rear admiral."

Nyurba's surviving commandos, all wearing gas masks now, clambered up the stairwells of the three missile control bunkers, knowing they didn't have a moment to lose. The explosion of three silos had repulsed one Russian counterattack, and the heat and toxic exhaust of three missiles launching later on had broken up an effective rally by hostile troops still alive in the area. But those two battalions of paratroopers, overheard on the bunker radio before the SS-27s took off, could be here very soon.

Watching things on bunker one's soundless and two-dimensional TV screens couldn't have possibly prepared Nyurba for the hellish situation he was engulfed in on the surface. Dense smoke, thick poisonous fumes, and billowing steam drifted everywhere, surrounding and partially cloaking what he thought resembled the site of a terrible airliner crash. The once wide-open missile field, within the fence enclosure, was impenetrably shrouded in deadly smog and persistent flames from asphalt and mangled debris. What passable ground still existed was pockmarked, cratered, and warped, and blackened *things* lay underfoot everywhere. Above the steady crackling and roaring of fires, and the staccato pops and bangs of ammo cooking off, Nyurba heard plaintive or agonized screams, but blessedly didn't see live victims, yet, only scattered body parts. He also heard occasional, halfhearted orders shouted far away, in voices he didn't recognize. AK-47s and the smaller-caliber AK-74s, their muzzle reports distinctive to a trained ear, sporadically fired in the distance, wildly it seemed and from random directions. Occasionally their rounds snapped by, harmlessly overhead. Whoever was shooting aimed high—assuming they were aiming and hadn't simply been driven mad or gotten blind drunk. No Russians nearby were in any shape to put up the slightest resistance.

Main opposition forces lack cohesion and discipline. Good.

The commando groups from the three control bunkers linked up amid this carnage and frenzy, Abakans trained on each other until they were sure they met with friends. At first Nyurba was enraged when he saw his medics and other men dragging travoises improvised from backpack frames, each holding a seriously wounded teammate who should have been lethally overdosed with morphine and abandoned. Platoon leaders said they *were* obeying his orders, making the wounded permanently unavailable for hostile interrogation—by bringing them home. He realized that, consciously or unconsciously, he'd phrased the order to give his team this out. He assisted a Green Beret lieutenant who'd taken shrapnel in one leg and had a bandaged, splinted compound fracture. He must have been in unspeakable pain. Using a bent metal rod as a crutch, the lieutenant was too proud and tough to be pulled, like so much baggage, on a travois.

Like the others with wounds, the medics had made the Green Beret's dressings especially thick. They knew, as Nyurba knew, that radioactive particulates could enter the bloodstream through breaks in the skin. There was plenty of nuclear contamination in the air all around them, outside their masks.

Nyurba did a head count: twenty fit, twenty badly wounded, and five wounded who were—generously speaking—ambulatory. He carefully verified with each squad that everyone not present was accounted for as definitely dead; Russian forensic pathologists would have rogue cadavers galore to analyze.

We'll never escape and evade through the forest like this.

"Change or hide insignia," Nyurba ordered through his gas mask. "Riffle the Russian corpses." Concealed by the swirling, noxious, opaque, and multicolored haze, the team removed their Spetsnaz wolf-formation badges, tore off shoulder patches or drenched them in gore, and grabbed uniform markings from bodies strewn everywhere. It was vital they not be recognized as the same unit that had talked its way in at the start of the battle.

Some of the corpses, on closer examination, weren't quite dead. Nyurba had to look a mortally wounded private in the eyes; he couldn't be over eighteen. Too weak from loss of blood and shock from burns to be able to talk, the teenager pleaded for help with those dark brown eyes. Nyurba watched the confusion cross his battered, sweaty face as he finished him off with his fighting knife—a gesture of mercy. The kid had no legs and his groin was nothing but smoldering ash. He knew he'd remember those trusting brown eyes for the rest of his life. He removed an insignia badge from the body and fastened it to his own chest.

Having kept his sense of bearings while his squadron regrouped aboveground, Nyurba told them to head for the entrance gate—or whatever was left of it. This would bring them to the route from the support base and Srednekolymsk. He had a hunch that Russian casualty-clearing efforts would have already started, and his intention was to blend in. *We were supposed to pass as Russians all along. We'll pass as Russians now.*

Nyurba's read of the situation paid off. As they trudged along toward the gate, the ends of the travoises scraping noisily on the concrete, more and more Russian medics scurried around, helping whomever they could. One directed Nyurba and his men—filthy, exhausted, coughing repeatedly inside their gas masks—to the field ambulance staging area.

"What happened to those missiles?" Nyurba asked the medic. His lungs hurt when he spoke; it felt like he was getting pneumonia. "Are we in a nuclear war?" He peered at the sky, but it was too smoke-obscured for him to notice any auroral effects.

"I heard someone say they were terrorists, sir. Two went off in space over Moscow. Everything near there got fried."

"Three launched."

"The last was a dud, sir. If you can believe the rumors."

That's all I needed to hear. He led his men toward the ambulances. They moved with renewed strength and spirit, knowing this mission phase was a success.

Most casualty transport were commercial trucks pressed into service for the emergency. A harried, emotionally dazed dispatcher said that hospitals at the support base and in the town were overwhelmed. Nyurba had no intention of going to any hospital. The most practical route of egress was the Kolyma.

He told a tractor-trailer driver to take his people to the waterfront. Nyurba sat in the cab. The trip on the excellent concrete road was short. The mines his men planted earlier were cleared. Their victim, the hulk of a blown-up tank, sat partly blocking one lane, turret-less, bathed in firefighting foam. Firemen used their engines to pump water out of nearby streams and ponds, to hold forest fires back from the sides of the road.

All roadblocks were for vehicles approaching the complex—sealed off against spies and journalists—not for those leaving with troops who badly needed trauma care. Regional authorities were muddled, psychologically overwhelmed by the SS-27 liftoffs. They focused on rescue and recovery, and further site defense from outward, not on interdicting escapees. Perhaps someone in charge, from optimism or face-saving ego, made the assumption that the attackers had all been killed, or committed suicide.

The EMP hitting the Kremlin, plus rigid central control, is buying us getaway time—but for how long?

Civilian and military boats, ships, hydrofoils, and hover-craft were tied up in a hodgepodge at the Kolyma piers. Reinforcements were still arriving for a battle that no longer raged, while wounded, some with hideous burns, were being rushed to other hospitals downriver. Nyurba picked what he wanted: an old Skat-class air-cushion landing craft, official capacity two dozen troops. The six-man crew made no effort to refuse when the commandos demanded transportation. They climbed aboard the vessel, using the troop ladders at both sides of its blunt bow. The casualties, wheezing inside their masks due to lung problems from the missile fumes, moaned louder with this mishandling.

His fit men easily bound and gagged the crew. The enclosed, soundproof passenger area became overcrowded with commandos. The separate tiny control cabin's fittings were worn and scuffed, but the small armored windshields on all four sides gave good views. A SEAL Chief knew how to operate the hovercraft—it wasn't very different from the U.S. Navy's LCACs, just smaller. An Army Ranger acted as radio man; a card by the transceiver gave their call sign of the day. He listened for news of pursuit or blockades downriver; static was extreme, but no cordon for rogues was set up. Nyurba's medics had Red Cross flags, since these could give certain protections under recognized rules of war. He ordered two to be flown from staffs on the Skat. They'd help the vessel blend in now as a regular unit bringing injured men toward aid. *When will the Russian dragnet gel? How far will it reach?*

The Skat was powered by two turboprops and one gas-turbine lift fan. The turboprops, in cowlings on tall projections at the stern, drove giant propellers; rudders in those tails worked just like those on airplanes. The turbine provided high-pressure air to a rubbery skirt surrounding the vessel's bottom. The fuel tanks were full; the crew had topped them off upon arriving.

With the lift engine pushed to full power, the Skat rose on a cushion of air. Mist blew out from under the skirt. The chief turned the Skat downriver, north, and shoved the throttles all the way forward. Soon they were making more than fifty knots.

Looking back at dumpy Srednekolymsk, Nyurba noticed something painted on one of the Skat's twin tails, so faded with age he could barely make it out—a hammer and sickle.

CHAPTER 27

Rear Admiral Meredov was quickly responsive to Jeffrey's request, and very efficient about it. His aide gave Jeffrey a course to steer at flank speed under the ice, to surface and meet a civilian icebreaker unaffected by the EMP in this far-eastern part of Siberia. She told him the ship had a helicopter pad—a common arrangement, to scout ahead for the best route through difficult ice conditions.

When *Challenger* rendezvoused, Jeffrey was surprised to see, on the photonics mast display screens, not a helo but a Yakovlev-38U, a two-seat trainer version of the Russian Navy vertical takeoff and landing plane. The old Yak-38 resembled a Harrier, except its fuselage was longer and thinner, and its wing and tail were distinctively Russian in styling. The helo pad had to have been reinforced to take its weight and withstand the force and heat of its lift jets. That and the fact that the Yak was being refueled on the pad implied that the so-called civilian ship was a naval auxiliary, thinly concealed. She flew the Russian Federation flag, three broad stripes, white over blue over red.

Lieutenant Bud Torelli, the Weps, noticed that her superstructure bore several long, thin rectangular boxes covered by tarpaulins. He said these were almost certainly antiship and antiaircraft missile launchers.

She's an auxiliary cruiser, an outright warship, disguised.

The other photonics mast showed that same Tu-204, Sable Seven, circling both vessels at a polite distance. It was there, Jeffrey assumed, for two disparate reasons. One was to help make sure that the rendezvous went off okay. The other was to make sure *Challenger* was really *Challenger*—not an American SSBN who'd tricked the Russians and snuck in close to launch its two dozen MIRVed missiles on flat trajectories with very short transit times. From this location, they'd reach anywhere in Russia in ten or twelve minutes. *I don't blame them for being very, very cautious. They think we think they just tried to nuke the U.S.*

Surfaced, her antenna masts exposed again, *Challenger's* radio room received fragmentary updates for Jeffrey and Bell. The earth's ionosphere and magnetic field were still distorted. The Van Allen belts were excited and swollen by nuclear gamma rays, X-rays, and ionized bomb debris. Several dozen unshielded satellites in low earth orbit had gone dead, and more would in the weeks to come from lingering radiation and energetic charged particles—although special methods of pumping high-frequency radio beams into space could ease this problem. Geosynchronous satellites and ones in high earth orbit were safe, as were ground stations outside the pancaked area. But reception was poor; transmissions via these satellites had to pierce the layers of persisting disruption from the exoatmospheric blasts.

The substantive news was that the Kremlin seemed harder hit by the EMP than expected. Jeffrey knew that shielding needed diligent maintenance or it wouldn't hold up. The slightest bit of dirt or grease where it shouldn't be, or one loose fitting, or a faulty backup battery, could cause even military-grade EMP protection to fail. Fiber-optic cables themselves might be immune to voltage surges, but their electrically powered signal amplifiers were vulnerable—and too many had been knocked out. It appeared that the Kremlin's minions were sloppy.

Technicians were scrambling to get the Hot Line hot again; in the meantime Russia's president was incommunicado, not by choice. Unfortunately, the American ambassador in Moscow, who wasn't forewarned for security reasons, had taken the weekend off with his top aides at a *dacha*— country cabin—in the affected zone, and couldn't be reached. Washington hoped that the German embassy was suffering similar problems. The U.S. and Russia were holding their H-bomb forces at DEFCON 2 or the equivalent, but the status quo of restraint was very volatile under the circumstances. The SS-27 warheads exploded in space at what had been 7 P.M. on a Saturday night in Moscow. Urban traffic there was at a standstill, gridlocked, the microchips essential to modern vehicles all destroyed. Aircraft near Greater Moscow had been rendered unflyable, their avionics cooked. Airports in the pancaked zone were unusable without the severest risks, their radios, radars, navigation aids, and landing guidance systems all inoperable. Most planes in the air at the time of the EMP had managed to make forced landings, but some had crashed—the death toll was already extending beyond the missile complex at Srednekolymsk. Berlin, ever opportunistic and ruthless, so far seemed to be treating events with a studious silence. Jeffrey hoped to deliver them a sucker punch very soon.

The opening act in this drama, now that the icebreaker was here, would be to keep the Russians waiting. Jeffrey went to the XO's stateroom to pack an overnight bag. And he took his own sweet time about it.

———

More than once, Nyurba ordered the SEAL chief to steer the air-cushioned Skat on shortcuts over tundra or swamps, saving miles compared to the wide, island-studded Kolyma's winding course in the Arctic lowlands. He, the chief, and the radio man kept coughing up thick phlegm that they spat on the vibrating deck. At least, here in cleaner air, the commandos were out of their gas masks. Other vessels rushed upstream; the Skat, one of the fastest things on the river, overtook many heading down. In the sky, planes and helicopters flew back and forth, but none approached the Skat, which could defend itself with machine guns and shoulder-fired missiles he intentionally left unmanned.

At a medic's request, Nyurba gave two pints of blood for the wounded, standing with a needle in his arm in the control cabin. His blood flowed from a vein to refill expended plasma packs—the wounded needed whole blood desperately. Two pints after a hard week was a lot; he felt dizzy. He drank water and ate field rations to replenish himself. He visited the men to offer comfort, distressed by how maimed they were in body and mind.

———

Jeffrey said good-bye to Bell, and wished the crew good fortune. Lugging the overnight bag, he paraded from *Challenger*'s hull into the icebreaker, up the ramp of a brow the big ship lowered from a gangway using a deck crane. He wore his winter greatcoat and formal hat and Navy blue dress uniform—including four gold rings that COB removed from Finch's jacket to sew on his sleeves that already bore three. Jeffrey was led aft by the icebreaker's weather-beaten master, a gaunt part-Asian man, fiftyish, whose fingers and teeth were stained by nicotine from cheap Russian cigarettes of which he thoroughly reeked. Now, he didn't smoke; the Yak's refueling had just been completed.

Looking over the icebreaker's side, Jeffrey saw the crane stowing the brow. *Challenger,* her bridge crew already below, was moving away. She dived, a magnificent sight.

She'd head north, to disappear under the ice cap, and Bell would make sure to lose any tail. Meredov's base was in range of her dozen-plus Tactical Tomahawk cruise missiles, from anywhere within a huge area stretching up to the North Pole; Jeffrey would refuse to move any farther once he got to that headquarters.

The pilot, a no-nonsense, thirtysomething very fit Slav, strapped Jeffrey into the trainee seat, giving him a flight helmet. He climbed into the rear seat and lowered the cockpit canopy. Engine noises rose from idling whines to bone-shaking roars. The aircraft jumped into the sky, carrying external fuel tanks instead of bombs or missiles—but it did have a nose gun.

The Yak-38 hit five hundred knots. After a blur of Laptev Sea icebergs and white caps and surf, then a stretch of desolate tundra, Jeffrey looked down and around at a crazy-quilt patchwork of untouched taiga forest, winding rivers and tributaries, repulsive overindustrialization, and open-pit strip mining. The pilot helped Jeffrey listen to a news update that Meredov relayed to the plane. Drunken looting and panicky riots had broken out in crowded downtown Moscow. With no government explanation forthcoming for the paralyzing fireworks in the sky, with police unable to mobilize and blazes burning unchecked, anarchists and hooligans seized the chance to unleash years of pent-up rage. The frenzied mob-rule lawlessness and violence rapidly spread. As paranoid as ever of interference from abroad, Russians lynched Westerners at random, and stoned embassies indiscriminately.

So much mayhem so quickly is outside the envelope of scenarios considered in the mission plan. We're going way off the map, into uncoordinated guesswork and ad-libbing.

CHAPTER 28

I n minutes the Yak landed at a base in the foothills of the snowcapped Cherskiy Mountain Range. A group of naval officers stood there to meet Jeffrey, led by a tall and bearlike figure, easily recognized from his photos, the unsmiling Elmar Meredov.

Meredov loped toward the Yak idling on the airstrip, trailed by his senior staff including a translator. He welcomed Jeffrey curtly, cautiously. Jeffrey insisted on carrying his overnight bag, hugging it in his lap in the van that took everyone on a short ride through the base. He chided himself immediately: the gesture with the bag was meant to establish antagonism and distance, but it was coming across as plain defensive. He sat there in stern silence, and no one else spoke a word.

A ceremonial honor guard of naval infantry, holding rifles with gleaming fixed bayonets, very smartly snapped to attention flanking the last part of the road to the headquarters building. Jeffrey wasn't sure if this was a courtesy to him, or a show of force, or both. A platoon of Army Spetsnaz troops arrived by helicopter a minute after the Yak, and followed the van in two trucks. They grimly established close-in perimeter security—terrorists, rogues, insurgents, or assassins could be anywhere in this crisis of unknown, imponderable dimensions. Again Jeffrey wondered. Was this a precaution, needed from the Russians' perspective to protect him and Meredov? Or was it to confine him, while Russia and the U.S. followed a path toward atomic war?

In Meredov's office, Jeffrey eyed the meter-long model of a NATO code-name Typhoon displayed on a bookcase. He reminded himself that Meredov once walked the decks of such a sub as assistant captain. During nuclear deterrent patrols, he'd been ready if ordered to help unleash wholesale Armageddon on America.

Jeffrey loosened up, for the first time in hours, when Meredov showed him a photo of his wife and their three grown sons. Meredov's pleasure at displaying his family to a professional peer—Jeffrey—was clearly genuine, and infectious. *This man has natural charisma. His staff draws strength from his calming influence. Inside, he's probably as nervous as I am.* He seemed an ideal role model of leadership based on compassion, self-confidence, and proven experience.

Other physical tokens of that experience festooned Meredov's uniform jacket. Russian practice was to give a separate medal for each award of the same decoration; the man's chest held rows of them. Jeffrey recognized five copies of the Medal for Courage, but he didn't know what most of the others meant. He was glad he'd worn his dress uniform with his own medals, including the five-pointed bronze medallion of the Medal of Honor on a ribbon around his neck. *We've got parity in the clothing department. This is a diplomatic face-off. Dress codes matter.*

Obliged to reciprocate, Jeffrey pulled out his wallet, showing Meredov pictures of his parents, and of his two older sisters with their husbands and kids. Meredov admired them, with apparent sincerity. He also admired Jeffrey's Medal, and, seeing the fourth ring on his sleeves, congratulated him on his recent promotion. He complimented Jeffrey on his Russian. Meredov didn't speak English, beyond a few basic phrases learned from TV.

Enough with the pleasantries. Both our families could go up in mushroom clouds soon if things are delayed or mishandled.

Meredov seemed to read his thoughts, which Jeffrey found unsettling. Meredov suddenly turned dour. "Come into my conference room, Captain Fuller. Let us get down to the urgent business, shall we?"

Maybe he didn't feel nervous inside after all. Maybe Meredov was incapable, at this point in his life within such an alien culture as Russia, of ever being made nervous. Jeffrey realized that he'd already shrewdly, smoothly, seized the mental edge. This concerned Jeffrey in a bigger context. Why was he playing, so soon, for such an edge? It made sense, given the political risks to his career, for Meredov to begrudge the role of unwilling back-door emissary—but even so he ought to want to tone down conflict, not raise it, for his own country's sake.

He also appeared to be very good at donning different masks from one moment to the next. Jeffrey wondered which of these personas was the real Meredov. Then it occurred to him that this might be the wrong point of view. Maybe they were all parts of the real him? If so, he was a complicated guy, unpredictable to someone who didn't know him well, a tough customer to deal with.

And Meredov had another advantage in this strange, developing confrontation. His best weapon was probably to tell the simple, honest truth as he saw it. Jeffrey, in contrast, had to constantly lie.

───────

Nyurba's Skat, still going all out, began to run low on fuel. They reached the harbor, Ambarchik, at the Kolyma's outlet to the sea. Nyurba, smeared with gore, talked to the fueling-pier workers. He scrawled an illegible signature on the requisition forms. They hurried, but the transfer of thousands of liters of gas via hoses used valuable time. The Skat took off again, heading east along the shore, passing promontories with lighthouses, and cliffs. They aimed for narrow Malyy Chaunskiy Strait, between the mainland and big Ayon Island, leading into huge Chaunskaya Bay, fifty miles from the Pevek naval base.

"Sir," the Army Ranger shouted, "we're being called on the radio." The Skat was so old that the control cabin's soundproofing didn't work very well. The whining drone of the engines and props made conversation difficult.

"Don't transmit!" Nyurba ordered hoarsely. "Who's calling?"

"I don't know what their call sign means."

"How's reception?"

"One by one." Poor signal strength, poor message clarity.

"Don't transmit." *The distant EMP's broader, persistent effects could've spoiled local surface ducting, and sea surveillance radar resolution could be messed up.* "They may have no way to tell where we are."

"Hydrophones can still track us," the SEAL Chief corrected sardonically. Nyurba was none too happy at the reminder. He had another worry as the Skat's engines continued to strain: How long before they broke down and the group was stranded?

―――――

Meredov's conference room was windowless, shielded against electronic eavesdropping. He didn't seem too concerned about that, since he left the thick door from his office open. He took the seat at the head of the table, so that through the doorway he could see his senior aide, a stocky woman, Captain, Second Rank Irina Malenkova, sitting at his desk and handling phone calls for him on less pressing matters.

In the middle of the table was the traditional plate of *zakusi,* a selection of various Russian appetizers that Jeffrey thought of as Slavic antipasti. Coffee, tea, and bottled water were arrayed on a sideboard; there was no alcohol. Jeffrey poured himself black coffee—it was several hours after midnight here, and many more hours than that since he'd last slept. Meredov, who also looked tired, preferred tea.

Jeffrey intentionally took the seat at the foot of the table, opposite Meredov, and picked only lightly at the food, to reestablish an adversarial atmosphere. Near the *zakusi* platter was a conference phone, with the lights implying the connection was live and the phone wasn't muted. There was another, regular telephone within Meredov's reach on the sideboard. The translator, a captain, third class—lieutenant commander—sat against a wall, being unobtrusive. That wall held a map of the Russian Federation and surrounding waters and countries. Another wall held a whiteboard with eraser and colored markers; faint streaks indicated the board was used, perhaps often. A third wall held a big, blank computer flat-screen display.

"Communications with Vladivostok have been tested," Meredov said, "and from there across the Pacific through the United States to Washington. The Hot Line to Moscow is still under repair but is hoped to be operational soon, Captain. Once that's done, we'll be patched into the discussion between our presidents. In the meanwhile, what do you want?"

"Who's on the other end of this conference call?"

"Senior admirals in Vladivostok who gave me permission to meet with you, and who want to listen in. They've told me they wish to keep their participation to a minimum. Also, I'm instructed to inform you that they're recording this discussion, to replay it for the Kremlin once communications are restored."

Typical. Centralized control is everything to these people.

"*Zdrastvuti,*" Jeffrey said tentatively into the conference phone. Hello.

After a long pause, a gruff old man on the other end answered with a grudging "Hello." His gravelly, unfriendly voice was a good conversation killer. He came through clearly and crisply, though, presumably by a fiber-optic trunk line, which led in the opposite direction from the pancaked area far to the west; Vladivostok would have been untouched by the EMP.

Jeffrey made a procedural arrangement with the translator. If he didn't understand something Meredov said, or didn't know a word in Russian himself, he'd raise his thumb. The translator would help while Meredov waited. The young man, thin and serious, said in English that he followed what Jeffrey meant. His English was accented but fluent. His voice was oddly nasal. *Maybe he has a cold, or just always talks that way?*

Jeffrey remembered Colonel Kurzin's advice from what seemed like ages ago, to not rush himself or be rushed, to set a steady and even pace and stick to it. He wondered how Kurzin's team was doing now, and if they were even alive. He cleared his throat.

"As representative of the aggrieved party, I believe I have the right to insist that you speak first, Admiral, and make your country's position plain."

"I have no experience in acting as a military emissary to a foreign state. I'm informed that you've done so before, successfully, in South America. But I'm not clear why you've come to me personally."

"You're a naval officer, qualified in submarines in fact, so you and I have important traits and attitudes in common. There's a potential rapport which I would not share with someone from your army or air force, and certainly not from your Strategic Rocket Forces arm. Your base happened to have been the closest one to my ship when this crisis erupted, and my ship happened to be the closest American nuclear sub to Srednekolymsk when back-channel discussions, as we call them in my country, became necessary. Your rank, as rear admiral, is not too senior to mine yet senior enough to give you . . . how do you say it . . . clout. And yet you in turn are sufficiently junior in the broader context that your statements can be treated by Mos-

cow as deniable at a later date if necessary. That's the recipe
for us meeting, alone, you and I, specifically, here and now,
given the disturbing events at Srednekolymsk and their
troubling potential aftermath. I'm sure those in Vladivostok follow my logic."

*And they understand how to cover their asses by keeping
safely separate from me, the foreign influence, the hot potato.*

The conference phone stayed silent.

Meredov nodded. "Then I suggest that we leave rank
aside right now, and I request that you, Captain, establish a
proper framework for what we must cover."

"I am here as an unofficial envoy, to resolve for better or
worse the many questions raised by the SS-27 launches.
Causes, intentions, who is responsible, and what retribution
by my country is justly called for."

Meredov winced. "I think there is more. You have come,
America's greatest submarine ace, as a personified demon-
stration of your nation's power and prowess in tactical nuclear combat. I believe you also serve as a high-value trip
wire, a significant test of Russian goodwill. If you are
harmed, your president will learn of it soon, and will judge
his next actions accordingly."

Meredov was to some extent playing to the audience on
the conference phone—some of those men were his bosses.
Jeffrey knew that, ultimately, because of the recording being made in Vladivostok, both of them were playing to the
Russian president. They also circled one another, verbally
and nonverbally, still sizing each other up. It was time for
Jeffrey to move in, hard.

"Your headquarters is under the guns of my ship, in the
hands of my capable executive officer, who is in constant
receive-only extremely low-frequency contact with Commander, U.S. Strategic Command. *Challenger*'s nuclear
Tactical Tomahawk land-attack cruise missiles can devas-
tate this base and most of the rest of your assets, from Tiksu
to Pevek, if the situation should so dictate."

"I presumed as much," Meredov responded dryly.

"There's more. My commander in chief has set a deadline for adequate resolution of the outstanding issues. The question of proper retaliation for Russia's attempted ballistic missile H-bomb strike at the U.S. homeland is serious indeed. What does the doctrine of flexible response mean in this situation?"

"What does it mean to your president?"

"My executive officer already has the emergency-action message and the target list. He also has the launch window. The timing has been set for midnight tonight, your local time. If the United States of America has not received sufficient explanation and agreed compensation by then, my executive officer, with *Challenger* hiding in the marginal ice zone, will launch a dozen cruise missiles at places within range. These places include not only your regional bases, Admiral, but also Anadyr, Vladivostok, and the cities of Yakutia and Magadan. The yield of each warhead is twenty-five kilotons." This supposed prearranged strike was a total lie, part of the script, but Russia had no way to find that out unless they dawdled. Jeffrey's purpose was to establish a frightening deadline, to motivate the Kremlin to get to the bottom of the SS-27 launches, yet not allow them—or the Germans—time to think too much.

Meredov's face turned red. "This is outrageous! Your nation has not been harmed and yet you'd attack our innocent cities? Call off this deranged order!"

"America not harmed? Not harmed with no thanks to you and your treacherous government. *Challenger*'s tactical nuclear strike will not be called off unless we find satisfaction. Her cruise missiles will surely reach most of their targets, given the confused state of your nationwide command and control."

"But if you nuke this base while you're here you'll be killed!"

Jeffrey forced a nasty smile. "You said I was a trip wire. I am, in fact, much more than that. Think of me as a walking dead-man's switch. No good news by midnight, which gives you less than twenty-four hours by the way, then the strike occurs regardless of my personal situation, what I say, and whether or not my government is even in contact with me."

Meredov jumped up from his chair. "Such a strategy by Washington is utterly reckless! It's madness!"

Jeffrey stayed seated, feigning calm. "You also said I'd come to test your good faith."

Meredov hesitated. "Yes?"

"I am here, given my value to my country and my experience, to demonstrate my government's resolve. I come in hopes of helping achieve a positive resolution to the murderous actions attempted but thwarted at Srednekolymsk. In order to avoid a full-scale nuclear exchange between our countries, if need be I'm prepared to give my life. Aren't *you*, Admiral?"

"I've always been prepared to give my life for the Motherland."

Jeffrey stared at Meredov. "Do we understand each other?" He glanced at the clock on a wall. "You have until midnight."

Meredov sat down and let out a long breath. "Yes. We understand each other."

"So who launched those missiles and why?" Jeffrey banged the table with a clenched fist. The translator was startled. Meredov looked pained.

"We do not yet know. It might have been rogues or invaders. I'm told this is being actively investigated."

"As far as my country is aware, and as far as my president sees it, Russia attempted a first strike against America. *Your* country, with the authorization of *your* commander in chief, and the rest is all lies!"

"But—"

"Verbal excuses will carry no weight! How can you possibly explain *this*?" Jeffrey reached into his bag and pulled out the transcript of the Hot Line call, before the SS-27s lifted off.

Since it was in English, Meredov gave it to the translator.

"Read it aloud in Russian," he ordered, pointing at the conference phone.

Meredov's face turned crimson as he started to understand what the transcript said. "I myself am puzzled. I do not think my commander in chief would mislead yours intentionally, on topics of such importance, when the likelihood of deception being found out was so great. Perhaps he was misled by intermediate-level commanders, who were confused or who sought to protect themselves."

"Between nations, Admiral, the whole is held responsible for the actions of its parts."

Meredov nodded reluctantly.

Jeffrey leaned forward. "Listen carefully, you and those in Vladivostok, and in Moscow when they hear this as a recording. . . . If extremists launched those missiles, in some analogy to the attempted provocation by the Golf-class sub in nineteen-sixty-eight, and other suspect events since then, the Kremlin is answerable. Answerable for failing to adequately safeguard its own thermonuclear missiles during a time of terrible international strife. And answerable for failing to maintain adequate internal security as to conspiracies and splinter groups within the Kremlin's own power structure. If we did not have our stealth space-based missile shield in place, tragedy would have occurred. Instead of us sitting here talking, our two countries would be busy fighting a strategic nuclear war! *Do you grasp how serious things are?*"

"What is this missile shield? I thought Russian rogues created the electromagnetic pulses over Moscow on purpose, or the missiles were aimed at America but detonated early due to some error in fusing inputs or a hardware or software fault."

This is the critical moment. To make it real, I need to keep it tight, almost as an afterthought, and sound blasé. Overexplaining or going verbose would only cast doubt.

The Hot Line would be used to convey its technical details—that part of the script wasn't Jeffrey's job, unless pressed.

"The shield's very existence is classified. I was informed by radio only because I had a need to know, as part of my tasking to meet with you. It has the capability to make enabled, unlocked hydrogen bombs on ballistic missiles launched against America detonate prematurely in the vacuum of space, after their boost phase is complete, to inflict punishment on the aggressor and discourage further provocation or escalation."

Meredov was astonished. "The nuclear explosions were caused by your missile shield?"

"The punishment inflicted is proportional, discriminate, appropriate, nonlethal, and nonescalatory. My government views this retaliation as entirely justified under international law."

"Such points, I am not qualified to debate. But why has such an amazing capability been kept secret?"

"I suppose to not tempt an adversary into striking before it was ready. . . . Don't evade me, Admiral. I repeat my question. Who was responsible for launching those missiles? And I don't mean who turned the keys. I mean who made the decision, issued the authorization? If you don't come up with some good answers soon, my commander in chief will feel righteously entitled to inflict more such pulses on Russia, beyond the tactical nuclear strike launched from *Challenger,* using *American* ICBMs. We will be protected by our special shield, while we send your whole country back to the age of the telegraph and the hot air balloon!"

Meredov's face turned white this time. "Captain, please. There may very well have been no authorization. The missile complex is a crime scene, a battlefield, and a toxic hot spot all in one. Vladivostok told me an investigation is under way. Such things always take time."

"Speaking of which, where's our patch into the Hot Line? The clock is ticking, and *Challenger* is lurking where you'll never find her soon enough."

Meredov turned to the doorway. "Irina!"

She appeared in a moment. "Yes, Admiral?"

"Call Vladivostok on another line and see what's causing the delay with us hearing from Moscow and Washington."

"At once, sir. And I didn't want to interrupt, but Rear Admiral Balakirev phoned you twice."

"What did he want?"

"He wants to know if he can fly here to meet Captain Fuller, and how is the computer analysis coming since it's been a while."

What computer analysis?

"Tell him the analysis is on hold due to more important problems, and whether he is invited to meet with our guest is up to his superiors, not me."

"Yes, Admiral. I would also like to speak with you in private for a moment."

Meredov sighed and stood.

"Excuse me, please, Captain. My regrets."

"Who's Balakirev?"

"Rear Admiral Balakirev is my counterpart in Anadyr, covering the coast and waters around the Bering Strait." Meredov spoke into the conference phone. "I am stepping from the room. I am muting the phone, and will return shortly."

When Meredov left the conference room, Irina beckoned for him to follow. Puzzled, he went to her office across the hall.

She closed the door. "There's something you need to see."

"Yes?"

"Regarding the computer analysis, Admiral."

"Go on. Quickly."

She placed a false-color image, a computer printout, on her desk. He examined it. "These are the spires in the strait?"

"Yes, sir."

"What are these red and orange dots and blobs?"

"Echo returns from the ships' and sonobuoy's active sonars, that our supercomputer eked from all the data Anadyr sent us."

The fuzzy colors traced the shape of a submarine in profile.

"So there *was* a hostile contact. It *did* just sit still and wait out the depth charges. . . . It used some sort of very effective out-of-phase ping cancellation to conceal itself."

Malinkova nodded. "That's what the computer center says."

"Can they identify the class of submarine?"

"Its dimensions as revealed by the dots indicate a length of about one-hundred-ten meters, and a beam close to twelve meters."

"That eliminates most possibilities."

"Yes, sir. The wide diameter of the hull is key, when combined with its length as a fast-attack. It can only be USS *Seawolf,* USS *Connecticut,* or USS *Challenger.* And our intelligence reports say that *Seawolf* and *Connecticut* are on the other side of the world, operating near South Africa."

"So it was in fact Captain Fuller's ship that Balakirev's forces pinned down temporarily?"

"Yes, sir. It appears quite certain."

"Does he know this?"

"Rear Admiral Balakirev? No, sir. I thought you should see this first, as soon as the analysis was ready."

Meredov started to think out loud. "And the depth charging was almost two weeks ago."

"Yes, sir."

"What's the distance from the Bering Strait to where *Challenger* first made contact with us by radio?"

"Less than two thousand miles, sir, even allowing for an indirect route."

Meredov did the arithmetic in his head. "So if she were moving constantly, she'd have made an average speed of less than seven knots."

"Yes, sir."

"Why would a vessel who's maximum quiet speed is at

least twenty-five knots move so slowly for such a long time?"

"I don't know, Admiral. It does seem odd, unless she had some mission in our waters."

"I won't mention this to Captain Fuller right away, because I don't want him on his guard before I'm ready to corner him with his own words. His being in the Laptev Sea when the missiles launched is awfully convenient. Too convenient."

"You think it wasn't coincidence, sir?"

"Who fired the decoy that pretended to be *Challenger*?"

"The real *Challenger,* maybe? But why?"

"I can think of several reasons, and I don't like any of them. . . . All right. Very good work, Irina. Express my thanks to the analysts. Inform Vladivostok immediately by secure line, but beyond that, you and the computer center are to say nothing about this to anyone. . . . Something here doesn't make sense. Something here doesn't make any sense at all."

Meredov folded the sheet, and put it in his jacket pocket.

When the Skat neared the Malyy Chaunskiy Strait and marshy Ayon Island, Nyurba removed the Red Cross flags, to alter the Skat's disguise. He told the SEAL to steer north, into the open East Siberian Sea, away from Pevek. The swells were mild; the hovercraft barely lost speed. Still making fifty knots, but running low on fuel again, they reached the long-planned rendezvous point, according to the inertial navigation readout.

"All stop on propulsion engines. Full power to lift fan."

They coasted to a halt, bobbing gently on the air cushion. He ordered two men to throw hand grenades over the sides, in groups of four, as if they were trying to kill escaping combat swimmers—a subterfuge meant for any snooping hydrophones or watching aircraft. The men hurled the grenades as far as they could, to not damage the lift skirts.

Each raised a spout when it detonated. The water was one hundred thirty feet deep. The grenades were the prearranged signal for *Carter.* Nyurba waited.

It's been five days. So many things could've gone wrong.

And if Carter *is compromised, then so is* Challenger—*and Commodore Fuller, ashore by now, is trapped in a fabric of lies.*

Suddenly, a dozen divers broke the surface at the bow, pulling coffinlike pressure-proof capsules, with built-in backboards and oxygen masks for bringing wounded through cold seawater into a submarine. Nyurba rushed to help the divers load the twelve worst stretcher cases. The divers said that Captain Harley had ordered both superstructure lockout chambers, and the trunk inside the sail, all to be used at once to save time; the top of the sail was only thirty feet beneath the surface.

After a nerve-wracking wait, the divers came back, their capsules empty. Ten more wounded were shuttled into *Carter,* along with the bodies of two commandos who'd, sadly, died on the ride in the Skat. Then waterproof equipment bags went, filled with digital cameras, top-secret manuals from the bunkers, and Nyurba's hard-won pollution data and environmental samples.

The fit passengers buddy-breathed with divers, pure oxygen easing their lungs, suppressing the worst of their coughing.

The hovercraft's crew might have somehow been useful alive, but not anymore. Nyurba shot them with his reloaded PRI. *If executing prisoners is a war crime, let Russia blame Germany.* The chief turned the Skat southwest, back toward the Kolyma as a ruse. Using duct tape, they fixed the rudders to hold that course. They shoved the throttles forward and taped them there. Before the Skat—horribly noisy outside—could gain speed, they jumped overboard. Buddy-breathing with two SEALs, they locked into *Carter's* sail trunk, ready to decontaminate.

CHAPTER 29

"My apologies," Meredov said as he reentered his conference room. He unmuted the phone. "Vladivostok, I have returned."

"What's going on with the Hot Line?" Jeffrey pressed.

"My aide is finding out. She'll let us know. The Kremlin was very hard hit by the twin electromagnetic pulses."

Jeffrey had achieved his initial goals for the meeting, delivered his pointed queries and table-thumping messages, and introduced the premise of a next-generation missile shield. But he wasn't supposed to work this as a lone wolf. And the artificial midnight deadline, meant to squeeze Moscow, was also putting a squeeze on him. Would the Kremlin, de facto, call that bluff, just by quietly, gradually running out the deadline?

"At least patch me through to my president."

"Preparations are still being made," that grumpy voice said over the speakerphone from Vladivostok.

While this could be true, it was also an age-old Russian excuse to stall, for their own inscrutable reasons. An uncomfortable Jeffrey saw that, in effect, they were holding him incommunicado. *What's going on behind my back, that even Meredov doesn't know about?* He let Meredov make the next move.

"I have to ask you some questions."

Jeffrey grew more cautious. "Certain things, I can't comment on."

"I understand. But clarity is necessary to piece together the clues we do have about what happened at Srednekolymsk. Allow me." Meredov stood and went to the whiteboard. He took a blue pen from the shelf and removed the cap. "I'm not sure who will centrally coordinate the investigation, Captain. For some things it might be helpful if you and I get a head start while Vladivostok listens."

The translator leaned over to the phone and murmured that Rear Admiral Meredov was drawing a diagram for Captain Fuller.

"The more information you can provide to me, Admiral," Jeffrey said, "the better for Russia's sake. An appearance of procrastinating will very much displease my commander in chief. Dissuading him from a harsh response is not part of my orders."

"The question remains, who is responsible for launching the missiles?" Meredov wrote on the board, "Who did it?"

Jeffrey nodded impatiently. *Is this a delaying tactic, or is he leading somewhere? And if the latter, is he helping me or laying a trap?*

"What I have been told by officials on the scene is that the group that attacked the silo complex and entered some of the launching bunkers gave every appearance of being Russians. That is, ethnic groups from the mainstream populations, such as Eastern Slav or Siberian. With equipment and language skills, even dental work assessed on initial examination of the corpses, that appear to be truly from the Russian Federation."

"So some of the attackers were killed?"

"Yes, about thirty-five."

Jeffrey tried to remain expressionless. "How many attackers were there?"

"Over two hundred, the few survivors of the initial firefight say. All very heavily armed. Which is consistent with the casualties they inflicted on our counterattacking forces."

Hah! That's triple the number of men Kurzin had. . . . But it also means he suffered almost fifty percent killed in action.

"Where are the others? Taken prisoner? Interrogate them!"

"None were captured. And where they went after missile liftoff is still a major mystery. They vanished amid the confusion and the casualty evacuations. . . . But this hits on two related questions, aside from who exactly they were or who sent them. How did they get there? And how did they escape? I suppose, come to think of it, we should make that second question present tense, since their escape is currently in progress."

Again Jeffrey nodded, wordlessly.

"We should start with a list of possible perpetrators. Being objective and open-minded."

"Put down Russian rogue faction," Jeffrey said.

"Yes. Motive being to embarrass or take over the government."

"And put down Russian government."

"But—"

"Write it! You agreed to be objective. The Kremlin has not been ruled out! Blaming unnamed rogues for your actions is too convenient to be so lightly dismissed!"

A funny look crossed Meredov's face. "Then also America."

"*What?* What could our motive possibly be?"

Is he fishing, or does he know something?

"You are displeased with our logistics support of Germany."

"Then put down Germany too if you put down America." This was Jeffrey's most critical task, to shape Russian thoughts to focus on Berlin as orchestrater of the Srednekolymsk raid.

Meredov was skeptical, even shocked at the suggestion. "What would *their* motive be?"

"Weaken both our countries, and then maybe attack you."

"Why would they attack us? We're already helping them."

"Our intelligence knows all about the bonds they give you. Payable with plunder they intend to confiscate from the occupied countries once the fighting stops and the bonds come due."

"You have the advantage of me on this."

"Trust me. It's easy enough to confirm. So greed would be a German motive. Instead of paying you, they conquer you. Or they sense they won't win the fighting, and fear you'll sense it too. Look. They're evacuating North Africa as fast as they possibly can, before the Allied advance in that theater resumes."

"This also is new information for me."

"And also easy to confirm. So what do you think they'll do with all those troops and tanks and aircraft once they're removed from Africa, and they've had time to lick their wounds? The Axis needs to reestablish their evil empire's outward momentum."

"Defend southern Europe."

"They can do that with nuclear cruise missiles alone, to make the Med impassable for Allied amphibious or airborne assaults. Cheap and effective. . . . I'll tell you what they'll do. Their main forces will turn east, and cancel their debts by canceling your sovereignty."

"Hitler tried to conquer us, and look what happened to him."

"Hitler was an incompetent who went completely insane, and he didn't have tactical nuclear weapons."

"We have strategic rockets with hydrogen bombs."

"Which when they leave the atmosphere are exposed to our space-based missile shield. The U.S. is unlikely to sort out where the rockets are aimed before setting them off right over your own heads. . . . Ground-hugging German cruise missiles on mobile launchers with fission bombs are effective weapons in a counter-city or counter-industry strike. They're an effective deterrent against you striking first from inside the atmosphere, say with cruise missiles or nuclear bombers of your own."

"I view a German attack on us of any sort as unlikely."

"But not implausible. And 'not implausible' is what counts in this context, not what's 'likely.' Your conventional forces are weak, spread thin. You know it. Germany knows it."

"Yes."

Time to plant the seeds, and let them sprout in the minds of everyone who hears this conversation. "Once your government realizes Germany has had too many setbacks already on land and at sea, and can't prevail against the Allies without doing something exceedingly drastic, Moscow will cut logistic support to Berlin since they'll never get paid. They'll refuse to deliver more Eight-six-eight-U submarines. There'd be bad consequences, repercussions, realignments sought in Berlin as a result."

"These are murky waters, yet there is logic to what you say. Germany would be cornered into attacking us, to grab what she can no longer buy. Provoking a limited nuclear exchange between us and America, to soften us up first, aids her cause on two fronts at once. . . . But German raiders could have programmed the missiles to go off over Moscow . . . which if true would suggest that your claimed new missile shield is in fact sheer flummery."

Jeffrey was ready and waiting for this one. He tore into the admiral. "I dare you to test it. Launch another armed SS-27 at the U.S. See what happens to Russia."

Meredov didn't even blink. "Don't taunt me. . . . A *test* appears unneeded. . . . If the Germans achieved armed launches at all, inflicting EMPs on Moscow squanders the missiles. It wastes the larger chance to hurt you *and* our joint relations, by landing warheads in America. Thus, positing the culprits were German does *not* imply your shield is a mere fabrication."

"So put it down, Admiral. Write 'Germany' on the board."

"And China? The war destabilizes world trade at a time that's bad for Beijing. They're displeased that we favor Germany in our exportation of natural gas and oil and weapons, which is also stifling China's economic and military growth."

"Displeased enough to frame you for nuking America?"

"I doubt it, but I'll put them down, too."

"Okay. That's our list of culprits. In other words, at this point, it could've been almost anybody. So, what next?"

"Events suggest the attackers infiltrated by submarine."

"Foreigners?"

"Maybe not. A rogue faction with penetration into the Northern or Pacific Fleet could have sent them."

"I see what you're getting at."

"But I don't think they were from Russia."

Bingo. "Why not?"

"The timing and speeds and distances aren't right. We know that a submarine penetrated the Russian side of the Bering Strait from the south and evaded attack by Balakirev's forces, then very slowly entered the waters for which I'm held responsible. . . . A decoy pretending to be *Challenger* is an especially baffling conundrum. Why was it launched at all? To mislead, or to draw attention? Why pretend to be *Challenger* in particular? Why send it on the specific course it followed?"

Whoops. Not bingo. Better think fast.

"I suppose I should be flattered that someone thought they'd gain, somehow, by pretending to be me. Which seems consistent with another country, not America, being the perpetrator and seeking to implicate the U.S. circumstantially. Doesn't it?"

"It wasn't you who launched the decoy?"

"No, I did not launch any decoys." Jeffrey wondered if

Meredov could tell that he'd just been lied to again. The admiral, a seasoned infighter and shrewd managerial gamesman, had a good poker face of his own.

Meredov began drawing a map on the whiteboard, similar to the one on the other wall, but with just the highlights of the northern coastal waters and islands. He wrote "Decoy" in the East Siberian Sea, added the date and time it was launched, and drew an arrow in the direction the decoy had headed. He didn't say or write anything about *K-335*. He did make a mark in the Bering Strait, with the date and time for that depth charging.

"The false report of detecting *Challenger,* the decoy, caused a heightened alert among submarine and antisubmarine units, including mine. But the Strategic Rocket Forces didn't pay it any attention. In retrospect they should have."

"Seems so." *It's taking an awfully long while for the Hot Line to get working.*

"But there was more. Some of my people who track drifting ice that might threaten the Northern Sea Route summer shipping lanes noticed a large piece of floe that was behaving strangely." Meredov drew more arrows, marked "Wind" and "Current." Then he drew a big "U" on the map, from the edge of the ice cap to the coast and back to the cap. He put in more dates and times.

"The floe had an ice hummock on one side. I thought perhaps this accounted for the odd course it followed, with prevailing winds and surface currents coming from opposite directions. But prior events had strongly aroused my suspicions. Having slept on the problem, I sent helicopters to locate the floe and make an examination. From very close. By landing on it."

"What did you find?"

"The hummock was gone."

"Melted."

"No. It was never a hummock to begin with."

"Admiral?"

"Holes and wear marks and fibers left on the floe made it

clear that a submarine had moored itself to the floe, gone south with it, then returned to the edge of the cap, cut loose, and disappeared under the pack ice."

"That's how the attackers came ashore?"

"I raised a second alarm at once. This time the army paid attention. They found tracks left by a group of commandos, roughly following the Alazeja River, coming inland, heading south. At first I was worried that they might be after my headquarters. But then we realized that the commandos had gone the other way, toward Srednekolymsk."

"What happened next?"

"All this took several days, you understand. But finally the Strategic Rocket Forces put the base complex there on highest alert against intruders. Even so, hours later the commandos made their attack. Which, as you know, was successful."

"So you're saying that your antisubmarine operations provided adequate warning, coupled with tracking by the Army, and *still* the base was penetrated?"

"Yes."

"It sounds more and more like the commandos had inside help. Either from the government, or from rogues hiding within the government. Sorry, Admiral, this doesn't support Russia's case. The Kremlin is so in bed with Berlin, and has been so unreceptive to American diplomatic urgings for true neutrality for so long, that the President of the United States will have his own list of culprits, and 'Russia' will be at the top of the list. For all he and I know, Germany is complicit as well. They could have dreamed up the idea first and shared it with the Kremlin. Or with rogues Berlin recruited in promise of taking charge of Russia, as their puppets, after a coup. Either way, Moscow is in deep trouble, the offender to American eyes."

"But now we come to *Challenger*."

"What about *Challenger*?" At this point, Jeffrey wasn't volunteering anything.

Meredov drew another mark, in the middle of the Laptev

Sea, and put a date next to it, today's. "Here is where you contacted me, at your president's orders."

"Sure."

Meredov began to draw dotted lines between some of the different places he'd marked. One nuclear sub could have been at all those different places easily . . . and the trail ended with an indisputable fact: *Challenger* breaking stealth to call Meredov.

He looked at Jeffrey hard. "Why did you sneak through the Russian side of the Bering Strait two weeks ago? What have you been doing in our waters ever since?"

"I did no such thing in the Bering Strait. I came across the top of Canada from the United States East Coast."

"Nonsense. We know you were in Australia too recently."

"I was not in Australia recently."

Meredov reached into his jacket pocket. Jeffrey saw he'd hit some kind of showdown with the man. It was as if Meredov, knowing he held a winning hand, was putting his cards on the table, with utter finality.

Meredov unfolded a piece of paper. He showed it to Jeffrey. "This is *you,* Captain, on the Russian side of the Bering Strait, heading north, outfoxing Balakirev's antisubmarine units in a way which is entirely in character for your known command style. I repeat the question. What were you doing there? And more importantly, what were you doing since then?"

"You know I can't comment on undersea warfare activities."

"Then you don't deny that this computer-generated image is indeed your ship, at the time and place so indicated?"

"I neither confirm nor deny anything. This aggressive cross-examination is inappropriate, and counterproductive. Anyone with graphics software could manufacture that imagery."

"Don't insult my intelligence!"

Bad move. He *knows that printout is real.*

"You have two choices, Captain Fuller. You can give me a good explanation of your ship's recent movements and intent, or you can decline to do so. In the latter case, I will have to tell my superiors that your ship is strongly implicated in perpetrating the missile disaster at Srednekolymsk."

The silence over the speakerphone was deafening. Meredov was turning up the heat on Jeffrey before a live but invisible audience—one that could swing things way out of U.S. control.

"All right. Don't make a confusing situation even worse. *Challenger* was tasked to blockade and sink the Eight-six-eight-U that we know you'll soon transfer to German ownership."

"By proceeding from the Bering Strait toward the far end of Russia on such pressing business *at less than seven knots?*"

He's too damned good. He's got me by the short hairs.

Jeffrey had to think fast, in the type of confrontation he most dearly wished to avoid: a battle of wits, face to face with his adversary, with every word being overheard and recorded.

"It's public that our subs do dwell near Russia for covert surveillance. Big deal. Ancient history. Why is that news?" Meredov didn't know of Jeffrey's long side trip east, to meet *Carter* near Canada. *He damned well better not ever know.*

"It's news because of the SS-27s that launched! I understand submarine operations, *remember?*" Meredov thumped the qualification badge on his own chest for emphasis. "Again, I warn you, do not insult my intelligence!"

I need to take the initiative and play a vigorous counter-gambit, or everything is doomed. . . . But how?

In a flash of insight, the pieces came together.

Jeffrey sighed, as if in resignation. "When you mention intelligence, Admiral, you strike at the core of the matter, closer than you realize."

"Explain."

"Your real problem is the coincidence of timing, between

my presence in the Laptev Sea and the SS-Twenty-seven launches, correct?"

"Correct."

"I understand now why it wasn't a coincidence."

"So you *admit* America's guilt?"

"No! Absolutely not! What I admit is that American undersea warfare operations have been compromised by the Axis."

"Go on."

"There were circumstantial indications for a while, that they knew in advance of some of our most important submarine missions."

"So?"

"Obviously, they knew about this one, *Challenger*'s tasking through the strait to snoop in your waters and then move toward their brand-new Eight-six-eight-U awaiting delivery."

"And what if they did?"

"They timed a commando raid on Srednekolymsk to coincide on the calendar in such a way as to incriminate me and my ship. Don't you see?"

"You mean they used their spies and scheduled their attack so the blame would fall in your direction?"

"Isn't that entirely consistent with the Axis High Command's own style, of disinformation and deceit?"

Meredov frowned. For a long time he didn't say anything.

Neither did Jeffrey. He was too busy silently praying.

Meredov breathed in and out deeply. "Either you're making all of this up, and you first revealed *Challenger*'s presence to me on the radio as part of a monumental double bluff, or you're telling the truth. . . ."

Jeffrey tried to be nonchalant, knowing he'd gotten a hook into Meredov now, and he needed to play the next move gently. The decision had to seem to come unforced out of Meredov himself.

"Yes," he said. "Logically, irrefutably, it's either of the two things you listed. I'm guilty or I'm innocent. Pick one."

Meredov stared at the ceiling. Frightening seconds ticked by. Then he began to think out loud. "A simple frame-up by the Germans is less convoluted than a double bluff attempted by you. . . . Hmm. . . . You've revealed to me valuable secrets about your country's counterespionage weakness which, now known, the FSB can validate or disprove, to hold you accountable. . . . I'm inclined to think you're telling me the truth."

"I would not have come to speak to you if I were living such a gigantic lie as you proposed."

"Then why did you launch the decoy? It—"

The admiral was cut off by the roar of a plane flying low over the building. Rather than being afraid of an attack, Meredov cursed to himself and went to look out his office windows; Jeffrey followed. The translator stayed behind, saying into the phone that Jeffrey and Meredov had left the room.

Jeffrey had trouble not trembling at the close call that he, the mission, and the world had just survived. *I pulled one out of my ass, and he bought it. I didn't know I had it in me.*

They saw a corporate jet on final approach to the airstrip.

"*Him,* of all people, *now,*" Meredov said angrily.

The phone rang on Meredov's desk. Irina Malenkova answered it. "Excuse me, Admiral, but Governor Krushkin is arriving."

"Yes, I know." He turned to Jeffrey. "Vladimir Krushkin is governor of the Yakutia *oblast.* Hand-picked by the president, who appoints all *oblast* governors. One of his top favorites."

"If Krushkin is such a favorite, Admiral, and no offense meant to you, what's he doing stuck in the middle of Siberia?"

"Not Siberia, Captain. Yakutsk in particular. The gold and diamond capital of the world."

"Money. . . . Why is he here?"

"I'm sure Moscow told him to come. As on-site observer."

"But if the Hot Line isn't working yet, how could your president talk to Yakutsk? Surely Yakutsk can get through to Vladivostok, and that linkage closes a loop with Washington, no?"

"Fine questions, Captain. I know better than to try to answer them."

CHAPTER 30

Both of *Carter*'s onboard trauma surgeons worked at a frenzied pace on the seriously wounded commandos. A hospital corpsman eventually got around to Nyurba, gave him a quick once-over, injected a mild sedative, and confined him to his rack in an oxygen mask. Nyurba lay there stressed out and numb; half his squadron's people had been killed. And the ordeal wasn't over, not unless and until Commodore Fuller did his job perfectly in Siberia, and *Carter* got away forever scot-free.

On this mission, there's no partial credit. The human race could still come to an end.

Later, a different harried corpsman came by to check on Nyurba. He said Captain Harley had ordered *Carter* north, to deep water, at twenty knots. He listened to his lungs with a stethoscope, seeming satisfied. But Nyurba's pulse and blood pressure were too high. He injected a much stronger sedative, and told him to sleep. Nyurba nodded off, feeling a drug-induced bliss.

When Jeffrey was introduced to Vladimir Krushkin, he was surprised. From Meredov's reactions he'd pictured a crude, overweight Russian *mafiya* type, flashy and boorish and overbearing, even violent. But the man was lean, had the healthy glow of someone who exercised regularly, and was neatly groomed, impeccably mannered, and wore a very expensive custom-made suit. *Saville Row, or Hong Kong,* Jeffrey thought. Krushkin also spoke perfect English, with a polished Midwestern accent. His wedding ring was a plain gold band, elegant, not gaudy.

"You spent some time in America, Governor?" Jeffrey asked.

"I have an MBA in finance from the University of Chicago."

"Very impressive."

"Thank you, Captain. Your combat record is very impressive too. But come," he said a little too smoothly, "let's not keep Vladivostok waiting."

They all went into the conference room and took seats, Krushkin in the middle of the table opposite the translator. He looked at the whiteboard, then gave Meredov a dirty look, as if of professional jealousy or annoyance. Jeffrey assumed that with his background in numbers and balance sheets, he could make sense of the map that Meredov had drawn there.

Krushkin leaned toward the phone and switched to Russian. "This is Governor Krushkin. Can you hear me well?"

"Yes, Governor," a younger voice answered.

Must be some admiral's aide. Vladivostok was in a completely different *oblast,* but the admirals there understood the Kremlin's extended power structure, and knew Krushkin's influential place within it.

"I bring information. Much evidence from Srednekolymsk has arrived by plane at Khabarovsk." A city a few hundred miles north of Vladivostok. "The regional police forensics laboratory and staff are being augmented by equipment and specialists flying in now from Japan, along with a United States Air Force military attaché stationed in Tokyo. He's been requested to observe the physical evidence and corpses and monitor the studies done using mass spectrometers and other relevant devices."

"Why was Vladivostok not used for this?" the old admiral demanded.

"The president has made his decision."

A power play, Jeffrey told himself. *Divide and conquer.*

"Then—"

The governor cut the admiral off. "Yes, communications have been reestablished with the Kremlin. The Hot Line will soon be repaired. By that I mean the secure system directly between Moscow and Washington, not some piecemeal roundabout linkage."

"Oh, good," Jeffrey said. "That's what we've been waiting for."

"Nyet." No. "We will not be participating. The President of Russia insists on speaking exclusively with the President of the United States. There will be no third parties on the call."

"Then what's the purpose of this meeting?" Meredov asked. "You flew a thousand kilometers just to tell us that?"

"I flew here to say that this meeting is adjourned. It's almost four A.M. Too much is at stake to continue working on and on while exhausted, particularly with the hard deadline set for us at local midnight. We will therefore resume at noon, after we have had a chance to sleep. Captain Fuller, you are a guest of the Russian government. I presume this is acceptable to you?"

"Yes, Governor."

"And you feel under no duress?"

"No."

"And we appear to be working in good faith to resolve the present situation?"

"So far as I can tell. I suppose we do all need to rest. The forensics will have a chance to progress in the meantime."

"Vladivostok, did you hear that clearly?"

"Da," the grumpy admiral said. Yes.

"You have it on the tape?"

"Da."

"Inform the American consulate in Tokyo accordingly."

"Can't an ambassador or an attaché be sent here?" Jeffrey asked. Krushkin switched back to English.

"No. This base is within the frozen zone established around Srednekolymsk by me as governor. The zone is closed to foreign nationals not already present until further notice, and none here may leave. The search for the guerrillas who attacked the missile complex is ongoing within the frozen zone. I've declared martial law, and my *oblast* militia troops will enforce this quarantine using deadly force if necessary." Besides Russia's regular army, each governor had a militia, like national guards. "You must surrender any radio or cell phone."

He hadn't brought such items, planning to rely instead on borrowed Russian comms gear, assuming that they would cooperate out of necessity, for self-preservation. Now Krushkin was singing the opposite tune, and insisting on a pause of eight hours, a full third of the time until the supposed ironclad *Challenger* cruise-missile nuclear strike deadline.

"Are you telling me I'm a prisoner?" Jeffrey was angry.

"Nonsense. You're our honored guest. To be credible, a forensic quarantine must be hermetic. No exceptions can be made. While you rest, experts in the research center of Akademgorodok, well equipped and far outside the area of EMP disruption, will judge the believability of America's secret new missile shield. As they do that, I'll review the full recording of your conversation with Rear Admiral Meredov. I see on the whiteboard under 'Who did it?' that one potential perpetrator is America. In that case, your missile shield is plainly a hoax. Captain Fuller, I find that a rather fascinating possibility. . . . Sleep well."

CHAPTER 31

In his guest quarters at a hotel-like building on the base, Jeffrey made a quick meal of bottled water and field rations he'd brought in his travel bag, then climbed into bed. The window shade failed to keep out that peculiar Arctic twilight. His mattress was much too soft, and lumpy. He tossed and turned.

He was startled at 11 A.M. by pounding on the door. After Krushkin's final comment, he expected FSB agents had come to arrest him, or Spetsnaz were ready to lead him to a firing squad.

It was Elmar Meredov. The man was visibly excited, but in a good way. "Get dressed. Skip a shower. They've found things!"

Jeffrey hurriedly put on his uniform, and followed Meredov outside. Irina Malenkova and several Army Spetsnaz bodyguards met them, and they drove in a van to the headquarters building. Jeffrey and Meredov rushed up into the conference room. The translator was already there. Governor Krushkin made a grand entrance like minor royalty, as perfectly groomed as ever, and even wearing a different suit and tie; he'd spent the intervening time on his luxurious private jet, staying in touch with Khabarovsk and Akademgorodok and the Kremlin, and catnapping.

Krushkin glanced at the whiteboard with Meredov's previous jottings. "The list of culprits has narrowed drastically."

"What's been happening?" Jeffrey asked, trying to hide the sickening feeling of failure in his stomach.

"I didn't mention this earlier," Meredov said, "but I ordered an auxiliary cruiser-icebreaker to retrace the route the intruding submarine took back north while moored to the floe. My deputy, flown out from Pevek, is aboard her, to make sure the job was done right, and to report. They searched the bottom using their active towed array as a side-scan sonar. They found an abandoned German mini-sub, flooded as if scuttled there, with its top hatch left open."

"You salvaged it?"

"Not yet. We sent down divers. It's in shallow water."

"And? . . ."

"Completely empty. Including the fuel tanks. We conclude it was abandoned after helping shuttle the big commando team."

"So the Germans did it after all?"

"All the forensic matches point to that," Krushkin said. "Bloodwork, metallurgy, never mind the details, but the Khabarovsk lab was definite and your attaché was convinced."

"Fast work," Jeffrey said.

"Your president put a lot of pressure on ours. He told him repeatedly about *Challenger*'s nuclear cruise missile strike scheduled for midnight. Our president passed the pressure down, and it produced results."

"Is Akademgorodok satisfied that our missile shield is real?"

"The way they put it was that they'd like a year to study the issue properly. But based on design specs provided by Washington, and given the obvious difficulties involved in subjecting your shield to an actual test, our experts deemed it 'not impossible in concept.'"

"What happens now?"

"Things are in flux. Your president told ours to sever all ties with Germany, both diplomatic and economic, today, long before midnight, as a form of reparations for what almost occurred with the missiles from Srednekolymsk. Or else. It certainly seemed that we had many good reasons to do so, only one of them being the threatened devastation from *Challenger*."

"And?"

"The German ambassador managed to make his way to the Kremlin early this morning. As you can imagine, there was quite a scene. He has now been declared persona non grata. He and his entire staff are being deported, on a sealed train routed through Belarus into occupied Poland."

"I'm glad the mystery of who attacked the silos was resolved, Governor."

"Not half as glad as we are. Your commander in chief was satisfied, and sent the order to *Challenger* to cancel her cruise missile attack. You should be back aboard her in plenty of time to doubly verify unambiguous receipt."

"That's a relief," Jeffrey said, faking it, knowing an actual attack was never planned—unless Moscow heated things up by launching more ICBMs.

"A tremendous relief for all of us. We were damaged enough by the high-altitude nuclear explosions. The last thing we needed is the thought of dealing with worse. So the pressure is off us and on Germany. But there are still big complications."

"Such as?"

"Proper retaliation against Berlin."

"But you said you severed relations."

"Yes, as a form of reparation to *America*, by *us*. There remains the vexed matter of reparation, or retaliation, *for* us. Billions of roubles of damage from the electromagnetic pulses, and hundreds of lives lost in the missile complex and in the area affected by the EMPs. Controversy on this issue rages."

"So what do you intend?"

"The president wants to speak to you." Krushkin turned on the speakerphone, pressed some buttons, and the big computer screen on the wall lit up. Now it was a video-phone, and Jeffrey was stunned. He thought the governor meant the President of the United States, but he was talking to the President of Russia.

"Captain Fuller, thank you for your assistance in this hard situation we faced together." The president was of av-erage height, barrel-chested and sixtyish, with rough, peas-antlike mannerisms; he'd always reminded Jeffrey of Nikita Khrushchev with hair.

Faced together? Before, he refused to even speak to me. Wait. Had he been listening in all along? "It was an honor to be of service, Mr. President." *When in Russia . . .*

"I want everyone else to leave the conference room and close the door behind them. Including the translator."

Soon Jeffrey was alone on the videophone with the Pres-ident of Russia, who spoke good English. Out of respect, he remained standing. The president sat in a plush leather swivel chair, behind a huge desk that didn't have a single thing on it. The wall behind him was paneled in dark wood. His body language was tight, stiff, and his mouth and his eyes weren't smiling. Jeffrey's mood of inner celebration vanished; unease returned.

"Your commander in chief thinks very highly of you."

"Thank you, sir."

"He offered me a substantial aid package, of which one detail might interest you."

"Sir?"

"We agreed to sell the Eight-six-eight-U and all addi-tional ones in the class that we can build to the United States."

"I'm delighted to hear that, sir. They're very fine ships." *And best kept out of German or Chinese hands.*

"I face a very grave policy decision, Captain, and I seek your advice. You have experience at fighting tactical nuclear battles, and winning them. Russia does not. We only have paper studies and training simulations. This gives you considerable prestige and credibility, to me and even to my hardliners."

"Er, I understand, sir."

"Unfortunately, the crisis at hand is far from over. My more hawkish advisors urge me to respond promptly and viciously to Germany's blunt refusal to pay immediate cash compensation for the damage and deaths they inflicted in their conspiracy to provoke us both into going to war. Emotionally, I'm inclined to agree with the hawks. I crave harsh revenge myself."

"The German economy is stretched thin, sir," Jeffrey said.

"We know. Had we not accepted their perverse bonds, in the belief that they would pay off, they might never have been able to launch their coup in Berlin and their war with the Allies."

"We see the consequences of that decision today, Mr. President. Very serious consequences."

"I offered your commander in chief a formal apology. He accepted it graciously."

"What were you referring to about your advisors, sir, and wanting my advice?"

The president glanced at his watch. "I'm due back in a cabinet meeting soon. . . . They want me to retaliate in kind against Germany. That would mean inflicting a high-altitude nuclear explosion's EMP."

"Only in theory would that be proper retaliation in kind, sir, and it might not be your optimal response."

"I know. For one thing, it's precluded by your missile shield. A low-altitude burst would produce such a pulse, but only locally, and mostly as a by-product of direct damage on the ground from heat and blast, and radiation and fallout."

"Precisely, sir."

"I asked your president if he would launch an ICBM and produce the EMP over Berlin for me, but he politely declined."

"Er, I'm not surprised." *Is he being tongue in cheek?*

"I want your honest counsel, man to man. You came to Siberia and helped us by your mix of threats and cajoling, kept us from making some potentially catastrophic errors of judgment and misinterpretation of facts. For this I am grateful to you."

"I was only doing my job, sir."

"I need your opinion, one I think that right now you're uniquely suited to provide. You know the horrors of nuclear war firsthand. You know what it means to fire atomic weapons in anger, and to have them fired at you. You've seen their effect on people, on those who die and the scars left on those who survive."

"Yes."

"What do you think is the appropriate level of response to retaliate against Germany's attack, especially given their first use of hijacked thermonuclear weapons? A heinous crime."

Jeffrey hesitated. "That's a very difficult question, sir. I'm not sure I'm qualified to answer it, or whether given my position vis-à-vis yours, it's even legal for me to discuss it."

Someone interrupted from off camera. The president irritably snapped at the functionary to go away, then glanced at his watch again. He turned back toward the camera, meeting Jeffrey's eyes. "The cabinet grows impatient. . . . Your president said to give me your recommendations."

For the first time Jeffrey noticed the conference room's camera, in a pinhole in the center of the screen.

He pondered. "It's best to take the widest possible view, sir, both geopolitically and in the context of future history."

"Yes?"

"What would other countries make of whatever plan you follow? How would that affect your world position, soon and later, in key ways such as diplomatic prestige, economic strength, national security, and current sympathy to you as the victim of Axis terrorism? . . . What would your own people think of you, today and in the years to come? That question has to be raised especially in the context of *oblasts* that are nominally autonomous republics on your periphery. Some may be motivated to break away if you take actions that they find too morally repugnant."

Jeffrey knew that secession, for real, by these border republics was a constant Kremlin headache—or nightmare.

"Wise insights, Captain. The problem is that factions among my supposed advisors, overambitious generals and minority-party opposition leaders as well, in the inevitable way of Moscow, are attempting to seize this issue to justify an opportunistic coup. To oust me as soft unless I retaliate fast and violently."

That sounds like they aren't being backed by the Germans, who have to be hopping mad since they *know America framed them.*

But Germany would have clandestine tentacles reaching for the helm in Moscow. They were the aggrieved party now, and would also be craving revenge in a most ruthless way. Keeping Russia from glassing Germany wasn't enough, as vital as that had become. Jeffrey had to help the now-friendly Russian president stay in power in this maelstrom, or Russia could backslide to the Axis.

"You must be bold and decisive, sir. Join the Allies?"

"Your president asked me that already. It would amount to declaring war on Germany and the Boers. We aren't ready to fight such a war. Soon, maybe, with proper aid and planning, but not today or next month. You referenced this yourself, quite eloquently, during your conversation with Rear Admiral Meredov."

"You've listened to the tape from Vladivostok?"

"Very carefully."

"A nuclear first strike against Germany would have dire consequences, sir, ones all Russians would come to regret."

"Tell me what they are. Be my devil's advocate. I need strong arguments I can use against the overly hawkish faction when I go back into the cabinet room, to prove that moderation isn't weakness. I stress, your personal word carries weight."

"You'd breach the threshold or firewall which has confined tactical nuclear combat to sea for most of the war. That's bad."

"Very bad indeed, but perhaps inevitable. . . . What else?"

This was the hardest oral exam he'd ever had to take, and Jeffrey dared not get a failing grade. He began to sweat, but knew he couldn't remove his uniform jacket in front of the Russian president. "Germany did not make a nuclear strike on you. They commandeered your missiles and attempted to frame you with a first strike against the U.S. The damage around Moscow was caused by our missile shield. America bears responsibility, in a sense, and our president has offered you aid as amends."

"But if the shield had not existed, or had failed, you would have suffered a strike from Russian strategic rockets, and would have retaliated in kind, and my country would have suffered far more serious damage than we did."

"That's probably true, sir. But it didn't actually happen."

"Too vague and hypothetical. Give me something better."

"Germany would retaliate, as I cautioned Admiral Meredov, and might substantially escalate, using cruise missiles that could penetrate your best antiaircraft defenses and destroy many cities and industries. Tens of millions of Russians would die."

"Thirty million died in our last war with Germany. Not counting Stalin's massacres."

"Isn't once enough? Do you want that level of death and destruction all over again, except happening in a day rather than over several years? Would you ever be able to recover, and rebuild, from such instant widespread devastation?"

"I see your point, but that still won't be convincing to the powerful extremists I have to contain."

Jeffrey tried to picture them, scheming, plotting in the cabinet room. He'd never felt such time pressure in his life. "Can't you launch a purge and just get rid of them?"

"When I'm ready. Things are too unstable now."

"Germany didn't try to frame you, or the Kremlin per se, sir. From the context as I understand it, the launches were definitely unauthorized and no one now questions that. This gives you the potent argument that the Germans tried to frame outcasts, rebels, rogues. So nobody can claim their scheme struck at the heart of your influence and authority."

"That's too abstract, and too arguable. You're a smart and clever man, Captain Fuller, but remember I have to deal with callous infighting bureaucrats, unsavory yes men, people who shift allegiance without the slightest compunction or warning."

"The strongest argument I can think of is to not nuke German soil so as to not cause massive slaughter among the Allied civilians they're holding as human shields in all their high-value target areas. That would gravely anger the Allied powers, and put Russia in a difficult position for her ongoing relations with neutrals, too."

"But you're asking me to give in to the German human-shield strategy, which is itself a war crime."

"Killing the hostages is not the best way to solve a hostage crisis, sir. Recent Russian history ought to show you that botched rescues where hundreds of innocents died did lasting damage to your country's reputation and credibility. You can't regain the superpower status you covet while showing such abject disregard for human lives. And remember, these hostages would not be your own citizens. They'd be Americans, British, and so on. You'd also kill many German civilians who are every bit as much victims of Axis repression as the people in the countries the Axis occupies. It would be calculated mass murder."

"And I suppose there'd be the problem of fallout knowing no borders or boundaries. We certainly took a battering in public relations after the Chernobyl plume hit half of Europe."

"Historians say that's one factor that brought down the

Soviet Union. . . . Furthermore, if you made such an attack, other countries including mine would start to think the supposed German launches had been done by the Kremlin after all, as a manufactured excuse for a preemptive strike on Germany whom you wanted a justification to invade. . . . Restraint is much better statesmanship than retaliation, sir."

"Good. This is the ammunition I needed. The specter of causing countless innocent deaths in Russia and other countries, making us become a weak pariah instead of a respected superpower, an abhorrent aggressor instead of a victim aggrieved. The resultant danger of a complete implosion of the Russian Federation, into dozens of fragments, with civil wars, or worse."

"A grim picture. But an accurate one, Mr. President."

"All right. I had these thoughts myself, but your independent confirmation is invaluable. I know what *not* to do. It's my job to convince my opponents and the fence-sitters."

Someone knocked hard on the thick conference room door, then came in. It was Meredov, breathless with excitement all over again. "Mr. President, I must interrupt. We've identified their egress route! The German raiders!"

"Explain," the president insisted. The translator returned to the room in Meredov's wake, since he only spoke Russian.

"We found a hovercraft drifting, abandoned, out of fuel, its crew shot in the head. Bloodstains indicate there had been many people aboard, some of them wounded. We were able to reproduce the hovercraft's route with an analysis of hydrophone recordings. The Germans escaped from Srednekolymsk down the Kolyma at high speed, and transferred to a submarine northwest of Pevek. The submarine appears to have then headed under the pack ice. Acoustic data suggest the vessel is an Amethyste Two."

"What are your intentions?" Jeffrey asked, stonefaced, knowing who was really on that supposed German Amethyste.

"Sink it!" the president commanded. "Do that and I'll have everything I need to deal with the upstarts in Moscow. Sink the submarine that brought the raiders and kill every person aboard! This is justifiable retaliation of the sweetest kind! Direct punishment in hot pursuit as they try to escape!"

"The punishment fits the crime, sir," Jeffrey said. "It carries a symbolic value that some indiscriminate atrocity against the German populace would lack."

"Captain Fuller, you certainly have a way with words. Can you get back aboard *Challenger* as quickly as possible and work in cooperation with Russian submarines in the area? Form a wolf pack to hunt down this German and destroy her. I can think of no better way to begin to build a partnership with America than that! An act of self-defense, short of outright war, fits the current situation extremely well."

"Yes, sir. Certainly. Then I need to get moving at once."

"One other thing before I end the call. Rear Admiral Meredov, for your vigilance and dedication throughout this difficult time, I'm promoting you to Vice Admiral."

Meredov grinned broadly. "Thank you, Mr. President!"

"You deserve it. I'll put the formalities in motion. You rate a more senior aide now, of course, so I'll promote yours to captain, first rank. . . . Captain Fuller, good luck to you, and good hunting." The president's image vanished. Meredov and Jeffrey glanced at each other, amazed, but still mutually wary.

"I need to get a message to Washington for them to send an ELF to *Challenger* telling her to raise a mast and signal her location to us, and once the mast is up inform her of the wolf pack concept. And I need transportation back to her. I also need the specs for your underwater acoustic communication systems, so I can speak to the Russian captains and make sure we coordinate and distinguish friend from foe. A map of any minefields. And of bottom-moored and under-ice hydrophone nets."

"Irina!"

The admiral's aide appeared at once. He told her she'd just been made Captain, First Rank Malenkova, by her commander in chief himself. She practically jumped up and down with glee. He ordered her to put everything in motion, messages and data disks.

"There's one other matter we need to discuss," Meredov said as Malenkova left the room.

"Yes?" Jeffrey was made apprehensive by Meredov's manner.

"All I can do is inform you now but give you no help later."

"Well, Vice Admiral Meredov, then inform me."

"Our latest-model UGST torpedo includes a new target homing sensor. Something specifically designed for use against nuclear submarines under the ice cap."

Jeffrey began to get worried. "Go on."

"The common tactic of hovering between ice keels to suppress radiated noise and avoid giving an echo to hostile active sonar?"

"I'm familiar with the concept."

"This new warhead has a miniature gravimetric gradiometer. Optimized to detect and attack the density discontinuity from the reactor compartment of a stationary nuclear submarine."

"This is actually operational, *now,* deployed on your subs?"

"Nine-seven-one-As, our *Bars*-Threes, what you call the Akula-Twos, do have them."

"I wouldn't want to be hit by such a weapon."

"That's why I'm informing you. You'll need to be careful with your underice tactics. Very careful. A friendly fire accident between a *Bars* and *Challenger* would spoil everything we've worked so hard for. Not to mention sinking your ship."

I must warn Harley somehow, pronto. Were Carter *sunk, she'd surely be identified. Blame would instantly shift back to America. Everything achieved today would be lost, in a way Meredov can't imagine.*

CHAPTER 32

Jeffrey was strapped in the front seat of the Yak, flying north at five hundred knots to land on one of Meredov's icebreaker-cruisers. The icebreaker and *Challenger* were already rushing toward each other at flank speed for a rendezvous.

Jeffrey was still under tremendous stress to act out a part, which was suddenly far more complex. Helping *Carter* escape, forever unidentified as who she really was to maintain the masquerade of German guilt, remained as critical as ever—but wasn't nearly enough. The President of Russia had to stay in power, amid unanticipated rough-and-tumble Moscow dirty politics set off by the missile launches and EMP. Otherwise a fulminating Kremlin might use hydrogen bombs against Germany after all, or a pro-German faction might seize control and reverse every one of Jeffrey's and Kurzin's achievements. The key to preventing an ouster or coup was to swiftly deliver what the Russian president personally demanded for revenge and closure: a sunken German Amethyste-II. Jeffrey had to do this while faking cooperation with Akula-IIs whose captains would keenly watch his every move.

The dead Amethyste's wreckage must *be real, and verifiable. The Russians have deep-submersible minis that can inspect any hulk and debris on the bottom well past ten thousand feet down.*

Just like when Meredov confronted him with imagery of *Challenger* hiding against the Bering Strait spires, he needed a convincing answer when there seemed to be no answer at all.

And then he remembered. He knew one and only one place in this theater where an Amethyste hulk did exist: in the Canada Basin, where Bell and Harley recently blew one to pieces. Because of the timing of that engagement relative to satellite overflights, the restricted geography, the terrible acoustic conditions, and the known lack of unfriendly hydrophone grids nearby, he was confident that the Russians knew nothing.

But he realized something else. Meredov was too smart. He could turn from back-channel friend into deadly enemy, if those fickle Kremlin winds indeed shifted drastically again. Jeffrey needed to get out of his jurisdiction, quickly, to keep open some plausible deniability if Meredov ever did change loyalties.

"Sir," the Yak's pilot said over the intercom, "the admiral is on for you. A translator is at his end in case required."

Jeffrey, expecting the call, used the headset in his flight helmet. "Admiral, we have an agenda to resolve without delay."

"Concur," Meredov said. "State the agenda."

Radio reception was much better, eighteen hours after the distant EMPs. "What submarines are available for the wolf pack?"

"Two Akula-Twos. *K-One-five-seven* and *K-Three-three-five*. Their names are *Wild Boar* and *Cheetah*."

"Both have the gravimeter-homing torpedoes."

"Yes."

"High-explosive, or nuclear?"

"Some of each."

"Where are they now?"

Meredov gave coordinates. They were charging toward near the place where *Challenger* would meet the icebreaker, *Cheetah* coming from northwest and *Wild Boar* from north, most of the time at their flank speed—thirty-five knots. They were using sprint and drift to not be blindsided by the supposed German, and to make a tactically safe linkup with Jeffrey's submarine. They'd all come together close to where Jeffrey knew Harley would be aiming for the end of the shallow continental shelf, which lay far northeast of Pevek, way up under the cap. And Meredov's hydrophone nets were catching whiffs of the Amethyste II—the actual *Carter*—enough to localize her general area.

Challenger, after dropping Jeffrey off at the initial meet with an icebreaker, had snuck east while Jeffrey claimed that Bell was lurking to make a nuclear strike. The plan had been for *Challenger* to stealthily escort *Carter,* bearing the commandos, safely home in the final phase of the mission. This plan had gone out the window, except Harley didn't know it yet and ELF was much too slow to send him a meaningful update. Jeffrey was glad the Yak pilot and Meredov couldn't read his face.

Jeffrey had to do things that made total sense to Meredov, but which somehow herded the pseudo-German sub toward the central Canada Basin. And he had to accomplish this without *Carter* getting unmasked or destroyed on the way.

How?

"Good, Admiral." Jeffrey spoke into his flight helmet mike, winging it—literally. "The Amethyste will certainly detect the three-ship wolf pack making so much noise. Given where the wolf pack units presently are and how they're converging, the Amethyste can best be driven east. That's my intention."

"You insist on command of the wolf pack?"

"I have the most experience fighting German submarines."

"Concur. Arrangements will be made. Messages will be sent to *Wild Boar* and *Cheetah* via Northern Fleet."

Jeffrey thought very fast.

"We need rules of engagement. Only I may go nuclear, at my own discretion. Akula-Twos may go nuclear only upon my specific order via acoustic link."

"I'm sure our commander in chief will agree, and will dictate such edicts at once."

"Have Rear Admiral Balakirev's forces seal the Bering Strait. Have the U.S. naval attaché in Tokyo contact Commander, U.S. Pacific Fleet at Pearl Harbor so he'll know to do the same." Moscow was still a disaster scene, U.S. embassy comms a shambles.

"Immediately. We can't allow the Amethyste to break out into the wide Pacific. She may have a covert tender hiding somewhere, for support, among neutrals."

Good, he bought that part.

"I want her confined under the ice cap, where the new gravimeter torpedoes give us the technical edge, and surprise." Jeffrey had an ulterior motive. Under ice, Akulas couldn't use their SS-N-16 Stallions, torpedo-tube-launched missiles that leaped from the water, transited many kilometers at high speed, and dropped an antisubmarine torpedo—or nuclear depth charge.

"How can my own forces serve you?" Meredov asked.

He needs a good role, to share in the "victory," so I keep him as a friend—and he can throw a bone to his pal Balakirev. "Use your surface and airborne units to patrol the marginal ice zone and the open waters south. The edge of the solid pack ice will be our line of demarcation. My wolf pack stays under the cap, and your aircraft don't fly over it." Overflights increased ambient noise; sonobuoys dropped through polynyas could be counterproductive. "Set off depth charges, and torpedo some icebergs at random, to make sounds to discourage the German from exiting the cap."

"I'll ensure that Balakirev does the same. May we fire on any undersea contact that does emerge from the pack ice?"

"Yes, until *Wild Boar* and *Cheetah* report that the battle is won. Then use your own procedures for avoiding friendly fire."

"An excellent concept of operations. Is there more?"

The punch line, the sleight of hand, to make it make sense to Meredov and the Akula captains.

"Ask Commander, U.S. Pacific Fleet to station fast attacks in a barrier line at the extreme eastern end of the Beaufort Sea. I don't want the German evading into the maze of Canadian islands that lead toward Greenland and Norway. Any available Canadian diesel subs that aren't blocked by the ice should also join this barrier. I want Allied subs there as an anvil, stationary, unyielding, against which my wolf pack can smash the Amethyste."

"Understood. But what if the German turns toward the pole?"

I'm glad you asked.

"I intend to see that he doesn't. He has a head start, but my wolf pack has higher flank speed, my ship especially. He's outnumbered three to one. I'll use the Alpha Ridge terrain to confine him to the Canada Abyssal Plain. In the deep water over there, *Challenger*'s crush depth gives decisive sonar superiority." Jeffrey glanced out the cockpit canopy. "Admiral, I can see your icebreaker, slowed, on the horizon. *Challenger* will be surfacing soon, and I'll be out of touch once we dive. So let me say good-bye, and thanks for everything."

"Godspeed to you, Captain Fuller."

That was the easy part. What Jeffrey had, as Meredov put it, was only a concept of operations. A myriad of details needed to be worked out. *The most daunting one of all is, how the hell do I turn a live* Carter *into a dead Amethyste right in front of multiple Russian witnesses who'll catch it all on sonar tapes?*

CHAPTER 33

His Yak flight and the rendezvous completed, Jeffrey jogged along *Challenger*'s hull and down the ladder inside her weapons loading hatch. Bell stood there in the passageway to greet him, while crewmen hurried to inspect and tightly shut the hatch.

"*Come on,*" Jeffrey said, lugging his overnight bag and heading for the control room.

Bell followed. "What's happening, sir? I got a message about some sort of combined task force with Russian subs?"

"It's gone all squirrelly, yeah. Get *Challenger* submerged and under the pack ice smartly. Before you ask, permission granted to go active on ice-avoidance sonar so we don't crash into something. Make flank speed until we're in acoustic-link range of *Carter*." Thirty nautical miles for the U.S. system. "We need to warn Harley. A pair of Akula-Twos are rushing to join up with your ship, Captain Bell, so that together we can destroy the German sub that brought the commandos who launched the ICBMs. The same German sub which you and I know is *Carter*."

"I expect Harley's people detected them. We just need to

elude the Akulas, which shouldn't be too hard, and we're home free."

"It's a hell of a lot more complicated. To cement the goodwill we've earned with the Kremlin, save the Russian president's domestic political backside, and avoid Moscow megahawks having a good excuse to glass Berlin, we must be *seen* to work with the Akulas and actually *sink* that Amethyste. Sink it where its hulk can be found, as positive proof of German deceit and aggression toward the Russian people and government."

They reached the control room. Finch, as junior officer of the deck—JOOD—confirmed via photonics mast that the brow from the icebreaker was clear. Bell began barking out orders to submerge the ship and get under way at flank speed. COB and Patel got busy at the ship control station. Finch went back to being sonar officer, and another lieutenant (j.g.) took his prior role as JOOD in the aisle next to Sessions, the XO.

Jeffrey zipped open his travel bag, yanking out the waterproof packet of data disks that Meredov's aide Malinkova had prepared for him. He gave them to Bell. "Have someone get these to the Systems Administrator. I want them up and running yesterday. Maps of Russian minefields and hydrophone nets. And specs for the undersea covert acoustic link used by our new comrades-in-arms, *Wild Boar* and *Cheetah*."

Bell gestured for the Messenger of the Watch; he grabbed the disks and headed below to the systems administrator's cubicle.

"Who commands the combined task force, sir?"

"I do."

"You're double-hatted, Commodore," Bell said with a lopsided smile. Assigned two different naval jobs at once.

"Lucky me. I've got two separate task forces, which secretly overlap in the form of *Carter*-as-Amethyste-Two, and my task forces are at war with each other. A war to the death, except if *Carter* is destroyed, the end effect will be that Russia joins the Axis."

"Can we sink the Russian subs? If we need to?"

"Aside from the fact that losing one or both in action would badly sully the Russian president's currently shaky position? And the other fact that Russian hydrophone grids are listening in, and a very smart man who's now a vice admiral could reconstruct events and get, to put it mildly, very pissed off?"

"You mean Meredov? *Promoted?*"

Jeffrey nodded. "Akula-Twos have double steel hulls, with inner and outer so widely spaced apart that they've got the highest reserve buoyancy of any fast-attack in service anywhere. And the inner hull has eight separate watertight compartments, right? They're nearly indestructible, unless we go nuclear."

"Would we?"

"Our odds of surviving a two-on-one duel like that with nukes are nil."

"But *Carter* . . ."

"I know. She is absolutely, positively not expendable. Our orders say *we* are. If this thing goes tactical nuclear, with the big yields on Russian warheads, Harley needs to run, not help us, and I don't see *Carter* surviving the whirlwind of shock waves and fireballs anyway. Do you?"

"No, sir." Bell was abashed, and worried.

Challenger's deck nosed down slightly, and the ship gained speed. As she approached her maximum, fifty-three knots, she began to vibrate—as she always did when the propulsion plant put out so much power. Things in the control room shook, squeaking and bouncing gently on their shock-absorbing mounts; mike cords hung on the overhead jiggled. The ship was making a heavy surface wake by doing flank speed so shallow, but that was the least of Jeffrey's concerns.

He tried to think ahead. Everyone in Control had heard what he'd told Bell, and they were tense. "I need two separate acoustic link setups. One for *Carter,* and one for the Akulas. Get your best Ru-ling in here to handle comms with the latter." A Russian language expert. "I think your

XO should continue to manage link messages with Captain Harley." Sessions, sitting at the command console, nodded, with what for the mild-mannered Nebraskan was the grimmest expression that Jeffrey had ever seen.

"Understood, sir," Bell said. He issued orders.

The senior chief, who was the best onboard Russian linguist, entered Control. "Use the console I was borrowing, Chief," Jeffrey told him. "I'll stand." Technicians were already installing the software needed to be compatible with the Russians' own frequency-agile, encrypted, digital undersea communications link. That link and the one used by *Challenger* and *Carter* had totally different formats and protocols, so neither could detect or interfere with the other. The Ru-ling reconfigured his keyboard to represent the Cyrillic alphabet.

"Sir," Lieutenant Torelli said from by the weapons systems consoles, "we have the overlay of hostile minefields and hydrophones uploaded now."

"Perfect." Jeffrey walked over to look at them on a fire-control technician's console.

"I sure hope Russian spies haven't stolen the specs to be able to detect and listen in on *our* comms link," Bell said. "And that Germans didn't nab the specs and hand them over to Russia."

Jeffrey remembered the mole, still on the loose somewhere in America's submarine warfighting personnel structure.

"Concur in the extreme. . . . And I better make damn sure I don't mix up which link is which, and send the Russians a message I mean for Harley. Everybody hear that? Backstop me if I make a mistake." Sessions and the Russian-speaking chief nodded.

Jeffrey studied the tactical plot. *Challenger* would reach the prearranged rendezvous point with *Carter,* from the old mission plan, only a few minutes before the Akula-IIs got within extreme torpedo range. They were all still over the shallow continental shelf, giving little room to maneuver or use fancy tactics. He had to work out a whole new doctrine for his strike group and convey it to Harley, all in a very short span of time.

"Sirs," Meltzer asked from by the navigating table, "may I offer a suggestion?"

"Go ahead, Nav," Bell said.

"Use one of the vertical wide-screen displays set up as a split screen."

"Nav?" Jeffrey didn't get it.

"Two tactical plots, sir. One labeled from the point of view of your combined task force with the Russians. The other from the point of view of the *Challenger-Carter* strike group. It'll help you keep things straight and manage two sets of strategies if you have the proper visual aides."

"Good thinking, Executive Assistant. The same four ships, except that on one display three are friendly and one is hostile, a German Amethyste-Two, and on the other two are friendly, us and *Carter*, while two are hostile, the Russians."

"That's what I meant, Commodore," Meltzer said.

"Okay," Jeffrey responded. "Captain, I need Lieutenant Meltzer's help full time for the duration."

"Of course, sir," Bell said.

"Let your assistant navigator take over here," Jeffrey told Meltzer. "You and I need to bone up ASAP on Akula-Two and Amethyste-Two strengths and weaknesses and their relevant antisubmarine weapons. We need some way to keep *Carter* alive for a thousand miles as she pretends to be an ex-French sub with half *Carter*'s real capabilities, while two Russsky skippers do their very best to try to destroy her. Let's use my office. . . . Captain Bell, have a messenger get me when we're five minutes out from effective acoustic-link range to Harley."

Jeffrey and Meltzer headed aft. Jeffrey stopped in his tracks. "Weps!"

"Commodore?"

"Get that Russian minefield overlay overlaid on both sides of the split screen."

One of Torelli's technicians typed keys, and more icons appeared on the display that showed two tactical plots.

This is gonna give me schizophrenia before we're done.

"Captain!"

"Sir?"

"What's in the tubes?"

"Four high-explosive ADCAPs, two high-explosive Mark Eighty-eights, and our two remaining Mark Three decoys."

"Perfect, for the moment." With the Russian sensor and minefield maps, *Challenger* didn't need to send out off-board probes. "Get the outer doors open on all tubes, *now,* while we're noisy. Prepare two ADCAPs for immediate firing at *Carter.*"

"Armed, Commodore?"

"Armed."

———

Several hours later, Jeffrey had updated Harley and given him orders to head east toward the hulk of the real Amethyste, continuing to emit the proper false acoustic signature. After warning Harley of what he was about to do, Jeffrey ordered Bell to fire a pair of live ADCAPs at *Carter,* programmed and wire-guided to barely miss. This would establish *Challenger*'s credibility to the Russians, while creating a sonar disruption that would help Harley begin to evade.

Bell gave orders, firing ADCAPs. The near-misses made very satisfying, ear-splitting roars. Shattered bits of pack ice, thrown high into the air, pattered down for minutes afterward. *Carter* vanished through this impenetrable acoustic wall.

Jeffrey established contact with the two Russian captains, and worked out a scheme to pursue the Amethyste into a trap in the Canada Basin, meanwhile wearing the German skipper down. He told them not to open fire at all unless he gave them orders, so as not to foul a shot from

Challenger with her superior capabilities. *Wild Boar* and *Cheetah* could dive below two thousand feet, almost twice an Amethyste's crush depth, but not nearly as good as *Challenger*'s. Akula-IIs were very quiet, the best fast-attacks Russia had, quieter than a real Amethyste, but noisier than the real *Carter*.

And aside from being nearly immune to incoming high-explosive fire, the Akula-IIs were very heavily armed by Western standards. They had ten reloadable torpedo tubes forward, plus six more external single-shot tubes that were loaded at a pier. Their torpedo rooms could each hold forty weapons. The Akulas' captains told Jeffrey via the link that they each carried twenty-five of the UGST torpedoes with new under-ice gravimeter homing sensors. All ten reloadable tubes were configured to fire these weapons. In a melee, the Akula-IIs could achieve an overwhelming rate of fire. Their weak spot was their sonars. Even the Russians admitted they were a fraction as sensitive as the ones on American subs. In the pursuit of the Amethyste, the Akulas would serve as Jeffrey's arsenal ships.

Jeffrey and Meltzer figured out, fast, that the key to *Carter*'s survival was convincing the Russians to keep their distance from her in her guise as the German. The reasoning Jeffrey gave *Wild Boar* and *Cheetah*, with the digital link working in effect as a three-way chat room, was twofold. If the Amethyste felt too cornered too soon—and considering what her commandos had already done at Srednekolymsk—her captain would likely go nuclear, even near land. If so, wide separation was needed to be able to take adequate countermeasures. Otherwise, even though the Amethyste had only four torpedo tubes and fourteen torpedoes maximum, Jeffrey's combined task force could suffer serious losses. The flip side was that, because the twenty-kiloton yields on the Russians' own nukes were so large—U.S. nuclear torpedoes used yields of a single kiloton or less—the Akulas had to stay well back or they'd be severely damaged or sunk by their own exploding fission weapons.

Wild Boar's and *Cheetah*'s captains, men seen only as disembodied responses in typed text on the chat, agreed with Jeffrey that, at least for the first stage of the pursuit, they'd all stay about fifteen nautical miles away from the German, half of maximum range for their UGST torpedoes. Plus, an Amethyste's F 17 Mod 2 torpedoes had a range of just under fifteen miles. Secretly, Jeffrey knew, for Harley's sake this was comfortably within the reach of the better American acoustic-link system.

The arrangement made even more sense from Jeffrey's conflicted point of view because the need to keep within Russian acoustic-link range for constant coordination—and yet maintain that adequate separation from the German—precluded a pincer movement to surround the Amethyste using the higher speeds of the three-ship task force. The Akulas and *Challenger* would have to spread too far apart to form the pincers, losing touch and leaving big holes in their formation that the German could easily slip through. Agreement on this was essential to the specific battle scheme vaguely forming inside Jeffrey's head. He held his breath. The Russian captains' replies soon appeared as Cyrillic text on the Ru-ling's console screen: they both concurred.

Jeffrey had contrived things so the battle would stay as a stern chase, proceeding along at the Amethyste's flank speed of twenty-five knots, and the Russians would be dependent on *Challenger* for meaningful target tracking data.

And nothing says I have to be honest when I answer.

Challenger had a maximum speed advantage over an Amethyste of almost thirty knots. Jeffrey would order Bell to put on bursts of speed and make end runs to the north, cutting off the supposed German each time Harley pretended he was trying to escape toward and beyond the pole.

CHAPTER 34

Jeffrey's pursuit of the Amethyste with the Russians was relentless. After twenty-four straight hours they'd covered half the distance to where the final reckoning, over the debris of a real Amethyste-II, would take place.

Jeffrey was doing this on purpose. He wanted the Russian captains, their senior officers, and the remainder of their crews exhausted. Each Akula-II had a total of about seventy men, barely half the size of *Challenger*'s and *Carter*'s crews. But modern Russian submarine captains did more delegating in battle than their U.S. Navy counterparts. Jeffrey was counting on his own combat-tested, iron constitution to outlast the Russian command teams, gaining a better mental—and tactical—edge. At Bell's urging, Jeffrey allowed modified watch rotations once the stern chase seemed to have settled into a routine. It was important, Jeffrey knew, for *Challenger*'s people to eat, sleep, and relax every day, so the ship would be in ideal fighting form. Over the acoustic link, Harley confirmed he was doing the same for his people—but like Jeffrey, he neither wanted nor could afford even a short catnap himself.

Challenger's battle-stations crew roster had recently rotated on watch again.

Then Jeffrey's plan to wear down the Russians back-
fired.

"Hydrophone effects," Chief O'Hanlon shouted from his
sonar console. "Torpedo in the water, Russian UGST!" He
gave the range and bearing. It had been fired by *Wild Boar.*

"Second torpedo in the water," O'Hanlon reported. "Also
Russian UGST!" This one had been fired by *Cheetah.*

In moments, each Akula-II fired a second torpedo.

"Target for all four torpedoes is *Carter,*" Torelli said.
Jeffrey eyed the new torpedo icons on the tactical plots.
They quickly drew ahead, chewing up the range to the
Amethyste-*Carter.*

Shit. I told them not to open fire without my permission.

"Ru-ling, how did they coordinate without us hearing the
conversation?"

"I think there was no conversation, sir."

Bell glanced at Jeffrey. "*Wild Boar* must've gotten
trigger-happy, and *Cheetah* used the excuse to join in."

"Weps," Jeffrey ordered, "confirm speed of the UGSTs."

"They're all making fifty knots, Commodore. That's
their maximum attack speed."

"Commodore," Sessions reported, "*Carter* signals, 'Torpedoes in water detected by echoes off bummocks. Torpedoes closing my ship. What are your instructions?'"

Jeffrey stared at the plots. They seemed to dance around,
and fade in and out of focus. He'd been awake for a lot more
than twenty-four hours. His plan to exhaust the Russians—
while pretending they all were ganging up to exhaust the
Germans—was having an effect on his own ability to think
straight. He hadn't made proper allowance for how much
his delicate negotiations and bluffs in Siberia drained him.

"Sir," Sessions stated, "*Carter* sends, 'Repeat, what are
your instructions?'"

"Ru-ling, make signal to *Wild Boar* and *Cheetah.* 'Why
have you opened fire without my prior order? By word of

your own commander in chief, you are under my command.'"

The chief typed on his keyboard.

"Commodore," Sessions interrupted, "*Carter* sends, 'Repeat, inbound torpedoes closing on me. Will impact before their maximum range if I maintain present course and speed.'"

"Okay," Jeffrey said. "Okay." He had an idea. "Make signal to *Carter,* 'Go silent and go to all stop. When you hear me making flank speed, make actual flank speed as *Carter* in wide circle, return to starting location after twenty minutes circling.'"

Harley signaled he understood. Jeffrey waited five minutes.

"Ru-ling, what reply from *Wild Boar* and *Cheetah*?"

"Nothing yet, sir."

"Repeat the message and add 'Response imperative.'"

The Ru-ling typed. Jeffrey waited another five minutes. The four UGSTs closed the distance to *Carter* faster than ever, making fifty knots while she sat still.

This was getting dicey, but Jeffrey realized he needed to pull off another subtle, dangerous sleight of hand to set up the Russian captains for later. "Ru-ling, response?"

"None yet, sir."

Jeffrey gave them five more minutes; the UGSTs would now be very close to where *Carter* went quiet and stopped. "That's *it.* As far as they're to know, they've gone too far and they're ruining everything. Captain Bell, make flank speed and cut back and forth in front of *Wild Boar* and *Cheetah,* at one thousand feet below their present depth. I want to teach them who's in charge here, and get them to behave themselves, but I do not want to break the wires to their torpedoes or we might lose *Carter*."

Bell acknowledged and issued helm orders. Patel acknowledged and dialed up flank speed. Bell ordered rudder turns and Patel put them into effect. *Challenger* vibrated and banked steeply into each turn, first to starboard and then to port and then back again. Jeffrey knew Harley would be kicking *Carter* up to her own flank speed, which slightly exceeded that of the UGSTs. He'd outrun the torpedoes until they ran out of remaining fuel. Meanwhile, Jeffrey anticipated that his own flank speed noise and maneuvers—his angry reminder of *Challenger*'s tactical and sonar superiority over the Akulas—would mask *Carter*'s actual signature.

Using their own rebelliousness to outfox them. I hope.

For Jeffrey's basic deception scheme to keep holding up, and for his gradually gelling final-engagement strategy to have any chance to work, it was vital that the guidance wires to the UGSTs not break, *and* that the Russian captains from now on did exactly what he said. Neither was guaranteed.

"Ru-ling, make signal to *Wild Boar* and *Cheetah*. 'Have lost contact with target, unable to regain, believe it hovering under ice to evade UGST homing sonars. Reduce your own-ship speed to five knots to retain separation against a German counterambush. Engage gravimeter sensors and steer your weapons to search area near last known location German vessel. And maintain task force discipline or I will personally tell Russian president to reprimand you.'"

The chief, as he typed all this in Russian, couldn't help chuckling at the tart tongue-lashing Jeffrey was giving to the captains of *Wild Boar* and *Cheetah*.

Jeffrey told Bell to maintain flank speed, while he kept an eye on the chronometer. If the Russians followed Jeffrey's orders, the UGSTs would search in vain near one place for an Amethyste reactor compartment that wasn't there. If they disobeyed, or had a fire-control malfunction, or the wires to one or more of their weapons broke, Harley could survive by outrunning the errant torpedoes—and would end up almost back where he started, as if he'd been an Amethyste, hiding, hovering all along and the Russian warheads had failed to find him.

Except. If a Russian captain's UGST somehow made,

and held, active and passive homing acoustic contact on *Carter,* with the guidance wire to his weapon still intact so he knew what his weapon and *Carter* were doing, he'd realize that something was way too fishy. The Amethyste would have seemed to go quiet only temporarily and then started racing around at twice her possible flank speed. The Russian couldn't dismiss this as just bad sound propagation—not when his UGST held a lock on the target.

Jeffrey began to sweat, despite the chill of the air fans. He told Bell to charge ahead, east, as if getting ready to deliver a coup de grace to the German from below, after she'd been hit by the gravimeter-homing UGSTs. Using UGST engine-noise data from O'Hanlon and Finch, Torelli confirmed that the Russians were doing what they'd been told to with their weapons.

The clock ran down; the UGSTs ran out of fuel and shut down. By now *Carter* would have reverted to being quiet and slow, so *Challenger* reduced her speed from flank to twenty-five knots. He told Harley to resume fleeing east, as a German sub once more.

It had been one of the most nerve-wracking half-hours Jeffrey ever spent in undersea combat—and this wasn't over.

Jeffrey ordered Bell to reverse course and steer toward the Akulas, to keep a better chase formation with them—if he drew too far ahead, he'd be vulnerable to fire from the Amethyste, including nuclear fire, without adequate Russian backup. And to any real German, *Challenger* identified as who she was, by the noise she'd made, would be a prize of such high value that going nuclear would be justified, even at the risk of self-destruction.

Challenger neared the Akula-IIs. The Ru-ling finally spoke up. "Sir, *Wild Boar* signals, 'Misunderstood rules of engagement. Weapons launched in error.' "

"Yeah, right," Meltzer murmured.

"*Cheetah* signals, 'Misunderstood actions *Wild Boar.*' "

"Ru-ling, make signal, 'Task Force Commander expects and insists that rules of engagement now clear.' "

"New passive sonar contact on the port wide-aperture array," O'Hanlon called out. "Tonals match Amethyste-Two class."

Torelli's target tracking team used the range and bearing data from Sonar to plot the contact's position and course. "Captain Harley is accelerating to Amethyste-Two's flank speed," Torelli said. "Course is due east." The tactical plots marked *Carter*'s new position; one plot showed *Carter* as friendly, and the other as enemy. She was slightly south of where she'd been at the start of her wide circling turn, and the maneuvers had cut target separation from fifteen miles to twelve, thus seeming to increase task force pressure on the German sub—Jeffrey's goal.

Both plots showed the Russians, on one as enemy and on the other as friendly. Jeffrey questioned, from the Akula captains' transparently disobedient behavior, which in the end they would turn out to be. "Ru-ling, make signal to *Wild Boar* and *Cheetah*. 'Contact regained. Resume chase.' Get the data from Weps and relay it. Then say, 'Target undamaged. You wasted ammunition and betrayed new UGST capabilities. Obey orders in future.'"

CHAPTER 35

For another day the grueling stern chase continued. From time to time Harley would fake another dash north, and Jeffrey would force him back east with the threat of a two-to-one advantage in torpedo tubes and speed, and a great advantage in crush depth. Jeffrey's behavior, by closing the separation menacingly if the Germans didn't turn away fast enough, was supposed to make it clear to the German captain that, at this point—frustrated or egged on by the Akulas' impetuous conduct—Jeffrey was willing to risk destruction in order to also destroy the Amethyste-II, a double kill acceptable for reasons of higher statecraft. This was consistent with his prior nearly suicidal tactics against real German subs, so if the Akulas had any intel reports from the Axis on Jeffrey's warfighting style, it would all be believable. If they didn't have such intel reports, they were finding it out for themselves, and he wanted them to know, to strengthen his psychological domination.

Wild Boar and *Cheetah* also continued the pursuit, and the combined task force gradually neared the eastern end of the Canada Abyssal Plain.

"We're moving into the endgame phase," Jeffrey said out loud, to no one in particular. He gulped down the last of what he thought must be his twentieth mug of coffee since reboarding *Challenger*; he used it to wash down the last of a ham and cheese sandwich, one of his favorite snacks when he was in the throes of deep fatigue during combat.

But he'd never pushed himself this hard for so long.

I'm too wired out, and stretched too thin. I need to wrap this chase up soon and send the Russians home happy. The only problem is, I haven't figured out yet how to pull the rabbit out of the hat, and make the Amethyste sink while Carter *escapes.*

Jeffrey stood in the aisle next to Bell and stared at the pair of tactical plots.

"Commodore," Bell said, "the assistant nav reports that at present speed, assuming no further misbehavior by the Russians, we'll reach the location of the genuine Amethyste's wreck in two hours. May I ask your intentions?"

"If I knew them, I'd tell you."

Bell frowned. "Sir, with respect, if we just keep running east we'll hit the line of Canadian islands and whatever friendly subs could get in position. If *Carter* keeps on going, and the waiting American and Canadian boats don't open fire, the Russians will know something's up. The distances are too great, and the closing speeds too high, for the submarines out in front of us to coordinate something with *Carter* fast enough to be effective and put one over on the Akulas."

"I know. I asked for those subs to keep Meredov and his cronies from getting suspicious, since if I really wanted the German destroyed that's one order I'd certainly give. It's what Commander, U.S. Pacific Fleet would tell Commander, Submarines, Pacific to do anyway."

"Concur."

"But it's up to us to fool the Russians."

"Sir, I know you do your best work under pressure, but the margins in time and space are getting narrow."

"Yup. They sure are."

"Do you want to order Harley to make another feint north? If we add some zigs and zags now, it could buy you an extra hour, maybe more."

"No. Good idea, but it only postpones the inevitable."

"Then what do you intend?"

"Let me think."

"Yes, Commodore. Of course."

Jeffrey looked at the tactical plots, the two different versions of reality displayed side by side, just as Meltzer had suggested so many mugs of coffee ago. The plots faded in and out of focus again. Jeffrey began to zone out altogether. Then he realized that he'd induced a state of near self-hypnosis.

Schizophrenia. That's what I told myself at the start. If I stared at these two plots long enough I'd give myself schizophrenia.

Jeffrey was feeling mentally punch-drunk. *What the hell does schizophrenia have to do with submarines?*

An hour went by, then more. And then he saw it. The win-or-lose gambit that would determine now and forever who won this crazy endgame—America or Germany, the truth or a very big lie. Just about the biggest big lie in military history.

He cleared his throat and spoke with new vigor. "Captain, man silent battle stations."

"Man silent battle stations, aye, sir. Chief of the Watch, on the sound-powered phones, man silent battle stations."

"Man silent battle stations, aye," the senior chief acknowledged. He spoke to the phone talker, and the order was relayed throughout the ship. Bell's control room first team began to arrive. COB looked like he'd been showering—his hair was still wet and his Latino skin had a rosy tinge from vigorous use of a scrub brush. Patel appeared, his facial features softened as if by sleep, but he sharpened up quickly. Meltzer and Torelli dashed in together, brushing crumbs off their clothes and still chewing the last bites of food—they'd been snacking in the wardroom. Finch, O'Hanlon, Sessions, and over a dozen technicians and chiefs arrived in a flood. Soon COB reported that the ship was at battle stations.

"Make signal to *Carter,* 'Man silent battle stations. Prepare to receive my orders for final melee.'"

Sessions acknowledged, typed, and reported that Harley had received and understood the message.

Jeffrey turned to the Ru-ling. "Make signal to *Wild Boar* and *Cheetah.* 'Man silent battle stations. Prepare to receive my orders for final melee.'"

The Ru-ling acknowledged, then the Russian captains did.

"I think we've worn down and lulled the Amethyste's poor German skipper long enough. Captain Bell, the key to beating an opponent who might go nuclear, using only high-explosive ordnance ourselves, is to stick to the fundamentals."

"Commodore?"

"Surprise, and overwhelming firepower."

———

A half-hour later, all the orders were relayed and acknowledged. All the torpedo tubes and weapons in them were ready.

"Make signal to *Carter,*" Jeffrey ordered, "'Implement. Repeat, implement.'"

On both tactical plots, *Carter*-Amethyste continued to behave as before, steaming east at twenty-five knots just below the reach of summer ice keels. But for the first time in two days, the tactical plots showed very different symbols.

On the real plot, the icon that was *Carter* stayed on track but changed into the icon representing a brilliant decoy, programmed to act and sound like the Amethyste. The icon for *Carter* split off and turned south, slowed to fifteen knots to stay quiet while getting out of the way, steaming south toward distant Alaskan territorial waters. On the fake plot, the one from the combined task force perspective—the Russian point of view—the icon steaming east continued to show the actual Amethyste. There was no icon there for *Carter.*

"Ru-ling, make signal to *Wild Boar* and *Cheetah.* 'Prepare to open fire.'"

Both Akula-IIs acknowledged quickly, their captains eager to go into action and share credit for an actual combat kill—not just a paper score in some training exercise.

Jeffrey kept a careful eye on the chronometer. Everything had to be coordinated to the second.

Now. "Ru-ling, make signal to *Wild Boar* and *Cheetah,* 'Open fire. Repeat, open fire.'"

The Ru-ling typed. The Russian captains didn't even bother acknowledging.

"Hydrophone effects!" O'Hanlon shouted. "Multiple torpedoes in the water! UGSTs!"

"Captain Bell, open fire. Launch the decoys in tubes seven and eight."

Bell began to issue his orders. Soon *Challenger* had eight units in the water, rising toward shallow depth from below the twenty high-explosive UGSTs launched by the Russians—a full salvo from each Akula-II.

Jeffrey watched the tactical plots. As he'd ordered, everything was targeted at the Amethyste. The Russian torpedoes began to spread out, horizontally and vertically, to leave the German no room to run—even accounting for several inevitable Russian torpedo malfunctions.

Not much longer. His heart raced. If the timing was off, if the coordination between *Carter*'s and *Challenger*'s decoys wasn't precise enough, if any of them broke down or had a programming input error or a software bug—or if Bell's units from tubes seven and eight were destroyed by shocks from the real weapons that they absolutely had to stay near—the whole grand deception scheme would collapse. If so, the next overwhelming Russian salvo would be aimed at *Challenger,* and would be nuclear.

Wild Boar and *Cheetah* between them could fire twenty nukes at once. *Challenger* only had eight tubes. Her better speed and crush depth would be no help against so many twenty-kiloton fission warheads. Russian nukes would surely get through, while none of her puny one-kiloton Mark 88 fish would reach the Russians. *Challenger* and all aboard her would die. The enraged Akulas would hunt down *Carter* and then go home and report the terrible truth of American treachery.

Apocalypse Soon, Apocalypse Later, Apocalypse Now.

———

The decoy that was the Amethyste began to give off the sounds of noisemakers and jammers. Already making flank speed, this was all her imaginary captain could do. According to Jeffrey's endgame scheme—reinforced by him scolding the Russians about having given away the UGST's special capability—the Germans had figured out, from seeing the search pattern used by the four torpedoes the day before, that the Russian weapons possessed some way to successfully search for a nuclear submarine hiding quiet and still against the ice. The Russian captains might wonder why the German captain didn't return fire, but decoys couldn't launch convincing phony torpedoes—and real torpedoes from *Carter* had entirely different sound signatures from the weapons used by Amethyste-IIs. Decoys from *Carter* pretending to be German weapons, coming at the Russians, would never fool them, and would leave irrefutable physical proof that the pseudo-Amethyste was really American.

This was a loophole in Jeffrey's strategy that he'd simply have to live with—or die with: the German captain would not return fire. Maybe he'd used up his few torpedoes and decoys days ago, approaching Russia, his weapons load drastically reduced to make room for so many commandos. Maybe he'd had a mechanical breakdown in the torpedo room. Or maybe he realized, with the geometries of torpedo maximum ranges versus ship flank speeds, that his countershots had no chance of being effective.

One tactical plot showed twenty-eight torpedoes quickly catching up with the Amethyste. The other plot showed twenty-six torpedoes and two decoys. Everything depended on those decoys doing exactly what Jeffrey needed them to do, exactly when he needed them to do it. They were the last two Mark III brilliant decoys *Challenger* had. They were preprogrammed, and fully autonomous once launched, with no guidance wire and no way to recover them. If something went wrong and they ran astray they'd be more forensic evidence unmasking Jeffrey's elaborate subterfuge. *The consequences will be far worse than Russians calling me a liar.*

Challenger's Mark 88 fish, launched from tubes one through six, were faster than the UGSTs, making almost seventy knots. Though they'd been fired from much deeper depth, they reached the target first. Jeffrey had counted on this. It was essential that *Carter*'s decoy be pulverized, but *Challenger*'s decoys had to survive because their indispensable tasks were yet to come.

Torelli crossed himself, and ordered his people to detonate their warheads via the fiber-optic guidance wires. Their massive high-explosive warhead charges caused tremendous, thundering blasts. Russian torpedoes began to explode right behind them, some command-detonated through intact guidance wires, others because the nearby blasts touched off their warheads sympathetically or spoofed their arming software, and a few because they'd been programmed for contact-fusing against anything solid they hit—including ice bummocks. *Challenger* was buffeted by many shock waves and strong turbulence.

Did the brilliant decoys survive? Months of mission preparation, weeks of hard work and bloody sacrifice and terrible risks, all came down to the next few moments. And then it happened. The blasts, echoes, and protesting ice cap were drowned out by a much louder sound, the unmistakable implosion of a submarine hull. A shower of wreckage of all shapes and sizes made flow noise as it fell, thudding into the seafloor.

The real tactical plot showed that these last effects were coming from Bell's two deep-capable decoys, emitting a modified rendition of a recording of the real *Amethyste's* death here two weeks before. As they dove for the bottom themselves, the decoys spread apart to give a better illusion on Russian sonars of a three-dimensional debris cloud forming.

The Mark III decoys still had crucial work to do. Jeffrey's acoustic smoke-and-mirrors ploy wasn't finished. The Mark IIIs were in the water, they'd eventually exhaust their fuel and might be found, and they needed a damned good excuse for being there.

Both decoys went silent, and rose back to *Challenger's* depth. They returned toward her, then altered their courses and headed in opposite directions, north and south. They began to sound and act like *Challenger* making flank speed—as if just launched to draw off return fire aimed at Jeffrey's task force.

So convinced were the Russian captains of the danger of German torpedoes—last gasps from the now-dead Amethyste, possibly nuclear, undetected while inbound through the deafening sea—that *Wild Boar* and *Cheetah* launched decoys, too.

But no German torpedoes emerged from the echoes and reverb and roiling clouds of bubbles and tumbling, shattered pack ice.

"Ru-ling, signal *Wild Boar* and *Cheetah*. 'Good shooting and well done.'" Both Russian captains acknowledged with thanks.

EPILOGUE

Two weeks later

Jeffrey sat alone in the Oval Office with the President of the United States, wearing his dress blue uniform with medals. The two men had had long talks before, starting the day that the President awarded Jeffrey his first, unclassified Medal of Honor.

The President was a retired four-star general, who liked to say he was hardly the first senior military leader to rise to the elected civilian rank of commander in chief—look at George Washington, or Eisenhower, to name just two. He'd taken a shining to Jeffrey, especially since he kept delivering important successes in this war. November was the next presidential election, which he reminded Jeffrey of whenever they met, as if suggesting there might be opportunities someday beyond the U.S. Navy for a war hero of Jeffrey's caliber. The President would be running for his second term; his winning depended on how the American public perceived the war to be going. Jeffrey was helping keep alive the aura of inevitable triumph and peace.

Jeffrey asked about the amnesty offer to the Axis leaders

that was supposed to follow the raid in Siberia; sneaking home submerged until just yesterday, and closely sequestered for security since then, he'd had no access to news reports.

The President told him that the South African reactionary leaders, seeing Germany evacuating North Africa after a recent, major defeat there, read the handwriting on the wall and jumped at the chance. They were already in Paraguay, which had agreed to grant them asylum, and a new interim government had been rushed into place. Jeffrey thought this was outstanding.

"I'm declaring next Monday a national holiday, V-A Day," the president said with a grin. Victory in Africa. "It takes time to plan the parades and celebrations."

But the advanced German nuclear sub that had been undergoing repairs in South Africa, the ceramic-composite-hulled *Admiral von Scheer,* had put to sea and evaded the Allied blockade and was on the loose somewhere. This put a bit of a damper on things. The German dictatorship refused to even consider an amnesty. They vowed to fight to the end at all costs, making threats about new weapons and alliances that would drive the Allies back and force an armistice favorable to Germany. The President declined to go into further details.

Jeffrey asked about his former lover Ilse Reebeck, and the status of the Axis mole. The president said that Lieutenant Reebeck had been known all along to be innocent; her arrest over a month ago was a ruse to help catch the mole. She'd just returned to her native Johannesburg, and was serving on a reconstruction and reconciliation commission under UN auspices. The real traitor had been identified, and confessed in return for the death penalty being commuted to life without parole. Jeffrey didn't need to know who the mole was, except it wasn't a senior official after all. It was a secretary who did it for the money.

Jeffrey's parents waited elsewhere in the White House, as did Dashiyn Nyurba and his parents, and Captains Bell and Harley and their parents and wives and kids, and Sergey Kurzin's parents. For security, Secret Service agents made sure that no one saw them. None of the relatives had any idea what their sons, husbands, or fathers had done to earn a meeting with the President, or how two of them were injured or killed—if secrecy held up as it needed to, they'd never find out, either.

"I think this sets a record," the President said. "Four Medals of Honor in one day. The toughest part for me is always giving one posthumously."

"I never got to know Colonel Kurzin, sir, but what I did see impressed me."

"Too bad you can't tell that to his folks."

"Yes, sir. I know." He looked at his hands, confused by mixed emotions. Jeffrey himself was receiving his second Defense Distinguished Service Medal, unclassified, for his superb management of a complicated mission that involved as much diplomacy as combat tactics, some of it public knowledge already.

Someone knocked on the door. "Come!" the President yelled.

It was the White House Chief of Staff. "Sir, the Russian Ambassador is here."

"Show him in." The President and Jeffrey stood.

Jeffrey had never met the Russian ambassador before. The man was short and fat and jolly. Some of that good mood, Jeffrey assumed, came from the suddenly improved relations between the United States and Russia. Some of it, though, seemed the man's natural personality.

The ambassador held a small velvet case in one hand.

"May I?" the ambassador asked the President.

"Please."

Jeffrey got the impression that the two had already talked about this, and something was being stage-managed here. An official White House photographer entered the room, followed by Jeffrey's parents, who walked over and stood next to him. They both were beaming. Jeffrey's father elbowed him proudly in the ribs.

"Captain Jeffrey Fuller," the ambassador said very formally, "it is my great privilege, in the name of the grateful people of my country, to award you this highest recognition that the Motherland has to give, the Gold Star Medal of the Hero of the Russian Federation."

GLOSSARY

Acoustic intercept: A passive (listening-only) sonar specifically designed to give warning when the submarine is "pinged" by an enemy active sonar.

Active out-of-phase emissions: A way to weaken the echo that an enemy sonar receives from a submarine's hull, by actively emitting sound waves of the same frequency as the ping but exactly out of phase. The out-of-phase sound waves mix with and cancel those of the echoing ping.

ADCAP: Mark 48 Advanced Capability torpedo. A heavyweight, wire guided torpedo used by American nuclear submarines. The Improved ADCAP has even longer range and an enhanced (and extremely capable) target homing sonar and software logic package.

AIP: Air Independent Propulsion. Refers to modern diesel submarines that have an additional power source besides the standard diesel generator and electric storage batteries. The AIP system allows quiet and long-endurance submerged cruising, without the need to snorkel for air, because oxygen and fuel are carried aboard the vessel in special tanks. For example, the German Class 212A design uses fuel cells for achieving AIP.

Ambient sonar: A form of active sonar that uses, instead of a submarine's pinging, the ambient noise of the surrounding ocean to catch reflections off a target. Noise sources can include surface wave-action sounds, the propulsion plants of other vessels (such as passing neutral merchant shipping), or biologics (sea life). Ambient sonar gives the advantages of actively pinging but without betraying a submarine's own presence. Advanced signal processing algorithms and powerful onboard computers are needed to exploit ambient sonar effectively.

Auxiliary maneuvering units: Small propulsors at the bow and stern of a nuclear submarine, used to greatly enhance the vessel's maneuverability. First ordered for the USS *Jimmy Carter,* the third and last of the *Seawolf*-class SSNs (nuclear fast-attack submarines) to be constructed.

Ceramic composite: A multilayered composite foam matrix made from ceramic and metallic ingredients. Alumina casing, an extremely strong submarine hull material significantly less dense than steel, was declassified by the U.S. Navy after the Cold War.

ELF: Extremely Low Frequency. Radio capable of penetrating deep seawater, used to communicate (one-way only) from a huge shore transmitter installation to submerged submarines. A disadvantage is ELF's very slow data rate, only a few bits per minute.

EMCON: Emissions Control. Radio silence. Also applies to radar, sonar, or other emissions that could reveal a vessel's presence.

EMP: Electromagnetic pulse. A sudden, strong electrical current induced by a nuclear explosion. This will destroy unshielded electrical and electronic equipment and also temporarily ruin radio reception. There are two forms of EMP, one caused by very-high-altitude nuclear explosions ("HANEs"), the other by ones at low altitude. (Mid-altitude bursts do not create an EMP.) The area on the ground affected by an EMP is called the "pancake." EMPs in outer space ("exoatmospheric" EMPs) will also cause damage to unhardened satellites in orbit.

Frequency-agile: A means of avoiding enemy interception and jamming, by very rapidly varying the frequency used by a transmitter and receiver. May apply to radio, or to underwater acoustic communications (see *gertrude* below).

Gertrude: Underwater telephone. Original systems simply transmitted voice directly with the aid of transducers (active sonar emitters, i.e., underwater loudspeakers), and were notorious for short range and poor intelligibility. Modern undersea acoustic communication systems translate the message into digital high-frequency active sonar pulses, which can be frequency-agile for security (see above). Data rates well over 1,000 bits per second, over ranges up to thirty nautical miles, can be achieved.

Hole-in-ocean sonar: A form of passive (listening-only) sonar that detects a target by how it blocks ambient ocean sounds from further off. In effect, hole-in-ocean sonar uses an enemy submarine's own quieting against it.

Instant ranging: A capability of the new wide-aperture array sonar systems (see below). Because each wide-aperture array is mounted rigidly along one side of the submarine's hull, sophisticated signal processing can be performed to "focus" the hydrophones at different ranges from the ship. The target needs to lie somewhere on the beam of the ship (i.e., to either side).

Kampfschwimmer: German Navy "frogman" combat swimmers. The equivalent of U.S. Navy SEALs and the Royal Navy's Special Boat Squadron commandos. (In the German language, the word *Kampfschwimmer* is both singular and plural.)

LASH: Littoral Airborne Sensor Hyperspectral. A new antisubmarine warfare search-and-detection technique, usually deployed from aircraft. LASH utilizes the back-scatter of underwater illumination from sunlight, caught via special optical sensors and processed by classified computer software, to locate anomalous color gradations and shapes, even through deep seawater that is murky or dirty.

LIDAR: Light Direction And Ranging. Like radar, but uses laser beams instead of radio waves. Undersea LIDAR uses blue-green lasers, because that color penetrates seawater to the greatest distance.

Multimission platform: A special extra one-hundred-foot-long, three-thousand-ton hull section added to USS *Jimmy Carter,* the last of the three *Seawolf*-class nuclear-powered fast-attack subs to be built, commissioned into the U.S. Navy in early 2005. By limiting the pressure-hull diameter within the central portion of the multimission platform to eighteen feet (the "wasp waist"), additional volume for larger weapons, off-board vehicles, and underwater fiber-optic cable tapping equipment was created between the wasp waist and the outer hull, called the "garage space." The full-width (forty-two-foot outside diameter) sections at both ends of the multimission platform include areas for special operations command, control, and communications, and for special operations forces berthing—

nominally fifty commandos, though more can be accommodated in an emergency. Reportedly, this extra hundred feet of "wetted area" of the outer hull reduces *Carter*'s maximum speed while submerged by less than one knot.

Naval Submarine League (NSL): A professional association for submariners and submarine supporters. See their Web site, www.navalsubleague.com.

Network-centric warfare: A new approach to warfighting in which all formations and commanders share a common tactical and strategic picture through real-time digital data links. Every platform or node, such as a ship, aircraft, submarine, Marine Corps or Army squad, or SEAL team, gathers and shares information on friendly and enemy locations and movements. Weapons, such as a cruise missile, might be fired by one platform, and redirected in flight toward a fleeting target of opportunity by another platform, using information relayed by yet other platforms—including unmanned reconnaissance drones. Network-centric warfare promises to revolutionize command, control, communications, and intelligence, and greatly leverage the combat power of all friendly units while minimizing collateral damage.

Ocean rover: Any one of a number of designs, either civilian or military, of a small, semiautonomous unmanned submersible vehicle that roves through the ocean collecting data on natural and man-made phenomena. This data is periodically downloaded via radio when the ocean rover comes shallow enough to raise an antenna above the sea surface. Ocean rovers can also be controlled and downloaded via fiber-optic tether from a submerged submarine, for greater stealth. Powered by batteries or fuel cells, ocean rovers move slowly but can have endurance of days or weeks before needing to be recovered for maintenance, reprogramming, refueling, etc. One U.S. Navy ocean rover is the Seahorse series, shaped like a very long, very wide torpedo.

Photonics mast: The modern replacement for the traditional optical periscope. One of the first was installed in USS *Virginia* (see below). The photonics mast uses electronic imaging sensors, sends the data via thin electrical or fiber-optic cables, and displays the output on large high-definition TV screens in the control room. The photonics mast is "non-hull-penetrating," an important advantage over older scopes with their long, straight, thick tubes that must be able to move up and down and rotate.

Pump-jet: A main propulsor for nuclear submarines that replaces the traditional screw propeller. A pump-jet is a system of stator and rotor turbine blades within a cowling. (The rotors are turned by the main propulsion shaft, the same way the screw propeller's shaft would be turned.) Good pump-jet designs are quieter and more efficient than screw propellers, producing less cavitation noise and less wake turbulence.

SERT: Seabee Engineer Reconnaissance Team. A modern breed of special operations forces "shadow warrior" drawn from among U.S. Navy Seabee (mobile construction) combat battalions. SERT teams, generally of ten specially trained men each, operate at the forward edge of the battle area, sometimes attached to Marine Corps formations. They use their special expertise to assess, in a warfighting environment, civil engineering requirements for tasks such as road-laying, bridge repair, and restoration of damaged or sabotaged structures and heavy machinery including power plants and waterworks. Their reconnaissance reports are relayed in real time to higher headquarters via digital network-centric warfare techniques (see above), for optimal rapid exploitation by follow-on mainline battle formations, aid relief workers, and democracy-building planners. Commissioned officers in Seabee units are members of the Navy's Civil Engineer Corps.

Sonobuoy: A small active ("pinging") or passive (listening-only) sonar detector, usually dropped in patterns (clusters) from an aircraft or a helicopter. The sonobuoys transmit their data to the aircraft by a radio link. The aircraft might have onboard equipment to analyze this data, or it might relay the data to a surface warship for detailed analysis. (The aircraft will also carry torpedoes or depth charges, to be able to attack any enemy submarines that its sonobuoys detect.) Some types of sonobuoy are able to operate down to a depth of 16,000 feet.

SSBN and SSGN: An SSGN is a type of nuclear submarine designed or adapted for the primary purpose of launching cruise missiles, which tend to follow a level flight path through the air to their target. An SSGN is distinct from an SSBN "boomer," which launches strategic (hydrogen bomb) ballistic missiles, following a very high lobbing trajectory that leaves and then reenters earth's atmosphere. Because cruise missiles tend to be smaller than ballistic missiles, an SSGN is able to carry a larger number of separate missiles than an SSBN of the same overall size. Note, however, that since ballistic missiles are typically "MIRVed," i.e., equipped with multiple independently targeted reentry vehicles, the total number of warheads on an SSBN and SSGN may be comparable; also, an SSBN's ballistic missiles can be equipped with high-explosive warheads instead of nuclear warheads. (A fast-attack submarine, or SSN, can be thought of as serving as a part-time SSGN, to the extent that some SSN classes have vertical launching systems for cruise missiles, and/or are able to fire cruise missiles through their torpedo tubes.)

Virginia-class: The latest class of nuclear-propelled fast-attack submarines (SSNs) being constructed for the U.S.

Navy, to follow the *Seawolf*-class. The first, USS *Virginia,* was commissioned in 2004. (Post–Cold War, some SSNs have been named for states, since construction of *Ohio*-class Trident missile "boomers" has been halted.)

Wide-aperture array: A sonar system introduced, in the U.S. Navy, with USS *Seawolf* in the mid-1990s, and also built into the *Virginia* class. Distinct from and in addition to the bow sphere, towed arrays, and forward hull array of Cold War–era *Los Angeles*–class SSNs. Each submarine so equipped actually has two wide-aperture arrays, one along each side of the hull. Each array consists of three separate rectangular hydrophone complexes. Powerful signal processing algorithms allow sophisticated analysis of incoming passive sonar data. This includes instant ranging (see above). Some *Los Angeles*–class vessels have been updated with retrofitted wide-aperture arrays.

ACKNOWLEDGMENTS

To begin, I want to thank my formal manuscript readers: Captain Melville Lyman, U.S. Navy (retired), commanding officer of several SSBN strategic missile submarines, until recently Director for Special Weapons Safety and Surety at the Johns Hopkins Applied Physics Laboratory, and now doing similar work at a major private contractor; Commander Jonathan Powis, Royal Navy, who was Navigator on the fast-attack submarine HMS *Conqueror* during the Falklands Crisis, and who subsequently commanded three different British submarines; retired senior chief Bill Begin, veteran of many "boomer" deterrent patrols; and Peter Petersen, who served in the German Navy's *U-518* in World War II. Thanks also go to two Navy SEALs, Warrant Officer Bill Pozzi and Commander Jim Ostach, and to Lieutenant Commander Jules Steinhauer, USNR (Ret.), diesel boat veteran and naval aviation submarine liaison in the early Cold War, for their feedback and support. In that latter category I must also include the many new friends and acquaintances I've made since joining the United States Submarine Veterans, Inc. (USSVI) as a sponsored Life Associate Member, and the Navy Seabee Veterans of America (NSVA) as an Honorary Life Associate Member, during 2004.

A number of other Navy people gave valuable guidance: George Graveson, Jim Hay, and Ray Woolrich, all retired U.S. Navy captains, former submarine skippers, and active in the Naval Submarine League; Ralph Slane, vice president of the New York Council of the Navy League of the United States, and docent of the *Intrepid* Museum; Ann Hassinger, research librarian at the U.S. Naval Institute; Bill Kreher, operations director of the Naval Submarine League; Chris Michel, founder and president of Military Advantage, Inc.; and retired reserve U.S. Navy Seabee Chief "Stormin' Normand" Dupuis.

Additional submariners and military contractors deserve acknowledgment. They are too many to name here, but continuing to stand out vividly in my mind are pivotal conversations with Commander (now Captain) Mike Connor, at the time CO of USS *Seawolf,* and with the late Captain Ned Beach, USN (Ret.), brilliant writer and great submariner. I also want to thank, for the guided tours of their fine submarines, the officers and men of USS *Alexandria, Connecticut, Dallas, Hartford, Memphis, Salt Lake City, Seawolf, Springfield, Topeka,* and *Virginia,* and the modern German diesel submarine *U-15.* I owe "deep" appreciation to everyone aboard USS *Miami* for four wonderful days on and under the sea.

Similar thanks go to the instructors and students of the New London Submarine School, and the Coronado BUD/SEAL training facilities, and to all the people who demonstrated their weapons, equipment, attack vessels, and aircraft, at the Amphibious Warfare bases in Coronado and Norfolk. Appreciation also goes to the men and women of the aircraft carrier USS *Constellation,* the Aegis guided missile cruiser USS *Vella Gulf,* the fleet replenishment oiler USNS *Pecos,* and so many other Navy folks.

The Current Strategy Forums and publications of the Naval War College were invaluable. Flying out to the amphibious warfare helicopter carrier USS *Iwo Jima* during New York City's Fleet Week 2002, and joining with her sailors and marines in rendering honors as the ship passed September 11th's Ground Zero, was one of the most powerfully emotional experiences of my life.

First among the publishing people deserving acknowledgment is my wife, Sheila Buff, a bestselling nonfiction author and co-author of books on health, wellness, and related topics. Then comes my agent, John Talbot, "spirit guide" for seven years now on all aspects of the writing profession. Equally crucial is my William Morrow editor, Mike Shohl, always full of keen insights on improving my outlines and manuscript drafts.